Another Family Reunion Novel
In The Wisdom of the Ancestors Series
— *Book 22* —

Regrets

Ann Jeffries

I bow in humble gratitude to:

Lois Evelyn Palfrey, 1924-2020

The Creator

My Ancestors

Jenetha Hollis, Editor
Quill Editorial Service

Jessica Tilles, TWA Solutions
Interior and Cover Art

Kelley Hazen, Narrator
Storyteller Productions

The Carolina Forest Authors' Club

My precious and faithful family, friends, and fans.
The journey continues and the struggle for literary
perfection shall never end.

I remain faithfully yours,

Ann Jeffries

Titles in the Ann Jeffries
Family Reunion-Wisdom of the Ancestors Series

In print and e-book formats:
Southern Exposures
Another Point of View
Northern Exposures
Uncommon Choices
An Unguarded Moment
Moments To Remember
The Better Part of Valor
Walking on Uneven Ground
Ask Me No Questions…I'll Tell You No Lies
Touch Me In The Morning
All Goodbyes Aren't Gone
A Different Frame of Mind
Judicial Indiscretion (Chi-Town Girls Saga)
Crystal Clear Persuasion (Chi-Town Girls Saga)
Sweet Justice (Chi-Town Girls Saga)
Bittersweet Memories
All in the Family
An Ulterior Motive (Alex-Mont Kids Saga)
A Forever Kind of Love (Alex-Mont Kids Saga)
Walking on the Wilde Side (Alex-Mont Kids Saga)
All That Glitters (Alex-Mont Kids Saga)

In audiobook format:

Southern Exposures, Producer Kelley Hazen
Another Point of View, Producer Glen Pavlovich
Northern Exposures, Producer CJ McAlister
Uncommon Choices, Producer Kelley Hazen
An Unguarded Moment, Producer Richard Dennis Johnson
Moments to Remember, Producer Richard Dennis Johnson
The Better Part of Valor, Producer Richard Dennis Johnson
Walking on Uneven Ground, Producer Richard Dennis Johnson
Ask Me No Questions…I'll Tell You No Lies, Producer Pam Dougherty
Touch Me in the Morning, Producer Ginger Walton
All Goodbyes Aren't Gone, Producer Julian Thomas
A Different Frame of Mind, Producer C. J. McAllister
Judicial Indiscretion, Producer Kelley Hazen
Crystal Clear Persuasion, Producer C. J. McAllister
Sweet Justice, Producer Kelley Hazen
Bittersweet Memories, Producer Kelley Hazen
All in the Family, Producer Kelley Hazen
An Ulterior Motive, Producer Kelley Hazen
A Forever Kind of Love, Producer Kelley Hazen
Walking on the Wilde Side, Producer Kelley Hazen
All That Glitters, Producer Kelley Hazen
Regrets, Producer Kelley Hazen

CHAPTER 1

"Are you going to be in the shower all night?" Satarah Josephine Johnson asked of her cousin, former co-worker, and BFF Mary Ella Baker. Satarah, known to her family as SaraJo, folded fresh towels and put them in the en-suite's linen closet while waiting for Mary Ella. When her cousin showed up unannounced on her doorstep after midnight, in the middle of the week, SaraJo sensed something was radically wrong. Mary Ella was not prone to surprises or impromptu behavior. Well, except that she did up and leave home four years ago on a whim when the handsome Dr. Mark Brooks asked her to go on an adventure with him. He didn't just ask Mary Ella to leave her home and everything she knew for the whole of her life in Summer County, South Carolina. Oh, no, Mark asked Mary Ella *to leave the continental United States!*

What a surprise that was! Steady, conscientious, sedate Mary Ella just up and left. It was so out of character for her that the mind boggled. Of the two women, Satarah thought she would have been more likely to do something so rash. No one, absolutely no one, would have thought Mary Ella capable of picking up, selling all of her worldly goods, and taking off for parts unknown with a man she had known for less than a year.

Well, he wasn't just *any* man, Satarah admitted as she continued to tidy the already fastidiously neat suite. He was Dr. Mark Brooks, after all, and a former Marine; handsome, intelligent, worldly, virile, and filthy rich Mark Brooks. Not that the money would have mattered one iota to Mary Ella. Oh, no. They met, and **WHAMMO**; instant heat!

Mary Ella isn't something the cat dragged, thought Satarah as she continued to cast a critical eye around the suite. On the contrary, her cousin was kind, considerate, and a steady calming influence in a crisis, an understated beauty. Not much rattled Mary Ella in the emergency room, where they both used to work as registered nurses. They were the same age and knew each other extremely well. After all, they went through school together from daycare up to and including nursing school. They were not only blood relatives but also the best of friends. All of their lives, people rarely saw one without the other.

Satarah felt she was viewed and had a well-earned reputation as the more adventurous one. On the other hand, Mary Ella had to be dragged into doing certain things, like dating the county's local bad boys.

Satarah sat on the bed, smiling to herself. They were "*so young, dumb, and full of cum,*" as Mary Ella's gram-mama, Amani, a full-blooded Cherokee, used to say. *She also told me not to date any man who didn't have a library card in his wallet.* Still, she, not Mary Ella, was the one who got knocked up at age fifteen by JoJeff Whitfield. Back in the day, she couldn't stay off JoJeff's Harley Davidson motorcycle or off of JoJeff. He was the consummate rebel without a cause and the most handsome guy in the county.

Mary Ella wasn't impressed with JoJeff or any of the other guys who rode motorcycles in their gang. Her cousin would go to the bike rallies, but she wasn't into any of the guys she met there. People sometimes accused her of being gay because she was so standoffish around guys. However, Mary Ella didn't care enough about what other people thought about her to defend herself against the accusations. She refused to be bullied and simply ignored her accusers.

She did date and went to high school and community events with different boys, but no one in particular. Well, maybe Dennis Lawson, Junior. They were hot and heavy the summer after high school graduation. Mary Ella confided that she didn't give up her virginity to him. When he went away to college in Florida, he would come back as often as possible to see her. Dennis tried to convince her to join him, but by then, she had moved on and was dating Eric Dixon. Eric was also in nursing school with them, and he and Mary Ella dated the whole three years until after graduation. Eric joined the Army so that he could continue his career in medicine at the military's expense. He asked Mary Ella to marry him and to come with him, but she declined.

Eric's career strategy worked, and he became a medical doctor. He came back home, bringing a wife with him, and was on staff at the Summer County Hospital. The wife couldn't hack the country living, and after two years, they divorced, and she moved back to Chicago. Satarah recalled that Eric often asked after Mary Ella. It was clear that he was disappointed to learn that Mary Ella left the county with Mark Brooks. Eric was still single, and Satarah knew he would be elated that Mary Ella was home again.

Now, her cousin was back just as unexpectedly as she left years ago. However, Mary Ella returned without Mark and was entirely too thin, much thinner than she was when she went away. Mary Ella had an enviable amount of beautiful, healthy, and thick hair, likely from her Cherokee ancestry. Now her lustrous hair, along with the desirable body curves, was all but gone, too.

Satarah understood, even back then, how much her cousin wanted to help alleviate a patient's pain and suffering. Mary Ella was a volunteer for the last four years with the non-government organization or NGO, Doctors Without Borders, DWB. Thankfully, Mary Ella was home again, but without Dr. Mark Brooks, the man she left home to be with. Something was definitely afoot, and Satarah intended to find out exactly what it was.

"Seriously, Mary Ella, are you going to be in there until the roosters crow?" SaraJo impatiently asked.

"Probably," Mary Ella called out to her cousin over the sound of the shower noise. "You should go back to bed, SaraJo. I'll be fine on my own. We'll talk later in the morning."

Satarah thought about it. She and her husband, Douglas, were in the midst of an all-encompassing love fest and getting to the really good stuff when Mary Ella arrived unannounced and carrying little more than a backpack and duffle bag. Douglas would probably be asleep by now, but he never complained when she woke him in the night. He told her she was the best type of gift to receive, no matter what time it was. She would gift him again tonight after learning what the heck was going on with her uncharacteristically crazy cousin. Why there were so many changes to her cousin's appearance would be among the first questions she would ask. Where Mark was would be the next. "You must be hungry. You usually can't resist my cooking. Maybe that will entice you to come out of the shower. I'll see what I can scrounge up and be back shortly."

"Okay," Mary Ella called back, though she really didn't have an appetite. *It was just good to be home,* she thought, *or, at least, it was good to be back in Summer County, South Carolina, safe and sound.* After being away and in danger for so long, it was a place she didn't think she would live to see again. In the time since she left, she had seen interesting parts of the world. However, they were not glamorous spots. Instead, they were some of the worst of what war, despair, degradation, poverty, and disease could do to the beautiful landscape and the humans who inhabited the lands. Man's inhumanity to man was on constant display. Then, again, it was what experienced nurses were expected to deal with. She did the impossible with nothing but sheer will and coped with the risks to life and limb as they came. The reward for those risks was the ability to help people who otherwise had no hope of survival whatsoever. To be able to put a smile on a child's face just before he or she drew their last breath was sometimes all her skills and abilities could garner.

There were occasions when, for days on end, she worked with little or no rest in the humidity and sweltering heat, reaching over 100 degrees in the shade or at night in freezing cold mountains and unbearable during the day. There were times when they barely had enough clean water to drink, and none to use for a bath or even to wash. One could only hope for a thunderstorm and torrential downpours and a sliver of soap to get clean. However, the rain only added to the high humidity at night and into the next day.

Toiletry items, like deodorant, toothpaste, soap or even a bath cloth or toilet paper or a blasted tampon, were like manna from heaven. There were no facilities to relieve themselves of natural bodily waste. Rather it was often necessary to find some place in the jungle to dig a hole and bury waste, hoping no deadly snakes, tarantulas or other lethal creatures, like alligators or crocodiles, took offense. In Africa and Asia, they were ever mindful of the big cats; lions and tigers could track scents for miles.

Being on the move, from one location to another not indicated on any map, prevented them from setting up a camp to rest and eat decent food. That is, except if they were assigned to a refugee region in some war-ravished country. They could share the food and other supplies airdropped into the area on parachutes by NGOs. Of course, those supplies could be anything, but they most often hoped for medicines to treat the ill and shovels to dig graves for the dead and wells for water.

Mary Ella luxuriated in the body sprays surrounding her as she slowly sponged her body clean. This was a luxury she missed most. Then she remembered Mark scrubbing her clean before making the most wonderfully exciting and joyful love to her in the midst of the jungle. They were like Adam and Eve, two nymphs in the Garden of Eden… until they were captured before making it back to their camp. *Where was Mark now?* she wondered, still deathly afraid he had not survived.

Then another vision kept intruding on her thoughts of Mark. Another man who touched her. A stranger who took her without her consent, but with a kind of single-minded determination that had her craving… *No! No! No! I can't think of that, of him. I won't think of him! What he did to her was wrong! She had to keep reminding herself of that.*

She had to put that behind her, the shrinks told her. So, she forced herself to focus on the here and now. As she shut off the water and looked around the large but purposefully old-fashion bathroom, she noted Satarah had done an awesome job restoring every detail of the antebellum mansion to its former glory and then some more beyond. With the family's help, the huge mansion was converted into a three-story bed and breakfast in time for the Alexanders' annual Juneteenth family reunion nearly five years ago.

The Alexanders hold a reunion each year for ten days encompassing the June 19, 1865, commemoration of Freedom Day, the date known as Juneteenth Independence Day for the enslaved people. An ever-increasing number of relatives attend to memorialize the abolition of slavery in Texas. More generally, they came together to celebrate the enslaved African Americans' emancipation throughout the Confederate South.

Although Mary Ella was related to Satarah's father's side of the family, the Alexanders were an inclusive dynasty of kinfolk and legion. They took her in as if she were a blood relative. In fact, Mary Ella took her nursing training under Satarah's aunt Sylvia Benson Alexander's careful tutelage at the Summer County Academy. She'd bet Sylvia, Satarah's mother's sister, was still the dean of the Academy Nursing School and the Director of Nursing at Summer County General Hospital. Mary Ella hoped Sylvia would hire her either as an instructor in the nursing school or on staff at the hospital where she previously worked in the emergency room before she met Mark. Otherwise, she'd have to contend with offering her services as a private duty nurse or maybe, if all else failed, she'd have to move on to a different city or state to find work.

Other than her cousin, Satarah, and Satarah's family, Mary Ella didn't have any real ties to the community where she grew up. Her parents were deceased, and she had no siblings. She had distant relatives among the Indigenous people of her mother's Cherokee family and widely dispersed family relations from her father's side of his family.

Still, Mary Ella didn't relish the idea of leaving again, particularly not now, but she didn't have many other options to work with at the moment. She was pretty much alone in the world. Most of her remaining relatives in her age group were scattered beyond Summer County, all except Satarah and Satarah's sister, Carlotta. Although Satarah and Carlotta's mother, Mariah, was formerly a relative by marriage, now she lived in Paris, France. The last anyone heard from or about Carlotta, she had run off with Satarah's husband at the time, Jonathan Jeffrey Whitfield, JoJeff, family members called him, leaving Satarah penniless with his and Carlotta's twin, male newborns behind for Satarah to raise.

If that wasn't adding insult to injury for Satarah to swallow, years later, after she divorced JoJeff in abstention and married Douglas Johnson, JoJeff returned to the county. He took one look at how prosperous Satarah had become in his absence with ownership of the successful bed and breakfast and tried to insinuate himself into her life. The last missive Mary Ella received from Satarah informed her that JoJeff was still trying to make trouble for Satarah and her new husband, Douglas Johnson. JoJeff had joined forces with Satarah's jack-leg preacher of a father, Obadiah Baker James.

Though Mary Ella detested Obadiah and resented the fact she was related by blood to him, through her now-deceased father, Robert Baker, Jr., and his older sister, Caledonia Baker James, she didn't wish him ill. Caledonia was married to Buster James and only had one son, Obadiah. All of her father's side of the family, the Baker side, were deceased now, except for a few relatives spread far and wide. Minnie Baker, a chef, lived somewhere in Atlantic Beach, South Carolina. Her brother Paul, a bakery store owner, and his son, a military man, were believed to be living in Los Angeles, California.

Mary Ella admitted to herself that she wasn't close to any of her father's other relatives the way she was with Satarah. They had grown up together, trained as nurses together, and remained best friends through the years. Although her cousin, Satarah's father, Obadiah, still lived in the community and pastored a church and congregation there, Mary Ella didn't care for him. The way he sometimes looked at her when she was younger and playing with Satarah as children made her decidedly uncomfortable.

Well, she had enough to contend with now and the reason she came back to the only close family member she had left. Her future was uncertain, she thought as she continued to prepare for bed. At least, she was not destitute. The NGO paid her back wages and covered her travel expenses. Still, having to re-establish herself was going to take time and patience.

Having plenty of both was established while in captivity, awaiting the rescue she wasn't sure would ever come. Yet, it did arrive one moonless night as she slept among her captors, the concubine of Kaseem, one of the fiercest warriors, or, at least, it's what she thought at the time. However, though she didn't understand why, it was nevertheless her belief that Kaseem actively participated in getting her out of the terrorists' camp. In retrospect, he protected her all of the time though she hadn't realized it until she was rescued.

He told her he had to take her against her will, or she would have been shared with the other terrorists in the camp and then killed as an infidel. He had to fight another man to keep her, and he won. The other man split off with a different faction taking Mark's unconscious body with them in a separate direction.

Captivity and being forcibly molested was devastating. Still, she replaced what was happening to her with images of sharing Mark's bed nearly every night before and after they left Summer County. Mark wanted to rejoin the NGO Doctors Without Borders, so they did. Her nursing skills were a valuable commodity to the NGO. She and Mark were fine until the night they were told of a limestone quarry, spring, and waterfall not far from the village where they made camp for the night. They worked for hours tending to the villagers' medical needs and, in the wee hours of the night, took advantage of a respite and the rare find of clean water in which to bathe and wash their clothes. Their native-born Libyan medical team and guides knew they sought privacy from time to time but cautioned them to be careful and not make noisy lovemaking sounds. Noises carried long distances in the otherwise silent night. They did make some noise, not a lot but were caught unaware while naked on the ground as they climaxed.

Taliban or Al Qaeda fighters overran the quarry and their camp; she didn't know which sect they belonged to. They may have even been ISIS or Boko Haram. The next thing she knew, she was wed to Kaseem the same night with Mark's scent still fresh on her body. Mark was taken away to a different terrorist camp, and she hadn't seen or heard from him since. Still, she had to put it all out of her mind for now.

Mary Ella rinsed the conditioner out of her short cap of hair in the sink before she dried herself. Jet lag was setting in, and she was weary from all the travel she had to endure to get to Goodwill. She took advantage of the little bottle of lotion in the gift basket and used the whole thing on her body. Her cousin made organic soap and lotion. Their scents were wonderful and served to soften her too dry skin. The sheets also smelled good and felt glorious on her nakedness, another luxury she hadn't had in years. It didn't take long for sleep to overtake her. She put her troublesome dreams away the way the shrink had taught her. Tomorrow was coming, and she had to sleep fast to be ready to face it.

When Satarah returned to Mary Ella's bedroom with a tray of food, she found her cousin sound asleep. She placed the covered tray on the little, gate-legged table by a rocking chair near the window, then quietly left the room. She got to her own bedroom and was surprised to find her husband sitting up in bed, reading a journal.

"How is Mary Ella?" Douglas put the Fireman's Journal aside and pulled the covers back for her to get into bed.

She disrobed and climbed in next to him, getting comfortable in his warm embrace. "I don't know, babe. There's something different. Something is off. I can't put my finger on it, but something has changed with my best friend." She curled into Douglas as he enveloped her more securely in his strong embrace, then she looked up at him. She loved that he cared about her family as much as she did. He took on her burdens as if they were his, too. She loved him for the man he was and thoroughly enjoyed being his wife. Rubbing his solid chest, she played with his plump, raisin-like nipples.

"What's on your agenda that you can move around to make time?"

"We're at full capacity in the cottages and near capacity in the main house, so I had to put Mary Ella into one of the last bedrooms up on the third floor. It's going to be a busy morning. There are two receptions planned for noon, one baby shower for about thirty people in the Rose Salon and one bridal shower with escalating numbers in the Parisian Room. Dixie Carter is so scattered she keeps adding people to her guest list without telling me. So, I don't have a good head count."

"There's the Low Country Book Club meeting at three in the East Library. They have a noted author, Adelaide Jackson, coming in for a talk about her latest novel and then holding a book signing after. She writes the Firelight Love series our book club is reading now. I wanted to make time to hear her and get her to autograph my copy of her book. The book club is set to read ***Hearth Heat,*** Ms. Jackson's newest novel. We're working on getting her to come back here while she's on her next book tour. I'm on the committee to try to make that happen."

"I've heard of her. Isn't she related to your cousin Vivian Alexander Montgomery?"

"She is, yes. Adelaide is Vivian's niece by marriage. She's Vivian's first husband, Derrick Jackson's niece."

"Now, I remember. Adelaide came with her family to the Alexander family reunion a few years ago. Adelaide is Grant Jackson's daughter."

"That's right. She's made quite a name for herself, and she's been on the New York Times' Best Sellers List several years running."

"Okay, now I've got it. What else is on your agenda for later today?"

"I've got to get set up for your Men's Club dinner by six. So, I probably won't have a lot of time to spend with Mary Ella."

"Then call in reinforcements and me and the boys to work for you. We don't have baseball practice today. I'll come home early with the boys, and we'll help you get everything done. Don't forget. I know your moves, babe. You've probably got everything already arranged for each scheduled event and only need labor to do the setup and clean up. Get some rest now. Mary Ella's home, so you'll have plenty of time to talk with her later today."

She smiled because he did know her well, but not everything. Reaching under the covers, she found him warm and responsive to her touch. He grunted in the sexy way he had of letting her know she pleased him. Adding tongue and breath to her mission, she had him flat on his back in the throes of bliss in no time at all. He turned the tables on her, so to speak, and had her gasping out his name in absolute euphoria. Oh, my, he certainly knew her well.

CHAPTER 2

The Summer House was alive, and so was she, thought Mary Ella, when she woke with the bright morning sun streaming in the bedroom windows. Her suite faced the east, and she thought of Mark somewhere in Africa or Asia, still a captive while she lay in a comfortable bed enjoying the familiar sounds of her home. Roosters crowed in the distance, cows made their displeasure with full utters known, and horses whinnied, romping in the fields. She hadn't heard the pigs and hogs and wondered whether Satarah rebuilt the pig pens further away from the mansion as she had planned.

Then her thoughts turned to someone else, and she wondered whether he faced Mecca and knelt on his sajadah or prayer rug for afternoon prayers. Five times a day, he stopped to participate in the mandatory prayer sessions with the others of the Muslim faith. Initially, she thought she could escape during one of their prayer sessions when she wasn't carefully watched. Still, there were always men on guard patrolling the camp's perimeter, making escape virtually impossible.

Escape finally came, and she was home now safe, if not completely sound. Rising from the comfortable bed, she attended to her morning needs, dressed in the only other clean clothes she had, and prepared to join the human race again.

When she brought down the tray Satarah left in the room much earlier that morning, Douglas and the children were eating breakfast in the kitchen at the round banquet table. The twin boys, Jonathan and Jeffrey, knew her well. However, Benson James Whitfield, Satarah's firstborn with JoJeff, had only been returned to her four years ago. Benson was born when Satarah was only fifteen years old. She was forced, by her father, to give Benson up for adoption at birth. Obadiah told her that a fine family adopted her baby, but when Douglas went looking for him, he found the preteen boy living on the streets in Chicago and brought him home to Satarah.

Shortly thereafter, Mary Ella left with Mark before she had an opportunity to bond with Benson, who was her cousin and now well into his teen years. Donovan Johnson, Doug's adopted son from his first marriage, was actually one of her patients and the reason Satarah and Douglas met and fell in love during a monster snowstorm that shut down all of South Carolina for nearly a week.

Now, in addition to the four teenage boys, since their marriage, Satarah and Douglas had two daughters, four-year-old Arianna Mariah, and two-year-old Katherine Lynn. Neither girl was born when she left, but Mary Ella loved them on sight. They were beautiful, bright-eyed little girls, both with a profusion of long hair like their mother's, which refused to be tamed. Though Jonathan and Jeffrey tried, both girls' hair resembled a cone of cotton candy. It was clear these little charmers had their teenage brothers twisted around their little fingers along with their father.

Mary Ella sat through breakfast with the family and answered a barrage of questions about her travels while Satarah and her helpers tended to the breakfast buffet for the bed and breakfast guests.

Even those who lived in the county frequented The Summer House for breakfast because they loved Satarah's cooking. Mary Ella admitted she missed it as well. The fluffy, plate-sized pancakes were stacked high and dripped with real butter and fresh strawberry or blueberry sauce. Thick, crispy bacon and little, hand-made hot sausages and patties lined a platter on colorful doilies. A whipping bowl full of scrambled eggs, with finely chopped peppers, onions, garlic, and cheese mixed in, was rapidly disappearing from sight. The grapefruit juice was ice cold and refreshing with lime wedges floating among the miniature ice cubes.

It tickled her to see Arianna and Katherine, known in the family as Ari and Kate, eating lemons as if they were sweet fruit. Still, the meal was hands down something dreams were made of. Notably, when in the jungle, their MREs, meals-ready-to-eat, ran out, and they had to eat whatever they could catch and kill. Sometimes they couldn't make a fire, so they had to eat the raw grubs they found under rocks.

The rainforests in the world were a veritable Garden of Eden if they knew what to look for. Mark was very adept at living off the land. More often than not, they were on foot. In some countries, horses or mules were purchased for outrageous sums. She had ridden camels and even elephants to reach settlements inland and well off the beaten track. Now, to sit eating the food she grew up with and often took for granted, she remembered how little some of the villagers in Africa, Asia, and remote areas of South America survived on.

"What's on your mind, Mary Ella?" Satarah sat down at the table with two mugs of aromatic coffee. Satarah's exceptional coffee was a dark-roasted blend combined with chocolate and mint. Passing one cup to her cousin and easing back comfortably in a chair at the breakfast table, she kicked off her shoes and put her feet up in another chair across from her.

That was when Mary Ella realized the kitchen was cleared and quiet. "Where is everyone?" She frowned, looking around. "They were just here."

"Thirty minutes ago. You've been zoned out for a while. Douglas left to take the children to school and head to work. He leaves a little early because he's teaching Benson to drive. My workers are clearing the hallway of room service trays."

"Doug took the girls, too?"

"Oh, yes, the Johnson girls, Miss Arianna Mariah and Miss Katherine Lynn, wouldn't miss a day of classes at the academy to spend with their mama. How soon you forgot," Satarah teased. "They take them young at Summer County Academy. Ari can read at four years old, and two-year-old Kate can write her alphabet and numbers. They're like sponges at that age. Douglas is so proud of his ladies that he's bursting at the seams."

Mary Ella smiled at Satarah. "He's not the only one," she teased her cousin. "You look so happy, SaraJo."

"That's because I *am* happy. I'm married to a man I trust, respect, and love, but enough about me. I want to know what's going on with you and not just the surface stuff about riding a camel or an elephant."

"There's really not much more to tell." She prevaricated.

"Then why didn't you tell me you were coming home? The last text message I received from you was when you and Mark were headed into the mountains somewhere in Timbuktu."

"Not quite Timbuktu. Though I've been there. It's in Mali," Mary Ella took another sip of her juice, avoiding the coffee. "We were in Libya on the Mediterranean Sea."

Satarah wasn't going to give up on this topic. "You didn't even hint you were coming home. Is this for a visit or are you planning to stay awhile?"

"I'm back for as long as I can stay." Mary Ella didn't know what the future held for her beyond the here and now. So, her comments were noncommittal. "I need to find a job, someplace to live, and to buy or lease a car. I plan to talk with Mrs. Alexander whenever I can get an appointment with her. Maybe she needs someone to teach a class at the academy or a position on the hospital staff."

"You're avoiding my question, Mary Ella. Did you and Mark have a falling out? Is that why he's not with you?"

"No, we're not at odds. Mark's, uh, still in Libya." Mary Ella had no idea where. Though she was rescued and sent home, Mark was still in captivity as far as she knew. She wanted to stay until he was found and brought back, but she had no papers, no resources, and the countryside where she and Mark had been taken was outside of the Libyan government's control. The NGO she worked for, Doctors Without Borders, got her out of the country and debriefed. They arranged for her to come back to the United States. There was nothing she could do to stay.

Currently, tribal militias, rebels, and various Islamist extremist groups ran roughshod and rampaged over the less populated areas and remote villages. They were nomadic people who took into captivity whole villages, sometimes killing the men and taking the women and maybe the children. They might set up camp one day and be gone the next.

Mary Ella knew there was a possibility of high risk to their health, welfare, and lives in some of the countries they entered to provide medical aid. The fact that Mark was a man of color, fluently spoke the languages, was a former Marine, and a medical doctor helped them through some sticky situations. Still, they were Americans regardless of their backgrounds or ethnicities.

However, she never expected to be captured and separated from Mark. When they were discovered, he bravely fought to protect her, but he was overpowered and knocked unconscious before he was taken away. She was terrified he would be killed, but she was told by the NGO much later after her rescue that Mark had been seen still alive and forced to provide medical aid to his captors.

Plans were underway to get him out the same way they had rescued her, but no date for his rescue was specified. On the surface, America was spouting the party line—they did not negotiate with terrorists. However, under the surface, she was assured that much activity was underway through back channels to rescue him.

Although she didn't know it when they met, Mark Brooks was an integral member of the über wealthy Townsend Pharmaceutical family. The majority of the relatives, both male and female, were prominent medical doctors and researchers. They married doctors and specialized in a wide array of medical specialties. The pharmaceutical company was among the world's most extensive research facilities. It created specialized medicines other companies found too expensive to manufacture.

What Mary Ella didn't know or understand was why Mark never told her about his family. She assumed he came up in life, pulling himself up by his own bootstraps, just as she had. However, nothing could have been further from the truth. Still, she loved him without knowing everything she should have known about him. Now, though she was married to someone else in a tribal ceremony without her consent, she still wanted Mark back home safe and sound.

Years earlier, before Mark and Douglas ever heard of Summer County, they were in the Marines together. She wondered whether Douglas knew how wealthy Mark was. She didn't know how to ask, but she knew she couldn't continue to field questions from her family about Mark.

"You're not listening to me, are you?" Satarah frowned.

"I'm not… It's not intentional, SaraJo." Mary Ella wearily palmed her face and then tunneled her fingers through her short crop of hair. "I've just got a lot on my mind at the moment."

"If one of your worries is accommodations, you know that you're welcome to stay here with us for as long as you want. This is your home, Mary Ella."

"I can't do it, SaraJo. You're running a very successful business here."

"It's a family business and you're my family."

"Yes, from the Benson side of your family. Your mother's family, not your father's family."

"According to the right reverend, it should be his because he was married to mama, but it's neither here nor there. If you don't want to stay in the main house, take one of the cottages in the back of the house. They all have a great view of the Santee River. They're small, less than seven hundred square feet, and furnished, but we've renovated them into two bedrooms and one and a half baths with a laundry closet, an open-concept kitchen, dining, and living area combined.

"As you know, they used to be slave quarters. We tried to keep the exteriors historically accurate and rustic. For those more adventurous types, in a few of the cottages, we left the interior the same as when built in the late 1700s, early 1800s. So, if you can deal with small spaces, it should work out for you to take one of the remodeled cottages."

"Thanks, Satarah. That sounds perfect, so I'll take it, but only if you permit me to pay rent."

"Sight unseen?"

"I just need somewhere to be until I sort out what I'm going to do next."

"Then it's a deal. However, I determine what the rent will be."

She named an amount that had Mary Ella shaking her head.

"That can't be nearly enough."

"It is if I say it is." Satarah grinned. "Grab your coffee while I get the keys to the cottages. The guests have cleared out, and the units have been cleaned. We have more people scheduled to register today, but you can pick the one you want before anyone else gets here."

"I'm a little dehydrated from all the traveling. So, I'll get a bottle of water for the time being."

"You do look a little off. Are you sure you're okay?"

"I'm fine, Mother Satarah Josephine." Mary Ella mildly accused. "In a few days, I'll be completely back on my feet."

CHAPTER 3

When his cell phone chimed, he was in his office looking at his patient's X-rays on a lightbox. Absently, he picked it up and answered. "Dr. Dixon."

"Eric! Did you hear? Did you hear?" his youngest sister, Hester, shouted excitedly in his ear, causing him to move the device an arm's length away and flip on the speaker feature.

"Hear what, Hester?"

"She's *back!*"

He continued to study the X-rays moving in closer and pulling his magnifier closer to a small shadow on the film. He circled the spot with a dry erase pencil and gave his sister more of his attention, "Okay, I'll bite. Who's back?"

"Mary Ella!"

That got his undivided attention—big time. Taking the phone off the speaker app, he frowned. "How do you know?"

"I overheard Jonathan and Jeffrey Johnson talking at lunch in the cafeteria at school. So, I asked, and they confirmed that, yes, Mary Ella got home sometime last night or early this morning. Isn't this great news?" She happily chirped.

He had to sit down, so he hiked his hip up on the edge of his desk and pinched the bridge of his nose. "Yes, of course."

"You don't sound too excited."

"I am, Hester. I'm happy that she's safely home. She's been away for a long time."

"The best part is that she came back alone. Dr. Brooks isn't with her."

Well, Eric thought, *that **was** something.* He liked what he heard about the man with whom Mary Ella left Summer County. She deserved to be with someone who would cherish her. Of course, it was disappointing to know she left the country with Brooks when she wouldn't even leave the county with him when he asked her to marry him.

Old regrets die hard, he thought.

"He may come later. You never know." Eric offered and sighed deeply, coming to grips with reality. "In any case, thanks for the heads up, but I need to get back to work. I've got a patient waiting for test results."

"Okay, but when are you going to see her?"

"I doubt that I will, Hester. I really don't know. I'll talk with you another time."

"Okay, I love you. Bye."

"I love you more. Bye." He put down the phone and palmed his face, briskly rubbing his five o'clock shadow, though it was only about three-thirty in the afternoon. *So, Mary Ella is back,* he contemplated. Eric had to admit, at least to himself, it was really good news. Still, it likely didn't mean she was back and willing to pick up with him where they left off years ago. *Hell!* They were what, seventeen or eighteen years old? That was more than ten years ago now. He recognized that he still had residual feelings for Mary Ella. Thoughts of her never really left him. After all, she was his first love, his endless love.

While he was away finishing his residency program at Chicago Med, he heard about her and Dr. Brooks. Hester was a fountain of information. He fully expected to return and find Mary Ella was married to Mark Brooks with a couple of kids to their credit. The news she left the country to join Doctors Without Borders with Brooks was staggering.

Then again, he and Ginger flew to Vegas and got married on a lark. His family was disappointed they didn't have a wedding at home. However, although he had a big family, Ginger's family was small. She had a brother living in Canada and a grandmother living in a nursing home in Alabama, the victim of Alzheimer's disease. Her grandmother raised her and her brother after their parents died. Ginger didn't see the need for a big shindig with such a small family and a few close friends.

Acquiescing to her edict, they spent a week in Nevada. After all, Ginger and he would start married life in Summer County, South Carolina. His family members and friends would surround them, and she would find family support she didn't have growing up. He wanted to bring her grandmother to live with them and invite her brother, a man he had yet to meet, to visit them. She wasn't high on those suggestions, so he let it lay for a while.

He and Ginger lived together in Chicago while he finished his residency program. He took the United States Medical License Exam. Eric waited for the results of his application to receive his South Carolina Medical License so that he could return home to practice medicine. He still had his nursing license, and it only took one call to his guru, Mrs. Sylvia Benson Alexander, the woman who trained him, for his medical license to be granted.

Ginger wanted him to accept an offer he received to remain at Chicago Med, but the bright lights and big city weren't for him. It was always his intention to return to Summer County to where he was born and raised in a family and community he loved. Both sets of his grandparents were still alive when he came home. Now, years later, he still had one grandparent, his paternal grandfather Junior Dixon. He had a feisty grandaunt, too, Lois Dixon Kennedy and her husband, Hampton Kennedy. His parents were hale and hearty, and his six siblings were all doing well for themselves. He was the middle child, and he was surrounded by a tightly-knit slew of cousins, uncles, and aunts. This place, Summer County, was important to him, and as he thought about it, so was Mary Ella Baker.

"Dr. Dixon?"

"Yes?"

"Are you leaving for the day?" one of the administrative assistants, Julia Hunt, moved toward him. He shared the admins with two other doctors in their suite of offices.

"I'm heading up to West 320 to see my patient; then I'm off duty. Why?"

"I thought you might want to join a bunch of us later for drinks at Jinx Juke Joint."

"Probably not. Have a good time. I'll see you on Monday."

He started away and was stopped, just out of sight of his office, by another doctor in the hallway for a quick consult. Still, he overheard one of the nurses, Carlie, say, "You really should give up trying to get next to Dr. Eric Hunk-a-mania Dixon, Julia. He's just not into you. He doesn't even call you by your name."

"That's all right. I know *his* name, so we'll see," Julia confidently responded. "He's been divorced for years now. A man as phine as he is has to be getting sex from someone. Why shouldn't it be me? I don't want to think he's jacking off in the shower or letting that fine body of his go dormant." She'd worked hard to be reassigned to Dr. Dixon's panel. She wasn't giving up yet. Not by a long shot.

"You may have better luck with one of his brothers. At least they haven't been married."

"No, I know they're all good-looking men, but there's just something about Eric that says we'd be simpatico."

"Yeah, right," her friend, Carlie, laughed.

When he moved on toward the stairs, he smiled to himself. Women on the hospital staff had pursued him, but Carlie was right. He wasn't into Julia Hunt. Eric knew her name, but she was only about twenty-two years old. He preferred women with a little more seasoning, so he wasn't tempted. Plus, he didn't use Summer County General as a dating pool the way his brother, Byron, the dental surgeon, did. The hospital didn't have any rules against dating co-workers. Still, in his off-hours, he preferred to date women who had other careers outside of medicine.

Rather than take an elevator up, he took the stairs two at a time because he liked to keep his body in shape and his options open. Still, he wasn't worried overmuch, but it was gratifying to know he still had a certain appeal to the opposite sex. Down the road, marriage and children were still on his radar, but for now, he had no one in his sights.

His cousin, James Dixon, and James' wife, Janice, set him up with one of the professors at the university where they worked. Dr. Vernice

Bradford Bond, an astrophysicist, Rhodes Scholar, and a Ph.D. in astronomy, was also a divorcee who traveled extensively and lectured at various universities in the United States and abroad. Vernice would be in Columbia at the university a few times a month for two or three days. She'd call ahead of time to let him know when she was arriving and departing, but if he couldn't get away to have dinner or anything else with her, she didn't take offense.

Vernice was happily divorced and intended to remain that way for the rest of her life. Though she wasn't a candidate for his long-term plans, their near-term acquaintance worked. They didn't make demands on each other, and their contact was infrequent enough that he wasn't waiting with bated breath for her return each month.

He couldn't say the same thing about Mary Ella Baker's return with any amount of detachment. She was exactly the woman he could see in his future so that bit of news today from his sister had rocked him to his core.

Reaching the last flight of stairs, he went through the door toward his patient's room. Eric stopped at the nurses' station to review the electronic chart and make a few notes. He didn't see anything troubling in the chart or film about which to be overly concerned. Still, he wanted his patient closely monitored overnight and, if there were no changes, he'd discharge the man in the morning and have him report for weekly outpatient visits for a while.

The door to W320 was ajar, but Eric still knocked and waited for permission to enter.

"Come in?"

"Mr. Winter?"

"Yes? Oh, hello, Dr. Dixon. I hope you've got good news."

"So far, so good. Let me take a listen." Taking his stethoscope from around his neck, he examined his patient's bronchial sounds. He checked the man's back and his chest while coaxing his patient to breathe in and out. He didn't hear anything to concern him overmuch. He hung his stethoscope around his neck and regarded his patient. "I've reviewed your test results and X-rays. I see one shadow on your lungs I want to keep an eye on. The nodule may have formed due to an infection in your lungs, which has cleared up. As you know, asthma is an inflammatory disease of the lungs. It makes breathing difficult and brings on coughing attacks, wheezing, tightness in the chest, and shortness of breath. I believe you've sufficiently recovered from your acute bronchial asthma attack to be released. I'm having you monitored one more night and, if all goes well, I'll be in to discharge you in the morning."

"That is good news. Thank you, Dr. Dixon."

"You're welcome, Mr. Winter. I'll want to see you in my office once a week for about a month. I also want to repeat your lab work a few more times, okay?"

"Yes, I can do that."

"Good. Any questions?"

"Well,…" he hesitated.

Eric took a seat on the foot of the man's bed. "What is it?"

"You see, the attack happened when I was, uh, you know, with someone."

"Okay, you mean you were having sex when your breathing was affected."

"Yes, that. I mean, I've been in here for four days. My friend will likely be the one to pick me up from the hospital if you release me tomorrow. Can I have, you know…when I get home tomorrow?"

Eric had to cover his mouth and jaw to keep the smile at bay. "I believe your lungs are sufficiently clear as not to be a problem with heavy breathing, but take it easy. You may want to test the waters a bit before going full bore."

Mr. Winter breathed a huge sigh of relief before thanking him.

"I'll see you in the morning." Eric shook the man's hand.

He visited the men's room before he left the floor and walked down the steps and out to the doctors' parking lot. He signed out via his smartphone and noticed a text message from his mother. He took off his stethoscope, white lab coat and put them in the medical bag he kept in the trunk of his SUV, along with a complete change of clothes and toiletry items. His mom's message didn't appear to be urgent, but he'd stop by the farm to see her since it was on his way home.

Ten minutes later, he entered his ancestral home.

"Hello, Son." Leroy Dixon smiled as Eric came into the house through the kitchen door.

"Hi, Dad. What're you cooking? It smells delicious."

"Beef Stroganoff. You wanna stay for dinner? I made plenty."

"I just stopped in because Mom sent a text to me, but if it's okay with you, I'll take some to go."

"I'll fix it up for you." His father nodded.

"Have you got any apple butter here at the house?" Eric asked.

"I think I can scare up a jar. You makin' biscuits?"

"For breakfast tomorrow, yes. If you want, I'll bring a dozen down to you on my way to the hospital in the morning."

"'Preciate it. Here, have a glass of this wine and take one to your mama." His father poured two goblets. "Your mother is in the den."

"Thanks, Dad." Accepting the wine, Eric headed for the den.

He walked through the big, old rambling farmhouse his paternal great-grandparents built with their own two hands with help from their families when they were young newlyweds. It always smelled of beeswax and lemon oil. The scent was a reminder of his youth when he and his six siblings were required to polish the furniture to a high sheen. Not a speck of dust was permitted to be on any surface in the front parlor then or now, nor would there ever be. That's where his grands always "received company," as they used to say. It was still kept in museum-quality condition, though it was rarely used these days. When they got together, they tended to lounge in the kitchen and lend a hand making the meals. All of the men in the family could cook, not so much the women. Most of the family had moved out, except Hester. She was a counselor at Summer County Academy, the only school in the county.

As one of the best schools in the United States, according to several boards of accreditation, including Mensa International, Summer County Academy operated year-round and had a very unique program. The students took only one class for six weeks, then had a two-week break before taking a different class for six weeks, changing subjects on and on throughout the year. As a result, students excelled because of their ability to focus on only one subject at a time. The students weren't grouped by age or grade, but by the proficiency level in each subject. Hester, a math advisor, wouldn't trade her position at the school for any other. She thrived there.

By specific standards, the United States was currently ranked number seventeen globally in education. Not so for Summer County Academy, which was ranked high in the ninetieth percentile in global education. Hester watched with great pride when her students competed on the world stage against countries of higher rankings and exceeded expectations.

Eric knew he'd find his mother in the den where she and their father used to sequester their seven offspring to do homework every day, including weekends. Mom managed the family's whole foods produce store on the edge of their farm while their father and grandfather worked the farm filled with fresh fruits and vegetables. They were up by five in the morning and their roadside market was open and serving customers by six. There were signs and billboards up for a few miles in each direction, announcing the fresh crops available, including the boiled peanuts. Hospital staff and restaurant owners came in early to buy fresh produce to serve during the day. Other patrons, particularly construction workers and road repair crews, came in early to pick up breakfast and fill their thermoses with coffee. Most would return to pick up lunch, too.

Many a day, the Dixon kids were out in the fields bringing in the harvest in the rain or hot summer days while people were steadily pulling into the parking lot and, if that was full, which it often was, they just pulled to the side of the road and parked. Their store had a wide array of barrels, flats, bins, and trays of freshly-picked produce for sale six days a week. On Sunday afternoons, Dad and Granddad would roast chickens on a spit and deep fry fish. They would sell dinners and added collard greens, potato salad, coleslaw, cornbread, and a slice of cake or pie. Cars would be lined up and down the road with people coming to pick up phoned-in orders. Those dinners helped put all six of Leroy and Sandra Miller Dixon's offspring through schools of higher education.

Now, thanks to their cousin, Dr. James Dixon, his father, Romelo Dixon, and the Alexander family, Leroy and Sandra Dixon, didn't have to work so hard. They had an Alexander-Dixon Industries (ADI) consortium of hydroponics farms specializing in specific, highly sought-after goods. They also had a crew of farmhands eager to learn the new farming techniques and were paid fairly in the process.

The LeRoy and Sandra Dixon contingent of ADI grew vine fruits like strawberries, blueberries, blackberries, and red, green, and blue grapes. Cantaloupe, honeydew, and watermelon were in a special section. They were closer to the vine grown vegetables of string beans, tomatoes, cucumber, and squash. They also grew root vegetables, like greens, kale, turnips and turnip greens, white and sweet potatoes, carrots, beets, and rutabaga. In the fall, they still had an acre dedicated to a pumpkin patch.

The new technology of growing foods in water turned two hundred thirty acres of their available farmland into a veritable Garden of Eden. They grew produce year-round in glass-enclosed, air-filtered, and controlled environments and experienced a higher yield of healthy produce using this method than they ever did farming only part of the year in the soil.

They distilled a few vintages of table wines and canned some of their produce for jams, jellies, and preserves. They also sold fresh off the vine locally or to boutique stores and restaurants all over the region and beyond.

Romelo Dixon managed ADI from a home office on his property, a mile down the road. Romelo and his wife, Olivia Alexander Dixon, Mayor of Goodwill, had twin sons, Donald and James, daughters-in-law, Cecile and Janice, both Ph.D.s, and a bunch of grandchildren. Donald Dixon, an MIT undergrad and Harvard Law grad, handled any business ADI had that required a lawyer. Still, all of Junior Dixon's three sons, Leroy, Albert, and Romelo's farms were used in the enterprise to benefit all.

That was the thing about the Dixons. They were a clan and tended to live within close proximity of one another on ancestral land they inherited along the Santee River. In fact, the road into this part of the county was called Dixon Lane with little spurs off the main, single-lane road, which were named for the children of the now-long-deceased elders, like Billie's Place. Eric's home was a two-story 1800 American antebellum farmhouse revival located on Gilly's Place. It was a home he built for himself and Ginger, but as life would have it, she didn't like the house, the farm or the idea of living in the country so far away from a major metropolitan area, like Chicago or New York City or Los Angeles. She left after only two years.

"Mom?" he called out.

"In the den, Eric."

He entered and found her exactly as he expected, comfortably in repose on her chaise lounge, bare feet, reading glasses in place, and a thick book with a provocative cover in her hands. She would knock off her workday at about three o'clock when an afternoon crew took over. She'd come home, get comfortable, and read until dinner time. The den was more a library with books shelved neatly on every wall from ceiling to floor, save the view of the Santee River through French doors to a covered and screened-in back porch. She loved to read but refused to use an iPad for reading novels.

"Hi, Mom."

"Hi, babe."

Eric kissed her forehead and gave her a quick squeeze before he handed the wine to her. He sat on a chair across from her and took a long sip of his wine. "This is good. Did Dad open another barrel?"

"He did, yes. He wanted to test it before he bottled it. It is good. We'll have to put a case of this aside for the holidays."

Eric stretched his long, long legs out, crossed at the ankles, leaned his head back against the cushion, and closed his eyes. "I got your text but didn't see it until I was leaving the hospital. What's up?"

"Your sister called me at the store all exercised because Mary Ella Baker is back in the county. She told me that she called you, too, but you didn't have time to talk with her. Of course, the drama queen thought you were just putting her off because you didn't want to talk about Mary Ella. Are you okay?"

"I'm fine, Mom. I'm glad Mary Ella is safely home. Her return does not affect me."

"Boy, are your lips moving because, if so, I know that's a lie, and you know it, too." She scoffed, laughing, looking at him over the top of her glasses. "When you were a teen, you loved that girl's last year's underwear."

He smirked at his mother without raising his head or opening his eyes to look at her. "Well, just a little white lie, but please don't tell Hester that. She'll be conniving ways to get Mary Ella and me in the same bed before the weekend is over."

"True that. Just have a care, Eric. You're still smarting from Ginger's departure."

"Yes, I am, but not so much. I'll be all right."

"I know you will. You're a Dixon. You love deep, hard, and long, but you're no fool. Your daddy and I didn't raise any stupid children."

"Thanks, Mom." He sat up and took another sip of the wine. "Is that why you wanted to see me?"

"Well, that and I want you to talk your grandfather into slowing down. You're a doctor. Maybe he'll listen to you."

"Ha! That'll be the day. Grandpa will be tending to this farm until the last breath leaves his body. He's eighty and healthy. I'll bet he'll be at the Friday night fish fry over in Goodwill dancing with every single lady in the place."

"You're right about that, and one of those ladies will surely take him home with her."

"You won't see him until the sun rises, and he takes that walk of shame Saturday morning. Just make sure he has gas in that old car of his. He tends to forget to fill it up."

"Quiet as it's kept, your father has already taken care of that. He also had JoJeff take it in for servicing. Are you staying for supper? I'm not sure what your father is making, but it smells good."

"Beef stroganoff, and no, he's making a plate for me to take home. I want to swim before it gets too late." He stood, stretched, and finished his wine.

"You don't need to hurry off, do you? After all, you do have lights in your pool, and the thing is heated."

Eric shook his head. "Stop fretting, Mom. I'm fine."

She huffed out a frustrated breath and sucked her teeth. "Okay, go on with yourself then. You don't believe cow horns will hook? See if I care," she scoffed.

He laughed, leaned down, and snuggled her around her neck until she giggled like a schoolgirl.

"Stop it, boy, or you'll make me pee my pants!" She laughed.

"Love ya, Mom."

"Love ya more, baby."

She picked up her book to resume reading and took another sip of wine before he cleared the den door.

"Guess your mama told ya Mary Ella's back in the county," his father commented as he entered the kitchen and placed his empty wine glass in the dishwasher.

"She did, yes. How did you hear about it?" Eric leaned against the kitchen counter and observed his father while he cooked.

"Hickok delivers for us over that-a-way. Said he was in The Summer House parking lot unloading SaraJo's orders and heard from one of the housekeepers he's been keeping company with that Mary Ella came in sometime during the night."

"Mmm, Hester called me at the hospital to tell me."

Just then, the back door opened and Byron Dixon, a dentist and dental surgeon, named by their mother for the English poet, Lord Byron, entered.

"Hey, Eric. I tried to catch you before you left the hospital. Did you hear…?" Byron started.

"That Mary Ella is back in Summer County," Eric finished for his brother and nodded. "Yes, I did, and I'm fine."

"Okay, just so you know." Satisfied, Byron quickly changed the subject. "What's for dinner, Dad? It smells good, and I'm starving."

"We'll eat in a few minutes. Go get your mama and grandfather and wash up." He sent Byron out of the kitchen. "Here's your share of dinner and a quart jar of apple butter. You sure you're all right?"

"I'm sure, Dad." He accepted the bagged food and then hugged his father. "Thanks for the grub. I'll bring the biscuits early in the morning."

"Thanks, Son. Now, be on your way before your sister comes home or she'll be all up in your business."

"Color me gone." Eric nodded and left in a hurry.

Ten minutes later, he was home and stripped down to his birthday suit.

His swimming pool wasn't inordinately large, but it spanned the distance across the entire back of his home between the conjoined kitchen and family room, making it big enough to host parties. It afforded him a comfortable way to swim laps for exercise in the early morning or afternoon. Even some nights, when he could not sleep, he'd come to swim or float on one of the inflated rafts. The entire outside area of the pool was a screened-in, seamless part of his home and severely cut down on the mosquito population that lived in this fertile area along the river banks. It certainly came in handy when he and Ginger made naked love in the pool or on one of the outdoor furniture pieces.

After swimming laps, Eric sat in the pool spa and let the hydro-massage feature relax his body. While he decompressed, he had time to think. What Eric told his mother was true. He didn't think of Ginger as much lately as he had. Her face didn't show up in his dreams or her voice enliven his need to mate. He wasn't going to have as easy a time ejecting Mary Ella from his thoughts now that she was back. Nope, but Eric promised himself he would suffer in silence for as long as he could before he would seek her out. For now, he did more laps until his hunger for his father's cooking got the better of him.

On Saturday morning, after rounds at the hospital, Eric was sweating, running up and down the basketball court. It was skins against shirts, and he was dragging. He always did better when his cousins, Donald and James Dixon, were in the game. Donald, a Harvard law graduate, and his twin brother, James, a Ph.D. researcher in Animal Husbandry and New Technology farming, were a hell of a lot of fun on the court. That was especially true when they brought their cousin, US Supreme Court Judge Vivian Alexander Montgomery, and her niece Whitney Alexander Cavenaugh, came along to balance out the team. Vivian's husband, nearly seven-foot-tall Dr. Charles Montgomery, was a basketball legend from his days in Boston College and a pro-NBA team for ten years. Also, out for some late morning exercise, was his famous cousin, Gregory "Alexander the Great" Alexander. His reputation in the world of professional sports was still spoken with reverence even now years after he hung up his famous basketball shoes while still at the top of his game. Then Gregory became a Wall Street trader with a reputation as stellar in the business industry as in the basketball arenas of the world. In addition to trading on the big board in the Big Apple, Gregory also owned and operated a basketball league made up of farm teams from the US Mid-Atlantic Region. One of those teams out of Richmond, Virginia, asked for an exhibition game today. Most professional NBA teams would give up their firstborn to play against talent, the likes of which were on the court this morning.

Eric played the game well, too, but not nearly as superlatively as other talented players on the court. It was still a helluva lot of fun to play a sports contest with his brothers, Byron, Frank, and Rick, cousins too numerous to name, and extended family members purely as a display of skill and entertainment for spectators, having no bearing on team or individual standings. However, basketball was in his family's DNA. They were all tall, athletic, and skilled.

He was open and Gregory worked the ball around the perimeter to him. He saw James put a body block on a defender, which left Chuck Montgomery free. Vivian was at the top of the key controlling the flow of the game. She had a deadly accurate three-point shot that won her Olympic Gold while she was still in college at Spelman. Vivian was also fast and could work the ball inside the paint and score. She continued to play the game all through law school and, although she's a sitting Supreme Court Justice, Vivian still plays weekly with Final Justice, a team of female law school students, lawyers, and judges in Washington, DC. The cousins played together enough to know timing combined with teamwork, pinpoint passing, and finishing was everything.

Vivian was a threat at the top of the key and was being double-teamed when she passed the ball off to him. When he met Chuck's eyes, he sent up an alley-oop, which Chuck caught in mid-air and put it in the hoop as a monster jam before touching the ground. They high fived each other as they started to trot up the court, but before they got to the midway point, Vivian stole the ball and, on a fast break, pulled up outside the perimeter and sank a three-pointer, which had spectators whooping and hollering.

The opposing team called a timeout to regroup.

"All right, Speed Racer," joked Eric.

"You better bet it, babe," Vivian rejoindered with high fives all around as she guzzled water.

Gregory shook his head. "Some people never learn. They've been keying in on Vivian since she walked on the court. They're not used to playing with a woman on the team, and they underestimated her until she started killing them with three-pointers."

"Yeah, but my SkyRocket taught them good and proper," Vivian grinned, referring to her nearly seven-foot-tall husband, Chuck Montgomery, an emergency room doctor. After his professional basketball career ended, he graduated from medical school and now owned Physicians' Hospital in a rural county outside Washington, DC.

"Eric's the one with good eyes. He's been styling all morning." James Dixon hi-fived his cousin.

"We're up by twelve." Dr. Bernard Alexander, Vivian and Gregory's father and coach of the team, nodded approvingly. "I'm going to put in some fresh horses." He sent in another group, including his son, US Air Force Jet Fighter Pilot, General Benny Alexander, and his son's wife, US Navy Admiral Stacy Green Alexander, and their daughter attorney Whitney Ivy Alexander Cavanaugh. Rounding out the team on the hardwood were first cousins Donald Dixon and Rick Dixon.

When the game resumed, Eric leaned back with his elbows resting on the bleachers behind him to watch the flow of the game. James and Gregory followed suit with their long legs out in front of them.

"So, Mary Ella, huh?" commented James.

"Yeah. So, you heard?" Eric deadpanned.

"Yeah, Janice mentioned it at dinner last night." James shrugged, speaking of his wife.

"Yeah, the news is making the rounds." Eric gave a dispassionate answering shrug.

"How are you hanging?" James looked at his cousin.

"By a hair, Cousin. By a hair."

"Have you seen her?" Gregory wanted to know. "That's a foul, ref!" he shouted.

"Not so far." Eric was still concentrating on the flow of the game.

"You ask me, which you didn't, take the plunge. Put on your big boy pants and go see her. I hear she's at The Summer House." Gregory never took his eyes from the game.

"So, I've been told…many times, but here's the thing. I'm not ready to swim yet."

"Understandable," commented Gregory.

"Hi, Dr. Dixon," a female voice came from over his left shoulder.

"Hi." He was not taking his eyes off the game either. They all stood when the play was stopped for an injury on the court.

"Gregory, go in for Benny." Bernard ordered as Benny came off the court, holding his thumb.

"Let's see." Eric took Benny's hand in his. He turned back to look in the direction of the blowing whistle, causing everyone to look around, too. In that split second, he snapped Benny's thumb back into the socket.

Benny cursed vehemently but was able to flex his fingers and thumb. Eric retrieved an ice pack in the interim and applied it to Benny's hand, wrapping it in a towel.

"Not bad for a sawbones," Benny teased.

"Trained by the best, Sylvia Alexander."

"You got that right," agreed Benny, referring to his mother, as they took a seat on the bleachers and resumed watching the game.

"So, Dr. Dixon, me and some of the others are heading over to the fairgrounds. Would you like to join us?" came the question from Julia Hunt.

"No, thanks. I've got a prior engagement." Eric absently continued to watch the game. Then thinking of how he must appear, he turned and looked at the three young women. "You might want to ask my brother

Rick. I don't think he has plans for later."

That seemed to capture at least two of the women's attention. However, Julia Hunt wasn't one of them. She was still focused like a heat-seeking missile on him. Eric didn't mind a little flirtation, but it seemed every time he turned around, Julia was asking him out. He didn't want to be rude or hurt the young woman's feelings, but her behavior was becoming problematic. Yet, he knew just the person to help him solve this dilemma.

"Gregory, is your mother in town?"

His cousin looked up and around, then nodded to the bleachers behind them. "She's sitting behind us with SaraJo and Douglas Johnson, Tucker Cavenaugh, your parents, and Uncle Romelo and Aunt Olivia. You want me to get her attention?"

"No, not now. If you speak with her before I do, would you mention I need to speak with her?"

"Sure. No problem."

Later, after the game, Eric found time to talk with Sylvia Alexander in private and laid out his concerns. She told him not to worry, and he wouldn't.

CHAPTER 4

"You're pregnant, aren't you?" Sylvia Alexander commented as more of a statement than a question. She was sitting with Mary Ella in one of the Summer County General Hospital's cafeterias for the last thirty minutes.

Mary Ella wanted to deny it, but she couldn't do it to a woman who was like a second mother to her. After her own mother died when she was fourteen, Mrs. Alexander, although she and her husband, Bernard, already had five children of their own, stepped up and provided the guidance her ailing father couldn't. So, too, did Eric's mother, Sandra Dixon. Mary Ella was seventeen when her father died, and Dr. and Mrs. Alexander became her primary caregivers. Leroy and Sandra Dixon were there for her, too. Dr. Bernard Alexander was the dean of the Summer County Academy through her high school years and throughout her training to become a registered nurse. Mary Ella loved all of them unconditionally and owed them everything, including the truth.

Mary Ella nodded. "Yes, I'm in my first trimester."

"Why isn't Mark here with you?"

Mrs. Alexander could be tactful, but she never minced words. She got right to the nitty-gritty of any issue. So, Mary Ella could be nothing but forthright. "He's still in Libya. He doesn't know about my pregnancy, and he may not be the father of the baby." Her eyes began to fill.

"Come with me." Sylvia briskly rose from the lunch table, dumping their lunch debris, and quickly exiting the building by a side door.

The hospital's garden they entered was lovely this time of the year, thought Mary Ella as she and Mrs. Alexander strolled arm-in-arm through the pea-stone pathways around the fragrant fauna and flora. The strategically placed tall trees provided dappled sunlight enough for the flowers to explode with beauty. The Sweet Grass, known as the Queen of the Garden, with its showy inflorescence, showed off against the backdrop of the Carolina jessamine and Yellow Honeysuckle.

When they were kids, she and Satarah would pluck the honeysuckle from the vine and suck the juice from the stem the butterflies and hummingbirds craved. As she looked around at the profusion of Yellow Indian Grass, its golden plumes shimmering in the sun, she was reminded that her lineage included Native Americans indigenous to this area. The evidence of the Catawba, Pee Dee, Chicora, Edisto, Santee, Yamasee, and Chicora-Waccamaw Indigenous American influences could still be seen in the faces and physiques of those mixed with other racial influences socializing in the hospital's garden. Even her Cherokee ancestry was still prevalent here in Summer County.

Strangely, she noticed similarities between her ancestry and those she found through her travels in Asia and Africa.

"Can you tell me what happened?"

The question snapped her out of her woolgathering. "I'm not supposed to talk about it to anyone."

Mrs. Alexander's voice was warm and comforting. "Is this why you've lost so much weight and cut off all of your pretty hair?"

"It's difficult to keep my hair clean and free of lice and ringworms in the jungle, so I cut it off." Mary Ella knew her words weren't exactly the gospel. Mrs. Alexander was very astute and likely knew it, too, but it was as close as Mary Ella could get to telling the truth. "Sometimes it was good that occasionally the extremists thought I was a boy. That way, I could avoid wearing a heavy, black burka in the high heat when we were in certain Arab nations. I have a beauty parlor appointment at Miss Minnie Mae's this afternoon for a new style. My hair grows fast, though I'll probably never wear it long again.

"As for my weight loss," Mary Ella continued, "there were times we didn't have food to eat, and we had to walk great distances to reach remote villages. So, I lost weight. Mark and I both did. The pounds just melted away, but I'm stronger for the trials with which we were forced to deal. My muscle tone is still good. The way Satarah feeds me, I'll put on the weight again, too."

"Not too much, though," Mrs. Alexander cautioned.

"No, I'll be careful. I just need to find a way to support myself and my child. I need medical coverage, and I know the various hospital plans here at Summer County General are excellent. Plus, you have all of the necessary specialties under one roof. I wouldn't have to go anywhere else for my or my baby's care."

Mrs. Alexander nodded. "Then I'll put you on staff at the hospital as the Head Emergency Room Nurse Administrator starting on Monday. You'll be working with Dr. Garrison St. Clair again."

Mary Ella shook her head, frowning. "I'm surprised Garrison is still heading the emergency room, but don't you have someone filling the head nurse's position?"

"Yes, I do today, but by Monday, Jenny Jones Sweeney will be taking an extended leave of absence. She's pregnant with her and Bob's third child, a girl this time. So, Jenny is leaving the position. With the little ones stair steps, she doesn't know whether she will return to nursing full-time before the last one is in school in about two years. That's assuming she and Bob don't have more children in the near future." Mrs. Alexander smiled delightedly.

"That's wonderful. I'll have to stop by and say hello to Jenny before she leaves. Are you sure you don't have anyone else who could step into the position? I mean, I prefer emergency medicine, but, really, I don't mind starting at the bottom again if there is someone else more qualified."

"I've wanted to get my niece, your best pal, Satarah, back on staff, but she's having too much fun at her bed and breakfast to consider returning to her old job full-time. She'll step in if I need her in a pinch, so will Jenny. So, your arrival works for me. No one I currently have on staff has your knowledge, experience, and credentials with emergency medicine. Although we've known for months Jenny was leaving the position, no one has come to Garrison or me and asked to step up to the challenge. Head of emergency nursing services is, as you're well aware, a very tough and demanding job. How does," she named a salary amount, "work for you?"

Mary Ella's eyes widened and filled again. This time Sylvia put her arms around her and just held her while she cried among the beautiful flowers, bushes, and trees.

Eric chanced to look out of his office window and did a double-take. His suite of offices was in the new wing of the hospital and had a view of the quarter-acre garden in the hospital's courtyard with its tables and chairs nicely spaced to allow for lounging and/or eating. If his eyes weren't deceiving him, Mrs. Alexander was standing in the garden, hugging someone who resembled Mary Ella Baker, except this woman had very little hair and was as thin as a rail. Before she left the county, his Mary Ella had bountiful hips, a narrow waist, and grapefruit-sized breasts he loved to get his hands and mouth on.

They used to make love in the house her parents once owned, which became hers when her mother and then her father died soon after. She had no siblings or close relatives except her cousin, Satarah Josephine, who was in nursing school with them and married to JoJeff Whitfield, one of the county's bad boys. Eric recalled that he practically moved in with Mary Ella. He loved her more because she had so few people in her life to give her moral support. Still, she didn't wring her hands or grumble woe is me. Instead, she put on her big girl pants and moved forward.

Of course, the Alexanders helped out, but they gave moral support to any and everyone. His parents and siblings would do anything for Mary Ella without being asked. However, she never asked. Mary Ella was a survivor, he remembered. She'd give the clothes off her back or the last morsel of food she had to a complete stranger in need. She worked hard and saved every cent she could to complete her nursing degree. Ultimately, she was forced to sell her family's big, rambling old home and farmland when it became too much to handle and rented a little house, but never complained about its size. She simply did whatever came next.

He wondered why she was with Mrs. Alexander in the garden, but his attention was diverted when his next patient arrived early for her appointment.

"I like that haircut on you. Miss Minnie Mae did a good job," commented Satarah of Mary Ella.

"Thanks, I agree. It will be less trouble to take care of. Miss Minnie Mae said to tell you hello and wondered when you'd be coming in."

Satarah smirked. "She and her customers just want to dish the dirt. They think just because I own a bed and breakfast, I know all the secrets about who is sleeping with whom in the county."

Mary Ella nodded her understanding. "True that."

"I presume everything went well at the hospital today." Satarah was having a snack in the screened-in lanai of the cottage Mary Ella chose. They were taking a break before the children got home from school.

She picked up a carrot stick to chew on. "It did, yes. I'm stepping into your old position as Emergency Room Nursing Administrator. You didn't tell me Jenny Sweeney is pregnant again," she mildly chided.

Satarah's brows furrowed. "Didn't I?" She shook her head, shrugging it off before taking another bite of her turkey salad. "Maybe I overlooked this bit of news, but Bob and Jenny are as happy as two pigs in slop. Their oldest, Bobby, Jr., and my Ari are in the same class at the academy during this rotation. The younger boy, Mitch, is a little younger than Kate and not quite potty-trained yet or caught up to the necessary maturity level of the academy. Bob and Jenny have him enrolled in the daycare facility at the hospital. I imagine they'll keep him there while Jenny is on maternity leave. He should be ready for the academy by then.

"Bob Sweeney is Doug's right-hand firefighter. He heads the Tactical and Training Unit on Doug's staff, and Jeff Logan, the Ambassador's son, is head of the Centerville Emergency Engine Company. Plessula Knight, you remember her, don't you? She was head over heels for my cousin, Benny Alexander."

"Ha! Who wasn't head over heels for Benny, Kenneth, *and* Gregory, I want to know."

"True that, but she trained as a doctor at Pittsburgh General, had a bad experience with some guy stalking her, and decided to come home. Now, she's heading Doug's fire department's medical staff and dating again. In fact, I think she's dating Eric's cousin, Davis Dixon. Louise McCrary is still here, too, with the fire department as the head investigator and living with Dr. Reynard Steward in his big house on the golf course. They have two daughters, but Louise still refuses to marry Dr. Steward. The man gets a boner whenever he walks past a woman who gets his attention. That's why Louise won't marry him. He looks, but to the best of anyone's knowledge, he doesn't touch.

"So, getting back to Jenny, she is so busy. She helps out her father on his farm when she can. He wants her and Bob to move to the farm with him. Jenny hasn't said what they've decided to do about it. Their little two-bedroom, one bath house is fine for two children, boys at that, but she says with a little girl on the way, they're going to need more space. With her father living alone with just a housekeeper in a big, six-bedroom house and farmhands in the bunkhouses, it would be an ideal place to raise children."

Mary Ella frowned. "I don't imagine any of Jenny's brothers or sisters plan to come back to Summer County to live."

"You're right. That's doubtful. The Jones family scattered all over the globe. Jenny is the baby of the family and the only one still living in the county. How long am I going to have to carry this conversation?" Satarah abruptly asked. "I've been around Robin Hood's barn and back again."

Mary Ella smiled indulgently at Satarah. "I thought you were doing a great job of it bringing me up to date on all the local news that's fit to print." Then she huffed out a breath. "Did you know Mark Brooks is extremely wealthy?"

Satarah shrugged listlessly. "According to Doug, Mark lives on what he makes as a physician. He doesn't trade on his family's name or their wealth. I do know he anonymously donated four fully-equipped ambulances to the fire department before you two left the country. I take it you didn't know about this?"

Mary Ella shook her head and took a sip of the water she had been nursing for over an hour to rehydrate her body. "No, Mark never talked about having a family."

"Well, he certainly wasn't hatched from purple people eaters," Satarah joked. "Still, I'm surprised he never mentioned them. One of his cousins, Dr. Rupert Townsend, was once married to Cecile."

"*Seriously? Don's* Cecile? Eric's cousin?" Mary Ella was shocked. "I didn't even know Cecile was married before. She and Don seemed to have been married since forever. Eric and I used to hang out with Don and James a lot. Especially when Don came home and built that house. Eric and I would go over every chance we got to help."

Satarah nodded. "Dr. Townsend and Cecile were married when they were working in Alaska on a big research project Janice told us about. You know she and Cecile are not only sisters-in-law but also best buds. They were housemates while at San Diego State University until they earned their doctoral degrees. Then they bought a condo together in the same building right on the beach where my cousin Benny has a condo. That's where Janice and Cecile met Benny and became friends. Cecile is considered one of the top oceanographers in the world. That's why she was tapped to head such a huge, important, research project in Alaska. Cecile and Dr. Townsend received the Nobel Prize for their work there. He's the head of the Townsend Science and Technology Foundation in Boston. He fully funded the Alaskan research project for two years. They weren't married long, though.

"Now Don and Cecile have five children, and they're expecting again. She's still traveling to deliver lectures on oceanography, and she and Janice, James' wife, conduct research projects at the university. Janice holds a doctorate in molecular biochemistry. Cecile's parents, sisters, nieces, nephews, and Janice's grandparents, and brother, Adam, were here for last Christmas. Those Dixon twin boys, Donald and James, are running neck and neck on the number of twins they produce." Satarah laughed.

"Speaking of the Dixons, Eric moved back home just after you left." That got her cousin's undivided attention, Satarah noticed. "He's a medical doctor now; a rheumatologist on staff at the hospital."

"That's great, but I'm not surprised. When Eric left after nursing school to join the Army, he intended to go to medical school. I'm glad to hear he succeeded."

"He was married when he returned."

She tried to control her surprise and disappointment at the news that her first lover; the person she gave her virginity to; the person who presented her with a ring and asked her to be his wife, married someone else. At one point, she thought she would spend her life with Eric Dixon, but that was a long time ago. They were just kids still in their teen years. She didn't know why she felt a little hurt by the news, but there was a definite tug on her heart at hearing that information.

Satarah continued. "Eric had his brother, Frank, build a home for him before he returned to Summer County. Frank is a carpenter and civil engineer by trade and owns the Dixon Construction Company now. It's a small operation, only about twenty or so full-time employees, but they're good and are in high demand. It's a really nice place Frank built for Eric and his wife on the other side of the Santee. He even has a screened-in pool area incorporated into the structure of his home."

"It must be in the Dixon compound." Mary Ella frowned.

"It is. It's on Gilly's Place. He invited a bunch of people over for a big barbeque to introduce his wife, Ginger. She's a pretty woman and so much like her name. She has ginger-colored eyes, hair, and complexion. Since his home is the only one, so far, on Gilly's Place, he had the street name changed to Ginger's Place."

Mary Ella smiled sincerely. "That's really sweet. Eric does things like that and deserves all the best. I hope she's a good woman who can appreciate what she has in a fine man like Eric."

"Not so good. Eric and Ginger's marriage lasted about two years before she left him and filed for divorce." Satarah frowned. "Fortunately, they didn't have children, so it was a clean break."

"Oh, no," Mary Ella moaned in sympathy. "I'm sorry to hear that they divorced. Is there any chance they'll get back together?"

"None. Ginger was in the Army as a high-ranking officer when they met. The last anyone heard, she'd gone back to Chicago and back into the military and was stationed somewhere overseas. Japan, I think. Eric said she's career Army and wants to climb the ranks as Benny and Stacy have."

Mary Ella was only half listening as Satarah continued to talk while they ate. She felt sympathy for Eric, but she was more curious now about why she never heard any of this information from Mark about his generous donation to the county fire department or his illustrious family's accomplishments in medicine. He wasn't from her community or anywhere in the south, she knew, because of his New England accent. From time to time, she did have the impression Mark was holding things back, but when she lived with someone, slept with someone for more than four years, she should have been told something about his background from him, at least where he was from or where he grew up. Four, fully-equipped ambulances could cost upwards of a couple of million dollars. Not that it matters one iota that he was wealthy, but he seems to be less than completely honest about who he was. That information was troublesome.

She mentally shrugged. All she wanted now was to have Mark back safe and sound.

Then what? she wondered. *If the baby she carried wasn't his, then what kind of future could they have together? Especially because of Kaseem.* She unconsciously rubbed her abdomen.

Now, things were beginning to fall into place, thought Satarah. *Mary Ella's pregnant,* she surmised, as she rubbed her own abdomen. Her cousin was keeping it a secret for now. Why, she didn't know. Maybe she hadn't told Mark about it or she had told him, and he hadn't reacted well to the news. That didn't seem to be consistent with the Mark Brooks she knew. However, Satarah knew that something brought her cousin home without Mark, and her pregnancy was only half of the story.

They were closer than twins in the womb, so she'd be there for Mary Ella when she was ready to share her concerns. For now, she had to get prepared for her Douglas and the rest of their family to come home.

"Want to help me get snacks on the table for the children?" Satarah languidly stretched. "Doug should be picking them up from school about now. They'll take their time because he'll let Benson drive home."

"Sure, I'll help, but I need to find a car to buy so I can return the rental to the airport."

Satarah rolled her eyes and huffed out a breath. "I hate to suggest it, but JoJeff is probably the best mechanic in the county."

Mary Ella frowned. "JoJeff? I thought we'd seen the back of him when he ran off with Carlotta. Why is he still here?"

"You know he came back after Ari was born. Benson wanted to know his biological father and asked Donald Dixon for help to find him. Donald found JoJeff out in Las Vegas and brought him back here."

Mary Ella shook her head. "I remember that, but please don't tell me Carlotta came back, too."

"No, as far as I know, my sister is still in Las Vegas." Satarah shrugged and continued. "JoJeff has a new car dealership and a full, used-car lot with SUVs and trucks he's reconditioned at his parents' garage over in Centerville. That's his new gig now. He's a new and used car salesman and a mechanic on the side. He always has to have some hustle going on. He hired a few people, but the used car business suits him."

Mary Ella shook her head. "Frankly, I'd rather not deal with him. JoJeff has always given me the creeps. What about Willis Greene, Stacy's father? He used to work on cars. He still owns the garage and gas station over in Goodwill, doesn't he?"

"He still does, yes, but he and my cousin, Gregory Alexander, went into the vintage-car business together. Willis still works on farm equipment here on our farm and for the other county farmers, county government's road repair equipment, and old cars now with Gregory in his spare time. They would probably have some vehicles on the lot, but I don't see you wanting to drive a vehicle manufactured in the 1900s to the 1970s.

"At least, JoJeff has cars manufactured in this century." Satarah laughed. "He buys new cars at auction that don't sell in the year they were manufactured and refurbishes older cars he takes as trade-ins. Grab

Douglas when he comes in from work and take him with you to return your rental car, and then take time to look at what JoJeff has on his car lot. I can't imagine you wouldn't, but if you don't find anything right away, you can always drive my old Jeep. It runs very well, thanks to JoJeff. I usually drive The Summer House van or Doug's pickup truck when I have errands. JoJeff takes care of the maintenance on those, too."

"Isn't it awkward for him?" Mary Ella frowned. "I mean, you're married to Douglas now, but you were once married to JoJeff."

"Yeah, and JoJeff claims I'm still legally his wife, but Douglas ignores the foolishness. It will be fine. We're thinking of giving Benson a used car for his sixteenth birthday. Doug and I were planning to look at what JoJeff has on his lot that would work for Benson."

CHAPTER 5

*O*kay, *this was going to be more challenging than he initially thought*, Eric ruminated. Word reached him that not only was Mary Ella Baker back in the county, but she was also going to be back on staff at Summer County Hospital as the new Emergency Room Nursing Administrator replacing Jenny Sweeney.

Oh, joy!

He usually didn't get called to the emergency room for a consult, but he was the only rheumatologist on staff. So, it wasn't improbable that he'd be contacted if there weren't any Allergists available, of which there were only two, and he shared a suite of offices with both of them. Because of the similarities in their specialties, they coordinated their days on and off duty. That could be problematic going forward.

Mary Ella was very popular among the hospital staff because she was previously employed there from the time they graduated from nursing school until she left with Mark Brooks. Everyone kept up with her exploits while she was with Doctors Without Borders romanticizing her departure with her true love to cure the world of its ills. In some of the places he had heard she worked in, he was sure her experiences were dangerous. Still, the buzz about her and Mark Brooks' hot affair could have been a movie on the Lifetime Channel.

Eric was still determined not to let this new bump in the road derail his plan to stay a reasonable distance away from Mary Ella Baker. However, he couldn't avoid the whispered chatter between his administrative staff going on just outside the open door of his office.

"She looks really thin, not like before, and would you believe she cut off all of her pretty hair?"

"No! Really!" I haven't seen her yet. Why would she do such a thing?"

"It beats me, but don't cha know, she came back alone."

"Where is Dr. Delicious, I wonder?"

"You don't think he dumped her, do you?"

"I hope not. You know Mary Ella and Dr. Hunk-a-mania Dixon used to date back in the day. Hester said he even asked her to marry him."

"See, I told you to give it up. Now that Mary Ella is back, Dr. Dixon might get it on with her again."

"That was so long ago they probably forgot all about each other."

"Ten years isn't that long when it's true love, Julia. You were what, all of ten years old ten years ago?"

"I was almost twelve," she huffed, insulted. "That doesn't make any difference now in the big scheme of things. My father is more than ten years older than my mother."

"That's what happens when there's a shotgun wedding."

Julia rolled her eyes and then suddenly quieted. "Shhh, Mrs. Alexander is coming up the hall. You better get back to work."

Okay, the tongues were already beginning to wag, thought Eric. *There would be absolutely nothing I can do about that. For the time being, until I can build up my resolve concerning Mary Ella, I'll simply stay out of her way. Damn it! All I wanted was a nice quiet afternoon of swimming, making a light dinner, and then relaxing with a good book.*

Hunk-a-mania? What?

Later at home, Eric flipped over and started back to the five-foot-deep, shallow end of his pool before he noticed his sister, Hester, sitting in one of the lounge chairs, elbows on her knees, hands on her chin intently watching him while he swam. He didn't break his rhythm as he flipped and backstroked in the opposite direction.

Eric was hitting his limit and knew he would have to face his younger sister sometime. He avoided her for the past few days and had no idea why she was at his home now. Whatever it was, he'd deal with it so he could get back to his plans for a relaxing evening.

Then he noticed sister number two, Kristy, helping herself to a hoagie and a glass of wine in the kitchen area. She looked almost normal today.

At least her hair wasn't cerulean blue as it had been a few days ago. Today she sported a shaggy hairstyle with hot chili pepper red tips that matched her lipstick. Her nails were long, but he knew them to be real, unlike the hair. The gold nail polish with silver designs was a little daunting in need of a heavy dose of Prozac, but to each her own. Still, he knew her to be an excellent barber. She tended to overdo it when it came to her beautician skills---except when it came to her face. She was radical about skincare and forced everyone in the family to follow suit. He guessed she was stylish in the dental-floss-sized, white cotton top, hip-hugger, micro-mini skirt, and wedged high-heeled sandals.

Kristy, the older of the two sisters, yet the two youngest of the seven siblings, couldn't be more dissimilar. Hester found the Annie Hall style to her liking and stayed there. She usually wore her thick hair in a processed pageboy style that just skimmed her shoulders and framed her face. Today it was in a ponytail that made her look to be about ten.

With his sister, Kristy, he never knew from day to day or even hour to hour what her hair, wig, or weave might look like. Yet, she practiced Ayurveda, a thousand-year-old type of traditional Indian medicine. She lectured the family and her customers that the practice aims to balance one's body system and incorporate many natural or plant-based remedies. She actually attended the Ayurvedic Institute in Albuquerque, New Mexico, and received her certification. Although there's not much call for her service in Summer County, South Carolina, she's a whole food farm girl and has access to her hair-care clientele, where she never fails to talk up her remedies.

He climbed out of the pool, and Kristy tossed a rug-sized terrycloth towel to him.

"Yo, Brotherman, you training for the Olympic trials or something?" Kristy observed him closely. She sat with her extra-long legs and bare feet up in a chair.

"Or something." Eric plucked the sandwich out of her hand to take a big bite. "Why didn't you put any meat on this sandwich?"

"You only had that fake, processed meat. I don't know what's in that stuff. For sure, no real turkey comes walking around the Alexanders' farm with teriyaki seasoning flowing through its' veins. I don't know how you eat that stuff when you're a doctor," Kristy complained and then got up to push Eric into a chair. She pulled a pin light from her back pocket, examining his face in minute detail. "It's bad enough you didn't have whole-wheat bread. I was forced to eat this white sourdough bread. Damn it. Your skin always looks healthy no matter what you stuff in your face." She sat and took her sandwich from him.

"Dad didn't bake whole wheat bread this week. You don't like what's in my kitchen, bring your own the next time you come. Why are you two here, anyway?" Eric frowned.

"Mary Ella was in my shop today to have her hair trimmed and styled." Kristy took another healthy bite of her sandwich.

Hester studied her brother. "Have you talked with her?".

Eric shook his head. "Not really. Why?"

"Mary Ella's lost a lot of weight. I mean, she doesn't look sickly or anything like that. In fact, she's got some muscles she didn't have when she left, but she could stand to add some serious pounds. I gave her a welcome-home facial. Her skin looks healthy. She had the works, a mani-pedi, too."

Eric picked up Kristy's wine and took a long pull eyeing his sisters. "You two came to tell me that Mary Ella is skinny and had her hair cut?"

"Why haven't you gone to see her, Eric?" Hester frowned, clearly annoyed.

"I'm bound to see her at the hospital or around and about." He got up, went into his outdoor shower stall, and turned on the water. Warm water shot at him from the rain-shower spigot above his head and several different body spray directions. The shower cleared away the chlorinated water from his skin. He quickly used a moisturizing body wash, dried himself, rubbed on lotion, jojoba oil in his hair and short beard, and then put on a dry pair of shorts commando-style before leaving the shower. Giving himself time to think and regroup, he went in through the mudroom door. Dumping his wet things in the washing machine, he started it. Entering his kitchen, he spoke loud enough for them to hear him through the open, fold-away glass walls, "I don't see why I need to track her down." There was a seamless connection between the screened-in pool area and the interior of his home.

He had a salad already prepared, which Kristy, obviously, helped herself to some of it for her sandwich. He added more raw chopped spinach, tomatoes, onion, garlic, black olives, anchovies, and slices of turkey and ham. After drizzling the balsamic dressing over the salad, Eric grabbed what was left of his loaf of sourdough bread, a glass of wine, and headed back onto the pool deck. He sat at the table with his sisters while they peppered him with questions, and using his fork, ate out of his bowl of salad.

"She was the love of your life," frowned Hester. "That's why."

"The operative word being 'was.' We were teens when we dated. We've both moved on since then."

"How do you know? Maybe she still has feelings for you, Eric."

He looked crossly at Hester. "If she doesn't, then what?"

"You can still try to get the magic back," Hester argued.

"This isn't a soap opera or one of your romance novels from your Low Country book club. Mary Ella and I aren't star-crossed lovers bound and determined to be together no matter what."

"I believe in love." Hester asserted, stridently.

"You believed in the tooth fairy until you were twelve. Some myths die hard," Eric retorted without heat.

"You should at least try, Eric. You never know what might happen."

His salad bowl was almost empty, and he'd only had a third of its contents. "I know what will happen if I lose my mind and put another one of my salads in front of either of you. If you wanted me to make dinner for you, you should have said something."

"That wasn't dinner. That was a snack," retorted Kristy. "What's the main course?"

Eric sighed and shook his head. Rising from his seat, he lit his grill and prepared to cook a large, thick piece of salmon he had marinating in preparation for his dinner later. The chicken breasts he planned to put on his rotisserie for tomorrow he skewered for today's meal instead. In his kitchen, he was preparing the food for the grill when his younger brother, Rick, walked into the kitchen, followed by Byron and Frank. At that point, he wouldn't have been surprised if his oldest brother Bishop, who lived in Florida, strolled in, too.

"What's for eats?" Rick went straight to the large double-wide refrigerator and opened the heavy doors.

"I was about to grill some fish and chicken. What's up? Why is everybody here?"

"Dad didn't cook today. He and mom went over to Grandaunt Lois' and Uncle Hampton's house with Granddad to have dinner and play cards."

"So, you all couldn't fix your own food?"

Rick shrugged. "Why bother when we can get you to cook?"

"So, I'm having lunch at the hospital with Luscious Lydia today," begins Byron conversationally while pouring a glass of wine for himself, Frank, and Rick. "She's one of the firefighters over in Centerville. Anyway, who should I see in the garden but Mary Ella Baker? Then the buzz around the hospital is that she's coming back on staff in the Emergency Room. Did you know about this?"

"Nope." Eric heard the splash into the pool. With three of his four brothers in his kitchen going through his freezer, pantry, and refrigerator, he didn't have to guess that his sisters were in the pool. Every one of his siblings kept swimwear in one of the cabinets in a spare bedroom. Even Bishop, the oldest member of their siblings, kept clothes there although he lived in Florida. Eric reasoned that his sisters must have changed into swimwear while he was preparing to cook.

What the hell, he mentally sighed, and pulled out a tray of thick steaks from the freezer and nuked them enough to thaw them out. While they marinated, he cut white potatoes into quarter wedges, bathed them in olive oil, seasoned them, and stuck them in the electric oven to bake. He made another salad, larger this time, and put it in the refrigerator to keep his brothers from eating it before they sat down for the meal. By the time he checked the grill, it was ready for the rotisserie chicken.

Byron sliced a pineapple from a fruit bowl and placed it on the grill while the chicken rotated. Rick grabbed fresh green, red, and yellow peppers, cored and sliced them before adding them to the grill. Frank was boiling water for the fresh, sweet corn he found in the pantry's cold box. He shucked the leaves off, washed them before placing them in the rapidly boiling water. The yellow skewers in the drawer would fit nicely into each end of the hot corn and would be handy for rolling the corn in the tray of seasoned butter designed for that purpose.

Eric cut fresh cauliflower and broccoli rosettes, washed and seasoned them, and then put them together in a large double boiler to steam. Rick came on to the pool deck in swimwear, cranked up the music on the whole-house iPod system, and then dove into the pool.

While he cooked, Eric's brothers and sisters held swim meets before playing a lively water volleyball game. *So much for his quiet evening alone at home reading a novel*, he thought, but he knew what they were about. Mary Ella Baker. His parents probably were out for the afternoon, but his siblings knew how to put together a meal when they wanted to. They didn't need him to cook for them. They were there to keep an eye on him. He didn't need it, but he loved them for the moral support they were always ready to furnish. They were not only his family but also his best friends.

CHAPTER 6

"Well, well. Look-a-here, look-a-here," JoJeff salaciously crooned, eyeing Mary Ella from the bottom up and grinned from ear to ear. She was always a good-looking woman. Sexiness ran in both of the cousins' families; Mary Ella's and SaraJo's. If he hadn't gotten SaraJo pregnant when she was fifteen and had to join the military or be hauled into court for statutory rape, he would have tapped that phine Mary Ella Baker next.

Then, of course, once he returned to the county from being in the Army for three years, he learned SaraJo's father had forced her to give up their son for adoption. Still, SaraJo was a tasty treat and the sexiest girl in the county at age eighteen. She could really whip it on him, have him speaking in tongues, so, since she was legal, he married her.

Once they were married, the first thing she wanted him to do was to help her find their son. He wasn't keen on the whole idea of having children in the first place. Plus, they were still young. He was twenty-one and wanted to live a little before settling down in Summer County. It wasn't a bad place, but after being in the Army and stationed at Fort Rosecrans in southern California around San Diego for a spell, he wasn't ready to do the family thing.

After SaraJo finished her nurse's training, he figured they could lite out to the west coast to someplace like Los Angeles or San Francisco, where the action is. Maybe even go back to San Diego. He liked it there and even learned how to surf. More often than not, he watched the pretty women wearing bikinis no bigger than dental floss. All that smooth skin on display was enough to keep him at half-mast most of the time. Yeah, he really liked it there, and SaraJo had people living in San Diego.

Her cousin, Benny Alexander, was some high-ranking muckety-muck in the Air Force and had one of those phat, two-level, high-rise condos right on the waterfront. Benny still owned the condo in San Diego, although he was stationed in Tokyo, Japan. Her cousin would do anything for SaraJo, so he bet they could live in the swank condo free of charge for as long as they wanted. With his mechanic's license and her nursing certificate, they'd do pretty good for a couple of young people without a care in the world. Babies just didn't fit in that scenario for the life he wanted to live.

Well, before he could convince SaraJo to leave Summer County for the left coast, her sister, Carlotta, older by two years, came sniffing around him while Satarah was doing her nursing job at an all-night clinic. She wasn't shy about telling him what she wanted. So, he gave Carlotta what she was begging for often and continuously whenever Satarah wasn't at home. SaraJo worked many nights and overtime to put a little extra money aside in a savings account, while Carlotta, a beautician, worked days and not a lot of extra hours. He and Carlotta were the same age, and it was a sweet deal having sex with sisters. He had Satarah during the day and Carlotta at night.

Then, wouldn't you know it, his little champion swimmers knocked up Carlotta with twins. Her father, The Right Reverend Obadiah Baker, put Carlotta out of his house, and she had no place to go other than to come to live with him and SaraJo in their little two-bedroom, one-bath home. SaraJo was none-the-wiser about what was going on, and he wanted to keep it that way. Still, she was a good wife, as sexy as hell, and could cook her ass off.

Carlotta was just a side piece. He sometimes let Carlotta talk him into tapping her phine ass with SaraJo in the house asleep in their bedroom. Carlotta loved to do crazy shit like that, and he had to admit it turned him the hell on, too. For Carlotta, it was almost like she was beggin' to get caught.

After the babies came, Carlotta said how if SaraJo didn't want to travel and see the world, she did. After six weeks, he was too through with crying babies, two A.M. feedings, and smelly diapers. So, one morning, after SaraJo came in from her night job, he tapped that phine ass of hers one last time good and proper. Then while SaraJo was sleeping, he and Carlotta packed up what they could in his vintage convertible ZX, took what money he and SaraJo put by for savings, and headed west.

He hated to leave his Harley Davidson motorcycle, but it couldn't be helped. He didn't have enough time to sell it, and he couldn't tow it behind his ZX. Carlotta could have driven his car while he rode his hog, but he didn't trust her enough for that, and they couldn't afford to take both his car and bike. As it was, he and Carlotta made it as far as Las Vegas before the money ran out. They slept in a shelter a few nights but got good jobs quickly enough. He worked in a gas station garage as a mechanic, and she put her skills to work in a beauty salon doing hair and make-up. They didn't need much, just someplace clean to sleep, but they didn't do much of that. They weren't homebodies, and Las Vegas was bright lights and big city all the way and all the time.

On the side, they learned to work various jobs in the casinos. Carlotta has a good voice, but not as good as her mother, the French Mariah, the toast of the European, Asian, and African entertainment industry. Still, he and Carlotta could carry a tune substantial enough for the strip clubs where they worked. He was ripped with good muscles and dance moves to drive the women wild. So, he did a lot of bridal parties wearing whatever costume the women wanted. Carlotta could sing and was built like a brick shithouse back home. When party jobs were slow, they even learned how to deal Blackjack at one of the big, fancy casinos.

Then Carlotta got propositioned enough she wanted to start an escort service. They did and hired a group of men and women to work for them. They were doing quite well for themselves until a bigger, mobbed-up group of La Costa Nostra moved in, putting them out of business.

Then Carlotta gets another idea to do some of them blue movies. So, what the hell. They were fucking like bunnies anyway, so they signed up and made movies every day and sometimes more than once a day for different companies. Before long, they were making big bucks again, enough to quit the other side jobs and just make the movies all day. He and Carlotta were living large in a big house with a swimming pool and rec room. They had lots of naked parties, orgies they call them, and charged people to attend. His reputation as a well-hung stud and movie actor spread. Some of them rich ladies wanted private sessions with him and sometimes with him and Carlotta. So, for the right price, he obliged them. Didn't bother him none to watch Carlotta get it on with some woman or some other man or a bunch of men. She was just buck wild like that. It took a lot to keep her entertained and satisfied.

Over the years, they moved up in the erotic film industry, and a couple of their films took top honors at a skin flick awards convention. They were in high demand after that. People even asked for their autographs and wanted to take pictures with them. They charged for that, too.

He and Carlotta were cruising right along. It was a sweet life until one day he looked up and there stood Donald Dixon, SaraJo's cousin. JoJeff learned from Don that crazy-ass Carlotta sent a postcard to SaraJo telling her the twins were his babies. The next thing he knew, Dixon snatched him up, and he was back in Summer County, expected to play daddy to his firstborn kid he had with SaraJo and the twins he had with Carlotta.

He felt he was still too young to be anybody's daddy. However, he didn't expect SaraJo to have divorced his ass and married someone else while he was away. She even sold his Harley though she knew what the bike meant to him. It was his first, and he practically built it himself from the ground up. She was the first girl he took riding on that bike when they were in their teens. They made love on it, and she was his wife for chrissake!

Yet, here stood Douglas Edward Johnson, Summer County Fire Chief, big and bold as you please with six children, correction four teenage boys, three of which were his, two little girls, and the tasty Mary Ella.

He really didn't see how he had teenaged sons when he was still in his early thirties. Yet the boys looked the spitting image of him at their ages. He ignored that fact, especially when he looked at the tasty morsel, Mary Ella, and could still get it up. Yeah, he really, *really* wanted to tap that booty back in the day.

Although Mary Ella was as pretty as she used to be, she was way too slim now. He preferred women with some meat on them. *"Didn't no male want a bone, but a dog,"* the old folks used to say. He heard that just before he was brought back to Summer County, Mary Ella left with a man, a doctor who was a friend of Johnson's, a former Marine. She wasn't sporting any wedding rings. So, even though she was too slim, maybe there was still time for him to make his play. After all, he had banged most of the available women in the county except her. He felt duty-bound to share himself with her, too. It would serve SaraJo right if he banged her cousin in retribution for selling his Harley, divorcing him when his back was turned, and for marrying Douglas Johnson!

"So, what brings you to me, Mary Ella?" JoJeff grinned. "Not that I'm complaining, mind you. You can come see all of me anytime you want."

Mary Ella gave him a cool, hard stare, which had him shifting from foot to foot, but it didn't knock the shit-eating grin off his still too handsome face. "I'm looking for a car, JoJeff. That's all. Something small and compact I can afford." She knew how to shut down a flirt. She'd had a lot of practice.

"I've got anything you want, baby, but I'm not small or compact. Far from it, and you can have me free of charge."

"Keep it clean, JoJeff," Douglas warned mildly. "Children here."

"You didn't have to bring an entourage to visit me, sweetheart." JoJeff smiled unctuously at her, ignoring Douglas.

"Doug took me to return the rental car I had. We're on the way home and decided to stop here before we tried any other car lot outside the county."

"Keepin' it in the family, huh? I like that. I've got the biggest and best deals in this part of the state. Step this way. I'll take extra special care of you so the Fire Chief can get those children home for their supper."

"Not on your life, JoJeff," Doug smirked. "The children are fine. It shouldn't take long to find something to suit Mary Ella's needs, and I don't mean you. Let's see what you've got in her price range. If we don't find it here, we'll move on elsewhere."

An hour later, Mary Ella signed the conditional sales contract, handed over a check for the down payment on the sharply discounted amount, and accepted the keys to her brand-new SUV. The purchase was financed through a new state bank owned by Gregory Alexander. JoJeff even threw in a year's worth of free oil changes, just to make sure she had a reason to come back to see him. He didn't mind selling it to her for five-hundred dollars over the wholesale price. He was sure she'd eventually show her appreciation in other ways. Yes, indeedy, she was a fine figure of a woman.

CHAPTER 7

The next morning, after breakfast, Mary Ella showed Satarah her new car.

"*Wow!* This is really nice." Satarah looked at it from several angles and then checked out the interior. "JoJeff did a fine job."

"He did, yes. I couldn't get over how little he charged me so I could afford an SUV, but he hasn't changed. He still looks and acts like he's in his teens."

"Good genes. Flirted with you, did he?" Satarah jokingly asked.

"Big time." Mary Ella huffed. "How are his parents and sister?"

"His parents still work in their garage over in Centerville, but they're slowing down some." Satarah shrugged. "They like to have their grandsons come and visit, and they include Donovan, even though he's not related to them by blood."

"That's good." Mary Ella nodded, pleased. "I remember you said they didn't particularly want Douglas to officially adopt Benson, Jeffrey, and Jonathan."

"That's true." Satarah nodded. "However, the boys voted and agreed that they wanted to be adopted and told their grandparents they'd always be their grandsons regardless of their surnames. Still, they feel Douglas is their father. JoJeff didn't object, and Carlotta didn't even respond to the proposal. So, Judge Holloway granted the petition, and now everyone carries Johnson as their legal surname."

"What about JoJeff's sister, Joy Alice?" Mary Ella rubbed her hand over the upholstery before they climbed out of the SUV and went into the cabin.

"I think she's still a television reporter or anchorwoman in Denver, Colorado. I don't hear from her much. Naturally, she's met the boys, but other than a birthday or Christmas card with a gift debit card in it, she doesn't keep in touch."

"Doesn't sound like she's ever coming back."

"I don't think she is, but to his credit, I think that's why JoJeff has stayed here to be with his parents now that they're older. He keeps a close eye on them and makes sure they keep up with their medical appointments. They're both in good health and come to the Friday night dances."

"JoJeff's sons are really beginning to look like him," Mary Ella commented.

Satarah huffed. "Don't I know it! The resemblance is uncanny. The young girls know it, too. There are many things to be said about JoJeff, but he's still a good-looking man with a great body. His boys look the spitting image of him. They're tall and well-built like him, too. That's where the resemblance ends. The boys are far more moral than JoJeff ever was."

"Didn't you say JoJeff is some kind of porn star?"

Satarah nodded. "Oh, yeah. Douglas accidentally found a few of JoJeff's movies on Benson's iPad. Since he was returned to me, he's been so focused on his father. He respects and cares about Douglas, but he wants a relationship with JoJeff, too. We had '*The Talk*' with Benson and the other boys but left it up to Benson to decide whether to delete the skin flicks from his iPad. Doug and I looked at the movies, too, to make sure they were what we expected, and they were triple-X-rated porn."

"You *watched* the movies… *with Doug*?" Mary Ella's eyes widened, aghast.

"Of course," nodded Satarah. "We didn't want to be talking out the side of our necks if we hadn't even seen them. When Doug and I talked with the boys, I approached it purely from a clinical perspective while Doug addressed the male response and responsibility aspects of having sex. Believe me, when I tell you, I found every video out there on copulation from a scientific and medical viewpoint. The discussion was useful. The boys aren't shy about asking questions, and Doug and I would prefer to have them ask questions at home rather than learn the misconceptions outside our house and family."

"I guess you're right," agreed Mary Ella, "but it has to be a shock for the boys to see their father in action, so to speak."

"It is, but they also know he sometimes still performs in these movies. That's how he started his car business. He, apparently, made a lot of money and received awards for his performances. When he goes away for extended periods, my boys know he's not just at some car auction," sighed Satarah. "The hardest thing for me is when Jeffrey and Jonathan see my sister, their biological mother, performing in some of the movies with or without JoJeff. They say it doesn't bother them because they don't think of her as their mother. Still, it bothers me for them."

"Oh, SaraJo," crooned Mary Ella in sympathy, taking her hand.

"It's okay, Mary Ella. I know who my sister is, and so do my boys." Satarah shrugged. "It's sad, but I don't want my boys being blindsided by this stuff and then blaming us for not telling them the truth. That could have easily happened. I know my own father has the entire collection of Carlotta's films to date.

"Ms. Clarisse Flowers, you remember her? She's one of the deaconesses at my father's church. She also cleans house for him, too. I think she would like to do a lot more for him, but he prefers much younger women. She found his stash of videos and could not get to Ms. Minnie Mae's beauty salon, where Carlotta used to work, fast enough to spread the word.

"Mama tried to reach out to Carlotta but got nowhere. Carlotta is who she is and does what she does because she likes it. Full speed ahead, and the devil take the hindmost. She's made it abundantly clear to me on more than a few occasions when I tried to talk with her about her sons that she didn't have any children. JoJeff takes the position what he does on film is honest work, and it's legal. If he wants to exploit his body for his benefit, ain't nobody's business if he does."

Mary Ella just shook her head. "So, what other news is fit to print?" She dismissed the craziness of JoJeff and Carlotta.

"Let's see." Satarah narrowed her eyes in concentration. "Oh, I know!" She snapped her finger. "Did I tell you Chuck and Vivian have a son?"

Mary Ella laughed. "That's news? They're always adopting children. In fact, one of the other doctors Mark and I worked with, Evan Michael

Cain, helped them adopt several abandoned Iraqi children in need of medical intervention. One little boy was badly injured, and his parents were killed by a car bomb. A brother and sister sustained shrapnel in several body parts."

"Oh, yes, I remember when they adopted and brought home the three children, but, no, I mean, they had a natural-born son. This time, Vivian finally convinced Chuck to name the baby Charles Patrick Montgomery, Junior. They call him Patrick. He and my Kate are around the same age."

Mary Ella frowned. "Didn't you text me to say Chuck and Vivian's daughter, Linda, married and has a child?"

Satarah nodded. "I did, yes. Linda married Will Hamilton."

"Will 'The Hammer' Hamilton, the baseball icon?" Mary Ella's eyes widened, surprised. "He has to be a little older than she is, isn't he?"

"He is, yes, about eight or nine years," nodded Satarah. "They have two sons now, and they're thinking of getting pregnant again and try for a girl.

"Linda opened a dance school and studio in New York City, but she still gives ballet or ice-skating performances for charity events. One of the ballets she created is in its second year on Broadway. It's very popular. We took the children to see it. It is a phenomenal production. It's co-produced by Trey Kennard.

Mary Ella goggled. *"Wow!* He's a real treat for the eyes."

"He is, but he's really good people," Satarah offered. "We ran into Chuck and Vivian's daughter Natalia and a guy friend, Glen Kennard; no relation to Trey. However, he's even more gorgeous than Trey Kennard, and, girl, is he built like a Greek god or what?"

Mary Ella laughed at her cousin's expression.

"Also, Linda found out she has a biological half-brother. He's a real cutie, too, tall, and very British. His name is Bradley Connor Smyth, II, and he's some type of computer genius."

"Didn't Vivian's brother marry, too?" Mary Ella frowned.

Satarah nodded. "The youngest one, Gregory Clayton, yes. He married Angelique."

Mary Ella's eyes rounded in surprise. "The supermodel and actress? *Wow!* I remember when she was just a kid. She and her brother, Miguel, were just getting started in modeling and the movie industry."

"Now Miguel is a super-star movie actor and high-fashion model. He also tours with the band Changelings," Satarah supplied. "He plays a mean electric guitar and sings really well."

Mary Ella nodded. "Changelings? I heard their music while I was helping with Pan-Africa disaster relief. They shared the stage with the group Ivy."

Satarah nodded. "Sometimes they tour together. Benny and Stacy Alexander's daughter, Whitney Ivy, is the lead singer with Ivy. She's an attorney now and married to a Marine who's a medical doctor, Tucker Cavanaugh, and he sometimes performs with Changelings. They were just in town to celebrate their grandparent's anniversary. They might still be in town."

"Tucker Cavanaugh is like Mark, then. He's a medical doctor and Marine." Mary Ella somberly sighed when reality reared its ugly head again.

Satarah was trying to keep Mary Ella's spirits up, but she could see she was failing. She comfortingly rubbed her cousin's shoulder. "Have you spoken with Mark since you've been back? He would want to know you've arrived safely."

"I'm sure, but I have no way of reaching him where he probably is now. He'll communicate with me when he can." Mary Ella could only hope that she was right, and Mark wasn't lying somewhere in Libya, Chad, Egypt, Sudan, Niger, Algeria, Tunisia, or some other country dead or dying.

"You look so sad, Mary Ella. I'm here if you need to talk."

She shook off the doldrums and rose to get another bottle of water and bring a pitcher of iced sun tea to the table for Satarah. "So, is Duke Patterson still here?"

Satarah accepted Mary Ella's abrupt change of topics. She understood that it was what her cousin needed at that moment. "He is, yes. In fact, he married Doug's aunt, Florence Johnson. She's a really delightful woman.

Though they were middle-aged when they married, neither one was married before. She's from Washington, DC, and used to work for this high-powered female attorney, Capri McAllister, who used to date my cousin Gregory. She's married now to the astronaut," Satarah snapped her finger, trying to remember his name.

"Do you mean Dr. Tate Kennedy?" Mary Ella smiled.

"Yes!" Satarah enthusiastically pumped her fist. "That's him. Anyway, remember, Duke was Doug's boss when he was with the Richmond, Virginia, Fire Department. They were longtime friends, so when Duke retired, he moved here."

Mary Ella's brows narrowed. "I didn't know Doug had a family other than Donovan. He was a widower when he moved here, and he never mentioned his parents." Just like she didn't think Mark had a family either.

"Yes, he does, but until recently, they weren't close. Doug's father, Chester Earl Johnson, Senior, lives in Seattle, Washington, and his older brother, Chester Earl, Junior, is in Peoria, Illinois. With his father's and Doug's help, Chester Junior just bought out his boss's interest in a used car lot. He and JoJeff are cut from the same cloth in that respect. They bonded at Jinx Juke Joint one night when Chester Earl, Jr., was visiting us. Doug's father and Florence, his father's much younger sister, came for a Thanksgiving holiday reunion. Actually, it was the first time Doug met his Aunt Florence. He didn't know his father had a sister, and he hadn't seen his father or brother since his high school graduation. Doug went right into the Marines as a teenager right after his mother died."

"Douglas told you about his life?" Mary Ella frowned.

"Sure. We spent a lot of time together during the blizzard. You remember how hard it was to get around, don't you? We had several feet of snow."

"The blizzard which shut down South Carolina is unforgettable. We triaged at the hospital for five straight days and nights without a break. There was a massive amount of accidents that paralyzed both the north and southbound lanes of I-95. That's when Doug drove through the storm to get here after he learned Donovan was seriously injured in the school bus accident. You saved Donovan's life and almost lost your medical license as a result. Some things can't be forgotten."

"I know." Satarah nodded. "Doug and I talked with each other a lot. He told me about his first wife, Lily. They were high school sweethearts. They married young, and he went to college after he left the military. Lily had several miscarriages, and later they discovered she couldn't carry a child. She convinced Doug to adopt Donovan. Then Lily committed suicide when Doug wanted to wait to adopt another child. Doug blamed himself for her death before he learned she was severely bipolar and off her meds. Lily's behavior was erratic, and it was why Doug wanted to wait to adopt again. It devastated him to discover he had no knowledge of her illness during the time they were dating or during their marriage. Apparently, her parents knew but never told Douglas."

As she continued to listen to Satarah, Mary Ella wondered whether there were secrets Mark held back from her about his family. She didn't think he was ever married before he met her, but she never asked him. She just assumed. He didn't wear a wedding band, but some men didn't. She didn't believe him to be the type of man to be unfaithful to a wife. No, no, it was too unseemly to think about, but to assume something was true made an ass of him and her.

What about Kaseem, though? she wondered. *Certain Arab men are permitted by the Qur'an to have multiple wives. Polygyny is permitted in the Bible, too. What could she tell this baby, if it's his, about its father? Kaseem translated meant Divided. If Kaseem fathered her baby, is she obligated to give it a Muslim name? If so, would she have to raise him or her in the Muslim faith?* The questions were mind-boggling.

At least she knew who Mark was related to, but she knew nothing at all about Kaseem, except he had exceptionally mesmerizing eyes and a full beard. His hair was long, ink-black, soft, and curly. She never saw him naked, yet she knew him to be solidly built and well endowed. She didn't know what it felt like to kiss him, but she knew what it felt like to have his mouth on her breasts. He never rushed when he took her. Instead, he brought her to her peak several times before he let himself fly.

Strange to realize now, after nearly two months as his captive, he never treated her like a piece of meat the way the other men did with the women and girls they took captive. Kaseem actually took time to… love her? Though he certainly never said the words, she, nevertheless, felt the sensation of being loved. Maybe even more than she felt it when she and Mark made love.

She realized she never even told Mark she loved him. The revelation surprised her, but they rarely had extra time to do anything other than help save lives. Still, it was no excuse for not telling him she loved him and defining what it was between them beyond excellent sex.

When they slept, they made time to make love. The high-stress situation they were in made them prone to live for the moment because the next day was never promised to them. She never knew that about herself until she left Summer County. She reveled in the excitement of seeing a new and different place and finding joy when they saved a life. What did it say about her, this country girl from a South Carolina farming community?

"When pigs fly," Satarah was saying when Mary Ella tuned back in.

"Ha! Ha!" Mary Ella scoffed good-naturedly.

"You're zoned out again. You're living inside your head these days."

"I apologize, SaraJo. I'm lousy company. I can't keep from mentally wandering off. What were you saying?"

"Nothing important. How about some lunch?"

"I'm really not---"

"That hungry. Mary Ella, I've heard the same song from you for too long. There is some leftover Chicken Parm from the Men's Club dinner last night. I might even have a few servings of prime rib. Or it wouldn't take long to put together a couple of subs."

Mary Ella sighed. "Okay, whatever is easiest."

Satarah smiled delightedly and hopped up from the kitchen table.

Though industrial-sized, the kitchen looked professionally designed, warm, and decidedly comfortable for a family. Her cousin designed and built the kitchen and the family room with her bare hands. She was proud of Satarah's accomplishments.

To her left, the spacious family room was where Satarah's children usually watched television or played board games under her watchful eyes.

It was convenient to have a space adjacent to the kitchen where Satarah could work and watch what the children saw on the big, flat-screen. They had private bedroom spaces on the first floor of The Summer House, where guests weren't permitted. She sat with the Johnson children the night before while Satarah saw to the Men's Club seven-course meal.

Satarah did much of the work in restoring the mansion. Her cousin was determined to do it all herself, and she became skilled at carpentry, tiling, electrical, and plumbing work. On occasion, she would permit her and Jenny to help her paint a room or grout the tile. Then Satarah's Aunt Sylvia, with the force of an invading army, stealthily brought other family members in to help complete the work in record time. It helped that Doug and Bob Sweeney were living in The Summer House after the blizzard before it opened for business, and both loved working with their hands.

Working together with the cousins, the bed and breakfast opened years before Satarah expected. Now, it was one of the places listed on the National Registry of Historic Homes. Over the years, Satarah turned the property into a working farm as it had been when it was built in the seventeenth century. People came from far and wide to tour the house and hold events in and around the estate, like the Men's Club meeting.

It was a working meeting, Satarah told her where the men in the community laid out plans for events they would host for the children, teens, and adults. They held a weekly Friday night fish fry and country dance at the fire station in Goodwill; a May Day dance called a Spring Fling and carnival in the spring, and a county fair and summer festival. In the fall, they held an Oktoberfest and Harvest in Summerville, sang holiday carols in the Goodwill town square on Christmas Eve, and had a big New Year's Eve party in one of the hangers at the county airfield.

These were the warm and fuzzy things Mary Ella remembered and was glad to see nothing changed in her absence. It made it a good homecoming for her and a place just to be until she could figure out which side was up.

CHAPTER 8

When Mary Ella answered the knock and opened the cottage's door, the tears sprung up and overflowed. Her breath hitched and choked her, and then the floodgates just opened and flooded.

"Okay, okay. You're okay now," Bernard Alexander crooned as he enveloped her in his powerful arms.

Mary Ella couldn't catch her breath, but she cried violently into his firm chest, clutching his crisp white dress shirt in a death grip. He just stood holding her as his wife, Sylvia, closed the door, put down her things, and found a bottle of water in the refrigerator.

Somehow, he managed to get her to sit down between them on the sofa, but the waterworks kept coming.

"Mary Ella, I want you to put your head between your knees and take long, deep breaths now. Do as I say, baby," Mrs. Alexander guided comfortingly, but firmly. "We have to consider the baby. This is too much stress on you and the little one you're carrying."

She did as she was told because she knew Mrs. Alexander was right. Holding in her fears and trepidations wasn't going to help her or her baby.

When Mary Ella sat up again, Bernard took her in his arm again and placed her head against his right shoulder. "Now, tell me what you can, Mary Ella. Let's get it all out."

So, she did. She didn't hold anything back while Mrs. Alexander handed tissues to her. "I was so scared that I was paralyzed with fear. I thought we were surely about to be killed. I wanted to ask them why they were doing this to us. We weren't bad people. We were there to help relieve the pain and suffering of others, but I couldn't get the words out. They just beat and kicked Mark and me. The more he struggled to get to me, to help me, to protect me, the more they beat him. I had to tell him I would be okay, but to please stop struggling. I didn't know what I was saying, but he wouldn't give up until they knocked him out. There was nothing he or I could do to stop it, to stop whatever was going to happen to us. I felt so helpless.

"They must have already been to the camp, but we didn't hear any shots, any noise or commotion. They told me everyone there was dead, but we were Americans, and even though we were people of color, they could trade us for money or other prisoners being held at Guantanamo Bay. In the meantime, we would serve them." Mary Ella took a deep breath closing her eyes at the horrific vision. "This one man wanted to take Mark and me with him, but another one, his name is Kaseem, he stepped up and said no. I couldn't see his face clearly because he wore a lungee turban and cloth over most of his face. Still, from what I could see, he had olive-brown colored skin and these pale, aqua-green eyes. Everyone else we'd met in the region had dark brown irises, so he stood out.

"I don't speak the Libyan dialect well, the way Mark does," Mary Ella continued while wiping away her tears, "but I understood enough to know this man, with the strange-colored eyes, intended to marry me. They fought over me, but not to the death. Kaseem won and covered my naked body with a madraga."

"A madraga?" asked Mrs. Alexander.

Mary Ella nodded. "It's a kind of dress Bedouin women wear, but it had this beautiful, intricately embroidered symbol on the sleeves. I was permitted to put on my tennis shoes, but that was all. I didn't have much: just some toiletry items and a few clothes in a backpack. My things were distributed to the other women being held captive. Then they held some type of wedding ceremony right then and there.

"Mark was covered with a lungee turban, too, and traditional Bedouin clothes. I can only surmise that it was to disguise his appearance and who he is. Like my things, his were distributed to others. Then he was taken away by the man who lost the fight and his group of Islamic fundamentalists. The last I saw Mark, he was still a captive and unconscious.

"We camped there right where Mark and I had just made love in the limestone quarry. I love Mark, but I couldn't… stop…" she tried to continue, but her breath hitched again. "He, the man, Kaseem, with the strange colored eyes… he had me right there on the ground in front of everyone. He kept whispering something in my ear as he took me, but I was too emotionally numb to understand his words. The others just sat there and watched him molest me while they ate their meals. He kept it up all night, and I…let him. I didn't try to fight him.

"The next morning, when he stood me up, I was weak and dizzy and felt his semen drain down my legs. It was so much I thought my period had started. Still, when I looked down, my IUD was there on the ground in a pool of blood and his… I don't know when it came… I didn't feel it, but they had punched me, beat me, kicked me. I don't know whether it came loose while I was with Mark or… the other man. They called me vile names because I was naked. I wasn't wearing a wedding ring… they have killed women for far less.

"Months later, I don't know how many, Kaseem, the man with the strange colored eyes, his name was Kaseem…" Her breath hitched again, and she knuckled her tears away. "I told you that already. I've said his name several times, haven't I?" She shook her head, frustrated, and knuckled away another flood of tears before she continued. "Kaseem woke me in the night. I thought he wanted sex again, and I was prepared to submit, but he whispered in English that I was going home and to be ready. He untied the sash he usually bound my hands with and said not to make a sound when they came for me. I was so blurry-eyed, tired, and numb I didn't immediately understand. Still, not five minutes later, this band of ninjas snuck into the camp, sprayed something in the air, put a cloth over my nose and mouth, and then took me away. I know Kaseem was awake, but he didn't move. He pretended that he was asleep while I was spirited away.

"I couldn't see the faces of the people who rescued me. They used hand signals and didn't speak to me above a whisper. There were about ten of them, but one of them had light, crystal brown eyes. I could see that in the moonlight. About a mile away from the camp, these bat-winged jet copters just seemed to appear out of nowhere without making a sound and took us away. We landed somewhere in the desert just before the break of dawn. I was transferred to a different helicopter and flown to a US Navy aircraft carrier surrounded by other Navy battleships. We had to be somewhere in the Mediterranean Sea because it didn't take that long to get there.

"I was given a thorough physical examination. Then I was psych tested and debriefed. That's when the doctor told me I was pregnant. He also said I was suffering from Stockholm syndrome."

"Stockholm syndrome?" Dr. Alexander asked.

Mary Ella nodded. "It's a condition that causes hostages to develop a psychological alliance with their captors as a survival strategy during captivity. The psychiatrist told me it results from a bond formed between captors and captives during intimate time spent together. Apparently, these feelings are generally considered irrational in light of the danger or risk endured by a victim. Still, if I wanted to have an abortion, I didn't have much time to decide. I was in no frame of mind to make that type of decision, given what I went through.

"I learned that Stockholm syndrome consists of strong emotional ties that develop between two persons where one person intermittently harasses, beats, threatens, abuses, or intimidates the other. From a medical, purely clinical perspective, I understand what I went through. I'm just not sure I've come out the other side of this thing unscathed.

"A few days later, a transport plane flew me and others in need of medical attention to Shaw Air Force Base near Sumter, and then a helicopter immediately took me to the Columbia airport. I was given a few clothes, a credit card, money and papers, my credentials and identification, so I rented a car and came home. I didn't know what else to do or where to go. I just drove straight to The Summer House and woke up Satarah. She took me in and gave me a room."

"You're still in shock, Mary Ella." Bernard squeezed her with a strong arm around her shoulders. "From what you've said, this was a very traumatic experience for you. It's not something you can just kick aside or pretend everything is all right. You've been wedded to someone you don't know, and you're pregnant. In addition to what happened to you, someone you care about may still be a captive. You shouldn't keep this kind of thing bottled up."

She leaned up, took another tissue, and wiped her eyes. "I was told not to talk with anyone about what happened to me or Mark's life could still be in danger. I didn't know who he is. We were lovers for almost a year before we left Summer County. Since I've been rescued, I did an Internet search on him. One of the doctors we worked with was joking with Mark because they were in medical school together. He mentioned that they went to Harvard. I was surprised by that, so I looked it up online and found out Mark graduated in the top one percent of his class. The information I found mentioned that his parents were also Harvard medical school grads. It led me to other references, and I looked up his entire family. He comes from a dynasty of medical doctors and researchers. He has a younger brother, Dr. Vaughn Cole Brooks, who's an expert hematologist. His parents, Gary and Judith Cole Brooks, are both medical doctors, as are his grandparents on both sides of his family. His paternal grandmother is Dr. Irene Townsend Brooks. She is not only the head of medical services at Mass General, but she is also a direct descendant, the granddaughter of Ashro Townsend, the man who created one of the largest pharmaceutical companies in the country. Her husband, Mark's grandfather, is Harlan Ellsworth Brooks, the former Surgeon General of the United States." She huffed, annoyed.

Mrs. Alexander sighed. "We know about some of Mark's family connections. His brother, Vaughn, came here to perform a stem cell transplant. He stayed a week."

"I have to wonder why Mark never mentioned any of this to me. We talked about medical science all the time and shared what we knew with the other medical professionals. There were many conversations with those who have an interest in medicine. He lived here in Summer County with us for nearly a year, helping us establish an effective and efficient firefighter's medic service. As I said, we were very close, even back then, and I left home to go with him when he asked me. We worked together, side-by-side, day and night, in all kinds of conditions and in different countries. We were a team, but he never talked about his family or his childhood. With him, it's all about the mission. If I didn't already know that Mark and Douglas were in the Marines together, I don't think Mark would have told me that either."

"What are you saying, Mary Ella?" Sylvia Alexander asked.

"I'm saying if he didn't tell me anything about himself, who is it I've been in love with for all of this time? If the baby I'm carrying is his, who do I tell my child his or her father is? How can I love a man I really didn't know? He has people who must care about him, but he doesn't indicate to me that he has people he cares about. How is this possible?" she asked vehemently.

"Those are questions you can ask him when he's rescued and returned to the United States."

"Will I even know when or if that happens? We weren't married. I'm not entitled to demand to know where he is or whether he's safe. I'm not even supposed to tell anyone, including his family, about what happened."

"For now, let's try to focus on your health and the health of the baby you carry. I presume you intend to keep the child?" asked Mrs. Alexander.

Mary Ella nodded. "Yes, I do. It's part of me now, and I don't want to give it up. I'm over thirty years old, and, thanks to you, I have a way to take care of myself and my child."

"I want to have you examined as soon as possible. Do you have a preference for an OB/GYN specialist?" asked Sylvia Alexander.

"No, not really. They're all board-certified at the hospital, so anyone there should be fine."

"Okay, then we'll arrange an appointment for you with the first available slot. In the interim, you know what you have to do to manage your care."

"I have to admit that I don't have much of an appetite," sighed Mary Ella. "I'm severely dehydrated, but I haven't had morning sickness."

Sylvia frowned. "Are the doctors sure that you're pregnant?"

Mary Ella nodded sagely with a bitter laugh. "Of that, there is no question. I haven't had a menstrual cycle since before I was taken captive.

I also took more than one pregnancy test. As best as I can determine, I should have been ovulating when I was captured. I just don't know who the father is. I had sex with two different men within an hour of each other."

"You made love with one man. That man is Mark. The other man was not consensual," Bernard Alexander reminded her. "You were abused, even though it was under cover of an Islamic marriage."

"That's not going to matter to the baby if it's not Mark's. I'd never tell him or her that he or she was conceived after some impromptu ceremony in the mountains, making me a wife and performed by a cleric whose language I didn't clearly understand. In the eyes of Islam, I'm the lawful wife of a man, Kaseem, who claimed me after a fight with another man who wasn't Mark. This situation is just too bizarre, Stockholm syndrome or not.

"If or when Mark is rescued and returns to the United States, what do I tell the man I love, but really don't know, about being married and having Kaseem's or Mark's baby? I don't even know whether I can get a divorce from Kaseem. Although divorce is permitted in Islam, it's approved only as a last resort. If it is not possible to continue a marriage, certain steps need to be taken to ensure that all options have been exhausted and both parties are treated with respect and justice. How can I do that when I don't even know who or where Kaseem is? I don't even know how to find out."

"You've studied this?" asked Bernard.

"I have, yes. I was working and living among people of the Islamic faith. I needed to know things about their culture and beliefs to be effective. I even studied to become more proficient with the various dialects and languages. I learned that when a marriage is in danger, couples are advised to pursue all possible remedies to rebuild the relationship. As I've said, divorce is allowed as a last option, but it is strongly discouraged. According to the Qur'an, The Prophet Muhammad once said, '*Of all the lawful things, divorce is the most hated by Allah.*' Even in Christianity, the wedding vows require that a marriage stays intact *until death do we part*. I don't wish Kaseem death.

"I believe I'm suffering from Stockholm syndrome, but the fact is Kaseem did save my life first by fighting the other man to keep me. He never beat, kicked or laid a hand on me in anger. Second, by marrying me, he guaranteed that none of the other terrorists would harm me. Finally, by somehow facilitating my escape. I don't know why or how he did it, but I'm sure he was involved. If it weren't for him, I don't think I would be alive today. Other than being an American, I just wasn't significant enough to anyone.

"I don't want to wake up each day for the rest of my life with regrets, but I don't think I have a way through or out of this situation. My baby will be a constant reminder of what happened to me, but I will not have regrets about bringing this new life into the world no matter what the future holds for us. I will love and cherish it, no matter who fathered it."

"You'll have to find a way to make peace with the reality that is your life, Mary Ella." Dr. Alexander looked at her squarely in the face and continued. "We won't ask you to see a psychiatrist because of what you were instructed to do, but we want you to come to us to talk through your concerns whenever the need arises the way you used to. Rest assured, we won't tell anyone what you've told us. Please don't keep this bottled up. You are important to us, and your feelings about Mark and Kaseem are important to you. That makes them important to us, too."

CHAPTER 9

She didn't expect it, but when she showed up at six-thirty on Monday morning, there was a surprise, welcome-home party waiting for her. It was going on time for a shift change at seven o'clock, but everyone gathered around to welcome her back to her old stomping grounds. She was just there in a different and higher capacity. Warm hugs and many smiles were making her feel welcomed. It felt good to see so many familiar faces and the people who were still in training when she left the country. Yet, she wondered why she hadn't seen Eric Dixon. He was on staff at the hospital, she knew, and most doctors made early rounds. They were friends, so she hoped he wasn't avoiding her. If they didn't cross paths soon, she'd seek him out… just to say hello.

"*Wow!* You look great," enthused Jenny Jones Sweeney, her big, pretty brown eyes alive with merriment, her shiny, platinum-blond hair curling madly around her still cherubic face and spilling down her back. Rosy cheeks and all, she seemed not to have aged one bit. "I used to be that slim," she sighed. "I used to be able to see my feet without having to bend over. When I do that, if I'm not careful, I could overbalance and face plant." She rubbed her motion-filled belly.

Mary Ella thought she'd be trying to balance her weight like that in a few more months. She smiled at her friend. "You look beautiful. You'll get back to that petite size in no time."

"I hope so, but I'll tell you the truth, Mary Ella, I just love having babies," she sighed. "Bob is just the sweetest man. I love him to pieces because he takes such good care of us."

Mary Ella remembered Bob Sweeney as a big, six-foot-five-inch, solidly built guy with curly red hair, a smile as wide as Texas, and pretty green eyes. "He loves you, too, and of course, he'd take care of you." She told Jenny. They used to double date back then when Bob and Mark first moved to Summer County to work with Douglas. Bob used to be one of Douglas' firefighters in Richmond, Virginia, and jumped at the chance to follow him to Summer County when Doug offered Bob a career change. They had great fun as a foursome. "Be sure to tell Bob I said hello."

"I'll do that. Bob was stunned, as we all were, to hear that you were back home. We've been living vicariously through the postcards you've sent to us from all over the globe."

"It's good to be back." She smiled at all who surrounded her, chatting and filling their plates at the buffet. They had coffee, tea, juice, donuts, and bagels nicely set out in the break room on a display table. A fresh watermelon rind was cut into the shape of a basket with a handle and filled with fruit. A banner was strung from wall-to-wall welcoming her home.

Even more people came in before they went on duty or came in after going off the night shift. So many people found their way to the emergency room's employees' break room to welcome her back home and share information about the goings-on since she left. Somehow it felt like slipping her feet into a comfortable pair of old shoes. She was safely home.

As much as she enjoyed the welcome home party and the people she had known and worked with for so long, she was anxious to get set up in her new office and get to work. Jenny came with her to help. Quite a few innovations had taken place in her absence. They were now a paperless operation. Jenny walked her through a straightforward process. Her office computer was like a control center. She could observe her nurses and the doctors providing care from her position at her desk. They could dial her up and see her face on their hand-held devices. All of the patients' charts were electronic and available at her fingertips. Reports and data streamed by on a wall-mounted monitor that was also hooked up to the community's cable television service. She could also see the face of anyone she was talking with via her monitor, desktop computer, cell phone or iPad. Everything had two-way video camera capability.

It fascinated her that a lot of the guesswork with quick and accurate diagnosis was taken out of the equation. Data fed into the hand-held iPad would deliver advice on what additional questions should be asked of a patient and what additional lab tests were recommended as a result. Past medical records, whether with their hospital or elsewhere, could be accessed and evaluated within moments. The innovations that had been made were delivered lightning-fast and at a substantially lower per-patient cost.

"I think you've got it," chirped Jenny excitedly. "*Wow*, it took me like forever to figure out how to move from one screen to the other, and here you've got it in ten minutes."

"You're a great teacher, Jenny. I'm really glad you had the time to do this."

"I had to drop one of my boys off at the academy this morning and the other in the daycare facility here at the hospital. I had nothing else on my schedule except helping to set up the welcome-home party we planned for you."

"Let's see the pictures of the boys. I know you have some."

Delighted, Jenny dug out her smartphone and started flipping through the views of the cherry-cheeked little cherubs with startling green eyes like their father but naturally wispy platinum-blond hair like their mother. They were too cute for words.

After Jenny left with the promise to call to set up a lunch date for the following week, Mary Ella sat rubbing her abdomen and wondering who her baby would resemble. She and Mark both had cinnamon-colored skin tones and medium brown eyes. On the other hand, Kaseem was more of an olive-brown skin tone, likely because of the sun's intense heat. His lashes were long and thick like his hair, but his pale, aqua-green eyes were unique. His voice was a deep, caressing purr. He never seemed to raise his voice but managed to command attention.

Command. That was an interesting word when applied to Kaseem. It sent an unavoidable sensation skittering through her body. Now that the threat to her life was retreating into her memory, bits and pieces of the experience were coming to the forefront of her recollections. Though he wasn't the leader of his sect, his words did command attention and even respect among the others. She counted forty to fifty men in the group at any one time and half again as many concubines. Men kept coming and going, groups forming and then dispersing, but the size of the faction she was with didn't change substantially. None disregarded Kaseem's directives.

Like her, the other female captives, girls really, were taken from their families, their homes and villages, and subjected to impromptu weddings. They were not given a choice about whether they wanted to marry or who their husband would be. The women were reluctant to speak openly with her. However, when they were set to the tasks of "women's work," some expressed a desire to wed Kaseem. Some even ventured that she was lucky to have been chosen by him.

Though she understood why they believed such a thing to be beneficial, after all, he was handsome, but she couldn't share their sentiment that she was lucky. All of her life, she had the freedom of choice about the directions she could take in her future. These freedoms were not embedded into these Middle Eastern girls' psyche. They may have wanted to rebel, but few would ever do so. Eons of oppression of women in certain Arab nations did not inspire a demand for freedom of choice. However, Mary Ella did not believe she would survive without it.

Each moment of every day, she thought of ways to escape her captors, escape Kaseem, but didn't see a way out that wouldn't lead to her immediate death or severe beating for disobeying her husband. Most of the time, he kept her tethered to him with a sash bound around her wrists. She didn't know what country she was in, what borders they crossed. She could only determine by watching the sunrise and sunset which directions they traveled. Many times, they journeyed by night and slept days in the sweltering heat in caves or mountain crevices. So, she bided her time and waited, serving Kaseem his meals, submitting to his sexual needs at his demand, and cleaning his clothes. She had little privacy. She wore no undergarments, making it easy for him to copulate whether from the front or back, lying down or standing up. It was only sex, she convinced herself, not love. So, she did not fight him but had no defense from his uncanny ability to make her respond to his touch. It was as if he had a road map of her body and knew the points of interest that would bring her to her completion. No matter how she tried to mentally block the natural reactions her traitorous body experienced, her body craved his touch. She was never successful.

As she continued to rub her abdomen, she refused to regret what he made her feel or the results of those daily encounters.

Later that day, Mary Ella sat in the garden adjacent to the hospital cafeteria, having lunch with Sylvia Alexander.

"How is it going so far?" asked Sylvia.

Mary Ella was sure this lunchtime meeting was arranged to ensure she ate a decent meal. The cafeteria food was surprisingly good. The turkey on whole wheat with a cup of tomato basil soup went down smoothly. She was still drinking copious amounts of water and staying away from caffeinated beverages.

"I'm amazed at all of the innovative things that have taken place since I've been away. The new wing on the hospital with the rooftop heliport is fantastic. Jenny Sweeney sat with me this morning and brought me up to speed. She said the new wing was a gift from all of the people who were helped or saved from death during that huge snowstorm years ago. That allowed the hospital to divert resources from the building fund to invest in new, innovative, cutting-edge, electronic equipment. Then a guy from IT, I've never met before, came in and customized my desktop unit and provided a laptop, smartphone with all of these gadgets and gizmos on it, and an iPad."

"Well, that was fast," commented Sylvia, somewhat surprised. "I just put the order in yesterday. Nevertheless, we're in the twenty-first century and heading toward the twenty-second," Sylvia joked. "I know you've had a full schedule, so I took the liberty of setting up an OB/GYN appointment with Alfred Quade for you. He's very conscientious about his patients, he's extremely competent, and he has a nice bedside manner. I didn't know whether you were still keeping your condition secret, for the time being, so Dr. Quade agreed to do your exam at Chuck and Vivian's home rather than in his office or the hospital. You might remember they have a fully-equipped medical facility in their home. Is that all right with you?"

"Yes, thank you for arranging this," Mary Ella spoke sincerely. "I'm not ready to answer a lot of questions about my pregnancy yet."

"Good!" Sylvia smiled brightly. "That's what I thought. I'll be there to assist Dr. Quade with the exam. Here are the date and time." She handed the card with the information on it to Mary Ella and then continued. "Chuck and Vivian are in Maryland and not expected back anytime soon, so I've arranged for the house staff to be off that day, and we'll have absolute privacy."

Mary Ella was genuinely appreciative. "I can't thank you enough for going to all of this trouble."

"It's no trouble at all." Sylvia shook her head. "With this new technology, I can access the physical exam performed on you aboard the ship when you were rescued, rather than have another one executed now for your medical insurance. I don't want to subject you to additional X-rays if they are not necessary at this point. I noticed you've selected one of the better medical plans with your employment package. It gives you one hundred percent coverage for you and the little one when he or she arrives."

Mary Ella nodded. "It was a little more expensive, but I don't have a lot of monthly costs to contend with. For now, I'm renting one of the cottages on the grounds of The Summer House until I find or build a permanent residence. I purchased an SUV for a good price. Satarah and I drove into Columbia on Saturday and did a little shopping for clothes and shoes. She won't let me eat meals alone, so I'm being royally fed."

Sylvia laughed. "I imagine she enjoys having another woman around to talk with."

"Well," Mary Ella smiled, "There is that. There's a lot of testosterone with five males at the table."

When Sylvia's smartphone beeped, she looked at the screen before checking the time. "I've got a meeting starting in about fifteen minutes. Are you okay?"

Mary Ella warmly smiled at Sylvia. "How could I not be?"

"Don't be a stranger, Mary Ella. Bernard and I want you to come to our home the way you use to. You're always welcome."

She nodded and stood to hug Sylvia before she hurried away. Then Mary Ella sat again to enjoy the garden for the next few minutes before she, too, had to return to her office. As she sat, mindlessly going through her afternoon schedule, she felt a strange sensation of being watched. When Mary Ella looked up and around, she didn't notice any other people who were having lunch in the garden paying attention to her. For the most part, they were people she knew and had grown up with. Many had stopped by the table to welcome her back but didn't linger overmuch. Since the sensation wouldn't leave her, she decided to end her lunch break early.

A little disconcerted, she got up from the table, dumped her lunch debris, and headed back to the emergency room and her afternoon challenges.

Toggling back and forth from camera to camera was made easy by the hospital's exceptional video and audio equipment, he thought as he watched Mary Ella. She was having lunch in a garden with an attractive woman with a shapely body, a full head of hair, and a great pair of legs. They seemed to know each other well and were having a pleasant time together. When he ran a facial recognition program on the other woman, nothing came up. *That was odd*, he thought. His system was one of the most sophisticated in use today. There were literally millions of video cameras in operation in the world, he knew. Surely the woman's face was captured somewhere. When he dug a little deeper, he still got nothing. *Curiouser and curiouser*, he thought and put it on his To-Do list for later. For now, he just wanted to watch Mary Ella for a while longer before he had to head out for a strategy meeting.

She looked entirely too thin but very shapely in casual business attire. He had been following her around for some time just to ensure she was where he expected her to be, doing the things she was familiar with. At least, that's what he told himself, but the reality was quite different from the facts. Still, there was nothing to be done about it now…or maybe ever.

Since the IT equipment she received was in place, he could monitor her morning, noon, and night. He would almost be able to hear her breathing. Still, he wanted desperately to taste her, to smell her exotic scent. Those olfactory sensations would be denied to him now and probably forever.

When she looked up and around as if sensing him watching her, he smiled. She had good instincts and, although this was the first indication that she felt his presence, it was a good feeling in his gut and below. He touched the screen when her image stood. She cleared her table and then walked away. Her face was enlarged to fill his screen. He froze the image and his eyes focused on her as he rubbed his thumb back and forth across her lips. He wanted that mouth on him. Had wanted that mouth for quite some time, years, in fact.

He let his hand drop from the screen and looked into her eyes again before deleting the image. There was nothing to be gained by torturing himself. He stood, repositioned himself in his clothes, and went out the door to his meeting.

CHAPTER 10

At the knock on her open office door, Mary Ella looked away from her computer screen and the report she was reading. The smile she was prepared to offer slipped from her face.

"Hello, Obadiah," she acknowledged to her older cousin, Satarah's father.

"How you been keeping yourself, Mary Ella? You been home nigh on to two weeks and ain't seen fit ta come see me. Why 'ount you come on o'va he-ya and give yo' kin some sugga?"

"Are you here to see me for a specific reason?" She did not rise from her seat or accept his bait. "If so, I didn't see your name on my appointment calendar for today."

"Why would your only'est kin need to make an appointment? We's kissin' cousins, ain't we?"

"State your business, Obadiah, or be on your way. I have work to do."

"Well, that ain't exactly the warm hello you should be givin' me. After all, I'm the rightful head of our family and the leader of our flock."

"I'm not in the mood, and I've never been a member of your congregation. I'll ask you again. Why are you here, Obadiah?"

"You're still tight with my daughter, SaraJo, and she's been mighty hard on me and her rightful husband, JoJeff. She's refusing to share in the profits from that house of ill repute her whoring mama denied me as a part of our marriage and her dowry. Now you're back. You should be able to talk some sense into that gal."

Mary Ella hooted a laugh. "You're a man of the cloth, but you want to benefit from the place you call 'a house of ill repute'? For chrissake, Obadiah, are you still beating that dead horse? Haven't you learned that dog don't hunt no more? Cousin Mariah and her brothers and sisters inherited that property from their Benson family members *after* you and Mariah were divorced. She and her siblings voted and passed the property down to Satarah Josephine *after* she and JoJeff were divorced. She took over and renovated The Summer House with her own two hands and without any help whatsoever from you. None of the other cousins on the Benson family tree wanted to take on the task of renovating that huge mansion and cultivating the farm, except your daughter.

"You kicked Satarah out of the little house you rented to her and JoJeff because she couldn't pay the rent after JoJeff left her penniless and ran off with your other daughter, Carlotta. If it weren't for Sylvia Benson Alexander and her siblings, Satarah wouldn't have had a pot to piss in or a window to throw it out of. She was raising your grandsons, Carlotta and JoJeff's twins, by herself, and you refused to help her. You forced her to give up her firstborn son for adoption when she was fifteen years old. Now you come around claiming she should share with you what you didn't earn through marriage or the sweat of your brow?"

"You don't know what you's talkin' 'bout, child! I'm the man of my house and the family I brought into this world. What's mine is mine, and what's theirs is mine, too. That harlot Mariah had no business givin' away what's rightfully part of the marriage bond!"

"You tried taking her to court over the ownership of that property and had your hat handed to you. There were eleven Bensons who inherited that property from their parents and grandparents. The thirty-eight first cousins, of which Mariah was only one, voted unanimously to deed the property to Satarah. You were not entitled to participate in that vote because you were no longer married to Mariah."

Obadiah raged, "It was them Alexanders that done it! They got Judge Holloway in their back pocket! He's been hankering afta that Sylvia Benson since he first laid eyes on her when she married Bernard Alexander. He loves her last year's drawers. I wouldn't put it past him to be that Vivian Alexander's daddy!"

"Get out of my office with that foolishness, Obadiah! Show some respect! Vivian Lynn Alexander Montgomery is a highly respected US Supreme Court Judge and Bernard Alexander's daughter!"

"I agree. It's time for you to hit the road, Jack," Sylvia Benson Alexander casually leaned against the doorjamb to Mary Ella's office. She spoke quietly, but the look in her eyes was purely that of a steel magnolia variety. "Are you in my hospital for medical reasons, Obadiah?"

"It's a public place! I can come and go as I please! My tax dollars pay your salary."

"Since you're always up on the tax rolls as delinquent, I highly doubt it. However, if you call my sister, Mariah, out of her name again anywhere within the hearing of anyone I know or if you impugn my reputation or that of my daughter, Vivian Lynn, I'll haul your rusty butt into court for defamation of character so fast I won't leave skid marks. Now, get the hell out of my hospital and have a good damn day!"

He puffed up like a Tasmanian devil, gave both women glacial stares, but left quickly.

"Are you all right, Mary Ella? He didn't upset you, did he?"

"I'm all right, but *wow!* You really can be scary when you're angry. How do you do that without raising your voice?"

"Practice. It's my 'mom' face. I have five children and a kit and caboodle of grands."

Mary Ella laughed. "Wow, I need to learn that technique."

"You will if it becomes necessary. Are you sure you're all right?"

"I am, yes. Obadiah doesn't scare me."

"I can arrange to have him escorted by Security if he has a legitimate reason for being on hospital grounds," Sylvia offered.

"Don't bother." Mary Ella shook her head. "If he becomes a nuisance, I'll call Security. Were you coming to see me about something?"

"Ah!" she scoffed. "I noticed you didn't change your name on your records. Do you want to continue to use your maiden name?"

Mary Ella's eyes widened, and then she just shook her head. "I didn't even think about it, but it's not necessary. In the Muslim faith, women keep their father's name. Even if I wanted to change it, I have no way of knowing what Kaseem's sir name is. I'll have to wait to figure out whose baby this is before I name him or her. If it's Mark's baby, I'll give him or her Mark's sir name of Brooks." She huffed out a breath. "I guess that's important for my medical records, too."

"You chose a family plan that would include not only your baby but also your husband or any future children."

"I hadn't thought of that either. Considering who Mark's family is, he certainly would not need to participate in any health plan I have. His entire family tree is full of doctors. Kaseem, however, might be different. I just don't know."

"I imagine it doesn't need to be resolved right now." Sylvia shrugged. "People in Human Resources might raise a question about why a single woman would need a family plan. I didn't want you to be caught off guard."

"Thanks." Mary Ella sighed. "I'll think about what I can do."

"That's fine. I'm on my way out. I'm taking off early to meet Bernard in Columbia. It's a date night for us. He has to be in the state capitol to participate in special Senate committee meetings tomorrow. We'll spend the weekend there and come back on Sunday night. Call if you need us."

Mary Ella warmly smiled. "Thanks. Have a good time, and thanks for intervening"

"You're welcome. I'll see you next week." Sylvia waved and left.

It was delightful that Bernard and Sylvia were still so romantic with each other after being married for more than forty years. They were such an active and attractive couple. He resembled the actor Sir Sidney Poitier, and she looked like the songstress Phyllis Hyman. All of their children, Kenneth, Benjamin, Vivian, Gregory, and Aretha, shared certain traits of their parents enough to know that they were indeed Alexander and Benson stock and siblings.

For a moment, she wondered about her own baby. Would he or she carry more of their father's traits or her Cherokee ancestry? She didn't know, but she would have DNA testing done if it wasn't apparent on the surface. Fortunately, she could just have her baby's cheek swabbed. Then the baby's history would be evident in the genetic tissue.

She was trying not to think of that prospect often. For now, she only thought of the baby she carried as hers. Her problem was she couldn't think of the baby without thinking about what it took to create the life growing inside her.

When she thought of Mark or Kaseem, her body had a natural sexual response. It was as if she were on autopilot where they were concerned. She shouldn't be thinking about sex at all since she couldn't have any now or maybe for the rest of her life. However, everywhere she went these days, she ran into happily married couples. Bernard and Sylvia, Bob and Jenny, and Douglas and Satarah. She had been asked out on a date by several men since she'd returned home but turned them down. There was no good reason to get involved with someone unless or until she could solve her situation with Mark and/or Kaseem. If she was legally married and couldn't get a divorce, she may never have a lover again. Indeed, that was a scary thought.

He was dog tired when he sat down before his computers, but it had been a while since he checked on her. Just like that, there she was sitting at her computer working. She wasn't alone, though. Instead, she was talking with someone in the room with her. He read her lips until he could open a split-screen and frame the man she was speaking with in the picture. He was an older man, slim and wiry, with what looked like long, shoulder-length, chemically processed hair curled like a woman's hairstyle. His speech pattern was definitely southern, but not particularly like someone with a good vocabulary. Something he was saying annoyed Mary Ella. It was clear she didn't like this man. Quickly, the watcher put on earbuds and brought up the volume.

"Why would your only'est kin need to make an appointment? We's kissin' cousins, ain't we?

"State your business, Obadiah, or be on your way. I have work to do."

"Well, that ain't exactly the warm hello you should be givin' me. After all, I'm the rightful head of our family and the leader of our flock."

"I'm not in the mood, and I've never been a member of your congregation. I'll ask you again. Why are you here, Obadiah?"

As he continued to listen, he wondered, *who is this clown?* Then he noticed the attractive woman he had seen before standing in the doorway. He opened another screen and focused on her as he listened to the conversation going on in Mary Ella's office.

The woman had a metal name tag on her jacket over her left breast pocket. He toggled in closer and read the name. *S. Alexander, Director.* Since he had seen her more than once with Mary Ella, he surmised she must be someone associated with the hospital.

Opening yet another window, he culled through the hospital hierarchy and found a picture in the database for a Sylvia Benson Alexander. She headed the nursing staff for Summer County General, but that was where the information began and ended.

This was very strange, but everything he learned about Summer County seemed to be unusual. For example, there was a phonebook for the county, but it only contained information for businesses, no listed names, addresses, or telephone numbers for individual people who lived there. Everyone couldn't be operating solely on cell phones. Someone had to have landlines into their homes.

He found a business, Alexander-Dixon Industries (ADI), but all it included was information about a hydroponics farm, food harvesting, and distribution. The data was all surface. The webpage provided an order form for goods that could be bought online.

He was about to fill in the information to place an order when he heard the Alexander woman's scathing rebuke of the man.

"… on the tax rolls as delinquent, I highly doubt it. However, if you call my sister, Mariah, out of her name again anywhere within the hearing of anyone I know or if you impugn my reputation or that of my daughter, Vivian Lynn, I'll haul your rusty butt into court for defamation of character so fast I won't leave skid marks. Now, get the hell out of my hospital and have a good damn day!"

Whoa, *this woman didn't mince words,* he thought as he watched the man puff up and strut away. Sylvia Benson Alexander had a commanding manner. He certainly wouldn't want to cross her. He continued to listen, but his attention was diverted to the point he had to power up another computer and track three drones in low earth orbit covering approximately one hundred miles. *"Damn it!"* he scoffed and pulled one earbud out to put on a headset with a face mic. He scrambled the message to translate into the Navaho language. "Grey Team, watch your six! Repeat! Grey Team watch your six! Unfriendlies on the northern tip! Closing fast! Look sharp!"

He continued to watch as the team leader, Wilde Wolf, held up his AK47 in his right hand and pumped it up and down in the air; the silent signal that the message had been received and understood. Then, with all due haste, the Grey Team turned away from the advancing tangos, shorthand for the targets or terrorists. The Grey Team was out of sight when the tangos rode into the valley where they would probably spend the night. There was water there and high hills where guards would be posted. He kept the drones sequestered enough so they wouldn't be spotted. Little did the tangos know a crack team of anti-terrorists was literally breathing down their necks.

Because his attention was diverted, he missed much of what was said between Sylvia Alexander and Mary Ella after the odious man left the office. It sounded as if it were personal and not a part of the job he sometimes listened to between Mary Ella and others just to hear her voice. The man claimed to be her "kissin' cousin." So, he jotted that information down in the dossier he started on her. She called him "Obadiah," so he added that info, too. Sylvia Benson Alexander mentioned a sister, "Mariah," and a daughter, "Vivian Lynn,"; tidbits of data he would take time to explore.

For now, he took pleasure in watching Mary Ella as she sat staring into near space. He wondered what she was thinking. With all the sophisticated equipment at his disposal, he couldn't get inside her head. All he could do was try to read her body language to determine her mood or state of mind. However, her body was a total distraction for him. Those grapefruit-sized breasts with pronounced nipples, narrow waist, and flaring hips lead to long legs, firm muscular thighs, and nicely sculptured calves. She seemed to be putting on a little weight, which was a good thing since she's a tall, shapely woman with pronounced hour-glass curves and a strong constitution. Those long, strong legs began at her earlobes. He had watched her curl them around Mark Brook's body often enough to know what a tight grip she could secure around him. As he watched her, his blood warmed just from the image those legs conjured in his head. He took several deep breaths to calm himself down. He wanted her with a passion beyond all tolerance levels. Still, he realized, with a deep ache in his heart, he may never have the chance to have her.

He was beyond exhaustion and desperately wanted to rest. When he disrobed and crawled into his bunk, Mary Ella's image was frozen on his computer screen. She was the last thing he saw when he closed his eyes and let sleep have him. He would dream of her and wake in need of her so great it would eclipse every other thought in his head.

CHAPTER 11

"You didn't think I knew this already?" Satarah asked as they sat in Mary Ella's cottage at a round table for four. She smiled knowingly.

"I didn't, no. How long have you known?"

"Since the second day after you arrived. You wouldn't drink my special blend of coffee. Before you left the country, you used to mainline the stuff through intravenous feedings. I noticed you've stayed away from anything with caffeine in it. We're chocoholics, but you wouldn't even eat my triple-chocolate cake. How far along are you?"

"Nearing the end of my first trimester as close as I can determine."

"Then we're running neck in neck." Satarah grinned from ear to ear.

Mary Ella enthusiastically smiled misty-eyed while squeezing her cousin's hands. "Oh, SaraJo, that's wonderful! I'm happy for you and Douglas."

Satarah grinned, squeezing Mary Ella's hands in return. "I'm happy for you and Mark. Have you found a way to contact him? He doesn't know yet, does he? He'll be over the moon——," she trailed off and narrowed her brows when Mary Ella abruptly stood and began to pace. "What is it? What's wrong?"

She dug her hands into the pockets of her shorts as she paced. "I, um, I don't know whether…I mean…you see, I may not be carrying Mark's…" she couldn't quite get it out.

Confusion grew on Satarah's face. "What are you saying, Mary Ella?"

"I was taken captive by a band of Jihadists rebels in Libya moments after Mark and I made love. There was a man who claimed me, wedded me by an Islamic cleric, an Iman, in the group, and then bedded me. He was unusually long and thick." She frowned, frustrated. She tunneled her fingers through her now slightly longer hair as she continued to pace. "His penis was larger than Mark's, though Mark is large, too. Oh, what the hell does that matter in the big scheme!" she scoffed.

"The next morning, when he pulled out of me and stood me up, my IUD had come loose from my uterus. He slept on top of me and woke periodically to…" she sighed as she continued to pace. "Well, I don't think I have to tell you what he did to me each time he woke up. I didn't fight him… Anyway, the IUD slid out of me and down my leg. It was on the ground at my feet mixed in with what I can only assume was my blood and his and Mark's semen. I don't know when or how it happened, when the intrauterine device dislodged from my body. I had the Hormonal-type IUD, which you know can prevent pregnancy for three to five years. Well, my time was up, and I was well overdue for a new one, but, of course, that's not easy to do in the middle of a frekken Libyan Civil War.

"So, this other man had sex with me often, several times a day, every day, in fact. Each time he…well, he had a lot of semen. The other men did the same with the women who were their captives. They would pray five times a day and rarely failed to have sex afterward."

"Oh, Mary Ella." Satarah stood and took her cousin into her soothingly, warm embrace. "You're afraid this baby might not be Mark's."

The floodgates opened. "I'm carrying twins, Satarah," Mary Ella cried, holding on tightly to her cousin. "I've seen Dr. Quade at your cousin Vivian's home, and your aunt Sylvia has been assisting him during each visit. He suspected it, but he confirmed today that I'm having twins. We saw two distinct images on ultrasound and heard what we believe are two heartbeats."

Satarah held her just that much tighter. "It's going to be okay, Mary Ella. We'll make sure it's okay. We've worked through problems before when it was just you and me. We'll do it again."

Mary Ella broke her hold on her cousin to retrieve tissues to blow her nose before she went into the bathroom to wash her face. When she came back into the room, Satarah was sitting at the table again, holding her head in her hands, a worried expression on her gamine face. She opened the refrigerator and pulled a bottle of cold water from the door rack. "Would you like something to drink?"

"Sure, but neither of us can have the hard stuff these days."

Mary Ella nodded and brought two bottles of water to the table. "I'll drink to that." She sat and passed one bottle to Satarah. They bumped water bottles in a toast before they drank long and deep. "I was just getting used to the idea of being pregnant, and then this happens. If it weren't for bad luck, I wouldn't have any luck at all." She sighed, much calmer now that she got that shock off her chest.

"You remember how frantic I was when the twins were left for me to raise?" A smile curved Satarah's lips.

Mary Ella nodded. "Oh, how well I remember. I nearly moved in to help you. You were getting no sleep, and you couldn't work because you couldn't afford a babysitter."

"You did move in, Mary Ella. You came to that little house I used to rent from my father, and you and Jenny changed your shifts at work to help me out. You two were with the baby boys and me around the clock for nearly a year until I got back on my feet. After JoJeff and Carlotta stole my savings, I could not afford daycare."

Mary Ella smiled at the memory. "We were all young and single then. I also remember when your mama laid our souls to rest because we didn't tell her you needed help with the expense of raising the boys and finding a decent place to live after your father evicted you. She helped you divorce JoJeff. Then your aunts, uncles, and cousins voted unanimously to sign over this property to you with the only proviso that it never be sold outside the Benson family."

Satarah nodded in agreement. "I look around at it now and wonder how we got through so much adversity. Now, I couldn't be happier or feel more secure. This will happen for you, too, Mary Ella. When Mark comes back, he'll be there for you just as Douglas is always there for me."

Mary Ella shook her head. "I wish that could be so, Satarah, but I'm not so sure. You see, under Sharia Law, I'm legally someone's wife, and these babies could be his and not Mark's. Even if Mark comes back and still wants to be with me, I can't be with him unless or until I get a divorce. If these babies are his, the only thing I can do is share them with him if he wants. If they are not his, I don't want to keep him from finding happiness with someone else or have him looking at the babies and realizing how they were conceived."

Concerned at what her cousin was willing to sacrifice, Satarah shook her head, "Douglas doesn't look at Benson and think that he's the product of sex between JoJeff and me. He doesn't look at Donovan and think he doesn't even share a blood connection with him. The twins don't share Douglas's blood because they're JoJeff's progeny. Douglas just loves and accepts all of the boys as his the same way he does Ari and Kate."

"Douglas is not Mark, Satarah. Your husband talked with you a great deal, and for a long time before you two even began a sexual relationship. You weren't just hooking up the way Mark and I did. You knew each other and exactly who he is and what to expect from him. He cared about the boys regardless of the fact he loves you to distraction, and the boys are yours. You're right, he loves the boys, but you two had a plan and a direction in less than a year of meeting each other. He knew you and the boys are a package deal from the get-go. I've been with Mark for nearly five years. I know little or nothing about him other than the fact he could make me cum at the speed of light.

"He never talked with me about his family or his life before we met. I knew not to expect him to talk with me about his military experience. For most military men who have been in combat, that part of their lives is hard for them to express. I never pressed for details for that very reason. Mark and I don't have a plan for our relationship, Satarah. We've never discussed where we want our liaison to go. We were just having fun being together. Now, it may be entirely too late to reset the clock and start over."

Satarah, unwilling to give up, pressed her point. "Douglas and Mark are terrific friends. They wouldn't be if they weren't cut from the same cloth. I have to believe Mark will respond positively to you regardless of who fathered your babies. However, what about how *you* feel about *him*?"

"I really don't know anymore." Mary Ella slowly shook her head. "I love him, yes, but am I *in* love with him? After all of this time, I'm not sure that I can trust Mark. I don't believe he ever purposefully lied to me, but he wasn't forthcoming with who he is. Of course, maybe he felt that I wasn't entitled to know certain things about him. Even if the answer is yes and I'm in love with him, my feelings aren't the only ones to consider now."

"Mary Ella, do you have feelings for the man who abducted you?" Satarah tentatively frowned.

"I don't know the answer to that question, either." Mary Ella shook her head. "You see, even though I never agreed to the ceremony, Kaseem saved my life by marrying me. He protected me from being attacked by any of the men who came into contact with us. Believe me, over the time I was a captive, there were hundreds of extremists who had absolutely no respect for women. What is so strange is that I know that he helped me escape. He always kept me close to him with my hands bound with a sash. I was tethered to him nearly all the time. He slept right next to me, practically covering me or on top of me. He was a light sleeper. The slightest noise would wake him. Yet, on the night the rescue took place, he had released the sash from around my wrists. He never did that before. I know he was awake and could have stopped my rescue, but he didn't. Somehow, I feel as if he facilitated my escape. I was his captive for nearly two months, but he never hurt me. Instead, he treated my scrapes with clean water, which is precious in the desert, and bound my wounds with clean cloths. He took care of me.

"The psychiatrist who saw me aboard the ship suggested that I would likely suffer from Stockholm syndrome. I can't deny that's what this is, but for sure, if he hadn't intervened, I'd be dead now."

"He repeatedly raped you, Mary Ella!" Satarah voiced hotly, vehemently. "Even if it was under the cloak of an Islamic marriage, it was against your will. No man has the right to rape a woman regardless of whether they're married to her or not."

Mary Ella nodded her agreement. "You're right, and these babies may be the result. However, after a while, I submitted. I stopped fighting. Still, here's the thing. If these babies are Kaseem's, I'm never going to tell these babies they are the product of being consistently raped. I can't let anything else take root in my head, Satarah. I can't let animosity color what I feel for these babies because of who fathered them. They'd pick up on it and not believe they're deeply loved and wanted. If they are his,

I don't know what I'm going to tell them about him other than he saved my life, which is the truth."

"Mary Ella, I understand why you would take that position. At least, with Mark, your union was consensual. So, I have to hope these little golden nuggets of yours are Mark Brook's offspring."

"You and me both." Mary Ella sighed as she rubbed the little baby bump she felt under her hand.

A few days later, on Sunday afternoon, Jonathan called out, "I've got the potatoes."

Everyone grabbed a dish of food and placed it on the dinner table in one of the smaller dining halls in The Summer House.

"I've got the roast beef," chimed in Bob Sweeney.

"Hot stuff coming through." Satarah, wearing oven mitts, with one bowl of piping hot collard greens in one hand and a bowl of green beans in the other, skirted the table.

"I'll say you're really hot stuff," teased Douglas with a wink.

"Who's got the ham, other than Dad?" Donovan sprinted, giggling out of Doug's swing of the dishtowel at his backside. He placed a bowl of Heavenly Hash salad on one side of the table and the bowl of Waldorf salad on the other.

"I'll get the ham," called out Benson, "and I don't mean Dad."

"See, you boys need to listen up and learn how to treat a good woman," prophesied Douglas. "Particularly one who looks like your mother and can cook like this."

Here! Here!" agreed Bob Sweeney. I'll drink to that!"

"Speaking of which, I'll get the sweet tea," announced Jenny after securing her sons in their high chairs at the table.

"Hold on, Kate," Jeffrey huffed as he sat his fidgety little sister in her high chair and gave her a carrot stick to chew on until they could all be seated.

She scrunched up her little face grinning up at him. He just shook his head and hid his smile.

When the side door opened, a voice had everyone freezing like a cartoon tabloid in place. "Well, look-a-here, look-a-here! Looks like I'm not late for Sunday supper." JoJeff grinned while rubbing his hands together with avarice. He made a beeline for Mary Ella, holding her chair out for her to sit, and then picked up Kate, high chair and all, and placed her on the other side of Mary Ella before pulling a chair from against the wall to sit beside her.

"Well, how yawl doin'?" JoJeff asked no one in particular as he began to reach for the bowl of whipped sweet potatoes with tiny, toasted marshmallows and cinnamon sprinkled on top. It sat on the track before him.

Doug rolled his eyes. "Donovan, I think it's your turn to say grace."

JoJeff quickly drew his hands back. Everyone joined hands around the table and bowed their heads. Mary Ella was forced to hold JoJeff's hand on her right and Kate's little hand on her left. During the recital of the grace, JoJeff held her hand under the table on his brick-hard thigh against his manhood. He rubbed his thumb back and forth across her palm. She didn't react or acknowledge him during the grace or after.

He turned his head and grinned at her. "So, you liking your new SUV, Mary Ella?" JoJeff helped himself to copious amounts of food. He talked and ate as if eating was going out of style and went back for seconds.

"Yes, it's fine, JoJeff," Mary Ella answered while transferring a scoop of mashed potatoes to Kate's plate.

"Ya know, it's fully loaded. It's got all these special features some people don't pay attention to," JoJeff continued. "Pass the hot rolls, would ya, Jonathan. I could show you after supper, Mary Ella. Wouldn't take long, ya know?"

Mary Ella rolled her eyes. "I've read the manual, JoJeff. I think I know all I need to know about how everything works."

JoJeff grinned at her. "I wouldn't want ya ta get stranded on a lonely road some night and not know where the lug wrench or the car jack is. Hey, is there any more of that apple and raisin stuff? What da ya call it?"

"Waldorf salad," supplied Douglas, and passed the bowl to JoJeff.

Mary Ella smiled wryly. "I've had cars before, and I know how to change a tire."

"Oh, a pretty woman, like you, shouldn't ever have to change a tire." JoJeff licked something from his thick thumb and eyed her. "You can always call me. I can be real handy when you want me. You got my number, right?"

"Oh, yes, I've got your number, all right, JoJeff," Mary Ella smiled sardonically. "Would you pass the green beans, please? I'm a little hungry because I'm eating for three."

JoJeff choked on his last forkful of food and gagged.

Mary Ella smirked and pounded on his back while he guzzled a glass of sweet tea.

"Uh, come again?" He wheezed, eyeing her abdomen while trying to get his breath back.

"Oh, haven't you heard? I'm pregnant with twins."

"Uh, no. I guess I missed the news bulletin. Well, this has been nice." JoJeff hoovered a plate full of food into his mouth as if he were in an eating contest. He guzzled the last of his drink, standing up. When he caught his breath, he nodded to the people at the table. "Thanks for the invite, but I really need to get along."

He was out the side door in a flash. People at the table laughed at his hasty retreat, but no one remarked otherwise.

Later, after dinner, the three pregnant women relaxed in the front parlor with their feet up while the men and boys cleared the dinner table, washed and dried the dishes, and put the food away. The little girls and the Sweeney boys sat at a child-sized table in the family room, making pictures on large sheets of paper with crayons and chalk.

"I feel like a slug." Jenny leaned her head back against the chair cushion with her eyes closed. "You are such a good cook, Satarah. I think I ate ten helpings of everything. Thank you for having us all over for Sunday supper. I'll tell you it seems harder to cook meals now that I'm not working at the hospital than it did when I was putting in eight-to-ten-hour days."

Satarah nodded. "You're welcome. You should take leftovers home with you to have for lunch tomorrow."

"I think I will if the guys don't eat it all up while they look at the football game."

Mary Ella frowned and cocked her head. "I thought they were looking at a baseball game."

Jenny shrugged. "It really doesn't matter. Men just loved to watch sports."

"I wonder whether JoJeff had to hurry home to catch the game?" Satarah grinned with tongue planted firmly in her cheek.

Both Jenny and Mary Ella hooted in laughter. Satarah finally broke down and joined in.

Satarah shook her head and eyed her cousin. "I don't think you'd better get a flat tire, Mary Ella. JoJeff probably won't answer your call."

"I hope you're right." Mary Ella laughed. "Who invited him to supper anyway?"

"Nobody." Satarah shook her head. "He knows we eat early Sunday supper. He'll come by and take the boys out for an hour or so on Sunday for any reason. Usually, he takes them to his car dealership to wipe down the cars in the showroom or on the lot and then brings them home when he knows we're about ready to eat. He pays them twenty bucks for the work they do, then he invites himself for dinner and eats up what he paid them." She laughed.

"Douglas takes it well," remarked Mary Ella.

"Douglas doesn't sweat the small stuff. He's game for whatever reason JoJeff makes time to spend with the boys. He's not insecure about JoJeff, but he'll dress him down in a heartbeat if he does or says anything to upset or disappoint the boys. As long as he's not showing them his latest film release, Douglas and I are good with the amount of time he spends with them."

"That's good, Satarah. That's really good," Mary Ella commented.

"Doug will be there for you, too, Mary Ella."

"So will Bob," chimed in Jenny. "All for one and one for all."

"Thanks. I'm not sure I know how to be a good mother, but being both a mother and a father to two babies will be challenging. At least I have the two of you to provide guidance along the way."

Jenny raised her head and looked at Mary Ella. "Are you planning to breastfeed?"

"*Whoa!* I hadn't even thought that far ahead. I think I probably will. It's the healthiest start for babies."

"Good. As long as you don't eat anything that doesn't agree with them, breastfeeding cuts way down on the colic. It helps with getting back in shape, too.

"I don't know whether you've had time to see the facilities in the new wing where you can nurse during the workday and, of course, the employee's nursery school is right next door to it." Jenny nodded and continued. "I felt comfortable having my babies close to me when I went back to work after our maternity leave ended. It's hard having to leave them in someone else's care for eight to ten hours a day. Bob and I were on maternity leave together, and we felt the same way. The nurses called to let him know when the babies were awake for a feeding. He and I would pop in to spend some time with them."

"Oh, my." Mary Ella buried her face in her hands. "There is just so much to think about that I really hadn't even considered. If I have two boys or two girls, they can share a room for a while, a few years, but if I have a boy and a girl, I'm going to need a bigger place. I've been thinking about buying land and having Dixon Construction build a place for me sooner rather than later. Then I think about all the expenses I'll incur and wonder how I'll be able to accomplish everything. I'll have to have two of everything, including car seats. What in the world did we do when Jonathan and Jeffrey were babies?"

"Survived," joked Satarah. "We did whatever came next. We'll do it again. You and I will be delivering these precious ones at about the same time."

"Somehow, I never really pictured myself as a mother." Mary Ella shrugged. "I mean, it was fun when the boys were little, but there were the three of us taking turns on eight-hour shifts, but we were in our late teens early twenties back then."

"Yes, and then they got bigger and potty-trained." Jenny sighed and smiled. "Life changed right along with them when they started school.

We took shifts again when they were at home sick with colds, needed a doctor's visit or whatever. We went to every school event, soccer, T-ball, swimming meet, and look at them now. They're practically ready to start driving a car instead of riding their horses or bikes. The next thing you know, they'll be dating girls and off to college or trade school. By the time we catch up, they'll be married with children of their own!"

"Wow!" Mary Ella lamented. "Did you really have to rush me through all of that so quickly? They're only about the size of a plump strawberry now. You've whisked me through to driving cars, dating, and off to higher education. Can we slow this down so I can catch up? It's way too soon for me to start thinking of myself as a grandmother."

"By the time they've been nesting inside you for nine months, believe me, you'll be praying for labor," laughed Satarah.

"I'm going to love every minute of it," Mary Ella smiled while rubbing her abdomen. "I should feel them moving in the next two weeks."

"Oh, yeah, and they'll play kickball on your bladder and do the River Dance on your kidneys, but when you hold those precious little ones in your arms for the first time, it will all have been worth it," Jenny commented. "You won't even remember the labor pains it will take to get them here into the world."

A roar went up in the family room. Shortly thereafter, Douglas, Bob, and Benson came into the front, downriver parlor carrying trays with warm apple cobbler topped with a scoop of vanilla bean ice cream, and hot butterscotch dripping down the sides.

"Well, aren't you just the sweetest man," Jenny cooed to her husband, her southern accent pronounced.

"Sweets for my sweet." Bob leaned over to kiss his wife's pink, Cupid-doll lips.

Benson hugged Mary Ella around the shoulders before placing the tray on her lap. Douglas noisily kissed Satarah's mouth.

"Bon appetite." Douglas smiled at the women and then turned to leave the salon.

"Don't let the little ones have too much sugar or they'll be bouncing off the walls," cautioned Satarah.

"Don't worry. The game is at halftime now. After it's over, we'll take the little people out for a long walk around the property and down by the river to skip stones. That should counteract the sugar they consume. Then, babe, you're all mine." Douglas gave a suggestive look and a wink for Satarah before he went back to enjoy the rest of the game.

"*Whoa!* That's hot!" exclaimed Jenny.

"*Ooh là là,*" contributed Mary Ella, grinning.

Satarah winked at them. "Oh, *yeah!*" she proclaimed. "I just love being married to Douglas."

The women laughed and continued chatting about inconsequential things while they ate their desserts. However, Mary Ella's thoughts drifted away as she looked through the wide picture window at the Santee River bordering the field of green lawn. It made her think of how her life would stretch out before her bending and twisting around the pitfalls that would likely develop in her path. She may have to live the rest of her life without the physical love, moral support, and warmth a good male partner could provide. To live a life with her babies and the memory of what physical love felt like.

"Mary Ella?" Jenny got her attention. "Have you met Amina yet?"

"Amina? No, I don't think so. Who is she?"

"After you left, Vivian and Chuck Montgomery brought twenty young girls to Summer County. They were rescued from an English boarding school in Africa that was overrun by the Boko Haram. The girls were the daughters of African nobility, but, in each instance, the girls' parents were murder victims. Each girl is like a princess in African culture."

"I hadn't heard that. I mean, yes, the abductions of girls and young women happen in remote areas of Africa and Asia, too, but I hadn't heard about this incident. So, what happened to them?"

"Families here took the girls in, and they've been living here ever since. Amina is one of them. She's the oldest at seventeen and a math and science genius. MIT accepted her on a full ride. She and her little sister, Aliyah, who is twelve, were adopted by Romelo and Olivia Alexander Dixon. Aliyah is one of Mrs. Alexander's patients' aides."

"That's wonderful. What about the other girls?"

"The girls were between the ages of five and fourteen when they arrived. Jefferson and LaiLoni Skye Hawkins Logan adopted three girls. They already have two young girls," offered Jenny and continued to list the other girls by name, who adopted them, and updating Mary Ella on what they were doing now.

Mary Ella looked between Satarah and Jenny. "Jefferson is still the dean of Summer County Academy, right?"

"He is, yes," Jenny nodded, "and doing a fantastic job. You remember, he has three sons from his former marriage: Jefferson Junior, Miles, and Stephen. They're heirs to the Montrose fortune and as rich as Midas. Jefferson Junior, we call him Jeff. He is Bobby's Deputy Tactical Officer and head of the medical team for the Centerville Fire Station. He's sweet on Amina and took her to the Spring Fling as his date. They've been training as nurses and keeping company since then. I wouldn't be a bit surprised if he applies to attend MIT with Amina."

"Stephen Logan is The Summer House evening manager," Satarah interjected, picking up the discussion. "He's still in school at the academy, but his interest is in hotel management. I don't know what I'll do when he goes away to finish college."

"Stephen Logan is twelve now," offered Jenny. "He volunteers with the county's veterinary doctors and at the animal shelter. He brought my boys two frisky puppies, and they love those dogs. Stephen is also really good with the horses and talked Jefferson into building a horse barn on their property. They go to the horse auctions with James Dixon to buy young colts and mares. Recently Tina Justice sent groups of her wild horses to him. Stephen wants to be a vet and/or breed horses. He hasn't quite figured out which yet, but he's still young." Jenny laughed. "He did convince Jefferson to add an equestrian class to the academy's curriculum. They took several blue ribbons at the Summer County Fair for two years running. They plan to enter the races at the state fair this year. I don't know whether you've seen it, but the Men's Club built a bridle path near the academy with a racetrack so they can train."

Mary Ella shrugged. "It's still hard for me to think of Jefferson as *Dean* Logan instead of *Ambassador* Logan."

Satarah nodded. "I know what you mean, but he's been the dean of the academy since Uncle Bernard left the post to become our state senator. Dean Logan has done great work there, too. Even though he's been called on from time to time to negotiate disputes between warring countries on behalf of the US, he's made a difference. He and his brother-in-law, Nathan Flack, work well together."

Mary Ella solemnly nodded. "I know. Dean Logan and Ambassador Flack worked with Mark to bring relief workers and desperately needed provisions to us when we were in the field."

"Did you know Nathan Flack and your Mark are cousins?" asked Jenny.

Mary Ella shook her head in confusion. "No, I didn't know that. What makes you think they're related?"

"Savannah told me. She and Nathan frequently come down to visit Jefferson and LaiLoni Skye. We went to a barbeque on their ranch, and Savannah and I got to talking. She's an OB/GYN specialist with this big medical practice in DC that Vivian Lynn owns. Remember, Vivian's first husband, Derrick Jackson, was a noted pediatric surgeon and pediatrician who developed the web/mesh system that revolutionized pediatric medicine for resetting bones and tissues. I think he was still in his thirties when he died of a heart attack.

"Anyway, she, Savannah, I mean, told me that her husband Nathan's grandfather, Dr. Hayden Townsend, and Mark's grandmother, Dr. Irene Townsend Brooks, are siblings. Mark's middle name is Harlan, right?" Jenny asked, but continued, "That's his grandfather's name, Dr. Harlan Ellsworth Brooks."

While Jenny went on chatting, she nor Satarah noticed that Mary Ella had been rendered mute. She didn't even know Mark had a middle name. Mark Harlan Brooks, named for his paternal grandfather, Dr. Harlan Ellsworth Brooks. *Wow! The hits just keeps on coming*, she contemplated.

Satarah noticed that Mary Ella had a sad, faraway look on her face. The discussion was making her cousin unhappy. She also noted that Jenny gave her a slight shake of her head. Obviously, Jenny noticed, too.

Satarah put a smile on her face. "Summer County Academy is still unique, but now they have several new campuses. There's Alex-Mont

Academy in Maryland, Justice Academy in Chicago, Baylor Academy in Washington, DC. Each one is rated in the top ninetieth percentile in this country. Their student exchange program competes on the world stage in academia and athletics through the junior college level. Did you know they won the Junior World Cup tournament in chess last year in Madrid, Spain?"

Mary Ella shook her head and frowned. "I don't remember receiving a text message from you about that."

Satarah sighed. "Maybe that's another of those news flashes I forgot to send to you."

"It's still hard for me to think of Jefferson's wife, LaiLoni Skye, as an heiress to the BlackHawk fortune," Jenny shook her head. "She's so down to earth and active with her children, the five little girls, and the children at the academy teaching them about nature and survival skills; things she must have learned as a child herself living on a Native American reservation in the Dakotas. She, Stacy Greene Alexander, Aretha Grace Alexander, and our own Satarah Josephine Johnson are still the top sharpshooters in Summer County. They beat out everyone else at the County Fair again last year during the Juneteenth family reunion holiday, and the four of them tied for first place.

"It's still a mystery what LaiLoni Skye did before she married Jefferson," continued Jenny. "Back then, she didn't know she was the daughter of Jake Hawkins. That was when she was known as Dakota Sinclair before she was discovered to have been a kidnap victim as a newborn."

"Don't start with your conspiracy theories again, Jenny," Satarah teased. "She could have learned to shoot like that at any time, maybe in a self-defense class."

Jenny shook her head. "I don't know, Satarah. She's in her mid-to-late thirties now, and I've seen her out jogging around the track at the academy. She's faster than anyone I've seen participate in the Olympic Games. On paper, there's no indication she was anything but a marketing and sales representative for Kenneth Alexander's company, CompuCorrect Global. At the same time, he was governor of California. But I'll tell you, someone with her skills and abilities to run and to shoot the way she does would seem to have a military background. Remember, she was with other industrialists' wives touring Africa to donate American goods with the Vice President's wife. She was supposed to be the wife of Vivian's friend and law partner, William Chandler, the supermodel and industrialist. That's when Ambassador Jake Hawkins spotted LaiLoni Skai in the entourage at his embassy reception in Africa and recognized her as his daughter. I still think she was some type of Secret Service agent sent undercover to protect the Vice President's wife. She's very athletic, and it's like she's got eyes in the back of her head.

"After all," Jenny continued. "That whole thing about her being the wife of William Chandler, all seemed to dissipate when LaiLoni moved here and married Jefferson Logan."

"Conspiracy theory," chided Satarah, though under it all, she believed Jenny's instincts were dead on. To her, it seemed one of Romelo and Olivia Alexander Dixon's twin sons, Donald, tripped her meter as someone who could be involved in clandestine operations for the United States government. Donald and Kenneth Alexander were first cousins and as tight as brothers. Kenneth owned CompuCorrect Global, the same company Dakota Sinclair, aka LaiLoni Skye Hawkins, supposedly worked for.

Then Donald moved back home with his wife and children after being away for years, and suddenly things around the county started changing. Aircraft stopped flying over Summer County, and the municipal airport was updated to accommodate larger planes at the federal government's expense. It also became the home base for Vivian's private aircraft fleet, Adventurer Executive Airline (AEA). She also noted that a new private, gated community sprang up in a remote area of the county. The people who lived there were all single men and women and seemed to all work in some aspect of supercomputer technology. Everything around the county and in all of the homes and businesses got upgraded intranet services through Kenneth's company free of charge. The academy and all of the county libraries were linked so that any and everything was available at their fingertips. Older homes and new ones were outfitted with smart-house technology. Roads and highways were monitored, and although there was no appreciable crime in the county, home security became a priority. They read about other places having their computer systems hacked, but none of that happened to anyone in Summer County.

Outwardly, Summer County still resembled a place the twenty-first century forgot. Still, nothing could be further from the truth. County residents were willing to let the world believe that nothing ever changed, but indeed, everything had.

Some years ago, rumor had it that the now-former President of the United States secretly flew into Summer County just to pick up Donald and his buddy, Lucas Hardesty. Don was home for the whole summer building his home when this was supposed to have happened. Lucas was someone Don met when they were both in Boston, Massachusetts, and he followed Don back to Summer County that summer. Lucas helped Don finish building that house until the President swooped in. Don sold Lucas the house, and he lived there with his wife, a local girl, Valerie Mitchell. They have four beautiful children. Lucas owned and operated a shoe manufacturing company, while Valerie was the general manager of her family's cable television franchise in Summer County and several of the surrounding counties.

Donald was a technology genius, just like Kenneth, and had an undergrad and graduate degree from MIT. Satarah believed Donald to have been instrumental in getting Amina noticed by his alma mater MIT. He also had a law degree from Harvard but didn't take on many cases except a few for Vivian's law firm in Washington, DC. It was the same firm where Bill Chandler, Dakota's supposed first husband, was a law partner to date. Donald also did legal work for ADI, his family's hydroponics business, Gregory's Wall Street firm, and Chuck and Vivian's many businesses, including the private airline. Yet, Donald and his wife, Cecile, lived simply, but well, in a very unique subterranean home and traveled extensively.

Once when Douglas complained that something always disrupted the GPS element in his truck, she had the presence of mind to mention it to Donald. After that, problem solved, and Douglas never complained about a problem with his guidance system again. She believed that Douglas knew more, but he would never betray a confidence even with her. Douglas and Donald always had their heads together in the Men's Club meetings.

Yes, quiet as it was kept, she believed Jenny was right and that they were living in a highly protected zone in South Carolina for some reason.

Mary Ella looked between Jenny and Satarah. "You mentioned that Jefferson and LaiLoni Sky have little girls in addition to the three older boys?"

Mary Ella's question took Satarah's thoughts away from feelings of clandestine operations and conspiracy theories about certain people in the county.

"Yes, Francine Sinclair, age four, and Skye Littlefeather Logan, age eighteen months," answered Satarah. "They have a manservant, Yates, who watches over the girls like a mother hen."

Mary Ella regarded Jenny. "I forgot about him and the fact that LaiLoni Skye is half Navajo. How about her sister, JaiHonnah? How is she doing?"

Jenny smiled. "Oh, she and Roderick Baylor have seven children now, and Jefferson's sister, Dr. Savannah Logan, and her husband, Ambassador Nathan Flack, have three stair steps."

"Goodness, was everyone just making babies after I left?" joked Mary Ella.

Jenny and Satarah laughed while they were polishing off their desserts.

Satarah swallowed a mouthful of ice cream and moaned with pleasure. "There was, indeed, a substantial baby boom, not including the addition of the twenty young girls. However, there is a bit of sad news. Stacy Alexander lost her baby while she was on some type of training mission. Still, she and Benny plan to try again."

As Mary Ella felt movement in her belly, the news about Benny and Stacy's loss was devastating. She hoped that she would safely carry her babies to term. Because no matter who fathered her babies, they were hers.

CHAPTER 12

News of her pregnancy spread like wildfire throughout the Summer County community. There was nothing she could do to hide her condition now that she was well into her second trimester. Her little plump strawberries were the size of potato spuds now and an active pair.

People stopped by to congratulate her on her pregnancy. Still, others, like Deaconess Clarisse Flowers, just came by to pick the bone clean of whatever gossip she could find and offer her own slanted opinion. She dropped little snide remarks about being pregnant without the benefit of a husband. *'Wasn't it a shame that the good Dr. Mark Brooks dumped her? Of course, when she ran off with a man she hardly knew, that's what happens. It was better if she stayed home where she belonged and married a local boy instead of traipsing all over who knows where. If she just wanted to help lost souls, there were plenty of those types around. She should come to her cousin's church and help out there. After all, charity starts at home. Them heathens in foreign lands should learn to take care of their own. Of course, she had opinions of who she should have considered marrying in the first place, like her son, Bonner, a good God-fearing man with a roadside vegetable stand business to his credit. Why Bonner had a future, and any girl would be lucky to have him. Her Bonner had always been sweet on her because Mary Ella had a lot of real injun blood on her mama's side of the family, don't cha know, and those injuns had a lot of money in them there casinos on them reservations,* Mrs. Flowers told her as if this was a news flash. She intimated that her Bonner may be willing to take her in, even though she was now damaged goods and would come with a ready-made family.

Mrs. Flowers overlooked the fact that Bonner had problems with personal hygiene and was pushing fifty... hard! She didn't mind that a man, who worked outdoors with his hands all day, would work up a sweat. She and Mark smelled a bit ripe between infrequent showers, but it seemed Bonner never brushed his teeth or bathed when fresh water and toiletries were plentiful. That was way too much for her.

Between Clarisse Flowers and Brother Phineas Roberts, treasurer of Obadiah's church, they were better at distributing gossip than a viral message trending up on Facebook. Phineas told her *she should come to Obadiah's church because there were good men in the congregation. Still, if she didn't find anyone to her liking, he offered up himself to take care of her sexual needs on the side. He could come to her several times a week and maybe take the odd weekend away somewhere like Myrtle Beach or Charleston. They would have to be discrete because his wife was a bit nosey. If she didn't agree to his terms, he could make her return to the county very uncomfortable for her. She was spoiled goods now so that no decent man would have truck with her. If she let him into her bed, he'd do what he could to protect her reputation.* She had a few choice words for him, and afterward, he skedaddled away from her like a scalded dog.

Most people assumed the babies she carried were Mark's and questioned her about his whereabouts. She kept it simple and offered that he was with Doctors Without Borders, which was, to the best of her knowledge, still true. As quiet as it was kept, he was a captive for many months now. She periodically contacted the organization to inquire about Mark, but they would not tell her anything. They only wanted to know when she was coming back to the organization to be redeployed. Not likely!

The NGO was in the world news every day, it seemed. They were ejected from the militancy-hit tribal districts of Pakistan; robbed of vital medical equipment and supplies in the Rohingya refugee camp in Bangladesh, and overworked in the cholera outbreak in the Ain Issa camp. Mark and she worked in each one of those areas. Thousands of people across Myanmar were displaced and unable to return to their homes.

When inter-community conflict erupted and continued tensions kept many in danger and in need of help, she and Mark were there, too. They had to stay on the move and a few steps ahead of marauding bands of terrorists. They did what they could, but the basic needs exacerbated other problems, such as the food and water supply.

Just before they were captured, a World Food Program needed immediate food assistance. Through his connections, Mark was in the midst of helping in that effort. Now that she had time to think about it, Mark was probably working through his cousin, Nathan Flack, the US Ambassador to the United Nations for that project, too. He may also have enlisted the help of US Ambassador to Seychelles, Jake Hawkins, a wealthy industrialist and father of LaiLoni Skai.

As she remembered it, Mark made contact with Islamic Relief USA and collaborated with his contacts at the United Nations High Commissioner for Refugees (UNHCR). He brokered the agreement between the two organizations. Mark was working hard and as quickly as possible to provide relief and humanitarian assistance to internal refugees in the Rakhine State and throughout Myanmar. However, although they were able to help hundreds of thousands of people, there were just that many more who needed to be supported. That's when time ran out on them, and they were captured.

Still, she needed to put those memories aside. She had problems of her own to concern herself with here and now at home.

She didn't want to think about the possibility that her babies could be born with exotic, pale, aqua-green eyes. As her Grannie used to say, *"People,"* like Clarisse and Phineas, *"who would bring a bone would carry a bone"* for generations. They would know her babies were not Mark's offspring and spread that gossip far and wide. She may have to consider moving away from Summer County before her babies were born to protect them from the ridicule of those who were gossips like Clarisse and Phineas. She didn't want to have to do that. However, if the need arose, she would do whatever was necessary for her children's welfare.

Eric was balls deep inside Vernice's warmth, but it wasn't getting him anywhere. He had the stamina, his Kegel muscles strong enough to hold his erection, but not the inclination. Still, Eric persevered, hitting her G-spots until she spasmed around him, her Kegel muscles gripping him tightly and vibrating like a plucked bow. He experienced the sudden involuntary muscular contractions her climax caused before his body twitched convulsively and released. His breathing erratic, Eric slowly pulled out of her and rolled over onto his back. Palming his face with both hands, he wiped away the sweat. He was getting his breathing under control when he heard Vernice's voice.

"What's going on, Eric?"

He didn't know what she was asking him. They had been out to dinner and dancing at one of the nicest restaurants in Charleston. Afterward, they took a long walk on the beach before heading to their hotel. They had steadily talked since they met when he picked her up from the airport on Friday afternoon. He had called her and asked whether she could come to South Carolina earlier than she planned and, if so, whether she would like to visit Charleston for the weekend. She agreed, and as far as he knew, they were enjoying themselves. So, her question had him stumped.

"I don't understand what you're asking, Vernice."

She leaned up on her right elbow and looked down into his face. "I enjoy you, Eric. You're an excellent lover; kind, creative, and considerate. You never fail to get me to where I need to go to be fulfilled and sated, so don't misunderstand when I say I'm not a marathon lover."

"I still don't understand. If I'm giving you everything you need sexually, is there something more you want me to do?"

"No woman could possibly want more, but that's the thing. You've had me on my back with my legs spread wide for a day and a half, nearly non-stop. This isn't like you. Generally, we do more than have sex. I thought coming here to tour the city was a great suggestion. I've never been to Charleston before. However, except for the three hours we spent at the restaurant and walking on the beach, we haven't been out of this suite. So, I'll ask you again. What's going on?"

Now he understood what she meant, and actually, what was going on had nothing to do with her. It had to do with the news that Mary Ella Baker was pregnant with another man's child. Likely Mark Brooks' child. She was going to have a baby, and he wished with every fiber of his being it was his child she was having.

Yeah, well, if wishes were horses, beggars would ride.

For now, he had some fence-mending to do. "I hope I didn't make you feel as if your sensitivities didn't matter." He placed his right hand behind his head and thumbed her left nipple with his left.

"Not at all. As I said, you are always, and I do mean *always* considerate and never fail to fulfill my needs and desires. It just seems as if you're in a certain mood or temperament that's unlike you. Believe me, I'm not complaining because I'm benefiting from whatever is on your mind. However, you've got to give a girl a break. I mean, I've never been multi-orgasmic before you, but if you keep up this pace, I'm going to need to be resuscitated. Where the hell are you getting your level of stamina, Eric?"

He had to laugh at Vernice's question, but in actuality, all he had to do was visualize making love with Mary Ella when they were teens. He certainly couldn't tell Vernice his inspiration came from thinking about another woman. His relationship with Vernice wasn't a love match, but he did respect her. From the first time they slept together over a year ago, they just clicked. They didn't have to have any long drawn-out conversations about what worked for the other. They went with the flow, and everything fell into place.

Vernice wasn't around that often; only once, maybe twice a month. She didn't want to meet his family, nor did he want to meet hers. They weren't carrying any emotional baggage into their acquaintance until Mary Ella Baker came back to Summer County. That's when his libido kicked up, and he began to crave copulation with his teen heartthrob. The possibility of being with her was now nil to none.

He shifted his focus from her nipple and palmed Vernice's face, rubbing his thumb back and forth across her lips. "How much more time do you need?" he smiled as his penis stood at attention.

She fisted him in a tight grip. "I'll let you know, but right now, something has my full attention." She smiled mischievously before leaning down and devouring him.

CHAPTER 13

It was getting close to the time of her staff meeting, thought Mary Ella as she checked her watch for the time. She had been working on quarterly evaluations all morning. Generally, she was pleased with the overall performance of her teams of nurses. However, there never seemed to be enough nurses capable of handling the insanity of emergency medicine. She remembered when she, Satarah, Jenny, and a few others were at the hospital during a record-breaking blizzard. The storm raged for almost five days and dumped nearly two feet of snow on South Carolina, a state that rarely even saw snow flurries. The entire state was ill-equipped to handle the situation in any manner other than as a natural disaster. They were the closest medical facility to the I-95 highway corridor and were forced to handle hundreds of accident victims and casualties.

The farmers rallied and, using their farm equipment, of which there was an ample supply in the county, kept the country road to the highway clear for the ambulances and four-wheel-drive vehicles. Those vehicles had to shuttle the six miles back and forth from the hospital to the interstate in a full-blown rescue operation. For many days during white-out conditions and after the blizzard ended, they worked to handle the load. All of the doctors who were in the hospital, regardless of their specialties, were pressed into service in the operating rooms. Farmers had to bring people to work in the hospital, too. No matter what they did, they couldn't save all of the victims.

Like Douglas Johnson, some out of state people braved the blizzard to be with their loved ones. Douglas drove from Richmond, Virginia, to be by his son Donovan's side. He and Bob were still here years later. So many patients were in too critical a condition to be moved, so many of their family members moved here and made a life they agreed was much better than the one they had where they came from. Some were still helping out at the hospital, but Mary Ella knew she didn't have nearly enough trained emergency room personnel for the tasks her nurses faced. Although there were clinics in each municipality in Summer County, the hospital was the only one serving county residents and the preferred hospital for people in the adjacent counties.

Fortunately, money wasn't an issue. The hospital, like Summer County Academy, always had wealthy benefactors. She did have the budget for hiring five to ten new emergency room nurses for all three shifts. She put out offers to nurses in the surrounding counties and to the state nursing association. However, so far, she hadn't received enough applicants to fill her needs. Next, she planned to advertise on the national medical and social media sites. For now, until times got better, she would have to extend the shifts to nine-or ten-hour days on duty for four days a week. Getting an extra day or half-day off may appeal to some, but not to enough employees. The plan could backfire, and she'd have a bunch of burnt-out male and female nurses.

She needed to get on Sylvia Alexander's calendar to determine whether there were any promising nurses in the current Summer County Academy classes or other nurses already on staff in the hospital who might be interested in switching to emergency medicine.

When she stood up, she heard the commotion going on in the emergency room. Three fire department ambulances were docking in the bays adjacent to the triage rooms. She grabbed her stethoscope and hurried out to manage the emergency and lend a hand where necessary.

"What have we got?" Mary Ella shouted to Jeff Logan as he wheeled in a patient on a fire department gurney.

"Commuter plane versus highway traffic on the interstate at rush hour," he shouted back. "Female, age approximately twenty-five, a passenger in a car on the highway. Plane's wing sheared off the top of the vehicle, an SUV, and the hair of the male driver. BP, eighty over fifty-five. We almost lost her on scene. Fractures…" he continued giving her the vital signs.

"Got it! Trauma Room C. Arthur?"

"On it, Mary Ella!" the young but experienced male trauma nurse acknowledged and took over.

Controlled chaos reigned well into the evening and night. The local, regional, and some of the national press and news entities camped out in the media room, waiting for any tidbit of information about the commuter plane that landed on a busy I-95 highway causing accidents galore. Family members and concerned friends descended on the hospital. They demanded moment-by-moment details on the conditions and prognosis of the pertinent patients. They had about fifty critical care patients, primarily from a group of Canadians on a bus tour of the American South. One of the plane's propellers cut clear through the bus from the front window exiting the back before lodging in the front windshield of an eighteen-wheeler trailing the bus. Trucks had jackknifed, sending cars and vans careening off the roads and tumbling into ditches. There were broken bones, abrasions, contusions, and a hellified mess getting people calmed down and coherent enough to give vital information about their medical history.

For Mary Ella, it smacked of the disaster they experienced years earlier during the blizzard. Fortunately, they didn't have to contend with a snowstorm. They had fire department helicopters to transfer patients from the crash site and fully equipped ambulances with well-trained medical teams aboard. It was a far cry better situation than before and a crack team of medical professionals who were about to deal with everything that came in the door.

Nurses from other parts of the hospital came in to lend assistance at the end of their regular shifts, while others came in on their days off or reported to duty early. It was a notable effort, but considering their emergency room was usually a busy place, it took all of her battlefield skills to make it all work. She had to press the orderlies into service to get patients into screened-off emergency bays with only two nurses per bay. Emergency room doctors scurried from one bay to the next, making snap decisions based on her nurses' advice and their own exams and observations. Patient discharges from other hospital departments were impacted until Sylvia Alexander activated her Blue Teens, teenagers, who were under her direct supervision as dogsbodies, and her Grey Ladies and Gentlemen, her group of senior citizens who were all volunteers.

Mary Ella was surprised to see Donovan come in wearing a light-blue vest with others in the Blue Teens' group. He nodded and absently waved to her but went about his assigned tasks without delay. Apparently, Dean Logan let the teens who were hospital volunteers out of school early to provide assistance during the crisis.

Later, after all of the patients had been evaluated and assigned out of Mary Ella's emergency room, Satarah came in with a picnic basket and corralled her. They went into her office, and Satarah sat her down.

"Put your feet up and eat," Satarah directed and stood with her arms folded over her baby bump. "Donovan says you've been on your feet for hours, and he hasn't seen you take a break."

"I didn't know he volunteers here with the Blue Teens."

"Oh, yes, he's very interested in going into medicine. When he's on duty here, he's usually in the children's area. He remembers how much it meant to him when he was a patient here. The Blue Teens came every day to entertain them during and after the blizzard."

"How well I remember. I'll bet The Summer House is full."

"It is, yes, but Douglas and others in the Men's Club are pulling the container homes out of storage and setting them up on the vacant land next to the hospital. The Grey volunteers are cleaning up the homes and preparing them for the arrival of families who have people in the hospital. I've been cooking all afternoon since I got the word."

Mary Ella plopped down at the small conference table in her office, took a deep breath before she opened the lid of the picnic basket. She toed off her shoes and put her feet up in a chair opposite her. A wide-mouth thermos of chunky and aromatic beef bourguignon tickled her taste buds. After a couple of warm mouthfuls, she sighed contentedly. "I planned to go to the cafeteria for a snack, but this is sooo good, Satarah." She closed her eyes and moaned pleasurably. "I'm glad I hadn't gone yet. Thank you."

"You're welcome. There's a little loaf of cornbread in there and a fruit salad. Home-made frozen yogurt goes well over the fruit salad for dessert.

I'm just glad that you've put on some weight and don't look like you're going to be blown away with the next breeze. How do you feel?"

Mary Ella shrugged. "Pregnant," she quipped and broke off a piece of the cornbread that was made with whole kernel Mexicali corn and finely minced onions, garlic, and green and red jalapeño peppers. It was a real treat for the taste buds, but she had to be careful since she was eating for three. "I'm not quite as agile as I'd like to be about now."

"I don't know what it's like to carry twins, but I think we should get away for a four-day weekend and drive to the beach. The McCoy Oceans Inn Resort in Atlantic Beach has the most amazing full-service spa, and they've added a culinary school on the premises. I try to go every year for Mother's Day, my birthday, and the weekend following Thanksgiving. In fact," Satarah grinned with all thirty-two showing, "since it's your birthday coming up, we have reservations for this weekend."

Mary Ella shook her head. "Geeze-o-flip, I forgot all about it. How old am I, thirty-one, thirty-two?"

"Who cares? We're the same age, give or take a month or two. We woke up breathing this morning. That's enough for me."

"I appreciate the sentiment, Satarah, but I don't know whether this is a good time to be away. I've got so much work to do. We're short-staffed as it is, and…"

"There is always work to do, and it will be here when you return. I've cleared it with Aunt Sylvia. She thinks it's a great idea. You've been pounding since you took over here, and you really need a break. I do, too, for that matter, and so does Jenny. Now that her Emily Rose is a month old, she's stockpiled enough breast milk to last for a month of Sundays. Douglas has given Bob the time off to take care of their household so Jenny can join us guilt-free. You're leaving all forms of communication here. No work allowed. So, you have no excuse. We're off to see the massage wizards at the McCoy Spa and Resort on Friday morning at seven. By ten o'clock, we should be in mani-pedi heaven!"

Where is she? he wondered. He toggled between all of the video monitors trying to pick up her image, to no avail. According to the GPS signal on her portable electronic equipment, she should be in the little cottage she rents on The Summer House grounds on the banks of the Santee River. He'd searched the security cameras there and at the hospital.

It had been months since he was stationary enough to use his equipment and check in on Mary Ella. The last time he saw her face, she was at her desktop computer concentrating on writing a report for a three-day nurses' conference in Atlanta, Georgia. She looked so beautiful with her hair growing longer and worn in a pixie style that complimented the shape of her face. Although he wasn't particularly adept at popular culture, his mother and older sisters were. Mary Ella and the actress Nia Long (as she looked in the film *The Best Man)* could pass for siblings, he thought. He and his father were of one mind; they didn't spend time watching popular movies or television shows.

Then again, Mary Ella would look exceptionally good wearing a burlap sack…or nothing at all, which was more to his liking. For some reason, she looked very healthy with a rosy glow to her cinnamon-colored complexion. Her high cheekbones didn't stand out and make her look gaunt and emaciated. She looked far better now than when she began working at the hospital.

Still, he didn't have much time to wait for her to return from wherever she was, but he wanted to see her again before he had to leave. He needed just one look to sustain him for the weeks and probably months ahead when he would be out of touch with his fantasy world, which included Mary Ella.

Frustrated, he shut down his equipment and stretched out on his back on his bunk. He really needed to shower and put on clean clothes; not too clean or that might draw suspicious looks in his direction. He couldn't afford to do anything out of the ordinary, or more importantly, out of character. Being away or out of sight for long periods of time could also prove dangerous, but so far, no one questioned when he and the others followed a different path.

His mind was tired and in need of rest… then he suddenly sat up in his bunk. What if something had happened to her, to Mary Ella? Could that be why her portables were in the cottage? There were places in the hospital where specific equipment could not be used.

He quickly logged into the hospital's patients' directory and searched for her name. He didn't know whether he was relieved not to find her listed or more concerned. There was an inordinate amount of patients in the hospital. It appeared that some disaster occurred, causing the hospital to be operating at better than ninety-eight percent capacity. That alone hiked up his concern for Mary Ella. If she wasn't a patient, then she should be somewhere in the emergency room area with her staff.

Not finding her anywhere in the hospital, he spread his search county-wide to the medical clinics and found his efforts blocked. He tried to break through the shields but couldn't get past the firewalls. Someone had major tech skills in Summer County. Then he tried to backtrack and go around the block. Usually, a public library was an easy way to get in, but not so much with this one. Even the Department of Motor Vehicles was heavily shielded. *Curiouser and curiouser*, he thought.

He backed all the way out, least his trail be discovered. Coming from where he was located might be construed as a threat. Then he went in through the South Carolina tax rolls, which were accessible online. He did a search on Summer County and found business names again, but not personal South Carolina tax returns. Real estate information was likewise scarce to non-existent. He wondered aloud, "What gives with this place?" Every avenue he attempted to access information was either blocked or non-existent. He tried accessing the top-ten most popular magazine distribution sites, and again, the publications were sent in the name of businesses. Someone had some serious tech skills and some very deep pull in the state to control the amount of information accessible through normal routes.

This was getting him nowhere. He may have to do something else to ensure that Mary Ella was well and healthy. He knew he would not rest until he knew all the facts.

"Alert! Shields up! Our bogey is back!" one of the techs announced.

"Are you locked onto the signal?"

"Right on his heels."

"Stick with it. Don't lose it."

"Copy that."

"Satin?"

"Yo!"

"Activate Wind Breeze."

"Copy that."

The line beeped three signals before the return signal was received.

"Acknowledged. This is Wind Breeze. The code of the day is being entered now. Go ahead."

"Verified, Wind Breeze. We've got a bogey fishing in your pond. Hold for ident and a coded message. Trace transfer embedded."

"Got it. Transfer complete. Wind Breeze is over and out."

CHAPTER 14

"Oh, my, this is heavenly," crooned Satarah as she received a full-body scrub from a very talented masseuse.

"I'll say," commented Mary Ella. "It's really clever to have a table with a hole in it for pregnant women so we can lay face down."

"Or for those of us who just had an eight-pound baby and haven't yet lost all the extra fat gained throughout the pregnancy." Jenny sighed. "My breasts are enormous!"

"I'll bet Bob isn't complaining about a few extra pounds of your petite frame," commented Satarah.

"No, he isn't. He just loves how large my breasts are. It fascinates him to watch me use my breast pump."

"*Whoa,* TMI." Mary Ella laughed. "If you ask me, you still look like a size eight Barbie Doll, Jenny. I don't see where you're carrying any extra pounds."

"Maybe for someone as tall and stacked as you are, the pounds don't show. Your body looks like one of those supermodels. Everything on you is proportional; thirty-six, twenty-four, thirty-six."

Mary Ella laughed. "Not quite those dimensions at the moment."

"Well, the cantaloupe-sized breasts are fairly prominent," Satarah deadpanned.

"Back at ya, babe," Mary Ella rejoindered.

"Me, not you, Mary Ella," countered Satarah. "Your breasts are still the size of grapefruits."

"I don't have the energy to even look at them." Mary Ella sighed contentedly. "This spa weekend is a really good idea. Thank you for suggesting it."

"You're welcome. It's a great way for us to get away and to celebrate your birthday."

Mary Ella drifted into a twilight snooze while the masseuse continued to scrub the back of her body from head to toe. Memories of her and Mark washing each other clean in a stream drifted into her mind. His hands felt so good all over her body. He didn't miss any nook or cranny when he bathed her. He sat in the water and brought her body to his mouth. He bathed her in another more intimate way with teeth and tongue until her muscles trembled from the heady sensations he could elicit. He had such skillful hands, a doctor's hands, and clever fingers that knew all of the secret erogenous zones to explore on and in her body.

It was so freeing to be out in nature bare-bodied to the sun and breezes. The gentle, warm rains dropped off the broad leaves of flora and fauna to cool their skin in the heat of the day. In the rain forests in different countries, they found little waterfalls over small shallow caves where the world didn't intrude. The streams ran cool over their moist bodies, heated from reaching the threshold of each level of ecstasy. With the transfer of breath back and forth between them, they enjoyed each other, challenging themselves to take their unions higher and higher. Hands on hips, they guided the action for one another, pumping each other hard for that just-out-of-reach passion they were trying to achieve. His voice in her ear, husky and smooth as he took her up, up and over… no, not Mark.

It was not Mark, but the other. The intimacy quietly seduced and the passion built on a razor's edge. Lips and teeth on her breasts elicited shaky, breathless cries of completion. His pale gaze so intense on hers. Her hands bound and stretched above her head, the rough hairs of his pubis against the softness between her widely spread thighs… Against her will, she luxuriated in the long and strong slide of his maleness in and out of her. The copulation aided by those fingers playing over her sensitive skin, tangling her senses in a greedy, explosive possession.

Her moan woke her before she went deeper into that twilight haziness and memory. The masseuse poured buckets of warm water over her body, taking the exfoliated dead skin away in its wake. Like the waterfall, only clean, soft, refreshed skin remained. Then an aromatic oil and deep-tissue massage followed. This time, Mary Ella promised herself she would not go back to her tangled memories of the two lovers. Otherwise, it would undoubtedly lead her unerringly to madness.

"What is this?" Jenny looked toward Satarah.

Satarah, Mary Ella, and Jenny sat in bathrobes, terry cloth slippers, and towel turbans at an outdoor patio on a bright sunshiny day, watching the Atlantic Ocean roll gently onto the shore.

"Shrimp scampi," Satarah looked at one of the smorgasbord of delectable dishes Jenny indicated. "It's got Cajun flavors cooked in it."

Jenny sampled it and then dug in for another mouthful. "It's really good. Can you make this, Satarah?"

"Probably. I think it's in one of the cookbooks on sale here in the resort's gift shop. Dr. St. Clair's brother, Jacque St. Clair, owns a Louisiana Cajun restaurant in Columbia, and he has a cookbook out."

"Really? Then maybe I can learn to make it."

Mary Ella frowned at her cousin. "Jacque St. Clair? Didn't you date him?"

"Yesteryear, for a hot moment."

Mary Ella smiled. "Mmmm, I thought the name was familiar."

Satarah regarded her friend. "Jenny, you might want to buy the ingredients on Monday before we leave. Otherwise, you'll have to order them online. The stores in Summer County don't carry these seasonings and herbs."

"There's a gift pack of herbs I can buy. I saw that…" Jenny frowned, bobbing and weaving to spy someone. "Hey, Satarah, isn't that your cousin, Gregory?"

"Where?" Satarah turned around. She spotted him on the other end of the patio, being seated with his little mini-me. At six-foot, ten-inches tall, he was hard to miss. "Yes, that's him."

Just then, Gregory looked up in her direction and did a double-take. She waved, getting his attention. He smiled, waved back, and said something to the hostess. She nodded and brought Gregory and his son to the table.

"Hello, Satarah, Mary Ella, Jenny." He hugged each woman in turn. "Mind if we join you?"

"No, we'd enjoy it." Satarah smiled. "Gezz, Gregory, your boy is getting so tall!"

"Hi, Miss Jenny, Miss SaraJo. I don't know your name, but hi," he looked to Mary Ella. "I'm three," the little spitting image of Gregory spoke up. "My name is Clayton Michael Alexander. This is my daddy, Gregory Clayton Alexander. He's not three. He calls me Clay. We have the same name…almost…and my uncle Miguel, too. That's Michael in American. My mommy's name is Angelique, but my daddy calls her Angel Face. She's not a real angel because she lives with us and they like to kiss a lot. She went to get her hair washed. I don't know why." He wore a confused expression on his adorable face and gave a little one-shoulder shrug. "It didn't look dirty to me. She took my baby sister, Anna Aretha, with her. She's one." He held up one finger as if to make clear what constituted the age one-year-old. "What's your name?"

"Actually, Anna Aretha is sixteen months, but who's counting," Gregory joked.

"Hello, Clayton Michael Alexander. It's very nice to meet you." Mary Ella offered her hand for a shake. "My name is Mary Ella Baker. I'm not three either, but today is my birthday."

"Happy birthday!" He brightly piped up and was joined by Gregory's warm embrace. "May I give you a birthday kiss like my daddy did?"

"You certainly may. I like getting kisses from handsome, young men."

The little boy obliged by giving her a tight squeeze and a big, noisy kiss and then crawled back up into his chair. "Can you keep a secret?" Clayton whispered.

"Is it a good secret?" Mary Ella frowned conspiratorially.

Grinning, he enthusiastically nodded. "We're having a baby. I get to be a big brother again. This time we're going to have a baby brother. He can't come out to play yet because he lives in Mommy's tummy."

Jenny's wide eyes glistened. *"Wow!* Is this true, Gregory?"

Gregory amusedly nodded. "It is, yes. We're due in time for Christmas."

"May I have 'nilla yogurt, Daddy?"

"Vanilla, Clay. Yes, you may." Gregory lovingly rubbed his hand over his son's close-cut head of hair. The boy beamed a smile up at his father that was just too adorable for words. Gregory placed the order for their lunches with a hovering waitress who smiled longingly at Gregory. Apparently, more intrigued by the placemat and small box of crayons the waitress put on the table before him, Clayton busied himself with carefully coloring the pictures on the mat. His little tongue was stuck between his teeth on the side of his mouth in concentration.

"He's awful shy, isn't he, Gregory?" Satarah teased."

"Yeah, a real introvert," he teased back. "Just like his cousins Ari and Kate. Mary Ella, it's good to see you. Mom told me you were back home. Angel and I planned to come by to welcome you home the next time we were in Goodwill."

"Thanks, Gregory. Your mother was kind enough to hire me back at Summer County General. I stepped into Satarah and Jenny's position."

"That's great. Angel and I will have to have you over to the house soon."

"Why are you here in Atlantic Beach, Gregory? I thought you and Angelique were still living in the Big Apple."

He laughed. "We do, for some of the year, but I like the slower pace here in South Carolina more than the hustle-bustle of New York City. Besides, I have business here in Atlantic Beach and the Greater Myrtle Beach area."

"Ah, yes, your bank."

"Yes, but also my semi-pro basketball league is headquartered here. Owners of the teams are meeting here for the week. We're gearing up for the new season and meeting here in Atlantic Beach at the McCoy Resort and Conference Center."

"Are you staying at Grand Aunt Hanna Ivy's house while you're in town?" asked Satarah. "I intend to take Mary Ella by to see her and Mrs. Lewis while we're here."

"Angelique and I purchased an ocean-front home further up in Atlantic Beach and had it renovated and remodeled. Since Aunt Hanna Ivy and Mrs. Lewis converted the first floor of her home to a tea room and gift shop, they're doing a brisk business. My little ones' curiosity gets the better of them, introverted souls that they are. If we let them, they'd spend the whole day talking to the customers who come in to relax in the tea room and to shop." He laughed.

"Wow, Gregory, this is wonderful. I didn't know any of this," smiled Mary Ella. "Congratulations. When did this start?"

"A year after I retired from professional basketball. I started a semi-pro league made up of both all-male and all-female teams. Initially, the teams were created in the mid-Atlantic states of Virginia, Maryland, and North and South Carolina."

"I gather there are places in these states that don't have major professional or big university sports teams," questioned Mary Ella.

"You're correct. We have ten leagues now across the country and the US territories. They're headquartered in second cities or what's better known as cities outside of the top one hundred."

"Gregory started a real trend," offered Jenny.

"Initially, I only got businessmen and women in cities, like Annapolis and Baltimore, Maryland, Norfolk, Richmond, and Roanoke, Virginia, Greensboro and Wilmington, North Carolina, and Columbia, Charleston, and Myrtle Beach, South Carolina, interested in grouping together and sponsoring semi-pro, basketball teams. However, the plan caught on like wildfire. Before I knew it, more communities, outside the top one hundred, came to me asking for semi-pro basketball franchises for their cities. It's entertainment. The fact that it's also lucrative is just a nice by-product."

"Not to mention the fact that Gregory opened a bank, which is one of the major sponsors of the league," commented Satarah with a big smile and a nod of pride in her cousin's success.

"There is that." He laughed. "If I was going to start the league, I couldn't also own a team in contention."

Mary Ella frowned. "So, you've given up trading on the New York Stock Exchange?"

"Oh, no, trading and parenting are my day jobs. I'm still a founding partner of Compliant Trading and Investments. I just don't have to be in

New York City to put in work. We live in a virtual-reality world. While Clay and Anna are small, Angel and I want to be able to travel as much as possible. In fact, we just returned from visiting your mother in Paris, France, Satarah. Angel accepted a modeling job for the designer Carlos Ortega."

Mary Ella was surprised. "Angelique is still modeling?"

Gregory nodded. "She does on occasions. This was a celebration of Carlos' admittance to the Designers' Hall of Fame. All of the supermodels who made his designs famous were asked to come to Paris and wear his signature designs. Angel modeled Carlos' line of maternity wear. Aunt Mariah was asked to perform for the event. As usual, she was awesome."

"Mom told me about it," nodded Satarah. "Actually, Douglas and I wanted to be there, too, but the boys didn't have a school rotation period open or coming up during the event."

Mary Ella regarded Gregory while she continued to eat. "Angelique still has her restaurant in New York City, doesn't she?"

"Oh, yes, Angelique's Place restaurant and The Run Way nightclub, bar, and grill are still in operation. Her brand is doing so well that she opened another location in Washington, DC. Part of the reason we're in the area this weekend is because she's negotiating with the Chef Daryl Mason to expand his culinary school here in Myrtle Beach."

"I've heard of him. In fact, since I've been back in the US, I've watched his cooking shows on the Gourmet Channel." Mary Ella nodded. "He's really very good."

Gregory nodded, too. "Angelique agrees. If it works out, she wants to join him and have a dormitory built somewhere in Atlantic Beach for out-of-state students to live while they're in training. She's been training at-risk high school students in both New York and Washington. Some of the kids can't afford the top culinary schools' tuition, room, and board. It costs less per student here in the south. So, for those who successfully come through her training programs in New York and DC, we'll sponsor them in the school here in Atlantic Beach for a full ride. If it all works out, she and Daryl plan to rebrand the school The Atlantic Culinary School of America. Clay and I have been out touring properties all morning."

He smiled at his sleeping son. "I think we need to get home for a nap. If you don't have dinner plans, why don't you come to the house around five today?" He stood to his six-foot-ten-inch height and lifted his sleeping son into his arms, the boy's head on Gregory's broad shoulder.

Checking with each other, Satarah, Mary Ella, and Jenny agreed.

"Great," smiled Gregory. "I'll text the address to you." He offered his farewells before he went to pay his tab and then left.

Mary Ella watched him go. For an extremely tall, solidly built man, he seemed surprisingly agile and light on his feet, even while carrying the weight of his sleeping son on his shoulder as if the boy weighed nothing. *Gregory is also a very handsome man*, thought Mary Ella, but even though they were uniquely different, all of those Alexanders looked like they stepped off the cover of *GQ* or *Stallion Magazine*. Gregory's older brothers, Kenneth, Benny, and a slew of his Alexander cousins, including the twins, Donald and James Dixon, were highly sought after in their teens by the young, local girls in the county. Yet, they never let their good looks go to their heads. They weren't vain or conceited about their appearance or accomplishments. Most were good-natured men who carried a smile as their default expression. Though they didn't wed local girls, they seemed to make good, strong, and lasting marriages.

Mary Ella smiled to herself. Her maternal, Cherokee grandmother, Imani, used to say that *"you couldn't sling a dead cat in a crowd in Summer County and not hit a cousin."* That was true of the families, particularly the ones in the Summer County municipality of Goodwill. The Alexander clan constituted the majority population of the town. The county comprised the descendants of a branch of the family from Alexandria, Egypt, a contingent of shipwrecked seamen from Barbados, and a mixture of the Native American populations of the area.

At one time, the region was considered a dangerous swamp, and for that reason, slavers avoided it. The rumors also made it an ideal path for those escaping slavery on the Underground Railroad. Many slaves sought asylum among the amalgamation of peoples, stayed, intermarried, and raised their families there through many generations. Long after slavery ended, that region became the fertile farming community of Summer County, South Carolina.

Her family tree was rich with a mixture of ethnicities to pass on to her babies. Once she had their DNA tested, she would prepare genealogy books for their posterity. Her babies would not only know *who* they were but also *whose* they were. It was essential to her that her children not lose track of their heritage. If these were Kaseem's babies, she'd have to cobble together a general history of the various sects who made up the Arab and African nations. Hope sprung that she was carrying Mark's offspring. His family tree was already in print all the way back many, many generations to his English and African roots. This was long before the Earth's Teutonic plates shifted, and Egyptians began to trade with people who became known as South Americans.

With stealth, Mary Ella's cottage was searched as her office had been the previous night. The intruders were skilled at this task and didn't disturb anything unnecessarily. However, they were successful in finding the bugs in her electronic equipment.

It was serendipitous that Mrs. Alexander sent a note to the hospital's IT department thanking them for the expeditious manner in which they handled Mary Ella's electronics installation and got her up and running in record time. Receiving the note of praise, the IT Department acknowledged her comments were appreciated but premature. Without making an issue of it, Mrs. Alexander casually mentioned the discrepancy to her son, Kenneth, with certain knowledge the matter would be brought under scrutiny. Afterward, she didn't give it another thought.

Her instincts were spot on. Kenneth's company, CompuCorrect Global, managed the hospital's cyberspace security from its corporate offices in California. It had a cyber threat facility in Goodwill staffed with people Kenneth implicitly trusted because they were tech superstars, and most were related by blood to him. Once the alert was sounded, a search for the IT installer was underway. Regrettably, he evaded capture, but a counter-intelligence watch was placed on Mary Ella's equipment.

She wasn't believed to be a threat to the country or to the secret installations in Summer County. However, considering where she had been over the last four, nearly five years, the consensus was that someone was trying to use her without her knowledge or consent. Now they had a means of backtracking the intruders without their knowledge while protecting Mary Ella from harm.

CHAPTER 15

"Pardon me, Miss." The middle-aged woman approached Mary Ella.

She, Jenny, and Satarah were standing in the McCoy Hotel lobby, waiting for Satarah's SUV to be brought to the resort's entrance by the valet service. They were leaving to have dinner with Gregory and Angelique Alexander when the woman approached her.

"Yes?"

"Is your sir name Baker?"

Surprise didn't cover the range of questions crossing Mary Ella's mind. The woman didn't look like anyone she remembered meeting before. She stared so long without answering the woman spoke again.

"I apologize. My name is Minerva Baker. My friends and family call me Minnie. My father was Golden Baker, and my mother was Hattie Ada Carrington. I'm a cook here at the resort. I saw you earlier today having lunch on the veranda, and I just couldn't take my eyes off of you." She took a deep breath and huffed it out. "I'm rambling, but you look the spitting image of my sister, Caledonia. Caledonia Baker James."

"Caledonia was my grand aunt, my grandfather Robert Senior's sister. My father was Robert Junior."

"Oh, my goodness! I was right!" exclaimed Minnie reaching to hug Mary Ella. "You're my little nephew Bobby Junior's Mary Ella. I'm your grand aunt."

She accepted the woman's embrace and smiled tentatively at her. "It's nice to meet you. These are my friends Jenny Sweeney and Satarah Johnson. Satarah is my cousin."

"Satarah? Satarah Josephine? You're Mariah and Obadiah's child, right?"

"Yes, I am."

"Oh, my, this is so wonderful! The last time I saw you, you were a little biddy thing in your mama's arms." She hugged her. "There's another one, a sister, right?"

"Yes, Carlotta."

Minnie snapped her fingers. "Yes! I remember. She's a couple of years older than you. My, my, my… Oh! Where's my head? I'm just so excited." She looked up and around. Then she turned to motion a man who was at the front desk over to them. "JC, you will not believe who this is."

He grinned at the three of them. "Three lovely ladies." He salaciously smiled at them. "However, it looks like I'm a little late to benefit from their acquaintances. Two are wearing wedding rings, and two are pregnant. I wouldn't want to sleep in anyone else's bed, so to speak." He laughed.

Something about him rubbed Mary Ella the wrong way and, if the quick eye roll she noticed Satarah giving her was any indication, she was feeling the same vibe.

"Stop with your flirting, man. This here is Mary Ella Baker!" Minnie gestured enthusiastically. At his shrug and blank stare, she shook her head and sucked her teeth. "She's your cousin, your grand Uncle Robert Senior's granddaughter. You see, Caledonia was the oldest child in our family." She smiled warmly at the group in general. "Then it's your father, Paul, then me and my little brother Robert who we called Bobby. There's only the two of us left now. Me and my older brother Paul."

"Really?" He obviously wasn't keen on or interested in the connections. "I remember my father mentioned his younger brother, Robert, had a son, but I don't recall ever meeting him or his son."

"Well, you were so young back then. Mary Ella, this here is my brother Paul's son, my nephew JC." She shook her head, frustrated. "John Calvin Baker. He prefers to be called JC. He's out of uniform today, but he's in the military stationed at Shaw Air Force Base. I haven't seen him since he was a young boy. My brother, his father, told him since he was so close, to come, make sure to see me." She laughed. "We're on opposite coasts, you see. Paul lives in Los Angeles on the Pacific shores, and here I am on the shores of the Atlantic Ocean. So, John Calvin came to visit with me for the weekend."

He stood straighter as he regarded the women. "I'm only at Shaw temporarily, though. I'll soon be called to a duty station in Washington, DC, at the Pentagon."

"You have to be patient, JC," commented Minnie. "I've told you this before. Good things come only to those who wait. Anyway, this is Satarah Josephine James, Obadiah, and Mariah Benson James' daughter. You've heard of the French Mariah, haven't you?"

"Of course. Who hasn't?" He took another look at her from the bottom up with greater interest. "She's the star of stage and screen in Europe, Asia, and Africa. So, she's your mama?"

"She is, yes, and my name is Johnson, Grand Aunt Minnie. My husband is Douglas Johnson, Summer County Fire Chief."

"Summer County?" JC injected urgency in his voice.

Satarah's brows beetled at his apparent name recognition. "Yes, that's where we live. It's located a few hours from here on the other side of I-95 along the Santee River."

"Do you know any Alexanders who may live there?"

"Yes, there is a huge number of Alexanders who live primarily in the Goodwill municipal section of the county."

"Kenneth and Benjamin Alexander?"

"I know them, yes. We're cousins, and our mothers are sisters. They have homes there, but they don't live there most of the time."

He laughed conspiratorially. "Well, I'll be damned."

Jenny smiled, observing the impromptu family reunion. "We're on our way to have dinner with Gregory Alexander now. He's Kenneth and Benny's younger brother. If you follow basketball, you've probably heard of him. He's a big basketball star, even though he's retired now."

"Is that so?" JC's eyes were alight with heightened interest. He wasn't a fan of sports, but he'd be sure to look him up. *Oh, yes, how the worm does turn*, he thought.

"You're right, Jenny. We need to hurry," suggested Mary Ella. "We're staying here at the resort, Grand Aunt Minnie. Perhaps we can get together for breakfast tomorrow morning?"

"That sounds just fine, Mary Ella. You girls run along now. Sorry to keep you, but when I saw you, I just had to ask because you're such a pretty girl just like my sister."

"Thank you. We'll see you…"

"Maybe I should come with you, ladies. It's been a long time, but I know the Alexanders. I used to be Benjamin's commanding officer years ago. His younger brother was still in high school when Benny was under my command. It would be interesting to see how he turned out."

"That would be…" Jenny began only to have Mary Ella cut her off.

"Another time, perhaps, JC. Please give my best to your father."

Once they were in Satarah's waiting SUV and pulling away from the resort, Jenny asked, "Why didn't you want him to join us, Mary Ella? That's not like you and Gregory wouldn't have minded. He's always so neighborly."

"You're right, but Gregory may be just one of the kids from our neighborhood to us, but to the rest of the world who don't know him personally, he's a mega-sports icon. He's a multimillionaire and television celebrity the sports industry calls Alexander the Great because of his skills and abilities on the basketball court and now in the world of high finance. I didn't feel comfortable inviting someone I don't know to his home."

"You know, I never got that memo. I didn't even think of that," admitted Jenny. "As you said, he's just Gregory to us."

The panoramic view of the Atlantic Ocean off the rear deck of Gregory and Angelique's stately home was awesome. Mary Ella and Satarah were chatting with Gregory while he grilled steaks and vegetable shish kabobs with meatballs. Angelique, Jenny, Clayton, and Anna Aretha built sandcastles on the shore. The ocean water was so blue and calm as evening approached, Mary Ella felt she could just drift away on the gentle waves. Across that vast expanse of water were Asia and Africa. Somewhere on that side of the globe was Mark and probably Kaseem.

"Gregory, do you know a military man named John Calvin Baker?" Satarah asked.

Gregory hesitated a pregnant moment. "J.C. Baker?"

She nodded.

"Yes, why?" He put down his grilling tool, wiped his hands, and sat to take a sip of his glass of wine. He eyed his cousin steadily.

"We met him today as we were leaving the resort. Apparently, he, Mary Ella, and I are cousins. From your expression, I gather he's not a friend."

Gregory nodded. "Do you remember when Kenneth testified before Congress about corruption in the handling of the military contracts and funding for goods and services?"

"I do, yes." Satarah nodded. "Mary Ella and I were in our first year of nursing school at the time. We came to Washington en mass to lend our moral support to Kenneth and help in any way we could. That was more than ten years ago."

Gregory nodded. "JC Baker was one of the military men behind the scheme to defraud the government. He tried to get Kenneth caught up in a mess by having his company accept and over price bogus requests for proposals."

"Yes, and I remember Kenneth blew up the whole conspiracy by secretly working with the Attorney General's office." Satarah smiled. "It was a hot mess. Didn't a lot of people go to jail?"

"They did, yes," Gregory nodded, "but JC Baker had a lot of connections in high places in Washington. He avoided being court-martialed but got busted down from Colonel to Second Lieutenant. He and a woman, Dr. Lisa Lambert, a real piece of work, should have been convicted along with the rest and imprisoned. They should still be serving time."

Satarah nodded and surmised. "In other words, they had blackmail evidence on certain people?"

"That's correct. They were in cahoots, and by all rights, they should have been convicted of several federal and state crimes and imprisoned. You say he's related to you and Mary Ella?"

Mary Ella nodded and sat forward in her seat. "He is, yes. His father, Paul, and my paternal grandfather, Robert Senior, were brothers. However,

I never met JC Baker before today. Now that you mention it, I remember that there were a lot of military men and women in the chamber during the congressional hearing, but that was so long ago. I don't remember the faces." She frowned at Satarah. "As I recall, Kenneth and that guy from Holly Hill, South Carolina, were the only ones to testify that day."

Satarah narrowed her eyes in concentration and then smiled and snapped her finger. She pointed at Mary Ella. "Yes, I remember him because he was a big guy and kinda cute. His name is Sam Yeager. He was JC Baker's driver."

"There you go." Mary Ella nodded.

Satarah sighed and sat back in her seat. "The same is true for me, Gregory. I didn't recognize him today, but my paternal grandmother, Caledonia, and his father, Paul, were siblings."

"Did he say what he was doing in South Carolina?" Gregory asked.

Satarah nodded. "Apparently, he's stationed at Shaw Air Force Base. He says he's waiting to be reassigned to a post at the Pentagon."

Gregory shook his head and cracked facetiously. "Yeah, right. When Hell freezes over, and the Devil goes ice skating. JC Baker used to be Benny's commanding officer and pretended to be a friend of our family. Then he does something so despicable as trying to involve Kenneth in a scandal of epic proportions that could have landed Kenneth in prison and damaged Benny's military career. Now, Benny's a five-star general with the Joint Chiefs of Staff as an advisor to the President and an Astronaut. We haven't talked about any of this in years, but I'll bet Benny would block any attempt JC Baker made to get back in the mix at the Pentagon. That's where the plan was hatched to defraud the government."

"Perhaps you should give Benny and Kenneth a heads up," Satarah suggested.

Gregory checked his watch before he pulled his phone from his pocket and dialed one number. "Hey, big brother, sorry to wake you. Hold on. I'm going to conference Kenneth in." When the connection was made, Gregory relaxed. "I'm sitting on the deck in Atlantic Beach with Satarah and Mary Ella. They just told me JC Baker is at Shaw and looking for a transfer to the Pentagon. Do you know anything about that?"

Mary Ella watched Gregory as he carried on a discussion with his older brothers, Kenneth, in Santa Barbara, California, and Benny, in Tokyo, Japan. He sat casually, relaxed with one long, long leg resting on the opposite knee, his feet bare. He wore a pair of loose-fitting shorts and a white T-shirt. The short beard did not hide any of his handsome face. Although he was seen regularly on sports shows, he looked like he should be the leading man in some blockbuster movies. As he talked, he tunneled his long, strong fingers across his close-cut hair, causing the large muscles in his arms and broad shoulders to bulge and ripple with the movement. He didn't have an ounce of fat on him anywhere. That move reminded her of Mark, who had a similar affectation when he was content and relaxed or concentrating on solving a medical problem.

Clayton bounded up the steps from the beach and, seeing his father on the phone, stopped from blurting out whatever message he was there to deliver. Gregory smiled at the boy, lifting him one-handed into his lap while he continued his conversation. Clayton contented himself by burrowing into his father's embrace and became fascinated with Gregory's watch. Absently, Gregory took off his wristwatch and placed it on his son's arm. It was entirely too large, but Clayton's little fingers successfully worked through some of the apps on the watch to a game.

"Yes, it was Satarah who thought you should have a heads up." He waited for a beat, listening, then laughed. "Yes, I'll tell her. Yeah, yeah, yeah, I love you, too." He disconnected the call and then turned to his son. "So, what's up, Champ?"

Clayton concentrated on the game on his father's multifaceted watch. "Mommy said to remind you that my baby brother is hungry."

"Okay, you can tell your mommy that anytime your baby brother is ready to eat, he should come and get it." Clayton turned in his father's lap, kissed his cheek, and returned his watch. Gregory kissed the top of his son's head before the boy climbed down from Gregory's lap and scampered away. He put on his watch and smiled after Clayton, pride showing in his eyes before turning to Satarah and Mary Ella. "Kenneth and Benny told me to say hello for them. Benny suggested if you want to give up ownership and working at The Summer House, he'll make sure you can take your pick of positions at the Pentagon, CIA or FBI. There are also opportunities at NSA and Homeland Security. They both appreciate the heads up. The last time either of them heard from JC Baker, he was working in a motor pool in Elmendorf Air Force Base in Anchorage, Alaska. They'll look into it."

It dawned on Mary Ella that Benny might be willing to look into the progress being made to find Mark and get him out of the Middle East. He certainly had the pull to accomplish it, but she wondered whether it would be asking too much of him. She was sure, given his rank and prestige, people were always asking favors of him. His parents, Bernard and Sylvia, would be the best people to ask about it. She would be guided by their recommendations. Then she thought better of it. She wasn't supposed to discuss the situation involving Mark with anyone. For the time being, she would leave Benny out of it, but if she didn't hear anything about Mark by the time her babies were born, she'd reconsider her decision.

Mary Ella still wasn't anywhere to be found, he thought while toggling back and forth between several locations where she was usually easy to spot. It worried him that he could not find her, but time was running out. He couldn't stay long or take more time to locate her. He'd have to wait until the next time he could safely check in for a debriefing. For now, dissatisfied, he was about to shut down his equipment and prepare mentally and emotionally to go back into the world when an alert using her e-mail address popped up in a box on his screen.

There she is! He could only see her face as she concentrated on her research.

He followed the links and found it curious that she was researching someone named John Calvin Baker, a military officer. He watched her go through several pages of information. She was a very good researcher and had even pulled up transcripts of hearings held on Capitol Hill years ago involving John C. Baker. Maybe he was a relative of hers she was searching for. He wondered what that was all about. He saved the sites she visited, marking the pages, sent them to his printer, and wondered whether she could speed read along with her medical knowledge. He imagined she was printing the copies because she was on a computer in the Business Center of a McCoy Resort and Conference Center in someplace called Atlantic Beach, South Carolina. He had never heard of the place before, but as she continued her research, he activated Google Earth and found the location near Myrtle Beach, South Carolina. It wasn't a particularly big place, but it was right on the coast between the Atlantic Ocean and the Intercoastal Waterway.

No wonder he couldn't find her. She was at the beach and didn't have her electronics with her. Why was she there without any form of communication equipment? He had her electronic calendar available to him, but he didn't notice she was scheduled for any meetings or conferences outside of Summer County. For now, he would have to content himself with the fact she was safe. A copy of what she was researching started printing on his system, and he left to dance with the Devil one more day.

CHAPTER 16

They had a wonderful time at Gregory's home with him, Angelique, and their two precious children. Angelique, born and raised in Peru until the age of eight, was teaching the children to speak Spanish. Clay enjoyed pointing to objects, including those on his face and body, and then having his mother tell him the words in Spanish. He would repeat the words and was reasonably adept at it. Anna Aretha, definitely a daddy's girl, though she would try to pronounce the words, too, was more interested in eating food from her father's dinner plate and feeding him in the process. Gregory dutifully ate whatever his daughter chose to share with him, but he drew the line at sharing his glass of wine with her. She was a little testy about that. All in all, they were a delightful, young family and a pleasure to be with.

Angelique, a supermodel and movie actress, was simply heart-stopping gorgeous in every dimension, effortlessly. She wore a simple, off-the-shoulder, summer cotton top that flared and covered her baby bump. Her shorts were maternity cut but showed off her long, long shapely tanned legs and bare feet to perfection. She and Gregory hadn't been married that long, but Angelique looked as if she could pass for someone twelve years old. She was very energetic and animated…and obviously happy to be the wife of Gregory Alexander. When she looked at him, the love for her husband and children was written all over her. There was no question that he adored her.

Although Angelique was a Le Cordon Bleu certified chef, Gregory did the cooking that day and did an excellent job. He wouldn't let her move a muscle if he could help it. Gregory cooked and cleaned up afterward while taking primary responsibility for watching the children.

He took the little ones in for baths, bedtime stories, and then bed, leaving Angelique to socialize and relax. Afterward, Gregory brought back baby monitors and rejoined them on the deck just as the sun was going down.

Gregory insisted the next time he and Angelique were in Atlantic Beach, she, Jenny, and Satarah should bring their families and spend time with them at the beach. They agreed to do so before summer's end if Gregory and Angelique were still in Atlantic Beach and when the children were on a rotation-change period, which occurred every six weeks. Mary Ella was looking forward to it. She enjoyed the McCoy Resort and Spa.

The next day, it was also interesting to have breakfast with Minerva "Minnie" Baker. There was a special employees' lounge set aside where generally the public wasn't permitted. Minnie set up a breakfast buffet there that had their mouths drooling. She was apparently an excellent chef, though she called herself a cook. However, the extraordinarily handsome and virile Daryl Mason was in town to visit Minnie and meet with the Resort's management team. The man Angelique was planning to partner with was a close friend of Minnie's. He actually cooked, especially for them. There were lumps of crab meat, lobster, and shrimp with a white sauce over big, fluffy, baking-powder biscuits, Spanish deviled eggs with onion, garlic, green and red peppers, on a bed of chopped, sautéed spinach, grilled fresh rounds of pineapple, baked salmon in a lemon and lime wash, with artichoke hearts, capers, and so much more. He kept the buffet stocked with delicious, delectable foods.

After such a great breakfast and the joy of spending time with a delightful grandaunt she didn't know, Mary Ella was reluctant to share the information she found online about Minnie's nephew, John Calvin Baker. She shared the information with both Jenny and Satarah. They believed, if Minnie Baker didn't know her nephew, she should not be left in the dark. She was family, after all. So, Mary Ella gave Minnie a copy of the newspaper accounts and the government hearing's official transcript.

"I thought something was amiss." Minnie shook her head. "He just didn't seem quite right to me, but I didn't imagine anything like this! This is terrible. I can't imagine my brother didn't know this, but he never said a word to me about it."

"Don't fret, Ms. Baker," crooned Jenny soothingly. "Maybe he's seen the errors of his ways."

"I'm not fretting, Jenny. I'm pissed. That young man came here all sweetness and light because I arranged for him to stay in one of the best suites in the resort free of charge. Butter wouldn't melt in his mouth. After you left to visit with your cousin and have dinner, John Calvin questioned me about you girls like I was on trial. Now I know what that was probably about. He's a real operator, that one, a user! I'm going to have a few words with my brother and ask him why he didn't tell me any of this. I appreciate you for bringing this to my attention."

Still, Minnie told them to let her know whenever they were coming to town. She would arrange for their accommodations at the resort. She was one of the employees who had been there the longest and knew the owner, Justin McCoy. Minnie told them Justin started working in the kitchen when he was just a young teenager. He lived not far from Atlantic Beach and was trying to make enough money to go to college. He came back to work there every chance he got up until he earned a master's degree in finance and management.

He saved his money, and a few years after working for a large textile company, he purchased the Oceans Inn and made it his flagship resort and conference center. The inn was poorly managed and about to be closed when Justin bought it, thereby saving all of their jobs. He now owned facilities all around the world, and his was among the top travel industry companies. Justin married, but that ended in divorce. Years later, he married the singing sensation Loretta, who actually got her start on the professional stage right there at Oceans Inn. Justin had a daughter, Jessica, from his first marriage. Jessica had a young daughter from an ill-fated relationship.

So, Minnie had friends in high places. They pledged to return and bring their families to meet her. They also invited her to come to Summer County to stay at The Summer House. She agreed and planned to come for Thanksgiving.

Fortified with a scrumptious breakfast, they spent the late morning and early afternoon shopping at the outlet stores in North Myrtle

Beach, an experience Mary Ella made clear she would be happy to avoid. However, she did need more clothes than the few outfits she had in her closet now, particularly as her pregnancy progressed. So, she gave her credit card a workout and found reasonably priced bargains. Jenny and Satarah were in shoppers' heaven, though most of their purchases were for their husbands and children. Still, they bought things for themselves. "Have visa will travel" was their mantra.

Mary Ella and the shopaholics piled their booty into the SUV. They headed for Point of View, the charming tea house and shop owned and operated by Satarah's grandaunt Hannah Ivy Benson and her friend Alma Lewis. The enormous Victorian sat on the shores of the Atlantic Ocean within spitting distance of the water. The three-story house with wide, deep verandas encircling the building provided unobstructed views of the ocean.

Afternoon tea was in full sway, and the ladies were enjoying their patrons' company when Satarah, Mary Ella, and Jenny arrived. The two women, well into their eighties, were quite a pair. They started the business not many years earlier. As spry as women in their fifties with not an ailment in sight, they had active lives and swam at the local YWCA pool every other day without fail.

Whenever Vivian's husband, Dr. Chuck Montgomery, came to Goodwill for the family reunion around the Juneteenth holiday, he would give both women a full physical examination. He called them his Golden Girls, and they giggled like school girls around him. His nearly seven-foot height couldn't be missed in a crowd, and he looked like a young Johnny Depp to boot. He was given to wearing cowboy clothes, boots, and a Stetson hat and could dance the Down N Dirty or Footloose like no one else. He had been a basketball star in his youth long before Gregory went to college, and his career skyrocketed. The ladies thought Chuck to be the cat's meow.

Nothing the shopaholics, Satarah and Jenny, must do but buy several unique blends of teas. While browsing, Mary Ella spotted the cutest child-size tea sets in pretty decorative baskets, one in pink, another in purple, and the last in yellow. She bit her lip in question, but she couldn't resist buying all three as Christmas gifts for Ari, Kate, and Jenny's Emily Rose. It would be a while before the newborn could appreciate it, but, in the interim, it would make a lovely decorative set in her bedroom, which Bob had painted a sunny yellow and white. While she was at it, Mary Ella picked up "just because" gifts for Bernard and Sylvia Alexander, Gregory and Angelique, and Minnie Baker.

CHAPTER 17

The weekend at the shore was a lovely respite, thought Mary Ella. However, now it was Tuesday morning, and work had to be done. Yet, she took a moment to savor the flavor of one of the herbal teas she forced herself to purchase from Grandaunt Hannah Ivy and Grandaunt Alma Lewis' Point of View Tea Salon. Although Hannah Ivy Benson was Satarah's great-grandaunt on her mother's side of their family, she told everyone to call her "aunt" as did Mrs. Lewis, who wasn't related to any of them by blood or love. She was born and raised in Washington, DC, and had lived there all of her life. Her husband and only son were deceased, but she had a grandson, a former Marine, she spoke with every day.

Mary Ella rubbed her abdomen thoughtfully while she considered introducing the "aunts" to Minnie Baker. They were about the same age and would probably get a kick out of each other, especially since Minnie didn't have family in Atlantic Beach. It was good to think her twins, and probably their families, would be there for her when she reached her eighties and beyond.

Well, that was at least fifty years in the future. In the interim, she hopefully had a lot of work to do. She put down her mug and got to it. A little after ten, there was a knock on her open door. When she looked up, a smile bowed her mouth.

"You don't write. You don't call. You don't text. You don't even send up smoke signals. What's a woman expected to think, I wanna know?"

Mary Ella quickly rose from her seat, rounded her desk, and, with arms open wide, engulfed US Supreme Court Justice Vivian Lynn Alexander Montgomery in a strong embrace.

"Believe it or not, they don't even have FedEx in some parts of the world," Mary Ella joked. "Still, it's so good to see you." Mary Ella gave Vivian an extra squeeze before holding her at arms' length.

"The feeling is mutual. You've been away from home for so long, and you were truly missed."

"Thank you, Viv. Is your family with you? I'd love to see them. I hear you have grandchildren, and you're still in your thirties!" Mary Ella led them to a small settee in the corner of the room where they could sit comfortably to talk.

Vivian smiled. "Chuck has a hospital board meeting here this afternoon that he chose to attend in person rather than via conference call or Zoom. So, I blew off a workday and hopped a flight down with him. Our grandsons are absolutely adorable, see?" She showed pictures of them on her smartphone to Mary Ella. "These two are Will and Linda's boys, and these two are Brian and KiLe's boys. This one is Chuck and my youngest son, Turner. KiLe and I delivered on the same day, last year on Christmas Eve. We were in the Pocono's visiting family in Monroe County where Chuck was born and raised."

"Oh, my, they are very handsome, and would you look at Linda? She's gorgeous and very pregnant."

"Yes, Linda and Will love being married. Brian and KiLe love each other to distraction and love having a family. As usual, we'll come for Thanksgiving here in Summer County. You'll be able to see them all then. Our children didn't come with us on this trip. Not that they have a lot of time for their parental units," she joked.

"How many is it now? Thirty, thirty-five?"

Vivian laughed. "More than that, but the number changes daily," she joked. "We added two young boys and one girl to our family. Dr. Evan Michael Cain brought them to our attention. I understand you were one of the first responders."

"Mark and I were in Iraq for a medical conference when the car bomb exploded across the street from where our meeting was being held. We realized the bomb's proximity to our location was no coincidence. There were so many people who were badly injured. We just broke up the conference and went to work literally moments after the blast. Evan dug one boy out of the rubble. His mother shielded him with her body. She didn't make it, and we weren't sure the three children we found in the chaos were going to make it either. I believe if we hadn't been right there, they would have perished, too."

"Well, miracles of all miracles, thank the Creator and the Ancestors, they're alive and getting better." Vivian nodded and smiled. "We're still working on the language barrier. My crew, who Chuck calls his posse, has got game when it comes to making themselves understood. So, they've got these computer apps they're using to communicate and teach each other to speak the different dialects."

"The different languages are the hardest things to overcome." Mary Ella sighed. "I struggled every day to learn to speak and be understood. Thankfully, people understand when you're trying to provide medical assistance to the injured. Mark is an excellent linguist. He only has to listen for a short time to understand what's being said and respond."

Vivian sighed. "I imagine you have to be knowledgeable about the different customs, too. We're working on that along with the language issues."

Mary Ella nodded. "That's true. Mark couldn't examine a woman in certain cultures, so I had to be his eyes and hands while he stood outside a screen. I couldn't go around with my head, face, and arms uncovered in certain countries regardless of the high heat index. Women could not eat in the same circle as men in some cultures. We had to know what was and was not permitted in each and every instance, or we could have caused an international incident of epic proportions."

"That is a part of your training with Doctors Without Borders, I imagine." Vivian frowned. "We decided a case that came before the Supreme Court, where a Muslim family, a man, and his three wives, were subjected to a strip search at an airport. When the man protested the male security guards putting their hands on his wives, he was arrested for having three wives." Vivian shook her head. "The authorities were clearly subjecting the man and his wives to racial profiling. They didn't have any other probable cause to search, detain or arrest the man or his wives. In my opinion, ruling against the Department of Transportation, I strongly suggested that they give their employees training programs to stem the flow of cases against them, which would, no doubt, often arise and end up before us on the Supreme Court."

"Do you think it will help?" Mary Ella asked.

Vivian shrugged. "President Gordon directed the head of the DOT to get busy."

Mary Ella laughed. "It's good to have friends in high places."

"*Ha!* Not me," Vivian scoffed good-naturedly. "I can't be seen to have close personal ties with the Commander-in-Chief of the US military forces when my brother, Benny, is a five-star general and sister-in-law, Stacy, is an Admiral under his direct command. I can't even have a hint of impropriety in the relationship."

"I hadn't thought of that, but you know the President and First Lady, very well, don't you?"

"Yes, extremely well." Vivian nodded. "He was Stacy's commanding officer when she graduated from the Naval Academy in Annapolis, Maryland. However, my association with President and Mrs. Gordon comes through my relationship with one of my Georgetown Law professors, Gustafson Fahey, a former California Senator. He and Clarence Gordon grew up together and are the best of friends. Professor Fahey is my guru when it comes to the law, and he continues to be my mentor. My former housemates, Bill Chandler, Alan Lightfoot, Melissa Charles, David Carter, Gloria Towson, and I were in an advanced group of first-year law students. He was our group's advisor and stuck with us through our graduation. My housemates and I ended up being partners in our own Washington, DC, law firm, Alexander, Carter, Chandler, Charles, Lightfoot, and Towson. Professor Fahey is the reason I'm sitting on the Supreme Court. So, when he issues an edict for my former law partners and me to be at his home for cocktails at six and dinner at seven with the President of the United States of America, we're all front and center no later than five-fifty five." She laughed. "In fact, it was his guidance that helped me and my law partners get information to the Congressional Committee investigating defrauding the government's military budget."

Mary Ella nodded as light dawned. "You spoke with Gregory," she offered as a statement, not a question.

Vivian nodded, too. "I did, yes, apparently after you, Satarah, and Jenny left his home. He's concerned because you're related to J. C. Baker."

"I am, too." Mary Ella nodded. "That same concern led me to do an Internet search on him. What Gregory told us is disturbing, but what I found is staggering. I copied everything and discussed it with Satarah and Jenny. We agreed to share what we found with Ms. Minnie Baker, who Satarah and I discovered is our mutual grandaunt. John Calvin Baker is her nephew. She didn't know anything about his character, but she appreciated receiving the information.

"Is this why you really flew in with Chuck today? You wanted to discuss this connection with Satarah and me?"

Vivian shook her head. "No, I actually wanted to come to see you when Dad and Mom told me you were home. I just didn't make the time. Mom is so thrilled to have you back just in time for her to hire you to step into Jenny's space. Then Gregory told me you and Satarah are expecting and were at the beach for a spa weekend. Then Chuck mentioned this morning, while we were getting ready for breakfast, that he was flying down here today for the board meeting. So, the stars aligned, I blew off a day of work, and *voilé*, here I am."

Mary Ella laughed. "I blow off a few days of work, and it's there when I return. You blow off a day of work, and empires crumble."

Vivian laughed. "I'm fortunate in that I have a legal team of young, eager, and brilliant attorneys who challenge me and prepare opinions in my absence. Chuck is the one whose absence is a life or death situation."

"Yes, you're right. The board meeting today is to evaluate our performance during last week's airplane disaster on the highway. I thought Chuck would have come down sooner."

"Believe me, he wanted to, but the minute he shows up anywhere, the story becomes all about him and his stellar basketball career, his relationship with Derrick, and my marriage first to Derrick and then him. Chuck and I agreed this situation didn't need any distractions. Now that the media coverage has calmed down to a dull roar, the real work can get done. He wants to ensure that the hospital met the challenges and did everything conceivable to save lives."

"I think we did. A great deal of credit goes to your mother for activating her Blue Teens and her Grey Ladies and Gentlemen."

Vivian smiled. "Mom is so proud of both groups. She says they add inestimable value to the work here at the hospital, and they have a sense of pride and accomplishment for their contributions."

"Viv, may I ask you a very personal question?"

Vivian squinted at her suspiciously. "Uh, yeah, but I reserve the right to take the Fifth," she joked. "What is it?"

"What makes it work so well between you and Chuck?"

Vivian laughed. "Why, because he wears cowboy attire all the time, and I'm not a country and western fanatic?"

"The way he wears it is a real turn-on!" Mary Ella joked. "I ask because you're an interracial couple."

"For sure, his attire is a real turn on for me, too, although I don't tell him that. Rather, the glue that holds us together is called love, trust, and respect. It took time for us to build our relationship; too much time that's full of regrets. Especially considering the fact that I married Derrick, Chuck's best friend, after being on the rebound from Carlton."

Mary Ella shook her head. *Wow! Carlton Andrews?* Talk about a blast from the past!"

"So true, but, nevertheless, one of my biggest blunders and regrets. Chuck was the one who helped me through that period of my life. He had feelings for me but was holding off telling me until I was completely over Carlton. I knew I had undefined feelings for Chuck, too, but we didn't do anything about it.

"Derrick didn't have any reservations about wanting to date me. He was everything Carlton wasn't, and I just went with the flow. Chuck and I realized later that we were in love with each other before I fell in love with and then married Derrick. We regretted that we didn't give our attraction to each other voice and just let it go.

"Then Derrick died less than a year after we married, and his death devastated me. When I learned that Chuck knew Derrick had hypertrophic cardiomyopathy, which you know is a serious heart condition, and neither one of them told me, I was so furious with Chuck that I would not speak with him for more than five years. I was inconsolable, but I never took into consideration that Chuck and Derrick were best friends since puberty. He knew Derrick for years before I even met him. What's even worse, Derrick knew how Chuck felt about me, but he also knew that he likely would not live long and that Chuck would be there for me after he was gone. When Chuck and I finally came together and admitted that we were in love with one another, we put away all of the animosity and regrets. That's when the healing process began for both of us.

"The fact that Chuck is my other half really does it for me. He's as eager as I am to help babies and children who have been abandoned and are in desperate need of medical care and a loving home. We jointly decide to bring these babies or children into our home and share with them what we've been so fortunate to have received. The fact that Chuck is white and I'm black is of absolutely no consequence to us. We are not ignorant of some views about our marriage, but we believe that it's not our emotional baggage to carry. We have a rainbow coalition of children in our home who span the distance between the amount of pigment in my skin and the absence of pigment in his.

"Still, that's such a curious question coming from you, Mary Ella. I wonder why you asked. Does your question have something to do with your situation? The last I heard, you and Mark Brooks, who is black, were still an item. Have you developed a relationship with someone other than Mark, who is not black?"

"For now, may I take the Fifth?"

"Of course, but only on the condition that if I can do anything to help, you'll let me know."

"Agreed. Thanks, Viv."

"You're welcome. Do you have time for an early lunch at The Summer House?"

"I do, yes. I'll give Satarah a call and see what's on the menu."

"No need. Chuck called her to let her know he was coming to town and wanted to plant his feet under her table. He dropped me off here so I could see you and then went to the fire department to meet with Douglas before the afternoon meeting. If I can catch a ride with you, Chuck and Douglas will meet us there."

"Works for me." Mary Ella got up to get her purse and keys. "I'm ready."

CHAPTER 18

"I tell you I never saw something that funny! I laughed so hard, I nearly peed my pants." Chuck laughed, his porcelain skin tone pinking more and more by the moment. "Ryan and Roger, our second oldest twins, are pushing the table from one side, and Brian and Vincent are pushing the table from the other, and the table wouldn't move! It was stuck in the middle of the doorjamb and wouldn't budge!" He laughed so hard he had to hold his stomach and wipe his tears at the same time. He could barely catch his breath. "Vivian and I had to sit there with straight faces while our sons tried to figure out how to get the table into the room. Then our six-year-old, Eden Ann, strolls into the room and watches her big, strong brothers trying to muscle the table into a room and then asks, 'what room did we want the table in'? I swear, at that point, I just lost it!"

Those at the lunch table were cracking up as much if not more at Chuck's manner of telling true stories about his and Vivian's children, teens, and young adults.

"They didn't think to ask which room the table was going into?" asked Jenny, between bouts of uncontrollable laughter.

Vivian shook her head while wiping tears from her eyes. "They were at it for forty minutes before Eden Ann came in. She is such a linear thinker that she immediately spotted the problem, asked the question, shook her head, and just strolled away. The boys were so nonplussed they just threw up their hands in frustrated embarrassment and walked away, leaving the table in the doorway. Chuck and I got up to move the table into the other room, but we were still laughing so hard we could barely stand up. That table stayed in the doorway for two solid days before our sons got over their pique at being outsmarted by a six-year-old and moved the table into the right room. We caught it all on video, and they haven't been able to live it down since."

"I tell you, children are funny." Chuck sighed, but he obviously enjoyed his houseful of rumbustious youths by the stories he shared.

"We probably need to get ready to leave for the hospital," suggested Bob.

Chuck looked at his watch. "You're probably right, but first, I want to thank you, Satarah, for feeding us so well. I had a taste for your southern fried chicken the moment I knew I was coming."

"You're welcome, Chuck, anytime. If you're free for dinner, you should come back after the conference is over and have dinner with us."

"I wish we could, Satarah, but Vivian and I have to get back to Maryland by six for dinner. We're taking Dad and Mom with us."

"Is something going on?" Satarah asked.

"Always," joked Vivian. "However, this has to do with our new additions. They suffer from a slight case of separation anxiety when everyone isn't where they're supposed to be. We don't want to put too much stress on them, particularly in these early stages. Dad and Mom have been a tremendous help."

Chuck nodded. "Our posse is doing yeoman's duty helping the children to get acclimated, so we've brought in a full-time tutor and a child psychiatrist of the Muslim faith to help them and us work through these early steps and stages. It's best when we're all there together to help with the process."

"That's a good thing you're doing, Chuck." Mary Ella nodded. "Mark and I encountered so many situations where this type of focused attention could make all the difference."

"It's what comes next and what we believe is necessary. The child psychiatrist is a longtime friend of ours, Ahmed-Sudah Ryheme. Vivian and I met him the same night we met each other during a horrendous blizzard in Washington, DC. I was returning from a ski trip, and Vivian and her family were returning from a Christmas holiday visit with Kenneth in California. We were on the same plane from Chicago to Washington, but we were delayed in Chicago for hours. When we finally got to DC, it was very late at night. Because cabs were scarce, I gave Vivian and Ahmed a ride home in my truck, which I had the foresight to park at the airport. Ahmed had just arrived in America from India to study medicine at Georgetown Medical. I was already doing my residency there. We hit it off and became friends. Later, I introduced him to Derrick, who already had a group medical and pediatric practice in operation. The relationship between Ahmed and Derrick turned out to be a good fit. Ahmed has been with the practice ever since."

"So, we have these group sessions with both the tutor and Ahmed." Vivian smiled. "Tonight happens to be one of them or, believe me, we would stay and return to Maryland tomorrow."

"Primarily because tonight is also our date night," Chuck offered. "I truly love our children, but when there are nearly forty in the household at the same time, Vivian and I make time to escape."

"We do that, too," Bob nodded, "and we only have three."

"You're not alone. With four teenage boys, we have built-in babysitters. Once we put the girls to bed after dinner, baths, and bedtime stories, we're outta here," Douglas joked.

"Okay, stop it! You're scaring me," Mary Ella joked while rubbing her belly.

They all laughed at her eye roll.

Chuck slung a big, beefy arm around her shoulder. "Did I ever tell you about the time Vivian and I..." he continued as they headed out of The Summer House to their cars.

"That was a good meeting." Vivian nodded as she, Chuck, her parents, Bernard and Sylvia Alexander, and Mary Ella stood talking as the conference room began to clear.

"You're right, though, Mary Ella, you could use more trauma nurses," Chuck agreed. "During regular rotation, you're barely covering your patient-to-nurses ratio. I'll circulate your employment notice to the nurses at my hospital in Maryland and at Georgetown Medical Center. Although I'd hate to lose any of them, some may be looking for opportunities for lifestyle changes."

"Thanks, Chuck." Mary Ella smiled. "I've heard about Physicians' Hospital from Evan Michael Cain, and, of course, Georgetown is one of the top hospitals in the country."

Chuck nodded. "Evan and several others are my partners. We created Physicians' Hospital to handle certain types of surgeries, but we're a full-service facility, and we do have trauma nurses. I'll let you know whether I find interested parties."

"Great and safe trip." Mary Ella hugged each one and waved goodbye as they left.

When they were all gone, she returned to the table to gather up her things. The report she worked on so diligently was well received. She was grateful that she had not only the administration's support but also the support of the hospital's board of directors.

"You done good, Mary Ella," a familiar voice came from beside her.

She looked up and smiled. "Hello, Eric, how are you?" She accepted the hug from her former guy friend, Eric Dixon. "I didn't see you in the crowd."

"I'm well, Mary Ella. I came in late and was sitting in the back of the auditorium. I heard your presentation to the Board. Do you have dinner plans? I'd like to make time to catch up."

She shrugged. "No, not really. Generally, I eat at The Summer House with Satarah and Douglas, but if you'd like to do something else, I'm game."

"Great. I understand you're staying in a cottage on the grounds of The Summer House. How about I pick you up, and we'll drive over to Columbia. There's a new Italian restaurant I'd like to try."

"Sounds good. I'm in Unit Two."

It was nearing seven o'clock when Eric and Mary Ella were seated in Solstice Saluda, a five-star rated restaurant in Columbia, South Carolina, the state capitol.

Mary Ella thanked Eric for seating her and then looked around at the charming décor. "This place is fabulous, Eric, but I feel woefully underdressed."

"You couldn't look lovelier than you do right now, Mary Ella. That black dress is saying something. It's talking to me loud and clear! Your pregnancy agrees with you."

"Thank you, Eric. I'll put your check in the mail soon." She joked, laughing. "So, first, tell me, how are your parents and siblings?"

"Leroy and Sandra Miller Dixon are hale and hardy. My sibs, Bishop, Byron, Frank, Rick, Krissy, and Hester are all still single and doing well. My grandfather is as spry as someone half his age, and he's keeping his options open when it comes to the single ladies in Summer County. I'm the first and only one to take the plunge and marry so far."

"I've seen Krissy at Miss Minnie Mae's hair salon, but please tell the rest I said hello, and I send my best."

"I'll do that. They're glad you're home again. So am I. I wanted to give you time to get your feet under you after being away for so long. You were missed."

"Thank you. So, what have you been up to since we were in nursing school together?"

He shrugged. "Well, as you know, once we graduated, and you wouldn't marry me," he joked. "I left in despair, took my broken heart, and joined the Army."

"*Ha!* You're not going to convince me that you left because I turned you down."

He laughed self-deprecatingly. "No, I left primarily to get experience working under different circumstances. I have lived here all of my life. I wanted to see some of the world. Don't get me wrong. I love living in Summer County, but I saw my cousins leave and have adventures before settling down. It's something I wanted to do, too. So, I did. I traveled as a part of the Army medical corps for several years. I met Ginger, my former wife, while I was still in the Army. She's Army, too; an officer. We weren't supposed to fraternize, but one thing led to another, and we had a decision to make. Either she had to leave the military, or I did. Since I wasn't an officer, I left the Army, took the MCATS, and was accepted to train at a few hospitals, but I chose Chicago Med. As you probably know, med school is a costly undertaking. Ginger and I were trying to make it work, but it wasn't happening with her traveling so much and me in med school and working all kinds of crazy hours to pay for the essentials. She agreed and resigned her commission so we could be together. We got married after I was a full-fledged physician.

"I always planned to come home, so I applied for a post at Summer County General, got it, and came back here. I was happy to be home, and I wanted to start a family. Ginger, not so much, but she toughed it out for two years. I couldn't blame her for wanting to leave. She's pure city and couldn't hack it in this much country living. I'm pure country and enjoyed the city, but I didn't want to live there. She went back into the Army, and her commission was reinstated. There were regrets, but no hard feelings. I think we consider each other friends, but we're happier apart than we were together with so many trials and tribulations in our way."

"I'm sorry this happened to you, Eric. You're one of the good guys."

"*C'est la vie.* Such is life."

"*Non, c'est le guerre.* No, such is war."

"You're probably right. It's war instead of life."

"I know it is, Eric. I was with Doctors Without Borders and saw war-ravished countries and villages up close and personal. Wars tear families apart and destroy dreams."

"I never saw combat duty, and neither did Ginger, but I worked with military doctors who were absolutely dedicated and fearless."

"Where were you stationed?"

He laughed. "The question is, where wasn't I deployed. They might parachute me in anywhere. I enjoyed Landstuhl Medical Center in Landstuhl, Germany, and US Naval Hospital, Yokosuka, Japan, the most. Every place else is a blur. Of course, Benny and Stacy are stationed in Tokyo, so we got to spend a lot of downtimes together. I actually met a distant relative of my father's there. His name is Colonel Riley Kennedy, and he's a Marine. His wife is Solange Brody, and they have two sons. You've heard of Matt Kennedy and his brother Tate Kennedy, haven't you?"

"Matt Kennedy, the golden-throat vocal artist extraordinaire? Are you kidding? His voice is what wet dreams are made of." Mary Ella swooned.

"He sounds like that other guy." She animatedly bunched her brows in search of her memory. "You know who I mean, Eric! We used to groove to his music! Blue lights, hot times, getting busy."

Eric laughed and nodded. "Oh, you mean Kem, with the band Kemistry."

She snapped her finger and pointed to him. *"When love calls, when love calls, when love calls your name, baby,"* they harmonized and laughed at the memory.

"Those were the days!" Eric nodded. "Were we ever that young?"

"Dumb and full of?"

"Oh, no, you don't." He laughed with her.

"'Scuzzie, would you and your wife like wine with your dinner?" the waiter asked.

"Uh, no, only for me. My lady is expecting. What's your house red?"

As Eric conversed with the waiter and worked out their dinner order, Mary Ella thought back on the good times she and Eric had together. He was her first lover, and he was so gentle with her. If the stars had aligned, as Vivian said about her regrets involving Derrick and Chuck, she and Eric should have had a life together.

Absently, she rubbed her abdomen. Now she was married to someone else, probably having his or Mark's baby, the man she loved, and reminiscing about the good old days with her first lover.

"I ordered a sparkling cider for you. Is that all right?"

"It is, yes. So, you asked me about Matt and his brother?"

"Yes, his younger brother, Tate Kennedy."

"Why do I remember that name? He came up in conversation recently."

"He's one of the astronauts Benny has flown missions to SPACEHOME with."

"Ah, yes. That's it. Tate Kennedy is married to an attorney, Capri McAllister. Capri and Gregory Alexander used to be an item while he was still balling before he retired, and he and Angelique got together."

Eric nodded. "There are truly only six degrees of separation between people. Capri McAllister's parents, Vincent and Charmaine Miller

McAllister, are military doctors. In fact, they saved my cousin, Riley Kennedy's life, when he had a heart attack. This Capri McAllister and Tate Kennedy marry. How is that for serendipity?"

"Can't beat it with a stick, but I'll do you one better," Mary Ella joked. "While Benny has been the shuttle pilot for SPACEHOME with Capri's husband, astronaut Dr. Tate Kennedy, Florence Johnson, Capri's former administrative assistant, she meets her nephew, Douglas Johnson, for the first time and ends up marrying Douglas' former boss, Duke Patterson and moving to Summer County."

"Okay, okay, you got that." Eric gave her a high five. "There is no way I can top that."

Just then, their meals were served. "Is everything all right with your meal?" Eric momentarily looked into Mary Ella's eyes and lost his heart to her all over again.

"It's perfect," Mary Ella said and thought, *Yes, there would always be regrets that she didn't marry Eric Dixon years ago. If she had, she would have left Summer County with him when he asked her, and she would never have met Mark, fallen for him, and ended up with Doctors Without Borders. She wouldn't be wondering whether she was pregnant with Mark's twins or Kaseem's. She'd be pregnant with Eric's baby, and everything would indeed be perfect.*

Later in the evening, Eric walked with Mary Ella to her door. "This was nice, Eric. Thank you. I had a good time."

"I did, too, and I'd like to do it again."

"Eric, I don't know whether that's a good idea."

"I assume your life is a bit complicated at the moment. Mary Ella, you know what they say about assuming."

"Yes, it makes an ass out of you and me, but here's the thing. We never gave a swift kiddie about what most people said about you and me."

"Exactly. So, I know you're involved with Mark Brooks, and I'm not going to get all up in your Kool-Aid when I don't even know the flavor. Still, I want my friend back, not my lover. We were as close as men and women can be as friends when we were in nursing school together before becoming lovers. That's who I'm looking for, my friend. I'm too raw still over the breakup of my marriage to try to rekindle a love relationship. So, pals?" Eric held out his hand for a shake.

What the hell, why not? she thought. "Pals," Mary Ella agreed, and instead of taking his hand, she tightly hugged him.

He hugged her back and kissed her on her temple. "Good night." He turned, leaving her at her doorstep, and walked away with his hands in his pants pockets.

CHAPTER 19

A few weeks later, Mary Ella hugely yawned as she walked barefoot a few steps from the kitchen bar to the living area sofa carrying a fresh cup of hot herbal tea. She was still wearing the nightclothes she slept in, which, of course, was a change because she usually didn't sleep in anything at all. Mary Ella never could reconcile the notion of getting dressed to go to bed. She didn't know why she didn't just take off her clothes and go back to bed now anyway. She was sleepy, but the "Goodwill Times" crossword puzzle had her stumped on twenty-three down. She had just sat down on the two-seater sofa and put her feet up on a hassock coffee table when someone knocked on her door.

"Come," she called out. "It's open."

"You decent?" Satarah called as she peeped in.

"Usually, but I make no promises," Mary Ella joked.

"Ha! Ha! You've got jokes." Seeing Mary Ella dressed, sitting on the sofa with her long bare legs and feet up on a hassock, Satarah came in and sat across from her cousin on the only other chair in the tiny space. "Was that Eric's car I saw in the parking lot this morning?"

"Probably. He spent the night. What's a word that means like holiday get-togethers?"

"Festive. Eric spent the night?"

"WOW! That's it! I've been trying to figure out that word for the last fifteen minutes. You're not just a pretty face; you've got smarts, too!"

"No, not really. The boys and Doug work the Sunday crossword puzzles all the time. So, the good doctor, Eric Dixon, is showing you his bedside manner, is he?"

Mary Ella hooted a laugh while continuing to work the puzzle. "No, not likely. We went to the Clemson football game yesterday." She yawned absently. "Eric's brother, Bishop, is an assistant coach for Florida State. The game ran late, but we managed to go out to dinner with Bishop and then get him to the airport in time to catch the team's flight back to Florida. By the time we got on the road to come back here, it was pretty late and very foggy. We had to slow down to a crawl because we could barely see six feet of the road ahead of us. We were both tired. It wasn't safe to drive, and it would take Eric another twenty to thirty minutes to get home in that soup. He slept in the spare room, and I slept in my bed…alone. He carries a change of clothes and toiletries in his car. This morning the fog had lifted, so he showered, we had breakfast here, and he went on his merry way. He said he had rounds at the hospital this morning."

Satarah looked suspiciously at her cousin. "You two have been out together several times lately. Are you sure you're not heating up again?"

"We're friends, SaraJo. Nothing more."

"I don't know, Mary Ella. He was pretty bummed out when you wouldn't take him seriously and marry him. Hester says he never really got over you."

"His sister is a dyed-in-the-wool romantic. She's always rooted for Eric and me to marry. According to Eric, Hester and Ginger never got along."

"Well, that's true enough. So, you two are just hanging ten?"

Mary Ella shrugged. "Yes. We're just laid back chillin'. Nothing heavy. He still cares for and about Ginger. He's not over her, and me?" She purposefully looked down at her baby bump. "It's still just me and my potato spuds."

"What are your plans for today?"

"It's Sunday. I don't have to go to the hospital unless I'm called in because something unusual happens, like a 747 landing on I-95. So, I'll probably take a nap."

"It's the first Sunday, Mary Ella. We're going to the Sunday Social. It's being held over in Goodwill this month. I baked a ham shank and a vat of whipped sweet potatoes. Do you want to come with us?"

"No, thanks. Eric asked me whether I wanted to go, but I'd rather not." She continued to work on her puzzle.

"Okay, but you can't stay away from community events forever, Mary Ella. People know you're pregnant and that Mark is still with the NGO."

"I know, SaraJo, but I get questioned about him all the time. Then they give me the *'poor pregnant girl got dumped'* look."

"You could go with Eric and *really* give 'em something to talk about," Satarah teased.

Mary Ella laughed. "Oh, yeah, and have Clarisse Flowers pouting, callin' me everything but a child of God because I wouldn't date her precious Bonner. No thank you very much. Let the tongues wag without me having to hear them."

"Okay, I won't insist, but if you change your mind, let me know."

"Thanks for the invite, but I won't change my mind. When I finish this crossword puzzle, I'll probably take a nap."

"Okay, but invite Eric for Sunday supper next week." Satarah stood up and took the three steps to the door.

Mary Ella's head finally came up and away from her crossword puzzle, frowning at her cousin. *"Wait! What? Why?"*

"See ya!" Satarah smirked, slipping out of the door.

A week later, Eric Dixon grinned from ear to ear. "I really appreciate the invitation to dinner, SaraJo, Douglas." He handed a pretty bouquet of flowers to her and handed to Douglas a two-bottle, gift-set box of vintage wine his family distilled and bottled on their farm.

Satarah grinned and buried her face in the flowers. "You're welcome, Eric. I should have had you over long before this."

"Hi, Dr. Dixon." Donovan hailed as he came into the back door with a load of fresh vegetables from their kitchen garden.

"Donovan, how is it going with the search?"

"It's hard to figure it out."

"You're right. Still, keep at it."

"What's this about?" Mary Ella helped set the dinner table.

"I asked Dr. Dixon about med school in Chicago."

Surprised, Mary Ella frowned curiously. "Oh, I didn't know."

"I've been interviewing the doctors at the hospital about the medical schools they attended. I want to know what it's like to live in different cities, not just how good the school is."

"What have you found so far?"

"Well, I know I don't like cold weather because I used to live in Richmond. Still, some of the best medical schools are in the north, like Boston, or in states that get really, really cold, like Illinois."

"Oh, yeah, it really gets cold there. The winters are brutal," Eric proclaimed. "You can't beat it in the summer, though. There's so much to do when people come out of hibernation. As an alternative, look at Stanford University Medical in Stanford, California, near Palo Alto. It's an excellent school, undergrad, graduate, and their professional schools, including medical. The weather is more temperate."

"That's a good idea. Thanks, Dr. Dixon."

"You're welcome, Donovan. SaraJo, is there something I can do to help?"

"You're fine, Eric. Today you're a guest. Next time you're a grunt." She laughed maniacally.

"I'm good with that as long as there will be a next time," Eric joked. "Your meals are legendary."

"I hear tell you're no slouch in the kitchen yourself."

"Well." He looked at Mary Ella and smiled. "I was inspired."

"I'll say," Douglas commented. "Stuffed pork chops, potatoes au gratin, and green beans amandine? Brotherman, you're putting the men in this county to shame."

"I learned at my dad's knee." Eric laughed. "He still does most of the cooking in our family home. Dad prefers receiving interesting cookbooks for gifts, and he uses them all the time. We never know what he's going to come up with, and unless we demand something specific, he usually doesn't cook the same thing twice. Every day is a new menu from soup to nuts."

Satarah smiled. "I've heard tell of his skills in the kitchen. I didn't know it's a like-father-like-son deal."

"Believe me, when it's two below zero in Chicago, you'd better be able to burn in the kitchen because no one wants to brave The Hawk."

Donovan frowned curiously. "What's The Hawk?"

"The wind," Benson answered.

Mary Ella turned to look at Benson, at the sound of his monotone voice. She'd forgotten he'd lived on the streets of Chicago until Donald and Douglas found him. Suddenly, her thoughts went back to children scavenging on the streets of bombed-out cities, towns, or villages wearing rags and without shoes. Their bodies thin from starvation and malnutrition. She touched her abdomen. It was heart-wrenching to see children dazed and dying because they had nothing to eat or drink for long periods. Her babies would never know that kind of despair or...

"Mary Ella?" Eric noticed she got a faraway look in her eyes sometimes, but until she was more comfortable with him, he wouldn't press for the reason why.

Eric's soothing voice finally penetrated her malaise. "Uh, yes?" She realized she was just standing in the smaller family dining salon staring into near space. She knew what triggered it. It was the comment Benson made about the cold weather in...oh, hell. She was doing it again.

Eric took the silverware from Mary Ella's hands and soothingly rubbed her back. She turned and curled into him, resting her brow on his shoulder. When Eric looked up, he saw Douglas watching them. Eric shook his head. Douglas acknowledged with a nod. He just let her linger, caressing her back while she slowly breathed in and out.

Douglas Johnson is a good man, thought Eric. A month ago, at a Men's Club meeting, when he asked Douglas how Mary Ella was doing, he said she was fine but could probably use all the friends she could get. Eric didn't know what Douglas meant by that at the time until news of Mary Ella's pregnancy began to spread. Unflattering rumors were started, by certain elements in the community, that Mary Ella had been dumped by Mark Brooks when he learned she was pregnant. Eric wanted to come to her immediately but was concerned about stirring up old emotions, memories, and disappointments that she didn't care enough for him to consider marriage in their future.

It was bad enough Ginger was jealous of Mary Ella and accused him of still being in love with her. Well, thinking back on it now, Ginger may have had a point. His relationship with Ginger could very well have been a rebound from losing Mary Ella. The timeframe was about right, and he was primarily just interested in having sex. Ginger pursued him from the beginning, even though, as an officer and him as an enlisted man, she knew their intimate relationship was forbidden. She wasn't in his line of commanding officers, though, and they took their encounters off the military base. She had a cottage far enough away that no one from the base was likely to see them. There was even a two-car garage where he could park out of sight.

Somehow, although the sex was good, he didn't like sneaking around doing something he knew was wrong and against the military code of ethics. That's when he decided they had to make a change or end things between them. Ginger didn't want to give up on their relationship, and he convinced himself that he didn't either. So, when his enlistment period was over, he left the Army. Ultimately, they married, and then later, he suffered through a divorce. It rocked him, but Eric admitted to himself that the demise of his marriage had not hurt as deeply as losing Mary Ella had. He was afraid she could hurt him again, but he was putting his fears aside to stand up as her friend against the vicious rumors. No matter what, he would always and forever be someone she could depend on the way she did when they were teens.

"Don't you ever get tired of coming to my rescue?" she asked jokingly.

"Would you ever get tired of coming to my rescue?" Eric parried.

She looked up at him smiling. "Nope."

"Enough said. Now, let's get this show on the road. I'm starving, and the food smells too good."

Dinner was underway, and the discussion around the table was jovial and often funny, as usual. *Eric fit right in and could tell a joke that had everyone falling over with gales of laughter so intense tears leaked from their eyes,* thought Mary Ella as she tried to recover from his last joke. She remembered that he could have a wicked sense of humor. She looked at the smiling faces around the table, Satarah, Douglas, Donovan, Benson, Jeffrey, Jonathan, Arianna, Katherine, the Sweeney family, and Eric.

Everyone was having such a good time, but she suddenly felt like crying. Here she was having fun, and Mark was still lost somewhere in Asia or Africa. She'd bet he wasn't enjoying a fine meal, good friends and family, fun and frivolity at a Sunday dinner.

She stood suddenly needing to get out of there or she'd start balling like a hysterical child. "Excuse me. I need to powder my nose." She hoped everyone believed her. Bob began telling a joke as she hurried away. Just as she was about to enter the powder room in The Summer House's public area, Miles Logan stopped her, taking her aside.

He frowned and quietly whispered. "Is Ms. SaraJo still at dinner?"

She nodded. "Yes. Why? Is something wrong?"

"Well, not really wrong, but there's a man at the front desk who wants to talk with her. He claims to be related to her, but I know I've never seen him before, and there's just something about him… I just don't know, and she has a strict rule. She doesn't like to be interrupted during her family time."

She did know and patted his arm. "Since you say this is personal and not business, I'll handle it. Don't disturb SaraJo. Just show me who the man is."

They walked back into the lobby of the bed and breakfast. Guests were milling around or coming and going to one of the dining halls or events being held in the salons. Miles led Mary Ella to the Rose Parlor, where a man stood with his back to the door looking at the framed photos on one of the walls. The broad shoulders, feet wide apart, with his hands interlocked behind his back, was a decidedly military stance. He wore a uniform. It was somehow familiar, but she didn't recognize him until she approached. "Hello, Sir. I understand you'd like to speak with…" she faltered when he turned around. John Calvin or JC Baker, as he preferred to be called, stood facing her.

"Well, I hadn't expected to see you here, Mary Ella, isn't it?"

"It is, yes, John. I'm surprised to see you as well."

He thoughtfully looked around before focusing on her again. "Quite an establishment our mutual cousin has here. I looked it up in the travel guide and found it's family property listed on the National Registry of Historic Homes." He looked up and around. "It's been completely restored." He looked around again. "This furniture looks real, too. Like they're antiques or something. Yes, mighty prosperous, indeed. I was just looking at the pictures of what it looked like when it was first built. It was a plantation house. Thirty-five bedrooms? Really?"

Mary Ella slid her hands into her pockets before speaking. "Some of those were servants' quarters on the third floor. I believe there are brochures in the library which include the history of The Summer House. However, the property was passed down through the Benson side of Satarah's family, not the Baker side of which you and I descend."

Baker nodded. "I've seen the genealogy tree about the ownership. It was built on the edge of a swamp."

"Yes," Mary Ella nodded, "it was, but that was eons ago. As you can see from this downriver view, it now sits on a knoll with a view of the Santee River. It's no longer swampland."

"You're a resident here?" Baker asked.

Her chin lifted a tad in pride. "I am, yes, born and raised."

He frowned inquiringly. "You've been away until recently? Something about a doctor's group?"

His question rocked her, why she didn't know. Her chin came up a notch more. "Yes, Doctors Without Borders. It's an NGO."

"*Ha!* That's a crock of bull. Bunch of government spies, if you ask me. Were you a spy, Cousin?"

"What I was and am is a registered nurse!" Her tone was vehemently delivered.

"*Whoa,* I didn't mean to get your dander up." He laughed.

Bored with the discussion, she straightened her back. "Why are you here, John?"

"That's JC to you, Cousin," his tone testy. "I was on my way from trying to see my father's sister in Atlantic Beach. You remember Aunt Minnie, don't you? You see, she comped my suite the last time I was there. That was when I met you and Satarah. Aunt Minnie wasn't available when I got there this time, and I got the distinct impression she was avoiding me. I couldn't convince the McCoy Hotel staff that I'm related to her. They wouldn't comp a suite for me. I was forced to stay at a lesser hotel chain that had availability during this high tourist season and gives military discounts. So, since it's on my way back to Shaw, I thought I'd just stop in Summer County and say hello. I wasn't expecting to find all of this." He waved his hands around, indicating the mansion. "This is quite an establishment. Maybe I can get a comp here for the night."

Mary Ella shrugged. "As you're probably aware, from what the desk manager told you, The Summer House is booked months in advance. It's always at or near capacity."

"That's what the kid said, but surely you can make space for a cousin for the night, can't you?"

Mary Ella shook her head. "I'm afraid not."

"You're just going to turn a cousin out on the streets?" Baker's tone was more belligerent. He stepped into her personal space.

Her chin came up another notch. "There's no room at the inn, JC." She stridently stepped into his personal space. He backed down and smiled through gritted teeth at her.

She felt Eric's hand at her back. "Everything all right here, Mary Ella?"

"All's well, Eric. I'll be back shortly. I just need to show this man to the door."

"Colonel JC Baker." He stepped forward, hand extended to Eric. "You must be the dude who knocked up my pretty cousin. I certainly can't blame you. She's put some nice meat on her bones since we last met."

"You're related to Mary Ella?" Eric ignored the man's hand and then looked at the insignia on his uniform, "Second Lieutenant?"

"Uh, yes, well, uh, you must be in the military. Just a little misunderstanding."

"That's quite a misunderstanding. You claim to be a Colonel in the Air Force, but you're wearing only a Second Lieutenant's bar in an Army uniform. That's a real stretch."

"I, uh, should be going. I'll be leaving Shaw tomorrow, Mary Ella. I'm being redeployed to Guam."

"Safe travels." She smiled but didn't mean it. It didn't surprise her that her and Satarah's talk with Gregory, and his discussion with Benny and Kenneth, may have been the catalyst that landed JC as far away from Washington, DC, and the Pentagon as humanly possible. She sincerely hoped she and Satarah were the facilitators for his redeployment. Whatever the reason, she felt good about it as she watched him strut away.

Eric nodded at Baker's retreating back. "Some character, huh?"

"Yes, but I didn't notice you clearing up his misconception that you're responsible for my current condition." Mary Ella smiled at him suspiciously.

"Didn't I?" Eric asked, an innocent expression on his attractive face.

Mary Ella crossed her arms and raised her left eyebrow. "You certainly did not and, come to think of it, when you took me to dinner that first time, you didn't correct the waiter when he referred to me as your wife."

Eric laconically shrugged. "Must have slipped my mind in my declining years."

Mary Ella's mouth dropped open, and her eyes went wide. "*Declining years?* Bull! You're thirty-two years old, and you have a mind like a steel trap."

Eric grinned and then beguilingly smiled at her. "Thirty-three the night I took you to dinner the first time, but who's counting?"

Mary Ella's mouth formed a perfect O. "Oh, damn it, Eric, you're right! That was your birthday, and you didn't say a word to me about it. Your family always makes a big deal about birthdays. You should have been home celebrating with them."

He shrugged again. "I was exactly where I wanted to be and with my friend."

Mary Ella smiled up at him shaking her head, then put her arms around him, hugging him tightly. "Happy belated birthday, pal-of-mine."

Eric closed his eyes, holding her just as tightly. He kissed the top of her head and just breathed her in. Then he felt one of the babies kick against his lower abdomen and laughed. "Someone is hungry. Let's feed the little tykes."

Mary Ella breathed him in before he released her. He smelled fabulous, like all things right and male. She felt things she missed about being held possessively in a man's arms. Things she remembered about being held in Eric's arms, in Mark's arms, and even in Kaseem's arms. Holding each other around the waist, they wandered back into the private side of the mansion and resumed having dinner with family and friends.

CHAPTER 20

Mary Ella recognized the tears for what they were… hormones. She was prone to cry at the drop of a hat and was not fit to be around. Yet, Eric didn't let her get away with the weepy state she was in. Not even when she claimed it was because of the onions he had her chop that caused it.

"Come here." He took her hands and guided her to the big, wide, farm sink in his huge, open-air kitchen. He flipped on the water without touching it, tested it for temperature, and then held her hands under the tall, goose-neck nozzle. Standing behind her, he cocooned her, holding her hands open with one of his and squeezing juice from a lemon wedge into her palms.

Mary Ella felt him strong and muscular around her, his vertical ridge against her butt cheeks as he squeezed lemon juice into her hands and rubbed them together with his. The scent of onions was immediately eliminated as he washed her hands and his in the sink. He diverted the water, spraying her face as she tensed and quickly turned her head away.

"Oops! Did I get you wet?" Eric's face was all wide-eyed innocence.

She looked up over her shoulder at him narrowing her eyes meanly. "You did that on purpose. See if I'll ever chop onions for you again, pal."

"It was purely accidental," he lied and then did it again, spraying water on her cotton shirt.

She squealed and wiggled against the solid wall of his body but couldn't escape. He was taller than her, and she was laughing too hard to scamper away from him. So, she turned in his arms and tickled him. That got her out of danger. Eric was extremely ticklish.

"It was an accident," he averred, trying desperately not to laugh while backing away from her, his wet palms out in front of him, warding her off.

She looked down at her wet clothes and pulled a mean face at him. "I'm going to get you for this."

Using a dishtowel, he tried halfheartedly to blot the water on her shirt, but he dearly paid when she snatched the towel from him and tossed it in his face. Then she yanked her shirt up over her head and smirked at him.

"If you just wanted to get me naked." Mary Ella smugly wiggled out of her damp shorts. "All you had to do was ask."

Eric's mouth went dry with the sight of a beautifully pregnant and naked Mary Ella. All of that smooth cinnamon-colored skin went begging to be touched. She turned, swaying those luscious, bare hips of hers on long, long legs and bare feet as she went into his combination laundry and mudroom. He heard her put her clothes in the dryer and start it. The mudroom connected to the side exit door, his three-car carport, the screened-enclosed pool, and the back stairs to his home's upper level.

When he heard the music, he figured she found his whole-house iPod system and turned it on.

For long uncomfortable moments, Eric stood rooted to the spot, thinking of her walking naked through his home and into his bedroom above his head. It took time to get his libido and breathing under control. A while later, when she returned to the kitchen area, she was wearing a pair of his loose-fitting, draw-string shorts and an oversized white T-shirt. She obviously found the clothes in his bedroom closet. *Mercy!* Thinking of her in his bedroom was a complete turn-on. What had him as hard as ipe was the knowledge she wasn't wearing undergarments. Her pronounced nipples pressed enticingly against his soft T-shirt. He wanted to put his mouth right there on those beautifully rounded globes! *Jeezuss!* He had to turn back to his pots and pans, or he would have been salivating and showing his excitement in the front of his own loose-fitting shorts.

"Are those canoes I see hanging upside down in your carport ceiling space?" Mary Ella asked.

"They are, yes. Byron, Frank, Rick, and I went in together, and Frank built two of them for us. Sometimes we get Dad to drive us up to the

Catawba River in North Carolina, and we take a few days to canoe back home. We've been up to where the Wateree and the Congaree rivers meet and spent a few days fishing on Lake Marion." Eric continued to cook.

Mary Ella frowned inquiringly. "Have you been to Lake Moultrie?"

"Yes, we have. Up by the Cooper River. When we can make time, we canoe to the Francis Marion National Forest and spend a week or so camping and fishing. If you like, when the river isn't rushing so strong, I'll take you canoeing to Santee Point. It's a nice stretch of the river down near Georgetown and not far from the Pee Dee River."

"I'm a strong swimmer, remember?" Mary Ella averred. "We don't have to wait until the river isn't running as rough."

Eric nodded. "I know you are, but you're also in the second trimester of your pregnancy." He looked over his shoulder at her, his face serious. "I'm not taking any chances with you and the babies."

"I understand, but I'd really like to go to Lake Moultrie," Mary Ella argued. "My dad used to take me there after Mama died, just the two of us, to go fishing."

"That's doable." Eric nodded as they continued to talk. "Maybe we'll get a chance one weekend before the weather cools off, and we can camp for a few nights?"

"I don't mind camping in cooler weather." Mary Ella shrugged. "When I was with Doctors Without Borders, we camped most of the time and in all kinds of weather. We usually didn't even have tents. Some of the villages were in the upper ranges of the hills and mountains above the frost-line."

This is important to her, Eric realized and acquiesced somewhat. "As long as I can ensure that you and your potato spuds are warm enough, we'll make plans to go camp and canoe at Lake Moultrie. Tell me more about the places you've seen."

Mary Ella sat on one of six stools at the massive quartz-top island in the center of his kitchen space while they talked. The island was so large it deserved its own zip code. She told as much as she could about her exploits, but not everything. Eric was a good listener and asked pertinent questions about not only the places she'd seen but also about the people she'd met. For a while, they listened to and sang along with the music from his whole-house iPod system while the kitchen air filled with the most enticing, mouth-watering scents.

While they talked, Mary Ella thought about his bedroom suite and could imagine him there. It was a dream come true, and the en-suite luxury personified. It was a man's enclave with a leather headboard and highboy, king-sized bed, and was exceptionally well done. He wasn't ruthlessly neat. A pair of flip-flops haphazardly lay on the hardwood floor by the foot of his bed. She desperately wanted to crawl into his massive bed naked and take a nap.

She could put two of the cottages the size she lived in inside his closet and still have room to spare. While sniffing his colognes, she found her favorite scent, the one she liked best on him. He had a reading area with books stacked on an adjacent table. Some were medical books and magazines as would be expected of a doctor who kept current with medical advances, but others were not. *Fifty Shades of Grey? Outlander?* What? He even had a copy of Adelaide Jackson's newest release in her Fireside Romance series. Okay, she could get with that. Intrigued and more than a little curious, she had rummaged through his orderly, tall chest of drawers until she found something to wear while her clothes dried.

He didn't have much in what appeared to be a hand-crafted cabinet-top, jewelry chest, a few watches, a high school ring, his college ring, his dog tags, and what looked like his wedding ring. What stopped her was the blue velvet box, which contained the engagement ring he offered her when he asked her to marry him. She took it out and looked at the inscription. *MEB forever ELD*. It was made of titanium. She looked at it for a while before putting it back and closing the cabinet.

When she returned to the kitchen, she watched him for a while chop vegetables like a Ginsu Master. Then turning, she looked at the large swimming pool, which was just an extension of his kitchen space. The glass walls rolled up to the ceiling above the pool as if they were garage doors. No other walls separated it from the rest of the kitchen, family room, and informal dining space. There was also a powder room connected to the family room. It was a seamless transition from the outside to the inside. A nearly invisible screened area encompassed the pool deck, flowers, and kitchen garden in the raised planters.

Beyond the screen was a generous expanse of thick, healthy, weed-free green zoysia lawn that led to the sandy shores of the Santee River. No homes could be seen on the opposite shore making it appear they were isolated. However, his family members lived in close proximity to what was known in the county as the Dixon family compound. It reminded her of the farmhouse where she grew up further up the river outside of the Dixon family's land.

"You know, Eric, this place reminds me of my old home." Mary Ella absently still looked out at the flow of the river.

"Does it?" He sautéed onions, chopped green, red, orange, and yellow peppers, and minced garlic in olive oil, then added sweet, Italian sausage to the mixture. He hadn't thought of it before, but his house actually did resemble her former home except for the absence of the entire, lower-level, back wall of his house.

When he started planning the design before returning to Summer County, bringing Ginger with him, this was the layout that was stuck in his head. He tweaked it here or there, but it was essentially the same. Instead of the single, unadorned front door, her farmhouse had, his home had a double-wide, wrought-iron and glass front door with glass and wood-framed, full-height, full-view sidelights and a tall transom window above it all. It faced the north and allowed for the greatest amount of light to enter the front and vestibule of his home. There was a skylight at the top of the stairwell, which illuminated the entrance bringing more light inside.

The formal living room had a big box bay window and was to the right of the entry. It led to his home office and library. The formal dining room, to the left of the entrance, had an identical box bay window. The dining room's rear led into a generous butler's pantry, which opened into the kitchen space.

Now that he thought about it, it was precisely the way hers was arranged. Straight ahead from the front door through the vestibule and wide hallway, which paralleled the open main staircase to the upper level, was the expansive view of the pool, the lawn, and the river beyond. In Mary Ella's house, the back was a family-sized, eat-in kitchen that always felt warm and inviting when they were growing up, and her parents were still alive. He guessed he must have been trying to duplicate that feeling in his own home, the type of emotion he felt in her home, and the home of his own parents.

The master bedroom was upstairs in the center rear of the house with sweeping, accordion glass walls across the back leading to a veranda which overlooked the swimming pool below. Frank wanted to install a sliding board from the upper veranda, which would curve and empty directly into the pool. Eric firmly vetoed his brother's idea without a second thought. However, he enjoyed coffee in the early morning on the veranda with the view of the Santee River for miles in both directions. When the sun rose, it made the river look silvery as it rushed by. It was astounding to think that the river had been flowing like that for eons. He got to enjoy it in his generation as many had before him during ages past.

Four additional bedrooms, two on each side of the master with Jack and Jill, shared, four-piece baths completed his home's second level. There were only three bedrooms in her house, including the master and only two, three-piece baths, not five beds, and three-and-a-half baths. So that was different as well. Yet, she was right. There were substantial similarities between his home and the one she used to own. The only real difference was the size, his being much larger and more modern. After her parents died, he spent a lot of time there at her home with her and wondered whether that had influenced his design. *Did he actually design the house with Mary Ella in mind and not Ginger? Could Ginger have been right? Was he unknowingly still in love with Mary Ella?*

"You had this built?" Mary Ella looked toward him.

Her question brought him out of his quandary. "Yes, Frank and his crew built it."

"He's a civil engineer, isn't he?"

"He is, yes."

"Did he come up with the design, too?"

"Uh, no. I came up with the plan as a wedding surprise for my former wife."

Mary Ella turned around to look at him critically, but he quickly turned back to his six-burner gas range. "I can't imagine her not loving it here. This is a perfect spot."

"Actually, she hated it on sight. It's a farmhouse, although it is not on a farm and has all the modern conveniences."

"You're kidding, right? She actually hated it?" Mary Ella was astounded.

Eric turned around, shrugged his muscular shoulders, and wiped his hands on the dishtowel he had tucked into the waistband of his shorts. "Nope, no joke. She played it off during the party I arranged to welcome her to the community and to meet my family and friends, but when we were alone, she let me know this house, this community, would never do."

"Wait! What? Are you telling me she didn't meet your family until *after* you married?"

"Well." Eric hedged. "We never found the time to come home for visits. She missed the rhythm of the city, even the noise at night. The crickets, owls, and other night creatures didn't do it for her."

"I really don't understand that at all." Mary Ella shook her head and looked out toward the scenic river again.

Eric poured a small amount of olive oil into the rapidly boiling water before dumping in the linguini. Then he briskly shook the pan with the vegetables and sausages to blend the juices with a cup of red wine. The steam billowed up and made him smile when Mary Ella moaned.

"That smells like heaven." Mary Ella came to stand beside him at the range to watch him cook and inhaled deeply.

Eric carefully added the freshly diced tomatoes to the mixture and shook the pan again, expertly flipping the ingredients so that they folded perfectly into themselves without bruising the tomatoes. He had his home-made marinara sauce warming in another pot. "This is almost ready. It needs about ten more minutes, and then we can eat."

Just then, an old Anita Baker song, ***"Giving You the Best That I Got,"*** came out of the strategically placed speakers. They looked at each other and laughed. That used to be their song back in the day. It actually won gold back in their grandparents' days, but they heard it, and Anita Baker's music played so often around their homes that it became their anthem.

Eric turned down the flame to let the food simmer and then took Mary Ella into his arms, coaxing her into a dance. She went easily into his arms, moving together with him as if no time passed separating them. They were mindful of their close proximity to the swimming pool as they sang the lyrics to the song, the words familiar, reciting them as their former pledge of allegiance to one another.

"We love so strong and so unselfishly
And I made a vow, so I tell you now
I'm giving you the best that I got, baby."

They didn't let go immediately when the final strains of the music ended.

"Oh, Eric," Mary Ella moaned into his chest as he held her. "What have we done with our lives since we were that young and in nursing school together?"

He held her tightly. "Nothing to be ashamed of or to regret, Mary Ella. Nothing that can't be made right. I'm here for you, and I know you're here for me. Beyond the physical lovemaking, we made a vow of lasting friendship. I'll listen for as long as you want to talk. We don't have to do anything or go anywhere. We can stay here and talk or not say a word and just be."

She squeezed him again before she let him go. He returned to his pots and pans. She leaned her back against a countertop and watched him as he took an oblong-shaped bowl from an open shelf and placed it in the microwave for a minute to warm. Then, taking the bowl out with an oven mitt, he poured drained linguini into it and topped it with the sausage and vegetable mixture.

"This is beautiful." Mary Ella enthused.

"How about getting the salad from the refrigerator and the garlic bread smells like it's ready to come out of the oven, please. I need to add the marinara sauce, the cheese, and chopped parsley. Then we'll be all set."

He carried the steaming hot bowl to the informal dining table, where the dishes were already arranged for two. After pouring wine into his goblet and sparkling cider into hers, he lit the candles and sat waiting until Mary Ella came to the table with the bread and salad. The lights, for inside and around his pool, were automatically coming up as the evening approached. He used a remote to douse the kitchen task lights, leaving the under-counter and ambient lights on as they sat in the evening's semi-glow.

After they blessed the meal, Eric waited while Mary Ella tasted her food. Her pretty brown eyes widened in pleasure, and she moaned as if she were deep in the throes of an orgasm.

"So, you say you found this Ginger person in an insane asylum? Did insanity run in her entire family?" Mary Ella looked up at him from under her eyelashes.

Eric laughed and toasted Mary Ella with his wine. "Are you saying she had to be insane to marry me?"

"No, quite the contrary. Remember, I know firsthand what you're working with, pal. You were an extraordinary lover at nineteen. Added to that, now you also know what you're doing in a kitchen. So, she had to be bat-shit crazy to walk away from this." Mary Ella held up a fork full of food.

He laughed at her antics. "Hey, you walked away, too, remember," Eric joked.

"You knew what to do between the sheets, pal, but you sure couldn't cook like this when we were teens," Mary Ella teased back.

It warmed his heart that she enjoyed his cooking. After all, that's how his grandfather snagged his grandmother and how his father seduced his mother. Maybe, just maybe, the magic would work a third time and be a charm for him and Mary Ella.

An hour later, the dishwasher was going at a pretty good clip. Mary Ella insisted on cleaning up the kitchen by herself and putting what little remained away in the refrigerator. Intermittently, they danced to music from their era and before. She was doing a passable rump shake to Bruno Mars' **Uptown Funk** as she hung the clean pots and pans she hand-washed among the ones hanging from the ceiling on hooks in his butler's pantry. On the other wall, she noticed he had a well-stocked group of dry goods and seasonings. There were all kinds of jams, jellies, and preserves, some, like watermelon rind, she'd never tasted before. The man was ready for any eventuality. She shook her head. Ginger really must have been off-the-chain insane.

Mary Ella turned out the task lights and moved toward the lighted pool looking down into the water. "What's that in the water?" She pointed toward the deep end of the pool.

Eric walked to the edge of the pool and looked down. "What's what…" he began and realized too late what Mary Ella was about. He surfaced, treaded water, and regarded her standing there on the pool deck provocatively posed with one hand on her impressive hip examining the nails of her other hand.

"Nice form with that dive, pal. Did you figure out what was in the pool?" She sauntered to the other end of the pool, where she removed his T-shirt and shorts before walking naked into the water. She swam toward him and, when she was close enough, dunked him and laughed like a loon.

He could have drowned, taking off his clothes underwater, tossing them on the kitchen floor. "Hey, if you just wanted to see me naked, babe, all you had to do was ask." Eric grinned and swam after her to the other end. They swam for a while back and forth, getting in a good workout after a heavy meal. When they tired, he pulled inflated rafts into the water. They climbed aboard and drifted while listening to the music play.

"Thank you, Eric. This has been wonderful. Just what I needed to solve the weepy state I'm experiencing. You're a perfect friend."

"You're welcome, Mary Ella. Any time you want to come for dinner, weep over the onions, and have a naked swim, you don't even need to call me. Just come on by."

"I want to sleep in your bed tonight, but would you understand if all I want to do is sleep?"

Eric chuckled. "I would, yes, and you're welcome to do so. I have four other bedroom suites to choose from."

They drifted a while longer before Mary Ella sighed. "You know, I really want to make love with you right now, but I can't."

"I know. You have issues to solve involving Mark Brooks, but when you do solve them, I need to make love with you again, too. For now, don't let what you want and what I need complicate matters for you. We're okay, Mary Ella. Whether it works out for you and Mark or not, I'm not going anywhere. I'll always be here for you."

"I know."

CHAPTER 21

"Is that him? Is it Mark Brooks?" the questioner whispered. "I need to get down closer to the camp. I can't see from this vantage point so far up in the mountain, and the drones would be spotted and shot down in this light. That would expose our position."

"We need Explorer One's tactical operatives again. How soon do you think we can get them in country?"

"I'll run it up the flagpole with HQ." He preceded to do just that. "Yankee Bravo One Two, One Two. How do you read?" he asked and then waited for a return signal. "It would be better if we can verify that's him," he suggested while waiting.

Hey! Look! I believe that's Imad Mohammed Azul coming in from the north on horseback. I count ten, no, twenty plus tangos," said another, who excitedly joined the discussion.

"I've got eyes on him and them."

"Watch the sun! If it reflects off the glass, we'll be FUBAR!"

"Copy that, Master Chief." They couldn't move around in these mountains or they could shake loose some gravel. Although they were up in crevices, someone would surely come to investigate a landslide, so they had to remain vigilant and as still as possible. The sun was going down, but they needed to keep track of who was coming and going from the camp full of tangos. Something big was happening, and they needed to know what it was. They also needed to verify whether Dr. Mark Brooks was with them. If so, this could be the first verifiable sighting of him in months.

"Damn! Look who else is coming to the party!" Another voice added excitedly.

Everyone turned to look through spyglasses over the boulders they were hidden behind.

"That's Atif Mustafa Salim!"

"Should we be offended we weren't invited to the party?" someone sarcastically asked.

"Get down! Get down! Helos incoming!"

They ducked for cover, their light-colored clothes shielding them and blending into the color of the rocks just as two helicopters flew in right over their heads. Two more followed, all landing near the camp and sending up a blizzard of dust and sand. As the men in the mountains watched and the dust settled, two men got out of the first helicopter and approached a group of about two hundred terrorists. They wore traditional desert clothing and exchanged typical Arab greetings with the perfunctory three kisses on the cheek before going into one of the tents.

"That looks like Sheikh Al Ghalbi and one of his sons, Prince Abdullah Ali Al Junaibi. What would they be doing here?"

"Intel says that the sheikh sometimes acts as a go-between for certain factions."

"Break radio silence, again. Speak Navajo," the order was given. "We need Explorer One on the horn… now!"

Moments later, a voice came in over the satphone. "Yankee Bravo One Two, One Two. You've got Helen of Troy via the Navajo Princess. Sitrep!"

"Requested Explorer One."

"You've got Explorer Number Two, and that's all you're going to get unless or until I get a sitrep!"

The caller sighed but responded as directed. "Multiple high-target tangos at this DZ. Four helos on-site with marking as follows." He described the markings on the sides of the helicopters. "Negative chance on a photo op. Eyeball only, Sheikh Al Ghalbi and one of his sons, believed to be Prince Abdullah Ali Al Junaibi."

Thousands of miles away to the east on remote islands in the Archipelagos, databases ramped up, cataloging the inputted information. Red alerts called into action specialized covert operators, and mobilization began. Within moments, bat-winged supersonic jets lifted off, heading east. In Tokyo, a specialized phone chirped three signals in rapid succession. A naked woman straddling a naked man, who was buried balls deep inside her, cursed like a sailor but rode the man to their cataclysmic mutual completion before acknowledging the red alert signal.

There were kisses, a quick joint shower, and frustrated goodbyes. "Saddle up, we ride," a voice commanded into the specialized phone with a face mic before crawling into a waiting military car. The passenger issued orders while being whisked to the Air Force base, where a supersonic jet was being fueled. Shortly thereafter, the craft was airborne at speeds approaching Mach 3, headed for a nuclear-powered aircraft carrier in the Mediterranean Sea. In less than twelve hours, six bat-winged, stealth jetcopters were taking on fully-armed, black-clad Ninjas.

Back in the hills above the campsite, the terrorist posted guards at the lower level in the hill, unaware that a contingent team of crack counter-terrorists was literally sitting above them in the mountains, watching every move they made and what was happening in the camp. When nightfall came, the spies could fly one of their smaller drones down closer to the man they believed to be Dr. Brooks. The terrorists had him tethered to a stake and guarded. He had a beard, and his hair was long and dirty, but he still fit Dr. Mark Brooks' description. It was eerie, but he seemed to be looking directly into the camera lens of the drone, the size of a hummingbird, and blinking his eyes.

"*Fuck me!* That's Morse Code! He's blinking in Morse Code! Wait! Let me read that back. '*Bomb the shit out of this place now!*' He knows we're here. He has to know we're here, but he wants us to bomb the camp? He's not trying to be rescued? What the fuck?"

"I have a bad feeling about this. We gotta get him outta there to find out what's going on. Do we have C4?"

"That's affirmative, but not enough to take out the whole camp. *Wait!* They're coming out of the tent."

The spies watched as rows of women strung together on long ropes, about thirty, each, were pulled kicking, crying, and screaming from the tent toward three of the helicopters, shoved on board, and tied down. An obviously heavy trunk was brought out of the first helicopter and carried by four men to the feet of the target terrorists. When the trunk was opened, the gleam of gold bullion was evident even in campfires' reduced light. It was tested and apparently found to be real. Two men, believed to be the sheikh and the prince, left the camp, boarding the first helicopter. All four lifted off and flew away. The remaining terrorists seemed to be bedding down for the rest of the night. Dr. Brooks sat with his head on his upraised knees. No more signals coming from him.

It was 0200 when a huff of air alerted the guards, and they woke the rest of the spies. They grabbed their weapons, ready to fire, until a decidedly female voice sounded, "Explorer One on board. You rang?"

Everyone relaxed as the familiar Ninja-clad figures infiltrated the group.

"You're a little late to the party, Explorer One. Four helos departed hours ago, three carrying a cargo of female captives."

"That's Thing One. We're tracking the helos and prepared to separate the women from their slavers as soon as they land." She looked at the watch on her wrist. "That's happening about now in three different countries."

"Copy that! We've got tango guards spaced along the ridge at six o'clock."

"That's Thing Two," offered another Ninja entering the group and holstering a bloody K-bar knife. "Guards neutralized. HOT, here on board."

"Helen of Troy?"

"How good of you to remember," she offered, wryly, but her face and hair were completely covered, as were all of the other Ninjas so that the faces couldn't be seen.

"Cammie up with your night visions," Explorer One ordered.

They looked otherworldly wearing night-vision goggles, but they got to work like a well-oiled machine. They used hand signals as they activated drones and sent them flying at a dangerously low level over the terrorists' camp and even into the tents. With the night vision glasses, the drones and fluorescent hand signals could be clearly seen in the now moonless dark. As they watched, anyone standing seemed to melt onto the sand until there was no one standing. Not even the pack animals or horses remained upright.

"What happened? They seemed to be neutralized."

"They were. We don't have time to go *mano a mano* or have a firefight. We used scopolamine. You may know it by its other name, The Devil's Breath. We use it to get the mission completed faster. Otherwise, it could be a real Charlie Foxtrot."

"The Devil's Breath? I've never heard of it."

"It's one of the tools in our tool belt, which, when sprayed in the air by our drones, eliminates a target's free will and can wipe the memory of its victims. It's a drug derived from a particular type of tree common to South America. If I tell you more, I'll have to kill you.

"For now, we need to double-time it before dawn and get the hell out of Dodge. Otherwise, we won't have any cover. Our transport is stealth capable, but it's not invisible to the naked eye… yet."

"You Grey Ops people are scary, but you have hot toys."

"Better living through technology." HOT nodded. "Now get the lead out. We're on the clock."

As they made their way down the mountain in the dark, the Ninjas led the way.

Then out of the darkness surrounding the camp came what looked like an army of skeletal-like, florescent Ninjas systematically swarming over the downed terrorists. Only the skeletal forms could be seen clearly through the night-vision glasses like some crazy, laser-light show. They took away the high-value targets, anyone of note, and cataloged all of the others with a photo, fingerprints, and mouth swabs for DNA. Finally, the tangos were tagged with an X on the back of the neck and the forehead and a dot on the tip of the nose.

"What's that they're doing now?" one of the counter-terrorists' spy team members asked, watching the process with AK 47 armed and at the ready.

"Watch." Explorer One showed an iPad that lit up with Xs in a green glow on everyone tagged.

"*Whoa!* What the hell?"

"It's an oil that stays on the skin like tattoo ink. It won't wash off, and it can only be seen through a certain light prism. Our night Vs' lenses are equipped with the refractors and can follow them anywhere in the world. Even without the night Vs, we can trace them. If they try to board a plane or ship, security will pick up the glow, and they'll be tracked or arrested." She shut down the iPad and stored it in a zipper pocket of her lite-weight Kevlar uniform.

"We're all hands, Explorer One. Forced Recon, complete," HOT reported.

"All right, gentlemen, we got what we came for. We're ready to exfiltrate. If you want to catch a ride to your AO, you need to raise your left hand high in the air and hold on to the rope."

"What rope?" One asked, just as it dropped like a spider into his face. He jumped back and looked up at the silent, bat-winged craft hovering overhead. He never heard it coming.

They each grabbed hold of a rope and were quickly hauled up and onboard the two jetcopters. As they were making their ascent, the other Ninjas were climbing aboard similar jet-copters that had silently settled on the sand and were preparing to lift off. Dr. Brooks was among the first loaded and immediately taken away at warp speed. Though the target terrorists were still asleep, victims of the Devil's Breath, without a fight, they were bound and gagged as if they were Hannibal Lecter in *Silence of the Lambs*. When they were all secure, the transports stole away without a sound at Mach 2 before the dawn creased the night sky.

Mark Brooks woke briefly and uttered two words, "Mary Ella."

Twenty-six hours later, the covers were pulled from the sleeping body. Kisses rained down on thick, muscular thighs, homage paid to the midsection all the way up the well-toned torso to a waiting mouth. "Now, where were we? Oh, yes, I remember now," the voice whispered, and, secured in place, the bodies fit like a hand in a very tight glove.

CHAPTER 22

He thought of nothing and no one else except Mary Ella. He had put her life in danger when she should have been safe and sound in peaceful Summer County, South Carolina. Still, she readily followed him and the band of doctors, nurses, and other medical professionals wherever they were needed or wherever they were sent. Every day since she was taken from him, he feared she'd been brutalized and killed. He couldn't let himself imagine losing her. Yet, women were ravished and killed when they outlived their usefulness or couldn't keep up with the frantic pace they were forced to endure with little or no food or water.

Mary Ella was physically and mentally strong. He had to remember that. She was also smart and resourceful. He prayed she'd use all of her wits and skills to survive and persevere. Mark thought he would go mad when he thought of her the last time he saw her. She violently struggled to get to him to keep him from being beaten without a care for her own safety. She pleaded with him not to fight them; she would be all right if he would just stop fighting. He couldn't do it. It took four men to hold him down while he tried to keep his eyes on hers. Then everything faded to black, and he thought he could still hear her cries.

When he woke, it was daylight, and he was in a cave where other men were. With little regard for women they ravished, the men kept up the torture. He looked from woman to woman, but none was his Mary Ella. None was his Allison. He was raging with fever from the untreated, infected wounds, and not coherent more than half the time. Delirious, he called out to Mary Ella, but Allison's face repeatedly appeared in his visions.

To remain sane, he touched the raised, puckered skin of the Marine medical insignia he had branded on his upper left arm and the Phi Beta Kappa insignia branded on his upper right arm. They stood furrowed and proud in his skin. That was enough to bring him back to his right state of mind and prompt himself to know who he was.

The captive women tended to him until his fever broke. He had tried to help them in return by giving them what little rations he was allowed. However, it usually only resulted in him and the women being severely beaten again and again. Women were killed as an example to him that to help the women would mean certain death for them. In his weakened state, he could not survive much more. Still, he had the will to live, the will to find Mary Ella, and get her to safety.

He was being kept alive to serve the medical needs of the terrorists. He was honor-bound to adhere to the Hippocratic Oath he had taken and suppress his desire to withhold medical aid to the terrorists. They were not his enemies; disease and illness were. He had to bargain to keep alive those battered in the villages that were overrun. If he refused to help the terrorists, the villagers would be lined up and summarily shot. For the most part, they were the older people who couldn't escape fast enough in advance of the terrorists descending upon them. That didn't stop the beatings, but they didn't waste bullets on the elderly. They had machetes for that. Those who were more firm managed to escape into the hills, leaving their goods and animals behind, and were hard to find when the marauders overran the villages. The animals were slaughtered and eaten by the marauders, moving from village to village. They took anything that could be used, and the villages were burned to the ground.

The terrorists spoke openly around him, unaware that he understood their languages and dialects. He pretended not to understand when he was directed to do something. Few spoke English, but some who did were used as interpreters and were charged continuously with guarding him. Mark didn't know how he knew, but he believed he would be rescued. He was a Marine, and they never left another Marine behind, but he feared for Mary Ella. She didn't speak the language well and wouldn't know what to expect. He just prayed she was still alive and would be found and rescued.

He recalled that the best day of his life was when his friend and fellow Marine, Douglas Johnson, asked him to come to some place called Goodwill, Summer County, South Carolina, to help train a fledgling fire department to stand up its medical corps. The first day he was in this place he never heard of before, there she was, this tall, shapely, gorgeous, smart, take-charge, registered nurse, Mary Ella Baker. They took one look at each other and were lovers the following week.

He had done her a real disservice. She was open and honest with him, but she never questioned him as some women would want to do after years invested in a relationship, and it had been years. He loved her spirit and her genuine goodness. She was a beacon of light in a storm, and when he met her for the first time, he was in the midst of a dark, depressive maelstrom. Still, she appealed to his better angels and helped him reconnect with society and life.

She didn't ask for anything except honesty and respect. She didn't play games but told him what she wanted from him. No push. No pull. No bull. He readily gave it up often and continuously. He stayed in Summer County for as long as possible, but he wanted to get back to his mission with the NGO, DWB. However, he couldn't stand the thought of leaving Mary Ella behind. When he asked her to go with him to join the organization, she agreed, and his life got a little brighter.

They were a team from the very beginning. They could anticipate each other's needs, whether in the operating theatre or between the sheets. She filled every crack and crevice of his soul, yet he never shared with her who he really was and where he came from. He didn't want that ugliness to taint what they had. She took him at face value.

He thought she or their relationship would change over time, but she never did. They became just that much more cemented together, first as respected friends and then as faithful lovers. He didn't look at or need anyone else but her, and she seemed to feel the same for him. He never felt he had to question her loyalty to him, and he never gave her a reason to doubt his devotion to her. Still, he harbored secrets and deep regrets he failed to share with her. Over time, he convinced himself that it wouldn't matter. She wasn't the type of woman who was impressed with wealth or position. She subscribed to the theory that people put on their big boy or big girl pants the same way; either one leg at a time or both at once.

She was a refreshing bit of sunshine he never knew existed or ever expected to find. Before her, he lived his life by a code not wholly of his own making. Women were respected for their intelligence, but beyond a good conversation, he just wanted to get laid. Life was so much more with Mary Ella. He needed to find her to make his world live again.

"Dr. Brooks? Wake up, Dr. Brooks," a woman's voice entreated him.

"Mary Ella?" he croaked, his mouth dry.

"No, Sir. I'm Dr. Melody Jenkins. You're on an aircraft carrier in the Mediterranean Sea. Would you tell me your full name and where you were born?"

"Mary Ella? Where is Mary Ella? You have to find her." He tried to sit up but was forced back down again. "I need to find Mary Ella."

"He's still feverish. I'm afraid I'm going to have to sedate him again for a few more days. You'll have to wait to question him."

"Look, Doc, we don't have a few more days. He may be in possession of critical information."

"Then I suggest you find whoever this Mary Ella is or he's not going to respond to your questions. That's who he's been asking for since he arrived. Frankly, the fact that he's alive and able to function is a minor miracle. He's suffering from malnutrition, dehydration, starvation, exhaustion, untreated wounds, vicious beatings, hairline fractures to both legs, and fighting to stay alive because of this Mary Ella. He's delirious with fatigue and fever. I can and will treat his body, but his mind is an entirely different matter. I understand your task is dependent on him telling you what he knows, but you'll have to find Mary Ella or wait until he's better able to respond.

"Happy birthday, happy birthday, happy birthday to you," they sang enthusiastically.

Benson grinned from ear to ear as he looked around at all the people gathered to celebrate his sixteenth birthday, particularly the pretty girls from his school, Summer County Academy, and Stephney Montgomery, his cousin, sort of. He'd have to ask his mother to explain how he and Stephney were related. Benson knew she was Cousins Chuck and Vivian's daughter, but he didn't know whether she was his cousin by blood or by love, as his mama usually said.

His mama also told him that he had to be careful who he dated because he was related to so many people in the county. Now that he was officially sixteen, his parents agreed that he could date. Many of the girls he knew at the academy were related by blood to his family. However, so many of Chuck and Vivian's family were adopted. He knew that for sure. He just had to find out whether Stephney Montgomery and her twin brother Stanley were.

When the singing died down to applause, Benson gave his speech about how it felt to be turning sixteen and how happy he was to be right where he was with his parents, Douglas and Satarah, and his siblings Donovan, Jeffrey, Jonathan, Arianna, and Katherine. His Grandmother Mariah came all the way from Paris, France, to be there, he noted, and so many came from far and wide. The ballroom of The Summer House was used for the celebration, and although it wasn't bursting at the seams, he was happy with all of the faces he cared about and the ones he had come to love since Douglas brought him home to his mother.

While people were up on the dance floor and the music played, Mary Ella stepped out on the front veranda to catch a breath of fresh air. It would be Fall in a month or so, she realized, and the temperature was already noticeably cooler in the mornings. She'd stayed at Eric's house again last night. He cooked dinner, she cleaned up, they played chess, and as was their habit when it got too late and the night was foggy, she crawled into his bed and went to sleep rather than drive to her cottage. He slept in one of the other bedrooms.

Today, they woke early enough to swim before breakfast, which she cooked. Eric heated the pool some because there was a chill in the air, and the water had cooled overnight. They dressed, and he left for the hospital while she went to her cottage in time to help Satarah and Douglas start preparations for Benson's sixteenth birthday party.

Since the party was an unqualified success, Mary Ella sat in one of the rocking chairs on the deep and wide front porch veranda and rubbed her motion-filled tummy. This was the first break she'd had so far today. Douglas, Satarah, and their family spared no expense to make this a memorable event for Benson. He even got a new car, well new to him, from JoJeff's dealership, which surprise, surprise, JoJeff gave Benson, free of charge. The deal was that Douglas and Satarah would cover the car under their automobile insurance policy. JoJeff would teach Benson how to do routine maintenance. Benson would pay for his gas out of the salary he earned from working at Gregory Alexander's bank office in the accounting department a few hours a day and full-time during rotation breaks. Benson was interested in becoming a certified public accountant, and, as Mary Ella sat thinking about it, it would be a good fit. He helped Satarah with the books for the businesses she owned and operated, like The Summer House, the farm, and the tree farm on her land across the road.

She was looking at that road when a car she didn't recognize turned into the long driveway of The Summer House. Initially, she thought it was a guest arriving for a stay at the bed and breakfast, but as it got closer and stopped on the circular drive, she recognized the vehicle as a military transport. When two military men got out of the car, she stood and held her belly, afraid they were there with bad news about Mark. She felt lite-headed as they started up the sidewalk toward the veranda.

Satarah came out of the house just as the military men, both officers, stepped up on the veranda.

"Good afternoon, ma'am. I'm Captain Toucan, and this is Lieutenant Avery. We're looking for a Mary Ella Baker?"

She must have let out a sound of distress because SaraJo and the military men turned sharply in her direction.

"Are you all right?" SaraJo helped her to sit again.

She shook her head as tears welled up and overflowed. The officers moved toward her, but she was afraid to ask. Thank goodness SaraJo wasn't.

SaraJo turned to the men. "Is your visit about Dr. Mark Brooks?"

The captain noticed the state of her pregnancy. "Are you Mary Ella Baker?"

"I'm not. I'm Satarah Johnson, Mary Ella's cousin. This is Ms. Baker. Now, we want to know why you're here."

The captain noticed her pregnancy, too. "Uh, Ms. Baker, we are here to escort you to," he looked pointedly at Satarah, "meet with Dr. Brooks."

"He's alive? You've found him?" Mary Ella's voice trembled as she batted away the tears which would not stop falling.

"Yes, Ma'am. He was rescued, and… we would appreciate it if you would come with us."

"Where is he?"

"We are not at liberty to say. However, you should plan to be away for several days."

After that comment, everything was a blur. Mary Ella rapidly packed a go-bag. Satarah agreed to step back into her old position at the hospital. She and Jenny would cover for Mary Ella while she was away. Mary Ella tried to reach Eric, but he was with a patient. He planned to attend the birthday party, but he was running late. Thirty minutes later, she was driven away from The Summer House.

CHAPTER 23

Many hours later, Mary Ella arrived at Landstuhl Medical Center in Landstuhl, Germany. She was weary but determined to see Mark. Because of the medical center's sheer size, she was driven through the wide halls on a golf cart to a secluded section that required a security clearance to enter. She was taken into a room with no windows, but it had what she was sure was a one-way glass observation booth. The room itself was comfortable. Nonetheless, she believed it to be an interrogation room.

She didn't have to wait long before the door opened, and Dr. Evan Michael Cain entered with two other people. She rose from her seat to greet him. His hug was strong but mindful of her condition. They had worked together from time-to-time over the four years they were both members of Doctors Without Borders and knew each other reasonably well.

"You look well, Mary Ella, but this is a pleasant surprise. I wasn't told you're expecting."

"We can catch up later, Evan, but for now, I want to know about Mark. What's his condition, and when can I see him?"

As Evan began to explain in detail what Mark's physical condition entailed, the tears came again, but she choked them back. She couldn't help Mark if all she did was weep, but her hormones were wreaking havoc on her.

"His mental and emotional condition may depend on seeing you, Mary Ella."

Her brows narrowed. "What are you saying, Evan? You believe he's mentally unstable, unbalanced? That can't be true. Mark has a mind like a steel trap. No matter what, he'd keep his wits about him. He's a Marine, and they don't break this side of death."

Evan nodded. "I believe so, but he's not Superman, Mary Ella. Still, you're all he talks about. When the authorities try to question him, all he says is your name."

She sat back in her seat, searching Evan's eyes while her mind worked at light speed. Then she stood up with everyone else following suit. "I want to see him now!"

"Ms. Baker, you may not understand his condition," offered one of the other people who, until this point, remained quiet, just listening.

Mary Ella turned piercing eyes on the woman. "Are you his physician?"

"I am, yes. I'm Dr. Melody Jenkins."

"You're his primary care physician?"

"Yes."

"Is his medical condition as Dr. Cain described it?"

"It is, yes."

"Then, who is his psychiatrist?"

"That would be me, Ms. Baker. I'm Dr. Lee Elders."

"Dr. Elders, do you at this point believe that Mark has suffered a psychotic break with reality?"

"You don't understand, Ms. Baker. It may not be that simple."

"I understand the pathology, Dr. Elders. A psychotic break occurs when a person experiences an acute primary psychosis episode, generally for the first time, though it may also be after a significant symptom-free period. Many things can cause temporary psychosis. Environmental triggers, such as losing a loved one, are known to contribute, as may excessive stress or the interaction of intense social demands with a pre-existing vulnerability of self.

"I understand that you've only just met Mark, but I've known him and been with him until five, no nearly six months ago when we were both captured by terrorists and separated. If he is suffering any of the symptoms of a psychotic break, I'll be able to spot them faster than you or anyone else.

"Now, I don't have time to fool around with you while you try to determine what *my* state of mind is because if you don't take me to see

Mark now, I'll go into my Sapphire Act and demonstrate what a pregnant woman with an attitude can rain down on the unsuspecting!" She didn't raise her voice, but they got the message loud and clear.

Evan grinned at her as he led her out of the room. Still, she had the feeling someone was behind that one-way glass watching. It didn't matter as she was led to a huge bedroom suite. A man sat in a chair, staring out at the panoramic view of a garden and a vineyard beyond. She approached him slowly, his back to her, but when she faced him, she uttered his name, "Mark," and went to her knees, her arms around him, her face buried in his chest, and silently cried.

"Mary Ella," he crooned soothingly. "My Mary Ella, oh, praise The Creator," he moaned and gathered her up until she was on his lap, his arms tightly around her, breathing her in. She was not a figment of his imagination, but real, tangible, and warm in his arms. She was alive! He just sat there, holding her, unable or unwilling to do anything but hold on to her. Then his mouth was on hers, hungry for the taste of her and lost in the wonder of her responsiveness to him. When his hand traveled down her body, he felt movement in her midsection. It was an odd feeling, and it took him moments to realize she was pregnant. When they broke the kiss, he looked into her watery eyes. A smile bloomed on her face as she leaned back against his chest, took his hands, and placed them on her motion-filled body.

"Twins." She continued to marvel at the joy she felt from knowing Mark was alive. Still, he was barely skin and bones, not the robust, well-toned body mass he had been before they left Summer County years ago. They both gained muscle working in the camps. However, because they were always on the go, they lost most of whatever body fat they had. Still, as they sat in the growing fall of the afternoon sun, she instinctively knew he would be all right.

"Thanks for the call, SaraJo." Eric ended the call. He had just learned of the visit by a couple of military men who came and took Mary Ella away. She was apparently being taken to see Dr. Mark Brooks. So many thoughts were going through his head at that moment; it was hard to focus on the beauty of the hospital's garden surrounding him.

Yet, he did have the presence of mind to make one phone call. "Donald." He spoke with his cousin for several moments before they ended the call. He continued to sit in the open air and think. He knew the possibility of this day happening would mean a change in his relationship with Mary Ella, but he wasn't ready for it, no matter when it happened. They were friends, she insisted, and was reluctant to let their friendship go any further. He was the one who found any excuse he could come up with to spend time with her.

He smiled to himself. Spending time with Mary Ella and her potato spuds were the best days he'd had since he returned to Summer County. He loved to make her laugh, to dance with her, to talk with her or just to *be* with her. He didn't wish Mark Brooks ill feelings, but he had feelings for Mary Ella, too. He just hoped that her feelings for him were more in-depth and more potent than her feelings for Mark. He wouldn't know until she returned.

"Hello, Dr. Dixon."

He looked up into Julia Hunt's smiling face.

"Hello." He wasn't in the mood for this, not today. Still, this needed to end.

"Is this seat taken?"

He looked around the garden. There weren't that many people out here on a Saturday afternoon, and plenty of seats available. He wouldn't have been there either if he hadn't agreed to take his suitemate's afternoon rounds for him. He had forgotten about Benson's birthday party when he agreed. If need be, he usually did his hospital rounds early in the morning on the weekends. If he hadn't been at the hospital, he would have been at the party with Mary Ella.

"Dr. Dixon?"

He looked at Julia, having forgotten she was standing there holding a tray of food.

"Yes?"

"This seat? May I sit with you?"

"No, I mean, yes. Have a seat."

"Thank you. I saw your name on the roster today, and I was surprised…"

"Have you ever been in love?" Eric asked her.

He'd apparently caught her off guard.

"I, uh, I'm not sure. Why do you ask?"

"Because I know how it feels to be in love with someone exceptional."

"Your wife, I suppose. I know you were married before."

"I'm not in love again. I'm *still* in love. Very deeply in love, and I can tell you it has nothing to do with fantasies and physiques. Still, she's my dream come true. I want to be with her all of the time, listen to her tell me about her day, and spend my nights loving only her for the rest of my life. I want her to be the first person I see in the morning and the last one I see at night. I want babies with her; lots and lots of babies. I don't want to share my life, my body with anyone else. She's my Alpha and my Omega; she completes me. If she comes back, I'm going to beg her to marry me. Do you understand what I'm saying?"

Julia just stared at him. So, he took her silence for assent, stood up, and walked away.

"I can't believe you're here. I was so worried I would never see you again."

Mary Ella palmed Mark's face with both hands and looked deeply into his eyes. "I felt the same way, Mark, but we need to talk."

Mark nodded. "I know, but first, I have so much to say to you."

"Before that, the doctors believe you've had a psychotic break."

Mark snorted. "I let them believe whatever they wanted to. I knew what they needed from me, but I wasn't going to give it to them unless or until they found you."

"Oh, Mark," Mary Ella moaned, shaking her head as her hands fell away from his face. "I was rescued six weeks after we were captured. Didn't anyone think to tell you that?"

"I don't think they made the connection. I'm not sure, but the people who found me weren't people I ever saw before. I was flown to a ship, and my initial diagnosis was made there before I was flown here to Germany. I didn't let on, even to Evan, that I still had my faculties intact. I just continued to say your name. It was probably Evan who made the connection. It worked, and now you're here."

"We still need to talk, Mark."

He closed his eyes and took a deep breath before he looked into her eyes. "I have an apology to make to you."

Mary Ella's brows beetled. "An apology? For what?"

"I haven't been entirely forthcoming with you.

"About what?"

"I think you believe that I was…"

"Poor? That you grew up alone?"

Mark looked askance at her and nodded. "Yes, but you weren't under that impression?"

"I was, yes, until I was frantic about what to do when I was rescued, and you weren't. I didn't know anything about your background or family, and no one would give me that information. So, I Googled you and found you were Phi Beta Kappa at Harvard undergrad and medical school. You were top of your class, and you're a member of the Townsend family of Boston and New England."

Embarrassed, Mark looked away. "I should have told you who I am, but it never seemed the right time, and you weren't impressed by privilege or wealth. So, I convinced myself it wasn't necessary. While I was a captive, I realized that with you, it is all about family, about being there for family no matter what. It's not about *who* you are. It's about *whose* you are. You used to repeat that to me all the time, and I never truly understood what it meant.

"When we met, Mary Ella, you had lost your parents, and you had no siblings, but you had a family. People you cared about and who cared about you in the most fundamental ways. You were this extraordinarily strong, self-sufficient, self-possessed woman who could care less whether I had two dimes to my name or a pot of gold at my fingertips. All you asked of anyone who came into your orbit was to be honest, trusting, and loving.

"I failed your requirements on so many levels, Mary Ella. I grew up privileged, and although I appreciated what my family accomplished, I didn't know anything about how the other half lived, so to speak. I was a kid and at home in Boston when 911 occurred. One of the airplanes had taken off from the Boston Airport, and that shook the foundations of my life.

"Without discussion with my family, years later, when I obtained my MD, I enlisted in the Marines as a medical officer. That's where Douglas and I met and became friends. It was his platoon that I was assigned to. He kept me safe under the most dire of circumstances. I told him that, if there was ever anything I could do to help him, he need only ask. When he contacted me, I was no longer in the Marines. I had signed up for The Ship of Hope and Doctors Without Borders. I was willing to go with whichever one came through first. Another friend and classmate, Evan Michael Cain, got the post to the Ship of Hope, and then Doctors Without Borders came in with an offer for me.

"When Douglas asked for my help, I delayed accepting deployment. Then, when I got to Goodwill, Summer County, South Carolina, there you were. I had never met anyone like you or your cousin, Satarah or Jenny. Douglas told me that you and Satarah risked your nursing licenses to save his son. You performed an unauthorized and unsupervised delicate surgery on Douglas' son, Donovan, which could have gone terribly wrong if you two hadn't known exactly what to do to save his life. I was amazed and impressed.

"You are this incredibly beautiful woman, Mary Ella, both inside and out, and all I wanted was to be with you. You opened to me, a complete stranger, and welcomed me into your life without hesitation. You took me to your bed and asked nothing of me except to be loved. You weren't trying to trap me into a commitment, not even marriage. You didn't want to play games with sex, and that's when I understood the difference between having sex and making love. Those two concepts are a world apart, Mary Ella, and you showed me how that worked for the benefit of both of us. Now, we're having twins…" He felt her shiver at that. "What is it, Mary Ella? What's wrong? Why are you crying?"

She shook her head and took a deep breath wiping away the tears. She had to tell him the truth. "I'm not sure. I don't know with any degree of certainty that these twins are yours and mine." Then she told him the whole story of her capture and ultimate rescue. When she finished, they were both crying and holding on to each other.

"I was afraid that this would happen to you. I would have done anything, paid any amount of ransom to stop you from being molested. I feared every day that someone was hurting you the way I saw the men treat the women they kidnapped. They called it a marriage because an Iman performed a ceremony, but that was so they could justify what they did to the women they took captive."

"There was a man who fought for me against the man who took you captive."

"Yes, I remember. He is called Kaseem Ally Ghailani."

"Yes. I only knew him as Kaseem." She took another fortifying breath before she looked into his eyes. "He didn't beat me or… hurt me. He had sex with me, but he wasn't brutal. After a while, I simply submitted. I didn't try to fight him."

"You were smart and did what you had to do to survive. If you had continued to fight, you would have been killed, Mary Ella. These men don't tolerate being challenged by a woman. If he didn't kill you, one of his patriarchs would have done it with or without his permission."

"I know." She nodded. "This man, this Kaseem, kept me tethered to him most of the time."

"He kept you from being molested by anyone else or gang-raped because you're an American."

"You understand his behavior?"

"I don't like what he did to you, believe me, but he managed to keep you safe. If you are right and he somehow secured your rescue, I'll buy him a beer before I try to beat him into poor health." Mark cupped her worried face and smoothed away the tears with his thumbs, which continued to fountain up and overflow. "We'll look into what it will take to get you unmarried, and then these babies will be born as ours. Mary Ella, I want you to meet my family and see whether you approve of them or still approve of me."

"Oh, Mark, that's not necessary. I only wanted to contact them to tell them you were being held hostage, but the NGO said not to do that, or you could be killed."

"They were right, Mary Ella. I have a standing Do Not Contact order with the NGO. They were only permitted to contact my family if I was dead, and they had my body as proof. Otherwise, my family was not to know anything unless or until I gave them permission. You were the only one I wanted to see. Now, I want to take you home with me to show you off."

It took two more weeks for Mark to be released from Landstuhl Medical Center. During that time, he was continually debriefed about what he heard and saw while in captivity. She wasn't permitted to participate in the debriefing sessions with him, but Mark insisted on being able to see her while he was being interrogated. She would sit or stand in an adjoining room looking at him through a sound-proof glass partition, but he knew she was there. She just couldn't hear what they were saying. However, the intelligence reports were apparently of vital importance because the people doing the questioning were in a constant state of agitation. There was a speakerphone in the center of the table where they sat. The dials were green when the phone was activated and red when they weren't. At times it appeared they were listening to someone talk, while at other times, it was clear Mark was giving them information. He would nod or shake his head and seemed to be pressing a specific point. Every once in a while, he would look up at her and smile.

This went on between the medical exams they subjected him to several times a day. Still, she and Mark were able to spend mealtimes alone together talking, mostly about his extensive family tree. His appetite substantially improved. He was losing the gaunt scarecrow look he had when she first arrived. It was refreshing to hear him talk about his precocious preteen cousin Chandra Rodgers who was hearing challenged but spoke more languages than he did. He claimed she was smarter than everyone else in the family except their cousin Rosemary "Rosy" Dominique Rodgers, who was a few years younger than Chandra.

They slept each night in the same bed together, but they didn't attempt to make physical love. There were still certain things that were difficult for Mark to do. They could kiss, but he abided by her wishes to solve the question of her marital status before they made love. She realized she needed the reprieve to sort out her feelings about Mark... and Eric. Even about Kaseem.

Mark was getting his muscle tone back, but it was slow in coming. Landstuhl Medical Center was massive, like a city within a city; too large to tour on foot. So, they took guided tours by golf cart inside the cavernous building. The hospital dealt with the troops serving in Afghanistan and Iraq. Because of its location in Germany, it also served the German military and more than three hundred thousand individuals in the European Theater. Nearly all of its staff of doctors, nurses, and technicians were registered in the US military, the guide told them.

"I understand that Dr. Vincent and Charmaine McAllister are US Marines who were once in service here," Mary Ella remarked.

"They were for several years. Do you know them?" the guide asked.

"I know of them." Mary Ella nodded. "One of the residents of Summer County, South Carolina, where I'm from, used to work for the doctors' daughter, an attorney, Capri McAllister Kennedy."

"Ah, yes, I remember her and her sister, China, and younger brother, Paris. They came to visit their parents when they were stationed here. Since I'm a part of the security team guides, I was responsible for taking them around on tour. I didn't know she married."

Mary Ella nodded. "Yes, she married the astronaut, Dr. Tate Kennedy."

"She's a real nice lady. I wish her well."

"I believe Dr. Eric Dixon was stationed here, too," Mary Ella mentioned.

"Doctor? Well, I'll be damned! He did it, did he? He was here for a time as a nurse, but he was planning to go to medical school. I'm glad he made it. When you see him, give him my best wishes."

Mary Ella nodded. "I'll do that."

"How many people here do what you do?" asked Mark.

"We aren't allowed to divulge certain information because we're considered a target-rich environment. You see, the Center has in residence not only the military staff but also their families. Families of injured military personnel are also billeted here for the duration of the stay of a patient. Even captured terrorists are brought here for medical care.

"We have churches or institutions of faith of every denomination, museums, vineyards, restaurants, theatres, schools, and so much more. The residents don't need to leave the center for any of their needs. They do just to go sightseeing, but, otherwise, there is enough here to keep us entertained. We tend to develop close friendships here. If you're here for much longer, I'll be happy to show you more. Since you and Ms. Baker are medical personnel, I'll introduce you to more of the staff of doctors and nurses. However, for today, your doctors only permitted an hour tour."

"Thank you, but I hope, if all goes well, we'll be leaving here tomorrow," Mark commented absently.

It was news to her, Mary Ella thought, but she would check with his doctors to determine whether he could leave. While Mark napped, she sought out the Doctors Elders and Jenkins and was able to consult with them immediately.

"Actually, Ms. Baker, we would like to have Dr. Brooks stay another couple of weeks with us to go through further therapy."

"Physical therapy?"

"Well, yes, that, too. However, Dr. Brooks is insisting on being released AMA tomorrow. Frankly, there is no medical reason for him to stay, especially given the resources he has at his disposal at home. I imagine you'll accompany him as well."

"I will ensure that he arrives at his home, but I have responsibilities of my own to attend to."

Dr. Jenkins nodded. "Yes, I'm aware. I spoke with the head of your hospital and your immediate supervisor. Both gave glowing reports about the quality of your skills and abilities. I also called Doctors Without Borders and received a full report about your heroic efforts while working with them for over four years. They would welcome you back. However, we would like both you and Dr. Brooks to join the medical center staff. We would welcome someone of your caliber here at Landstuhl Medical Center. You, Dr. Brooks, and your family." Dr. Jenkins looked pointedly at Mary Ella's distended belly.

Mary Ella left them but made no commitment about whether she would be interested in considering their offer.

CHAPTER 24

Mary Ella didn't know why she thought they would be flown from Germany in a commercial aircraft. Oh, no, medical professionals helped them board an Adventurer Executive Air medically-equipped luxury jet and they flew for over seven hours in style to Boston's Logan International Airport. Upon arrival, they were met on the tarmac by a stretch limousine. They weren't even required to go through Customs. After leaving the airport, it wasn't until they turned off the main thoroughfare and into a gated tunnel that her stomach began to do summersaults and her nerves went on edge.

When they came out of the tunnel before them was a place that rivaled the Biltmore Mansion in Asheville, North Carolina. Mary Ella had visited the Biltmore as a child on a school trip. She never could imagine anyone living there, even though some of the family's descendants still did. She had visited Vivian and Chuck's ranch in Maryland and thought it was humongous. However, what filled her field of vision as she leaned forward to look through the limousine's front windshield was beyond description.

They drove for what seemed like a mile beside a vast unyielding stretch of green land with round, pool-sized fountains in the middle billowing up water spouts that were hypnotic to watch. No trees obscured the view of the landscape, but a similar road, like the one they were on, was on the opposite side of the green space and fountains.

As they grew closer to what looked like a castle crafted of centuries-old boulders with its many towers, turrets, balconies, and spires reaching into the sky, she thought of Disney World's Castle or the Mormon Tabernacle in Bethesda, Maryland, or again, the Biltmore Estate. They drove through another tunnel into an expansive, square courtyard, centered with green grass and another fountain, this one larger than the others, where they finally stopped halfway around the square before the tallest glass doors Mary Ella had ever seen.

"You should see your face." Mark smiled wryly at her. "I want to apologize now before we go in."

"Mark, this couldn't possibly be your home." Mary Ella eyed him incredulously.

"You saw that expanse of lawn with the fountains?"

"Yes, why?"

"My sixteenth-birthday party was held out there on the lawn under twelve circus tents. The place was packed."

Mary Ella just sat staring at him, unable to speak. When the driver opened the rear door to offer her his assistance in standing, she was jolted out of her fugue state. That's when she saw a group of people who were obviously staff lined up and excitedly peeking into the limo. After she stepped out, applause rose as she and the driver helped Mark to his feet. The applause faltered only momentarily until Mark smiled and waved.

Mary Ella could see that the long travel, even in luxurious style, was taking its toll on Mark. A tall, very distinguished-looking, well-dressed man in a rigidly formal suit and tie stepped forward, taking Mark's hand reverently in his.

"Sir, what do you need?" he spoke quietly to Mark.

"Great-grandmother's tram ought to do it, Mr. Masters."

"Right away, Sir." Then Mr. Masters spoke into a device the size of a cell phone. Shortly, a two-seater buggy rolled to a stop before them.

"If you don't mind, I'd appreciate it if you would drive, Mary Ella."

"Of course, but do we have enough breadcrumbs to find our way out again?" she joked, hoping to take some of the fatigue from his eyes.

"We'll have to make do the way we did with the NGO." Mark smiled back at her slightly.

It was a simple, electric buggy or golf cart that didn't have much zip to it. Still, it got them going, and the staff of servants fell in behind them. They appeared to be thrilled to have Mark back home again.

Mary Ella looked up and around as she drove into a large vestibule. "So, tell me, how large is this place?"

Mark shrugged. "I haven't been here in more than five years, but the last time I was in residence, the whole estate, including the grounds and the waterways, was about seven miles square. I'm surprised they haven't put in a runway to land jets…yet." Mark joked. "The house is perhaps one hundred and sixty thousand square feet. I really don't know. Although I was born here and grew up here, I haven't seen all of the spaces."

Mary Ella's mouth dropped open. "Summer County Academy isn't that large, and it's the largest facility in the county. Come to think of it, the state house in Columbia isn't that large."

"That's old Ashro Townsend's doing. Slow down and look up to your left."

She slowed to a stop and looked up and up to a bigger-than-life oil painting of a man dressed in 18th-century wear of cutaway coat with long tails behind and a tall standing collar. The lapel was large, and the shirt appeared to be made of linen with a wrapped cravat tied fashionably about the neck. A wide cummerbund circled his trim waist. The form-fitting britches were snug and showed off an impressive musculature of hips, thighs, and long, strong legs down to leather shoes with tassels. His face was just a shade darker than someone who might have had a tan, but the patrician nose, dark eyes, poetic mouth, and a face surrounded by dark, curly, long hair was purely aristocratic. He was all in all quite strikingly handsome and starkly masculine if the vertical form in his crotch was any indication.

He stood posed regally beside a chair where a pretty woman with a Mona Lisa smile sat cradling a baby in her arms.

"That's Ashro Townsend and his wife, Dilly, one of his former prostitutes or mistresses as they were known in those days. According to Ashro's diaries, he fathered many children but only married the first woman to give him a son. That woman was Dilly Peters. Although he was married to Dilly, he continued to sleep with other women. You see, Ashro descended from English nobility, a Lord Townsend in the Court of Saint James. It's the royal court for the Sovereign of the United Kingdom.

The court is named after St James' Palace, the most senior royal palace of the British Monarchy. A royal court has existed since the Kingdom of England before 1707 and the Kingdom of Great Britain 1707–1800, but Ashro was a bastard child and, from the age of fourteen, gave his father competition with the women at the royal court. That would never do in the Court of Great Britain. So, when Ashro was in his later teens, Lord Townsend staked him to a few steamer trunks full of gold and precious gems and shipped him off to the colonies.

"Ashro's mother was an Ethiopian woman named Shiloh. She is said to have been a highly celebrated, extremely beautiful princess in her own lands. She was the daughter of Ethiopian Emperor Tewodros II. You see, Ethiopia was the only territory in Africa to defeat European colonial power and retain its sovereignty.

"Between 1755 and 1855, Ethiopia experienced a period of isolation referred to as the *Zemene_Mesafint* or Age of Princes. The Emperors became figureheads, controlled by warlords like *Ras* Mikael Sehul of Tigray, *Ras* Wolde_Selassie of Tigray, and the Yejju Oromo dynasty. *Ras* Gugsa of_Yejju, who later led to the 17th-century Oromo rule of Gondar, changed the language of the court from Amharic to Afaan Oromo.

"Ethiopian isolationism ended following a British mission that concluded an alliance between the two nations, but, as I said before, it was not until 1855 that Ethiopia was completely united and the power in the Emperor restored, beginning with the reign of Tewodros II. Upon his ascent, he began modernizing Ethiopia and recentralizing power in the Emperor. Ethiopia began to take part in world affairs once again.

"You see, the Townsends lost a lot of resources trying to overthrow the Ethiopians. In retaliation, they stole an Ethiopian national treasure— Princess Shiloh. She was abducted from her home and spirited away to one of Lord Townsend's castles in the English countryside. Initially, he held her for ransom but ultimately fell in lust for her and decided to make her his concubine, much to his family's dismay. She had free reign inside the castle where she was imprisoned, but Lord Townsend had her securely guarded by everyone on his staff. The Townsends still wanted more riches for her return than they lost, but the Emperor refused to pay the ransom.

"The Princess was not only beautiful but also very smart and resilient. She taught her son, Ashro, by Lord Townsend, about the use of herbs to make medicines and other potions. He became quite proficient and used his skills in making drugs to put women 'in the mood.' He was very popular among the gentile women of England's social order and, later, Boston's blue blood society as much for his drugs as he did for his prowess between the sheets."

"You really know your family's history, Mark." Mary Ella was impressed. "So Ashro is the beginning of the legacy which built this castle."

"As do you about your Cherokee roots, Mary Ella. You're a walking encyclopedia about your Cherokee heritage. However, the genealogy and DNA of my family track back to Ethiopian scholars. Shiloh told Ashro of great civilizations in Africa before its infiltration by the English. We have her name and much of her history only because she could read and write and taught her son her language. He kept her diaries with his own when he was shipped here.

"She, as most mothers do, had a strong influence on Ashro," Mark continued. "Shiloh told him he descended from Emperors who were smart, bold, and fearless, and to never shrink from a foe. She gave him the tools with the herbs to defeat his enemies silently with the combinations of the drugs and potions she taught him to mix. So began what is now Townsend Pharmaceuticals Global, the parent company and its offshoots and subsidiaries, a Fortune 100 company. Each of Ashro and Dilly's offspring is well taken care of under the terms and conditions of their wills.

"Ashro bought this land and named it Shiloh when no one thought much of it because it sits so close to the water. It gets very cold here, and people built homes close together in Boston to guard against the nor'easters. Ashro built his place of thick boulders like the pyramids his mother told him about. He enclosed botanical gardens and continually heated the stones to grow his herbs and make his potions year-round. Although he came to Boston as rich as Midas when he was a teen, his legacy came from his mother's side of the family tree. He was over a hundred years old, even wealthier, and very influential when he died.

"Ashro reviled his father, Lord Townsend, an Englishman of inherited wealth and position, for the manner in which his father treated his mother. Ashro considered his father as merely a sperm donor. It is posited that Ashro is the only one of Lord Townsend's many offspring to have survived beyond childhood. As a result, Ashro inherited his father's wealth, properties, and status. Some theorize that Shiloh had a hand in the children's unfortunate deaths as revenge for kidnapping her and sending her son away from England."

"Who is this next set of people?" Mary Ella moved the buggy forward.

"Ah, here we have Dr. Rupert Alvin Townsend, Senior, and his wife, Rosemary Dwyer, a woman who was born on the wrong side of the blanket, so-to-speak, to a high-society Boston man and one of his slaves. No one exactly knows how or where Dr. Townsend got a medical degree since he had Ethiopian blood running through his body. Still, his father, good old Ashro, knew everyone's deepest secrets. He learned by putting key people under the influence of certain opiates, then sleeping with their wives, lovers, or whoever he could seduce information from. Quite a scoundrel, our Ashro." Mark grinned wryly and continued.

"Rupert and Rosemary begat five children, all *bonafide* medical doctors: Milton, Dominique, Rupert Jr., Irene, who is my grandmother, and Hayden. Each one married medical doctors. It was the next generation which kind of broke the trend." He pointed out the family portraits as they proceeded down the long, wide gallery.

"This is Grand Uncle Milton Townsend, MD, and his wife, Avery Todd. They only had one child, Charlotte Townsend Whiting, who you may have read about. She is crazy as a loon and held Attorney Capri McAlister's administrative assistant at gunpoint."

Mary Ella nodded. "Yes, I know her, Florence Johnson. She's now married to Duke Patterson. It happened after we left Summer County."

Mark nodded. "I didn't know that. Well, Florence was held hostage at gunpoint by Grand Uncle Milton and Grand Aunt Avery's daughter, Aunt Charlotte. Inbreeding is suspected as the source of her insanity. So, DNA testing is now a required part of the prenuptial agreement to ensure we're not bedding one of Ashro's lesser-known descendants."

Mark went on naming his other grand uncles and aunts, their offspring, grandchildren, and in some cases, even great-grandchildren of the Ashro and Dilly Peters Townsend dynasty.

"That's you up there." Mary Ella stopped the buggy to stare up at the bigger-than-life portrait.

"It is, yes." Mark nodded. "That was painted when I was here last. That's my grandmother, Dr. Irene Townsend, and her husband, Dr. Harlan Ellsworth Brooks. My parents, Drs. Gary and Judith Cole Brooks, me, and my younger brother, Dr. Vaughn Cole Brooks. A new portrait is commissioned every year the way the Alexander family takes that yards-long picture at their Juneteenth reunion. Apparently, my parents haven't had a new portrait commissioned since I left. I have a feeling that will be one of the first things they'll insist on me doing. This time, I don't think I'll complain about it because it will be done around the Christmas holidays. That's when our little potato spuds will be about the size of fat eggplants when they're born."

"Mark." Mary Ella sighed in mild censure.

"They are ours, Mary Ella, regardless of the sperm donor. They are descendants of the great Cherokee nation and Ethiopian Emperors. Great peoples all."

"We've talked about this, Mark. I have an obligation to determine the parentage of these twins before I can agree to anything."

"I understand that. Tomorrow I'll speak with my lawyers and find out what needs to be done."

"No, Mark, I'll handle the legal work through someone I know. I'll let you know the outcome."

"Okay, but for now, I need for you to make a left down the next corridor."

She followed his instructions as they turned down one maze of wide hallways after another until they came to a set of doors that opened into what looked like a large bed and sitting room. A woman reclined on a large divan facing an expansive view of the Boston Bay. Another woman in uniform put down a book she had apparently been reading aloud and stood as Mary Ella drove the buggy into the room.

"Welcome home, Dr. Brooks."

"Thank you, Tanya. How is she today?"

"There is still no response. However, we keep hoping something will break through. I'll leave you alone with her." The woman turned and left.

Mark got out of the buggy using a walker and, with Mary Ella's help, moved to sit on the foot of the divan facing the woman.

Mary Ella recognized that the woman was in a catatonic state and asked, "Who is she, Mark?"

"Her name is Allison Virginia Bond, of the New England Bond banking industry Bonds. She's a longtime family friend. We were sweethearts in private school together. She was a fellow med school student and a graduate of Harvard. She was my fiancée, who protested vehemently my decision to enlist in the Marines without discussing it with her. Our arguments grew to epic proportions. Two days before our scheduled wedding, our quarrel boiled over during our wedding rehearsal dinner in front of her prestigious family and mine. She ran out of the catered dinner for over a hundred people, gunned the custom-made Lamborghini I gave to her as an engagement gift, and sped out of the parking lot. A mile down the road, she skidded out of control on black ice and ended up in the ice-cold waters of the Charles River.

"She survived but was in a coma from which she wasn't expected to recover. She did recover from her injuries, but she's essentially been in this vegetative state since then. She breathes on her own but has to be tended to twenty-four-seven. Although my attorneys told me marriage to her wouldn't be legal, I married her anyway in a civil ceremony conducted by one of her uncles, New Hampshire Chief State Court Judge Terrance Bond, before my parents and hers. At the time, I believed we were expecting a baby. I wanted to be solely responsible for her care and the care of our unborn child.

"Then her doctor told me she was confused about why I was under the impression that Allison was pregnant. According to conclusive tests, Allison was never pregnant, and there was no child. I couldn't understand her duplicity. We were lovers and in love since we were post-adolescents, but she wanted to push up our wedding date. I hadn't really asked her to be my wife, but it was a foregone conclusion we would marry after knowing each other since we were toddlers and our families are the closest of friends.

"One day, I went to the hospital to be with her and found a classmate of ours, kissing her hand and crying. I didn't understand his behavior until he broke down and admitted to me that he and Allison were lovers all through med school. He was already married and expecting his first child when their affair began. Allison was distraught about her lover having a baby with his wife, so she claimed she was pregnant, too, with his child. When he wouldn't leave his wife, she convinced me that she was pregnant with our child and started making wedding plans with me to make her lover jealous. He believed that the accident was his fault because he wouldn't divorce his wife to be with her."

"Oh, Mark, that is so sad," Mary Ella moaned.

Mark turned ravished eyes on her. "No, the sad part is that her parents still wanted me to impregnate her so that they could have grandchildren. You see, Allison is their only child. She graduated with me at the top of our class in both undergrad and medical school. We were seen as a team during our residency program at Mass General. Marriage between us was a status symbol for her parents. When I came to you, I was running away from this. I couldn't bring this ugliness into your life, so I left out all of the things about my life before I met you. You were the beginning of everything for me, Mary Ella. My biggest regret is that I never told you the truth, and I led you into such a dangerous situation because I was selfish. I couldn't bear the thought of leaving you behind."

"It's not your fault, Mark. At the time, I couldn't bear the thought of you leaving without me. Until you came to Summer County, I lived such a simple life. Although I was in love with a special man, I wasn't ready to settle down and become a wife to him and the mother of his children. Your offer to join DWB came at a perfect juncture in my life.

"We did extraordinary things, Mark, and we helped save hundreds, perhaps thousands of lives. I have no regrets about what we helped to be accomplished. Regardless of the outcome, don't place the blame for our capture and resulting situations on your shoulders. I love and cherish these potato spuds." Mary Ella smiled into Mark's moist eyes.

"See, that's it. That's just the type of selfless person you are, Mary Ella, and have always been. That, in addition to your beauty, is what captured me from the first moment we met. That's the qualities of the woman I want to marry and live with until my last breath."

He kissed her softly, and she nearly forgot he was sitting at the feet of his fiancée-cum-wife. He had issues to solve, too. How much was he still tied to Allison's life? That was as large a concern as hers about being the wife of a man she didn't know as Mark hadn't really known Allison.

CHAPTER 25

It was evening when Mary Ella woke from her nap. Mark wasn't in bed with her, where he also slept the afternoon away after lunch was served in Mark's palatial section of many suites and salons. It was a relatively modern decorative motif in about five thousand square feet of floor space, he told her. It had interesting and different frescos on the walls and ceiling in each area with touches of vibrant or muted silver-greys and blues. Custom-made sheets and comforters matched the color scheme and somehow nicely set off the sofas and chairs arranged in clusters in the bedroom suite's sitting room area. She recognized them as those manufactured in Summer County for Natalia Montgomery's Pleasure series.

When she rose from the bed, she went into a spa-like bath suite, clearly decorated only for the use of a woman. The man's bath en suite was on the other side of the master bedroom. She took a refreshing shower and wrapped her body in one of the terrycloth robes and a fluffy white towel around her hair like a turban.

When she returned to the bedroom, Mark was sitting on the side of the bed with his feet in a sling he used to exercise his arm and leg muscles. She sat down beside him to watch him work and not let him overdo it. He had a good rhythm going, pushing the spiral sling with his leg and thigh muscles and pulling against the tension with his arm muscles. After working out for about thirty minutes, he was breathing hard, and his body was moist.

"That's very good, Mark, but that's enough for now," Mary Ella warned.

He nodded his agreement, blotted the moisture from his body, using a towel he had around his neck. He turned toward Mary Ella and opened the sash around her waist, revealing her breasts and bloated belly.

"You are so beautiful." He reverently touched her breasts and rubbed her nipples with his thumbs until they peaked. His mouth joined his hands in worshipful appreciation, his tongue smooth against her sensitive nerve endings. His mouth moved down to kiss and caress the active babies in her womb. Mark laughed and kissed every spot where a foot, knee or elbow protruded. Then he went lower, widening her thighs and causing her to melt back in surrender against the zillion-count sheets and comforter.

A cataclysmic orgasm was on her before she was prepared for it, and Mark didn't stop there. He continued to bring her to a state of heightened euphoria until she was as weak as a wet noodle. Then he brought her onto his lap, facing him, and guided himself into her wet portal.

"You're so tight, Mary Ella," he breathed out with difficulty as he attempted to penetrate her to the hilt. Once seated, he guided her movements with his hands firmly on her hips until she began to ride him and tweak his raisin-like nipples between her fingertips. They were both lost in the motion their bodies greedily shared for ponderous moments until she crested, and Mark's dark-brown eyes glazed and went opaque. They were both breathing hard with difficulty in catching their breaths.

"Okay, so that's working well, but for now, you've had enough." Mary Ella breathlessly sighed.

"Mary Ella, I apologize, but I admit I'm not sorry. I had to have you. I was selfish because I needed to feel you around me the way we were all those months ago. This was all about me. While I was a captive, I dreamed about you; about being deep inside you and feeling how you used your Kegels to milk me. Dreams and thoughts of you and the symbols on my upper arms are the only things that kept me sane. When I dreamed, I could taste you, capture your scent, and feel your warm body against mine. I was determined to find you again if it took my last breath." He sat up and put his arms around her burying his face in the cleavage between her sweet breasts while still buried deep inside her.

She palmed his face, guiding it up to look into his eyes. "I don't regret what you make me feel, Mark. Sex between us was never an issue. I love being loved by you. I love feeling you inside me, the way you touch me. We always have fun like this together. I just wish it didn't come with so many uncertainties in my life and yours. We, neither one of us, are free of obligations. I have such mixed emotions that I can't think clearly all of the time. You'll have to help me with that as I will be there to help you sort out things once we know about the babies and going forward beyond that."

Mark nodded his understanding. "That will never change, Mary Ella. Regardless of the babies' origins, we'll always be there for one another. However, right this minute, I need you again in the best possible way."

They spent another period in lustful abandon.

"What's this?" asked Mary Ella as she found several racks of fashionable clothing in the woman's changing section of the closet.

"What's what?" Mark called out from where he still reclined naked on the bed.

"There are racks of clothes that weren't here when I found my luggage here before."

Mark laughed. "Mary Ella, you can hardly call a duffle bag 'luggage.' All you brought with you to Germany were jeans, tops, underwear, and toiletry items. You purchased a few things while we were there, but nothing to wear to dinner."

"Mark, we don't have to go out to dinner. Actually, the lunch we had here in your rooms today was quite good. We can have more of that… why are you laughing?" She came into the bedroom to look at him. He was stretched across the bed, unabashedly naked with his hands folded under his head, seeming well sated. "What's so funny?"

"You are. Yes, you are correct. We could have our evening meal served here, but it would be a bit difficult with sixty plus people in attendance. I don't think we have time to have all of the tables, chairs, and various, sundry items transported here." He leaned up on one elbow and ruefully shrugged, narrowing his eyes. "I've never had it done before, but it would give Mr. Masters an interesting conundrum. Heaven knows The Fives and me tried his last nerve when we were much younger, but he always came through. He's come to expect the unexpected from us."

"Mr. Masters?"

"Yes, the head butler or majordomo of all things Shilohland."

"The Fives?"

"My cousins, the fifth generation after Ashro. Now, let me finish explaining. Cocktails are served in one of the salons promptly at seven and dinner at eight. I don't know which rooms yet. My groomer will have that information. All in residence are expected in attendance dressed in evening attire of specific colors."

"You're joking, right? This isn't Downton Abbey, pal."

"It's a close second." Mark laughed.

"All of your family lives here in this house?"

"All of the ones descending from Ashro and Dilly, yes. Now, of course, there are those who are house and field staff who, even after generations of being employed here, bear a striking resemblance to the rest of us. I dare say that, if we did a DNA test on the staff, a substantial number of them would show traits matching Ashro's. I'll have to mention that to Grand Uncle Milton. He's the family's titular head because he's the eldest and his four siblings are only about a year apart after him. When you and I marry, you'll probably have to have a DNA test just to ensure that Ashro's line didn't extend south to the Cherokee Nation."

"Unbelievable," Mary Ella huffed.

"Believe it or not, Mary Ella, that's what being born into this family means. Ashro built this place to house generations upon generations of his offspring in perpetuity. Everyone is expected to make this our primary residence and to raise our children together, never to lose sight of *whose* we are and where we come from. That was very important to Ashro, and it's one of the things that has become very important to us generations after him. It makes us a very closely-knit family. The history is taught to us from the time we are babes in arms until we are in private high schools. Knowledge is The Holy Grail in Shilohland.

"Even for us, in a place this spacious, we can tire of each other's company. So, homes have been built in other places, like Palm Springs,

California, Caracas, Venezuela, and Les Chouettes, France, by the Dordogne River and Le Plongeoir at Du Point Le Garrit just outside Cyprian. The family has a grape orchard and a winery there in France. I got my first passport when I was less than a year old.

"Before I left to join DWB, there were discussions of finding land in Ethiopia to build a home similar to this one outside of the capital city of Addis Ababa, somewhere like Adama in the Oromia Region or Gondar in the Amhara Region. Someplace to pay homage to Shiloh and the emperors from whom she descended. My generation of offspring traveled there periodically for several months. When we were growing up, we traveled all over the world."

"That's where your skill with languages and dialects came from, isn't it?" asked Mary Ella.

Mark nodded. "We were home-schooled here within these walls until we were high school age. Languages, customs of other countries, and science, math, and technology were stressed, and, unlike the curriculum in Summer County Academy, we got no breaks in our schedules. Even when schools were out for vacations and holidays, our education never ended. That's when we had to study the hardest in preparation for travel to different parts of the world. We had to know the customs and the languages of the places we visited to a certain proficiency level. So certain traditions are still sacrosanct in this household. Dressing formally for dinner is one of them. So, let's see what suits you."

They went into a closet together, where Mary Ella selected gowns to consider. However, every time he got her naked, he found an interesting means of making love to her. He had her back on a bench with her legs up over his shoulders. She had to balance herself on the bench when he straddled it and found his way inside her.

Eventually, they settled on a golden-colored sheath with off-the-shoulder long fitted sleeves and a gold-colored, strapless bra that elevated her breasts noticeably. The shoes were flat and matched the dress perfectly, causing Mary Ella to be suspicious.

"Did you pick these outfits?" Her eyes narrowed menacingly. "They're awfully revealing, and they fit, even the shoes."

He held up his hands in a placating motion while grinning at her. "Actually, all I did was to tell the dresser your size, age, and the trimester of your pregnancy. He did the rest. I think he did a great job. By the time your hairdresser, manicurist, and make-up artist are finished, we'll be ready to go down to dinner and meet the maddening crowd. Before you accuse me of being sexist, I'm also having a haircut, manicure and pedicure, and a facial. I hope it will camouflage some of what my family will no doubt see. They're very perceptive since most of them are medical doctors. We'll have to be early since we will form the receiving line of two to meet the family, so they'll get a good look at me up close and personal."

"Mark, isn't this going to be hard and tiring for you? We could postpone this until you're a little stronger," Mary Ella suggested.

"If I don't manage this tonight, my family will have me hospitalized before the soup course is served. I also recognize that you dropped everything to come to Germany and to come here with me to Boston. I understand that you're obligated to go back to Summer County. It will be as cold as a witch's tit before long here, but it won't be nearly as uncomfortable for you there in the south. Your blood is too thin to survive Boston's deep freeze, particularly because you're pregnant. I'll come to you when I'm stronger and not so much of a burden as I am now."

"Oh, Mark, you're not a burden."

"I feel as if I am. Believe me, Mary Ella, I want you to stay with me here while we wait for the babies to be born, but for the next few months, I'll be deep into physical therapy here at Shiloh. I won't impose on you while you feel as if you still want to work, but you know, if you say the word, I'll be wherever you want me."

She understood his need to do this next phase of his recovery independently, and she applauded his determination.

CHAPTER 26

When Mark informed her that there would be sixty or more for dinner, he wasn't off by much. Mary Ella stood next to him while he partially sat on a tall stool at the entrance to a salon, one of several anti-rooms for the dining hall.

First came the eldest, but by no means infirm, Dr. Milton Townsend with his wife, Dr. Avery Todd Townsend. She wore a slender, muted red dress that fit perfectly on her svelte frame, and Milton wore formal evening attire with a cummerbund of the same shade as his wife's dress. Since their daughter was currently in a mental institution, the son-in-law, Judge William Turner Whiting, and the grandchildren, William Junior, Everest, and Natalia Whiting, all teenagers, were in attendance and all in formal evening wear.

Next was the second oldest, Dr. Dominique Townsend Fitch, and her husband, Dr. David Fitch. Their only daughter Dr. Norah Fitch Rogers, and her husband, Dr. Alvin Baxter Rodgers, accompanied them. They had eight stair-step children beginning with Dr. Ted Rodgers. His absentee socialite wife frequently gained a bit of notoriety in certain casinos and other venues on the European continent, leaving Ted to raise their hearing-challenged adolescent daughter, Chandra, alone.

Mary Ella could not believe how beautiful and impish the young girl was when she sign-languaged something that made Mark burst out laughing. Ted and his daughter were followed by his single siblings Robert "Bobby," Cole, Shiloh, Alan and his wife Sharon, and Ross, all doctors, and Michael with (surprise, surprise) Mary Ella's homegirl, Kayla Hill of the Columbia County, South Carolina, high-society Hill family.

"Kayla." Mary Ella broadly smiled as they hugged. "The last time I saw you was forever ago. Are you still with the State Department in Washington, DC?"

"I am, yes. This is my guy friend, Michael. We're one of the few couples in this family who are not medical doctors. Michael's an attorney."

"It's a pleasure to meet you, Mary Ella. I've been to Summer County and tried to convince your cousin, Satarah Johnson, to sell The Summer House to McCoy Hotels. I'm the corporate vice president of the hotel chain. Of course, being a very smart woman, Satarah turned me down and laughed in my face about it. I didn't know at the time that my cousin, Mark, was a possible ally."

"It wouldn't have done you a bit of good if you had known." Mark laughed. "The Summer House is in the right hands with Satarah and her family. Her husband, Douglas Johnson, is a fellow Marine and a pal of mine. I suspect The Summer House will remain in Satarah's family for generations to come."

"I believe you're right, Mark," Michael agreed, "and it's good to have you home again after so long. I hope you'll stick around for a while, and you, too, Mary Ella."

"Thank you, Michael." Mary Ella nodded noncommittedly.

"We'll make time to talk," Kayla suggested to Mary Ella with a tight squeeze. Mary Ella thought Kayla looked stunning in a form-fitting, money-green sheath that left her shoulders and arms bare.

As they moved on, Mark laughed and hugged the youngest of Alvin and Norah's offspring, US Air Force jet fighter pilot Captain Shawn Baxter Rodgers."

"Well, look what the cat dragged," Mark joked, hugging Shawn before he reached for Shawn's wife, Helen Marlow Rodgers, for a kiss on the cheek and tight squeeze.

"Are you two still in Hawaii?" Mark inquired, looking between the younger couple.

Helen shrugged. "Most of the time."

Something in her voice triggered a memory or thought or maybe just a dream, which was fleeting when Shawn lifted his and Helen's daughter,

Rosemary "Rosy" Dominique Rodgers, so that the youngster could hug Mark and Mary Ella around their necks.

"Wow, Rosy, you're trying to grow up on me," Mark remarked.

"I'm going to be all grown up before you know it." Rosy grinned cheekily, then whispered, *sotto voce,* "I still want a little brother or a little sister, but Dad and Mom aren't cooperating," making everyone laugh.

She was as pretty as a picture, but her mother, Helen, looked like someone whose face and figure should be up on the next high-fashion magazine cover, Mary Ella thought. Helen wore a flame-red tube but looked like she'd be more comfortable in gunslinger attire with a have-gun-will-travel banner slung across her body. From her stance and demeanor, she'd be an ideal Bond Girl or one of the female super heroes, Mary Ella thought. Despite Helen's undeniable beauty, there was something about her that warned in a life or death struggle, Mary Ella would definitely want Helen on her side. It was a feeling her Cherokee blood wouldn't let her shake. This woman was a warrior, not merely a US Navy officer.

The line moved on to Dr. Rupert Townsend Junior, his wife, Dr. Evelyn Ames Townsend, their only son, Dr. Rupert II, and his wife, Dr. LeNora Hicks Townsend. Mary Ella began to dread the introduction to Rupert II and LeNora's only son, Dr. Rupert Townsend III.

Rupert III hugged Mark and then took Mary Ella's hands in his, kissing her knuckles. "It's a pleasure to meet you, Mary Ella. I understand you're from Summer County, South Carolina."

"I am, yes."

"Then you, no doubt, know Dr. Cecile Jordan Dixon."

"I do, yes. I'm best friends with her husband's cousin, Eric Dixon." Mary Ella immediately felt the man's sadness and loss, though she sensed Rupert III still tried to hide it and smiled at her. This is the man Satarah told her was briefly married to Cecile, Mary Ella recalled. He was certainly a tall, distinguished-looking, none-the-less handsome man, but not as tall or as strikingly handsome as Donald Dixon. Not that she believed Cecile would base a marriage on appearance. Cecile was not a superficial woman, and it likely had nothing to do with wealth.

Donald was financially secure as were all of the Dixons. Still, Rupert III was among the one-percenters, the über wealthy, like Chuck and Vivian Alexander Montgomery, in terms of wealth. Mary Ella didn't know what brought an end to Cecile's marriage to Rupert III, but she was clearly happily married to Donald with a growing family.

"Please tell Cecile and her family I said hello." Rupert III nodded.

"I'll do that." It broke Mary Ella's heart to see the wistfulness in Rupert's eyes when he mentioned Cecile.

"Thank you." Rupert III nodded. "Good to have you home again, Mark."

"Thank you, Rupert. I'll call to set up an appointment with you so that you can bring me up to speed on what you're doing at the Science and Technology Foundation."

"We've got a lot of interesting things happening in sea-based biomedicines. Cecile and I worked on a project in Alaska that yielded hugely beneficial products. Let's make time soon to talk about it."

"Will do." Mark nodded as Rupert III moved on.

Then it was Drs. Harlan and Irene Townsend's faces who frowned at Mark, looking at him from the bottom up.

Irene kissed her grandson on both cheeks and then gripped his jaw tightly. Looking closely into his eyes, Irene mildly frowned. "Boy, you look like warmed-over shite. Where have you been for the last five years that you look like this? Where are all those muscles you used to have? Gary, come look at your boy," Irene ordered her son.

That's when Mary Ella realized Mark's family was unaware he'd been a captive.

"I'm sure he's fine, Mama." Dr. Gary Brooks stepped forward and hugged his son tightly.

"Bull shite!" Irene scoffed. "Judith, look at your son and tell me he looks well."

"Nothing that a few good meals and a lot of rest won't cure." Dr. Judith Cole Brooks, Mark's mother, stepped forward and hugged him, too. "Frankly, I hope my son is the reason this pretty, young woman is what, in the second trimester? It's about time we had some babies in this branch of the family." Judith eyed first Mark and her other son, Dr. Vaughn Brooks, over her shoulder. Vaughn looked wise and otherwise avoided his mother's glare.

Mark put his arm around Mary Ella's shoulder. "Mary Ella, the irreverent, doll-faced woman, and the suave, debonair man are my grandparents, Drs. Harlan and Irene Townsend Brooks."

"You ain't never lied about my pretty Irene." Harlan pinched his wife's butt. She squeezed his rear, too, making everyone laugh. It brought levity to the look of concern on every face.

"Next, we have my always brilliant, grounded father and my sometimes sweet and discrete mother, Drs. Gary and Judith Cole Brooks. Hiding from my mother is my little brother, Vaughn."

"Hey!" Vaughn scoffed. "Enough with the *'little'* bull." He took Mary Ella's hand. "Please tell me there are more like you at home and unattached."

"Sorry, I'm it, but there are plenty of available women in Summer County." Mary Ella laughed.

"Wait! What? Summer County as in South Carolina?"

"Yes." Mary Ella nodded, surprised. "Do you know it?"

"Heck, yeah. We have a bunch of women in this family who are from or connected to Summer County. Besides, Mark called me several years ago from East Jablip Land on the other side of the moon and ordered me to go to Summer County to perform a surgery on the prima ballerina Linda Lewis Montgomery. She donated bone marrow to her half-brother, an English bloke, Bradford Smyth, I believe is his name. I hoped Linda had more like her at home. Of course, she did, but they're a rainbow coalition belonging to Chuck and Vivian Alexander Montgomery. None of them are prima ballerinas, though. Do you know them?"

"Chuck and Vivian, yes. I grew up with the Alexander family. I've seen Linda perform on Broadway."

"Man! She is awesome!" raved Vaughn. "I was truly bummed when I couldn't steal her away from Will Hamilton."

"My *younger* brother is an aficionado of live theatre, particularly ballet," Mark interjected.

"Mary Ella, I can be anything you want, even if you have two left feet. We can ditch Gimpy and—"

"Not on your life, ace." Mark teasingly pushed his brother away from Mary Ella. "Go find your own Dream Girl."

"Looking for her every day, but a word to the wise, brother." Vaughn leaned in closer to whisper to Mark and Mary Ella. "If you thought your act of being hale and hardy fooled anyone of the thirty or so doctors in this room, you've got another thought coming."

Finally, the end of the line was in sight. Mary Ella felt Mark's fatigue even though he was valiantly fighting not to show it. Turning toward him, she leaned closer. "Mark, you need to rest."

"I know, but this is the last of my grands." He leaned toward her and then turned to smile at Dr. Hayden Townsend, the youngest of the grands, and his lovely wife, Dr. Stephany Kirkland Townsend. "Mary Ella, this is Grand Uncle Hayden, but be forewarned. He cheats at golf. It takes a strong woman like Grandaunt Stephany to keep him honest."

"*Ha!* That'll be the day," Stephany joked, looking up at her husband over her shoulder. "Mark's right, though. Don't play golf—"

"Or cards with my father. My mother is right. He's a terrible cheat," their daughter interrupted. "Hello, Mary Ella. I'm Dr. Priscilla Townsend Flack. This is my husband, Dr. Wendell Flack. Welcome to Shiloh. We've heard good things about you."

"Thank you, Dr. Flack, but I pay Mark to say nice things about me. I think I'll have to put him on retainer," Mary Ella joked.

"Oh, Mark, I like her. She's a real keeper, this one. However, Mary Ella, Mark would sing your praises, without payment, I'm sure. No, no, we have it on good authority from our daughter-in-law, Savannah." Priscilla looked around. "Where is your wife, Nathan?"

"First, Savannah went to check on the children," Nathan Flack answered his mother. "Then she had to take a call, Mom. One of her patients has gone into early labor at Georgetown Medical in DC. Savannah is monitoring her patient's progress. We may have to fly back tonight. In the interim, hello, Mary Ella. I apologize for the absence of our three children. They've come down with the flu, and we don't want to infect everyone." He stepped aside and clamped his hand on another man's shoulder. "However, this, Mary Ella, is my older brother, Dr. Robert Flack."

"Robert, a pleasure to meet you. I've heard your name associated with the Woods Hole Oceanographic Institute, haven't I?" Mary Ella shook his hand.

"You're correct, Mary Ella. I'm currently the head of the Institute. You know Cecile Jordan, don't you?"

She nodded in surprise. "I do, yes."

"Cecile was one of my students and research assistants at San Diego State University before I came to Woods Hole. I'm so proud that she won the Nobel for the work she and my cousin, Rupert III, did on climate change and molecular biochemistry."

Mary Ella released his hand and listened to his and Nathan's discussion with Mark. However, she got the distinct impression that Robert's feelings for Cecile Jordon Dixon went far beyond a teacher-to-student or research assistant's relationship. That was true, especially since neither Rupert III nor Robert was currently married. *Geeze*, Mary Ella wondered *how many men have been in love with Cecile and still have strong feelings for her?* This trip was shaping up to be very surprising.

"So, how are things at the United Nations?" inquired Mark of his cousin, Nathan, the US Ambassador to the UN.

"Touchy, with so many renegade countries threatening nuclear holocaust. Actually, you were in Africa this last tour, weren't you?"

"Uh, there and the Mid-East." Mark shrugged noncommittally. By the time he was rescued, he didn't know for sure what country he was in. "Thanks for the help you gave us."

"Think nothing of it. Recently, I've been getting reports that a great deal of money changed hands to insurgents for the purchase of spent radioactive fuel to make dirty bombs. Did you hear anything like that where you were?"

Just then, Dr. Savannah Logan Flack, Nathan's wife, joined them. "No shop talk, honey." Savannah and Mary Ella hugged warmly. "We're celebrating Mark's return after being away for so long."

Mary Ella picked up on Mark's unease about any discussion of his whereabouts for the recent past. She was happy to steer the conversation in a different direction. "It's quite a surprise to see you here, Savannah."

"That's true, Mary Ella, especially since I haven't had an opportunity to visit with you when I come to visit my brother, sister-in-law, nephews, and nieces. Have you seen them since you've been back?"

"Yes, in fact, I saw Jefferson and LaiLoni Skai at Benson's sixteenth birthday celebration recently. Of course, you know that Jefferson's son, Miles, works at The Summer House part-time. I haven't seen Jefferson Junior that much, but Douglas and Bob Sweeney tell me he's doing a fine job for the fire department's Centerville medic squad."

"He's got the hots for Amina Dixon, I understand." Savannah winked conspiratorially. "Nathan's family is trying to woo Jefferson Junior into applying to Harvard for undergrad and then medical school. Especially if Amina accepts the offer to attend MIT. The next thing you know, my youngest nephew, Stephen, and their baby sisters, will be grown."

"Not too soon, I hope," Mark interjected. "I think we need to be seated if you don't mind. I can escort you lovely ladies to the table."

Mary Ella and Savannah wrapped an arm around his waist while he put his arms around their shoulders. They appeared to be leisurely following Robert and Nathan, Savannah's brother-in-law, and husband, respectively, into the dining hall. However, Vaughn, Mark's brother, followed closely behind, ready to assist if necessary.

Mark nodded to his brother when he was finally seated, and Vaughn looked relieved. Standing in the receiving line and chatting with his family members and close family friends was meaningful because until a few weeks ago, he wasn't sure he would ever see them again.

Mark felt Mary Ella's hand on his thigh and turned to look into her eyes.

"Eat a good meal, Mark, because shortly after, I'm taking you back to bed," she whispered for his ears only.

"That works for me." He smiled at her and squeezed her hand.

"I don't think we have the same thing in mind, pal, when I say I'm taking you back to bed," Mary Ella joked. "I'll ask for the buggy and explain I'm fatigued because of my condition."

"Mary Ella?" Judith put her elbows on the table and leaned in to get her attention. "I understand you're a registered nurse. Were you with Mark while he was with Doctors Without Borders?"

"Yes, we were paired together. That's generally how it works. We work in teams of two or more."

"You're no longer with the NGO?"

"That's correct. I've moved back home to Summer County, South Carolina."

"Are you nursing there?"

"Actually, I manage the Summer County General Hospital's emergency room nursing staff."

"Really. I imagine that's a tough position to hold."

"It is a challenge," Savannah offered before Mary Ella could speak. "As you may recall, Judith, my brother, Jefferson, is the Dean of the Summer County Academy. They offer a fully accredited nursing school curriculum there. Jefferson has told me how much they value Mary Ella's insight into emergency medicine since returning to the county. She periodically lectures at the school. Her experiences in Third World countries add an extra level of knowledge to the school's program.

"Mary Ella, didn't I hear that Jenny Sweeney just had a baby girl?" Savannah continued and steered the conversation away from what could have been an uncomfortable situation. As the wife of a diplomat, Savannah knew that specific topics about America's intrusion into certain foreign lands could be highly sensitive.

"She did, yes. Her name is Emily Rose. We call her Rosy," Mary Ella smiled at young Rosemary "Rosy" Rodgers.

"Would you ever consider moving away from Summer County, Mary Ella?" asked Gary Brooks. "My wife is the head of Emergency Medicine at Mass General. As a physician, she's a real taskmaster. However, as one of Mass General's key administrators, she'd probably try to steal you away from Summer County. Me, on the other hand, I'm a plastic surgeon. There usually isn't a need for an emergency in my field."

"I'm a high school principal," Wendell Flack interjected, "and I've heard quite a lot of good things about Summer County Academy. I'd like to pick your brain about that."

"I'd be happy to talk with you about it since I'm a graduate of the unique system of education there. However, the best source of information is Savannah's brother, Jefferson Logan, Dean of Summer County Academy."

"The Ambassador, Jeff Logan?"

"Yes, the same. If I'm not mistaken, he's a Harvard undergrad and Harvard Law grad," Mary Ella offered.

"Is that true, Savannah? Is your brother Ambassador Jefferson Logan?"

"It is. I thought I introduced you to Jeff at the wedding."

"Oh, my, Savannah, there were so many people at your and Nathan's wedding. I don't know who I did or didn't meet."

"Actually, Jefferson escorted me down the aisle."

"Oh, yes, of course, now I remember him. You'll have to give me his contact information."

"Certainly, Wendell."

"I think Wendell is beginning to suffer from a little dementia," Vaughn whispered to Mark across Mary Ella. "Jeff Logan has been here with his LaiLoni and their family several times. We're going to have to have Wendell tested." Vaughn sadly shook his head.

"I hope it's not early-onset Alzheimer's," Mark whispered. "Wendell is only in his sixties."

"He wants to talk with me about Summer County Academy. I'll make a point of talking with him tomorrow and let you know whether I notice anything."

Vaughn smiled. "Thanks, Mary Ella. That would be very helpful."

"I want time with you, too, Mary Ella," Savannah whispered. "I want to give you a checkup."

Mary Ella sighed and nodded in agreement.

"Good. Who's your OB/GYN?" Savannah asked.

"Alfred Quade."

"Ah, good man," Savannah offered. "I tried to steal him away from Summer County for my practice in DC. He wouldn't budge."

"He's happy there." Mary Ella smiled.

"I can understand why. I'll give Alfred a call in the morning. You look a bit dehydrated. I want you to force fluids tonight and be completely hydrated by tomorrow morning."

At the clock chiming the eight o'clock hour, everyone at the long, long, beautifully dressed and set dining table quieted. Milton, the eldest and patriarch of the family, stood and offered a prayer for the blessings bestowed on the family and friends and included a heartfelt appreciation for Mark's return to Shiloh. After the prayer, everyone, except Mark, stood and hoisted their glasses of wine in a toast to the return of the prodigal son. "A cheer! A cheer! A cheer!" they all hailed Mark in unison and then took a sip of wine before sitting down again. Waitstaff, who were lined up on both sides of the long, bowling-alley-length table, were given the nod by Milton to Mr. Masters to begin serving the evening meal. As one course was finished, the staff skillfully removed the dishes and provided the next course with the precision neurosurgeons ply their trade.

Although there was a great deal of chatter at the dinner table, Mary Ella had never experienced such formal surroundings. Place settings with place card holders, individual salt cellar and pepper shakers, utensil setting for eight courses included a charger plate, dinner napkin in the napkin ring, bread plate, individual butter dish with lid, butter spreader on crystal knife rest, cocktail fork, soup spoon, fish knife and fork and crescent-shaped bone dish for fish bones, entrée knife and fork, ice cream spoon (for sorbet during palate cleansing course), relevé or main course knife and fork, salad knife and fork, dessert fork and dessert spoon.

Also, stemware for water goblet, sherry glass, white wine glass, red wine glass to a champagne flute were precisely situated on the table. The salad course was served in European fashion at the end of the meal. Sherry was served during appetizer and soup courses, white wine was served during fish and entrée courses, red wine during the relevé course, and champagne during the dessert course. Coffee or tea was served after the dessert course.

Mary Ella thought, *thank goodness for Satarah*, who she helped set up for formal dinners before or she would have been as lost as actress Julia Roberts' character, Vivian, was in the old movie *Pretty Woman*.

Although extremely long and filled to overflowing with fresh flowers, long tapers, and colorful decorations, the table was dwarfed by the thirty-foot-high, barrel-shaped ceiling with painted frescos in muted shades of red, green, and gold. The paintings depicted what appeared to be scenes of African origin. Mary Ella wasn't sure, but one scene could have been Hannibal at the Gates of Rome. She didn't want to be too obvious, but the hand paintings on the ceiling and walls looked to be very old, at least by a couple hundred years. Every space appeared to be dedicated to learning about historical events.

"You're right," Savannah whispered to Mary Ella across her husband Nathan, as if she could read her mind. "I had Nathan taking me from room to room and explaining everything. It took months!"

"Indeed, she did," Nathan agreed. "Savannah is like a sponge. She soaks up every bit of information she can find on a subject. I'm hard-pressed sometimes to feed her insatiable appetite for knowledge. Especially since Mark, I, and the others in our generation grew up being required to know every detail about Shiloh. Savannah still has me wandering the salons giving tutorials at night whenever we're here."

"It's fascinating to see this much history depicted in one place other than a museum. These murals bring that history to life. Jefferson and I grew up in a one-stop-sign town that's barely on any map. Our parents were both teachers and were returning from a convention when their plane crashed." Savannah continued to look up and around. "Jeff was eighteen, but I was only twelve. We were paid out of the insurance they had, and the airline paid insurance claims. Jeff fought for custody of me and won. We sold the house we grew up in, and Jeff put me in a private all-girls boarding school in Asheville, North Carolina, while he went to Harvard undergrad. We spent the summers and holidays together. When I graduated from high school, I went straight to Spelman, where I met Vivian Alexander. After college, I went to medical school at Georgetown. Vivian was at Georgetown law.

"Jefferson and my parents instilled a passion for learning in us from an early age. So, when I see a place like this that's steeped in culture, history, and information, I'm in the search-for-knowledge overload. Thankfully,

Nathan and I have children who share our craving for education and experiences."

"I can understand why. I can't imagine what all of these images mean, and the colors are so vibrant." Mary Ella looked around, too.

"Each salon is dedicated to one of the top one hundred kings and queens of Africa," Mark offered. "The frescos you see depicted report the significant contributions each person made in history."

"We had to learn about each and every one of them." Nathan ruefully shook his head. "At the time, I protested, saying when would I ever use this type of information and low and behold here I am as the US Ambassador to the United Nations." He laughed. "You can't imagine how often these historical people come up in conversation over cocktails and dinner."

"That's part of the reason I force Nathan to take me from room to room." Savannah grinned and winked. "The rooms are called salons here at Shiloh. Sometimes we spend hours sitting and talking in each salon or making out. We bring our children with us when we come, but considering they're so young, they mostly sleep through our discussions," she laughed, "but it's good to know this resource will always be here to teach each generation another aspect of world history."

Mary Ella touched her belly, thinking about the history her twins, if Mark's, would share. She would want them to know their family, both hers and Marks'. If they were not his, there would be a great deal of history she would have to learn so that she could teach her children about their heritage.

Just then, she felt Mark reach for her hand. She realized that she had stopped eating and was just staring into near space, lost in the conundrum her life was turning out to be. She squeezed his hand in acceptance of his obvious offer of moral support.

CHAPTER 27

Later that night, as Mark and Mary Ella were preparing for bed, she turned from the dressing table, still removing the makeup from her face, and regarded Mark. "You weren't kidding about the formalwear for dinner. What was with the reds, golds, and greens? It seemed as if everyone was wearing those colors, even the men with the cummerbunds. The table was beautifully set, and I also noticed those colors were prominent in the décor."

"Have you seen the Ethiopian flag?"

"Probably. Why?"

"I'll show you." He pulled up the image on his iPad.

"Ah, I see, and this Ethiopian anthem is in the vestibule as you enter the castle."

He laughed. "Yes, but this place is not a castle."

"It's not *'There was an old woman who lived in a shoe. She had so many children, she didn't know what to do. She gave them some broth without any bread. Then whipped them all soundly and put them to bed,'*" she animated, teasing him with her antics and had Mark hooting in laughter.

"No, I think we had more than broth tonight." He still laughed at her.

Then Mary Ella turned back to the dressing table and regarded him in the mirror. "Mark, what did Chandra sign to you that made you laugh?"

He laughed again. "The imp told me that she thought I stayed away from home for so long because I had gone gay. She said she believed that because I haven't brought another woman here since Allison." He used a remote-control device to open a long line of drapery to reveal a balcony and an expansive darkened view of the Charles River. He reached out a hand for her to come to him.

Mary Ella laughed, too, as she joined him on one of the divans facing the view. "Chandra is quite something. She reads lips?"

Mark put his right arm around her, drawing her to snuggle in against his chest. "She does extremely well and can communicate in more languages than me or anyone else in the family. She challenges her father, Nathan, Michael, Shawn, and me to read her lips and say what language she's speaking. She's stumped us the majority of the time."

"So, you can not only read lips but also read her sign in different languages?"

"Yes, all of us know how to sign and read lips. However, she prefers for us to speak to her as if she can hear us. She doesn't like to feel as if she's not a part of the conversation. We just have to remember to face her enough so that she can read accurately. If we are facing away from her, she'll sometimes feel our vocal chords to figure out what's being said. The only time we sign to her is if she asks us to when she's sitting too far to read the speaker's lips or that person isn't signing."

"Chandra is quite a remarkable young girl." Mary Ella leaned back against Mark's shoulder and raised her feet to the oblong hassock next to Mark's.

"You don't know the half of it. I truly expect she'll take the MCATs before she's fifteen. Her IQ is off the charts as it is. Talk about someone with a thirst for knowledge; she's it."

"You mentioned that her mother isn't in the picture?"

"Ted's wife, Victoria Stanton Rodgers, hasn't been in this hemisphere since Chandra was born. She spends her time jet-setting around the globe with one man or the other, but she won't give Ted a divorce. She grew up privileged in a wealthy family, just like Allison, but Allison was more grounded because she wanted to go to medical school and practice medicine from a young age. However, I believe Victoria only married Ted for the status symbol he represents. He's a noted surgeon and the Chairman of Massachusetts's State Medical Board. Victoria and Felicia Montrose grew up together."

"The heiress? Didn't her father, Tyler McKenzie Montrose, go to prison for arranging to have Jefferson Logan murdered and creating an international incident in the process? I understand that he died in prison."

"Yes, Felicia became pregnant purposefully to trick Jefferson into marrying her. I always thought she was a few French fries short of a happy meal," Mark joked. "She did outrageous things in defiance of her family. Marrying a black man was one of those things even though he's Harvard Law Phi Beta Kappa. It was clear that Jefferson Logan only agreed to marry Felicia because of his son, Jeff Junior. Then came Miles and Stephen, so Jefferson was committed to making the best of a bad situation. Felicia was the heir apparent of Montrose Global, one of the world's top one hundred monoliths. However, she died tragically, riding on the hood of a speeding Rolls-Royce in the Georgetown section of Washington, DC, Lady Godiva style, stark naked. Her lion's share of the company passed to Jefferson and their sons. Tyler fought Jefferson for custody of Jeff Junior, Miles, and Stephen. When he lost in court, he conspired to have Jefferson murdered." Mark sighed and continued.

"Felicia and Victoria were constantly in the news for some outlandish things they did. I mean, The Fives, my cousins and I, have done some pretty wild and stupid things in our sometimes-misspent youth, but Victoria and Felicia took crazy to an entirely new level."

"The Fives, those of you who are in the fifth generation since Ashro," Mary Ella acknowledged.

"Ah, you're catching on." Mark smiled. "You may not have done the headcount, but there are sixteen men and only two women in our generation. You can't possibly imagine how much mischief eighteen, closely-knit cousins could get ourselves into, considering we were all raised and educated in this house. We are all about the same age or within ten years of one another, so we still speak the same language. Our motto was *'Lead us into temptation.'* Mr. Masters took charge of us and was not averse to warming our bottoms, justifiably so, from time to time. Chandra, Rosemary, Nathan and Savannah's three, and our potato spuds constitute the sixth generation. We'll brand them The Sixes. However, despite her mother's craziness, Chandra knows who and what her mother is, but she doesn't seem to let it bother her. She knows we love her and communicates with us all the time."

"She says I have a southern accent." Mary Ella laughed.

Mark looked at her askance and narrowed his brows. "You do have a southern accent."

"I do not," she protested with an elbow to his solar plexus.

"Ouch!" He winced. "You don't have to get violent, babe. I don't mean that you sound like someone from the Mississippi Bayou, because I can tell the difference, but you do have a slow, husky quality to your voice. You should record yourself sometime and listen. Frankly, I love the way you speak, particularly when you whisper seductive words in my ears or when you tell me how I make you feel loud and clear when we're making love."

She elbowed him again, laughing. "I'm not going to say anything else seductive until I listen to myself speak."

"Hey, was I complaining?" He winced and rubbed his chest.

She noticed his apparent discomfort. "Are you in pain, Mark?"

"Not so much."

She stood and reached a hand out to him to help him to his feet. "Yeah, no, I don't believe you. Come with me."

"Is this where you take me to bed?"

"Not yet, pal." Mary Ella supported him and walked slowly into the men's en-suite to a massage table. "Okay, drop your drawers and get up on the table face down."

"This dominatrix personae had real promise until you ordered me to lay face down," Mark joked.

"Oh, you have jokes, do you?"

"When it comes to you and my body, it's no laughing matter, babe. I'm yours to command." Mark laughed.

Mary Ella was pleased to witness the return of the old Mark she knew and loved. Somehow, she also knew that being here at his home with his family gave him strength and the power to heal. Much the same way she felt about Summer County. It was like going to the source of her endurance.

Mark followed her instructions, but each movement was agony. When he was face down, Mary Ella began giving a deep-tissue massage to him that had his eyes nearly rolling back in his head. *"Damn!* That feels good," he pleasurably moaned.

"You're strung tighter than a bass drum, Mark. Your muscles feel like bricks. Why didn't you say something?"

"If I had known you'd strip me naked and give me this kind of treatment, believe me, I would have."

Mary Ella smacked his naked bottom.

"I draw the line at S&M, babe." His laugh lapsed into moans of tortured gratification.

"Mark, did you get a vibe from Shawn's wife, Helen?"

"All the time. Now that you mention it, and I don't know why you did in connection with my comment about S&M, but I had a strange sensation while talking with her tonight. I mean, it's happened before, but tonight I couldn't figure out why that was true. Obviously, you did, too, and I know your instincts to be spot on."

"What's her story?"

"Yeah, there, right there." She dug her thumbs into his spine. "Uh, oh, yeah. That's it. Okay, Helen Marlowe. Local DC girl. She grew up in the foster care system, moving from one home to another because the men couldn't keep it in their pants around her, but she managed the pull-herself-up-by-her-own-bootstraps kind of thing. She was about eighteen years old, a junior in college at Howard University, and working in an upscale men's club as a cocktail waitress to pay for her education. Two jokers came back night after night, demanding to be seated in her section of the club. They consistently harassed and propositioned her, and she declined their advances." Mark moaned and continued.

"One night after closing, these two miscreants attempted to take what Helen wasn't willing to give freely. She put them both in the hospital. One has a detached retina, and the other will never father children. What the men didn't know is that she was a martial arts master in high school and college. She was also ROTC at Howard as another source of funds for her education. However, these men claimed Helen provoked the altercation in an attempt to rob them. Because of her juvenile record of fighting, she was arrested and went to court, where some Georgetown Law school students were monitoring court cases as a student project. They thought Helen's attorney was illiterate for letting her juvenile record be introduced into the court record. As a result, they believed she got a raw deal because the bozos had money and high-priced lawyers. Instead of the men being charged with attempted rape, Helen was charged with solicitation, prostitution, and attempted robbery. The students were doing the project for a class assignment given to them by your pal, Judge Vivian Alexander Montgomery.

"Apparently, Vivian agreed with the students. Although she was a DC Circuit Court of Appeals Judge at the time, she arranged to have one of her former law partners, Melissa Charles Lightfoot, take over the case as Helen's legal counsel. Ms. Lightfoot requested the District Court submit the case for judicial review. Vivian, because of her prior knowledge of the circumstances, abstained from hearing the case. Three other judges, one of whom is the Chief Justice Harry Hathaway, reviewed the case and overturned Helen's convictions. The DC State's Attorney wisely didn't attempt to refile charges against Helen, and the matter was dismissed.

"As the unofficial story goes," Mark continued, "Vivian then called her sister-in-law, Admiral Stacy Greene Alexander. She had Helen tested out of her final year of college at Howard University and then inducted into the Naval Officer Candidate School. Helen's record as a standout student and her success in the Reserved Officers' Training Corps at Howard University was legendary. Vivian and Stacy kept tabs on her progress. Helen graduated with flying colors.

"My cousin, Shawn, told us he met Helen while at a three-month training seminar at the Norfolk military base. Shawn was already an Air Force jet fighter pilot, and Helen was a US Navy Lieutenant. He told me that he took one look at Helen, stuck a fork in it, and called it done. It was pretty much the same way I felt about you.

"Shawn has a private jet the family gave him for his twenty-first birthday. One weekend he flew Helen and some of their other friends, who are also officers, to Las Vegas for some R&R. You know what that means, right?"

"Yes, R&R means rest and relaxation."

"Well, technically, yes, but among The Fives, it means a lot of wine, heavy partying, and lots and lots of sex. However, for Shawn, it meant to put a ring on it. So, after copious amounts of champagne, Shawn had himself and Helen driven to one of those all-night wedding venues where he made himself her husband and her first lover. Helen didn't remember the wedding and thought Shawn was joking when he told her they were legally married.

"To put it mildly, Helen was angry, but according to Shawn, it was FUBAR." Mark shook his head.

"Fucked up beyond all recognition," Mary Ella recounted. "I recognize the acronym."

"Exactly, so when they got back to Norfolk after the R&R in Las Vegas to continue their military training courses, Helen refused to have any contact what-so-ever with Shawn. After the training ended, they went back to their duty stations; hers in Louisiana and his in California. Two months later, after trying every way he could to talk with Helen, Shawn received a text message from her stating that she's pregnant. Shawn knew Helen was a virgin until their wedding night, so he didn't question that the baby was his. Still, Helen refused to see him while she was pregnant and didn't even tell him when she went into labor. After Helen delivered their daughter, she had a nurse notify Shawn and promptly disappeared for five years, during which time Shawn raised Rosemary alone. Well, except for all of us pitching in when he would allow us to."

"It was happenstance or maybe not," Mark continued. "I've been on aircraft carriers before. They're so large that you can go for months without seeing the same person twice. That they were both on the same aircraft carrier in the Pacific during RIMPAC exercises and bumped into each other is more than a coincidence to my way of thinking. Nevertheless, after all those years apart, neither one had filed for divorce. Instead, they formed a tenuous alliance for Rosemary's sake. They're both stationed in Hawaii, still married, and live together in the same house."

"That story reminds me of Benny Alexander and Stacy Greene's story." Mary Ella frowned. "They went through something similar."

"Yeah, that's why there's a question of whether Shawn and Helen met accidentally on the aircraft carrier or whether the situation was contrived by Benny and/or Stacy." Mark stretched. "You see, Shawn is one of Benny's jet fighter squadron leaders, and Helen is a top training officer under Stacy's command."

"That does sound suspicious." Mary Ella continued to work on Mark's body. "Still, I hope it works out for them. The way Shawn looks at Helen, it's clear what his feelings are."

"She's beginning to warm up to him, too, but she never had a family before she became a Navy officer. Shawn says Helen regards the military as her home and her military command as her family. She's still uncomfortable around wealth."

"Well, that's understandable. This is a bit much." Mary Ella laughed.

"*Ha!* Remember where this all came from, Mary Ella. A scoundrel and a prostitute. We have skeletons in the closet like any other large, complex family."

"Every one of your family members is an upstanding citizen," Mary Ella scoffed.

"*Au contraire, mon amour.* You're forgetting about our own crazy cousin, hostage taker Charlotte Townsend Whiting. Did I mention that in the Rodgers branch of the family, we have cousin Alvin's brother Xavier Rodgers? He's out in Las Vegas and lives with his lifelong female companion, Chickie Day, star of the porn industry? They have a daughter, Rita Rodgers, who is a talented and much sought-after choreographer of stage and screen. However, she's prone to stalk her lovers long after the lovemaking part is over. Xavier owns a string of high-end strip joints and gentlemen's clubs, mostly out west. Chickie owns a porn movie production company where she stars in many of the movies and subjects her potential actors and actresses to casting-couch interviews. Sometimes, Xavier likes to get into the act, too, with Chickie and other men."

Mary Ella stared stunned. "You say she produces, directs, and stars in blue movies in Las Vegas?"

"She's all but cornered the market in the blue-movie industry. So, don't put this family up on any pedestal," Mark confirmed.

"Interesting."

"Why? What's interesting?"

"Satarah's former husband, Jonathan Jeffrey Whitfield, and her sister, Carlotta, are blue-movie stars in Las Vegas."

"JoJeff? I remember people talking about the scandal when I was there the year we met."

"Yes, and just after we left, JoJeff returned to Summer County."

"Bummer. Are Douglas and Satarah okay?"

"They're fine. Satarah and Douglas are expecting again. She and I should deliver at about the same time."

"Good. As I recall, JoJeff was a real piece of work. So, you understand, the Townsend descendants have our own share of regrettable family characters. We don't have the right to laud our resources over anyone. Still, Shawn says Helen won't allow him to spend a red cent on her, but he's deeply in love with her and determined to make a family with her. At least he still has a fighting chance to make it work. For now, he pilots the space shuttle to SPACEHOME. That allows Helen to have quality time with Rosy so that they'll get to know each other better. Shawn wants more children with Helen. As I said, he believes that they have a chance at making a family situation work for them. However, my sympathies are for my cousins Rupert Townsend and Robert Flack."

"You noticed that, too?" Mary Ella frowned.

"I did, yes." Mark nodded. "It's hard to miss when two men are so deeply in love with the same woman, and neither one has a chance in hell of having her come back to him."

Mary Ella nodded. "I sensed it was something like that, and you're right. Cecile is over-the-moon happy with her husband, Donald Dixon, and their six children."

"You mentioned something about being best friends with Donald's cousin? Is that your former flame, Eric Dixon, you're referring to?"

"Yes, it is," Mary Ella acknowledged. "He's been a rock since I've been back in Summer County."

"You two were in love at one time."

"We were, and I still love him dearly, but we went our separate ways years ago. He went into the Army, then on to medical school, became a doctor, got married, and moved back home. Regrettably, the marriage didn't work out, and they divorced. He has residual feelings for his former wife that he's working through."

"He, no doubt, still has residual feelings for you, too. As I remember you telling me, he was your first lover."

"He was, yes, and he was there for me when I lost my parents. He's always been a source of strength for me. I consider him to be among my closest friends."

"Babe, a man never forgets what it feels like the first time he truly falls in love with a woman. You two were together for three years during nursing school."

"He moved away and married someone else."

"Uh-huh, and did he first ask you to marry him?"

"Well, yeah, but we were just kids then. I certainly wasn't emotionally or mentally ready to jump the broom when I was barely out of my teens."

"Yet, he asked you first, Mary Ella. That's significant."

"Is that how you feel about Allison?"

"I feel an obligation to her because her accident came as a result of an argument we had immediately preceding the tragedy. Besides, I never really asked her to marry me. I've thought of that fact over the years with regret, and I still wonder why I didn't formerly get down on one knee, present her with an engagement ring, and ask her to be my wife. However, had I known that she was in love with someone else, we never would have gotten as far as we did in the marriage plans. We certainly wouldn't have been at our wedding rehearsal dinner party two days away from tying the knot before a confirmed wedding guest list of nearly a thousand people. She would still be able to function as a brilliant physician. I will regret that stupid argument for the rest of my life."

"Turn over," Mary Ella instructed him. When he was face-up on the massage table, she leaned over him and gently kissed his mouth. "You should have no regrets, Mark. She is an adult responsible for her own actions. If she had been driving recklessly and injured or killed someone else, that would have been on her, not on you. She was your childhood friend, your first lover. Take care of her because that's who you are, but please stop carrying her emotional baggage when it's not yours to bear." She kissed him again slowly, deeply, and then continued his massage. Ultimately, she gave him a happy ending that drained all conscious thought from his mind.

CHAPTER 28

Sure enough, the next morning, Mark was roused out of bed by five and subjected to a three-hour panel of examinations and tests in the medical facility in one segment of what Mary Ella called "The Castle." That made him laugh, but what his family subjected him to was no laughing matter. He was poked and prodded from stem to stern, so-to-speak, but he understood his family's necessity to ensure his recovery was achievable. What they didn't know, and never would know, is that Mary Ella's ministration the night before subjected him to the *La petite mort,* more than once after which he experienced the first, real, deep, recuperative sleep he had since being rescued.

Nevertheless, after a round-table discussion with his family of specialists, he agreed to a regimen of steps and stages that would take about two months to achieve his full recovery. Since it was essentially consistent with his own diagnosis, he couldn't argue the points. His parents, grandparents, and brother couldn't be a part of the physical examinations. They were breaking the rules as it was by tending to a family member. Still, he sat through another discussion with his immediate family while they reviewed all of the test and examination results that were available so far.

"So, you see, I'll be fine." Mark smiled at the conclusion of the discussion.

Irene abruptly stood and began to pace the room full of family members who were physicians. "I'm your grandmother, Mark Harlan Brooks, and I love you more than my next breath, but I know what I see in those results. You were tortured often and consistently! So, don't you dare treat this situation glibly with your usual damnable devil-may-care attitude!"

"Mom." Gary tried to console his mother. "My son is home safe, if not completely sound… yet."

"Don't you try to mollycoddle me, Gary! You're just like your father. You two are so damn stoic; you readily suffer in silence. Someone put their hands on my flesh and blood to hurt him! That simply will not be tolerated! Someone will be held responsible for that and rue the day he was born into his miserable life!"

When the tears formed in his grandmother's eyes, Mark slowly rose and walked toward her, standing in her path. "'Mollycoddle' and 'rue the day' in the same rant? Wow, Gram, I'm scared of you," he deadpanned.

She stopped pacing and stood to look up at her grandson for perilous moments, a myriad of emotions passing across her gamine features until the dam broke, and she was weeping in his arms. Irene, the youngest female of her generation but the fiercest, could turn anyone to stone with just a look from her dark, flashing, and intelligent-looking eyes. As the head professor of orthopedic surgery at Harvard Medical, she struck fear in the hearts of her young doctors and students. She had always been the kick-ass taskmaster who Mark both respected and adored. To see her distraught was heart-wrenching for Mark.

"I'll mollycoddle and rue if I want to, you big oaf." She snatched a tissue from his hand that he held out to her. "You always were such a big pain in the arse!"

"An oaf? Now I'm a stupid, uncultured, or clumsy person and a pain in your arse? Careful, Gram, your English is showing," Mark teased.

"Oh, just shut up." She hugged him fiercely, burying her face in his chest and just breathing him in.

"Come on and sit down, Mom," Gary cajoled. "We're not finished with this discussion yet."

"We're not?" asked Mark as he seated his grandmother and resumed his own seat. "We've reviewed the results inside out and upside down. We have a plan of action, and I'm prepared to work the plan, including taking daily naps. What more is there to discuss?"

"I want to know whether your father and I are about to be blessed with grandchildren," Judith inserted. "Are the babies that lovely Mary Ella Baker is carrying going to be Brooks?"

"Oh, no, you don't, Judith!" Her father-in-law sternly shook his head, frowning. "Don't answer that, Mark. This is not our way. Mark is a grown man capable of taking care of himself and his business. All of our children are raised to be strong, independent thinkers. If or when he is ready to talk with us about his relationship with Mary Ella Baker, he will do so. If he asks for help, we'll be there for him. Until then, we will stay out of his affairs, and I do not mean that in a pejorative way. Is that understood, Judith?" Harlan demanded.

She sighed, nodded her head, "Yes, Sir," and regarded her father-in-law.

"Good! Now, Mark, I speak for this branch of the family and for others here, too, I'm sure. If Mary Ella is your choice for a mate, be assured she'll be welcomed into the family with open arms."

"Thanks, Granddad."

"All I want to know is why all the best women, like Mary Ella, are already taken?" grumbled Vaughn.

"Because, my other favorite grandson, it's the early bird that catches the worm. You're a night owl."

Mary Ella was up and having breakfast with the non-medical family members and Savannah.

"How are your children today, Savannah?"

"I haven't a clue. The children conned Mr. Masters and their father into taking them somewhere in this house this morning before I woke up. Those men are pushovers when it comes to Nate, Junior, Logan, and Paula," she huffed without heat.

Mary Ella laughed. "How is your patient in DC?" They sat at a round breakfast table in a sunny salon with a view of the Charles River. Mark arranged for one of the house staff to assist her that morning and lead her to one of the smaller breakfast salons, although it could seat forty with room to spare.

Savannah yawned. "After all that melodrama, she was experiencing Braxton Hicks contractions. My staff of on-call doctors kept me up half the night with reports on her condition."

"What's that?" asked Natalia Whiting, who outwardly was the picture-perfect pampered princess. She wouldn't be seen without every hair follicle rigidly in place and makeup professionally applied.

"It's false labor." Mary Ella told the girl, who appeared to be in her mid-teens. "It's also known as prodromal labor or practice contractions."

"Did that happen to you?"

"No, not that I'm aware of. There are sporadic uterine contractions that sometimes start around six weeks into a pregnancy. However, they are not usually felt until the second or third trimester."

"You're in the second trimester?" the teenager persisted.

"Yes, soon to be in my third and rounding the bend, so-to-speak, to my own personal labor day."

The girl purposely shivered and frowned. "I don't want ever to have somebody living inside me. It's like having an alien, a mini-me feeding off your insides. That is so gross!"

Chandra smiled while Kayla, Rosemary, Savannah, Helen, and Mary Ella laughed.

"That's how you got here, silly," Chandra signed, with Kayla translating for Mary Ella's benefit.

"I know that," Natalia huffed, "but I didn't know I was inside my mother eating what she ate." She frowned, her face scrunched up. "Do you think I'll be crazy like she is?"

"No." Savannah immediately shook her head. "Your mother is emotionally challenged. I promise what she's going through didn't come from what she ate while you were inside her womb."

"I hope not. Otherwise, I'd have to go on a diet, and that would really suck sideways!"

"Don't have a nutty, Nat. If you want, I have a book which explains all about babies when they're growing inside a body," Chandra signed and simultaneously spoke the words.

"It's Natalia, Brainiac," she huffed without heat.

"Actually, I want to examine Mary Ella." Savannah looked in her direction. "If you agree, maybe you'll let them see the ultrasound image."

There was no way Mary Ella would deny Chandra this opportunity to see babies in utero, but she was saving the surprise about there being twins.

After Chandra led the way to the medical suite, Savannah did the preliminary tests for height, weight, blood pressure, temperature, etc. Then, she had her recline on one of the tables.

"During the first six weeks of the third trimester," Savannah began as if providing a classroom lecture, "a baby will more than double in size–growing from approximately one to three pounds. He or she will also grow in length from about fourteen inches to almost seventeen inches. The baby's growth during this period is an important indicator of his or her health, so let's see what we have here." Everyone gathered around while Savannah turned on the ultrasound and began moving the scope across Mary Ella's belly.

"Why does it look like there are two babies in there?" Chandra signed to Savannah and spoke.

"Because there *are* two babies in there." Savannah laughed. "Did you know, Mary Ella?"

"I did, yes."

"I think I can see the sex of the babies. Do you want to know?"

"I'd prefer not. I'll wait and be surprised."

"As you wish."

"Wow!" breathed Natalia reverently. "They're just like, you know, floating around in there like they're in a pool or something. May I feel it, I mean them, Ms. Mary Ella?"

"You may, yes," she agreed and let each one put hands on her belly.

"Look! You can actually feel them moving around!" chirped Natalia excitedly. *"Cool!"*

"That's way cool," Kayla agreed.

"See, Mommy, you can have two babies, and I'll have a brother and a sister," Rosy piped up.

Helen shook her head. "Uh, I'm not so sure we can have two at a time, Rosemary."

Mary Ella could sense that Helen was uncomfortable with the idea of being pregnant with twins.

"Thanks, Mary Ella." Kayla smiled. "This is truly a first for me seeing twins in utero."

"You're welcome."

As Savannah continued Mary Ella's examination, they answered questions for Chandra, Rosemary, Natalia, and Kayla. However, Helen was noticeably silent but seemed interested. When the others left the exam room so that Mary Ella could dress, Savannah stayed, filling in data for her report to Mary Ella's primary OB/GYN specialist.

"You seem to be under a certain amount of stress, Mary Ella. Your blood pressure is elevated. It's not dangerously high, but I think you should do whatever is necessary to reduce your stress level."

Mary Ella nodded her agreement. "I'll be heading back home in a few days. Getting back to my routine will help me get back on an even keel."

"I hope so. You're a damn good medical professional, so you know what you have to do. I don't need to lecture you on the importance of a balanced diet and bed rest."

"You're right. I know what I have to do. I'll check in with Alfred Quade when I get back. What about you, Savannah? When will you be visiting Summer County next?"

"Nathan and I trade off holidays here at Shiloh. Jeff and LaiLoni Skye come to DC or we go to Summer County. I have to check our calendar to figure out where we're scheduled to be when." She laughed. "You'll probably have to do the same thing once your babies are born. We'll have to synchronize our schedules so that we're not like ships passing in the night."

"Do you ever go to Texas when Jeff visits LaiLoni's Hawkins family?"

Savannah laughed. "Uh, that's a definite no. You see, before Nathan and I married, I was also having this hot affair with Jacob Hawkins."

Mary Ella's mouth dropped open, and her eyes rounded to the size of silver dollars. "Oh," she breathed. "Awkward, much? You were dating your sister-in-law's older brother?"

"Big time. It's not a secret or anything like that, but it's a period in my life I sorely regret. From my perspective, I wanted to taste the forbidden fruit, so to speak, even though I knew it wasn't good for me."

"Okay, I don't get it. Why is Jacob Hawkins forbidden fruit? I mean, I've seen him. He came to visit LaiLoni a couple of times since I've been back… oh, does he come to the county when he thinks you may be there?"

"Uh-huh. So, I stay out of harm's way."

"I still don't understand the forbidden fruit angle."

"Headline: International Playboy Jacob Hawkins, President of BlackHawk International was spotted with the heiress Contessa Lolita Viejo Dela Porte of Spain at Château de Louronie on the French Riviera or same headline, and this time he's spotted with former Miss America beauty pageant runner-up Geneva of Geneva Cosmetics or he's spotted with socialite Victoria Stanton Rodgers, wife of Dr. Ted Rodgers, etc., etc.

"Jacob sleeps with an exclusive set of big money people. Before he was killed, Jacob's best running buddy was international, wealthy financier Calvin Chapman, his sister, JaiHonnah's former husband. Jai divorced Calvin and fell in love with Roderick Baylor. Jai and Roderick were named as the co-chairpersons of BlackHawk Holding. As Jake Hawkin's firstborn child, Jacob was expecting to hold that spot when his father became an Ambassador. So, Jacob harbors ill feelings because his sister divorced Calvin, Jacob's pal, and married the man who sits in the seat Jacob believes he should have been given as a birthright. So, I used to date Roderick before his marriage to Monique and JaiHonnah. Jacob believes that, through me, he can disrupt Jai's marriage to Roderick, thus causing Roderick to resign from the chairmanship of BlackHawk so that he, Jacob, can step into the position he believes is rightfully his."

"It didn't work out that way," Mary Ella proffered.

"No, it didn't, but it hasn't stopped Jacob from trying. I'll admit Jacob has this kind of raw, animal magnetism. His Native American features, long hair, dark mesmerizing eyes, tall, buffed physique are like a magical love potion or a potent drug to any woman with a heartbeat. He's a smooth operator. For a while, I rode that magic hobbyhorse and may have stayed on that merry-go-round for a while if Nathan hadn't made it clear I couldn't have him and Jacob, too. That's when reality struck. I recognized there would never be anything real between Jacob and me and that I am, without question, in love with Nathan. I could have lost Nathan in an incident that occurred some years ago. It woke me up to realize for him I am a priority, not a pastime as I was to Jacob."

"I imagine a man, like Jacob, wouldn't like being dumped," Mary Ella surmised.

"That's putting it mildly. So, Jacob instigates these scenarios where he can insinuate himself into our lives. Nathan laughs in Jacob's face because he knows what Jacob is up to. Still, when Jacob's obviously been with Ted's wife and the media picks it up, Jacob knows what hurts Ted also hurts Nathan."

"Well, at least you're surrounded by doctors for lively conversation," Mary Ella joked. "Geeze-o-flip, Savannah."

"Believe me. It's refreshing when I don't have to talk shop."

"Oh, that reminds me. I intended to talk with Nathan's father about Summer County Academy."

Savannah laughed. "Oh, that. Not to worry. There's not anything wrong with Wendell. He's not senile. He was running interference to keep Judith off your scent. She's very proprietary where Mark and Vaughn are concerned. Judith is thrilled that Mark is showing an interest in a woman again after the way Allison disgraced him two days before their wedding. There is a considerable disappointment that Mark still chose to tie himself to a woman who was so duplicitous. Although everyone knows his marriage to Allison isn't legally binding, the fact that he hadn't been with anyone else until you was bothersome. If left up to Judith, she'd arrange Mark's marriage to you today if it meant she could keep him from going back to Doctors Without Borders and guarantee she could finally fill her arms with grandchildren. She's a strong woman, but she's been unsettled since Mark joined the Marines and then the NGO. Judith feels Mark stayed away because Allison's parents continue to pressure him to impregnate her. Even if he wasn't vehemently opposed to doing such a despicable thing, Mark told Nathan that Allison was having an affair with one of their friends, who was also a classmate, which is a complete turn off for him.

CHAPTER 29

It was the last day she would spend with Mark and his family at Shiloh. Instead of rushing off to work or other places before six o'clock in the morning, they all stayed to have a farewell breakfast with her. Mary Ella appreciated the gesture, and they couldn't have been more kind, but she was ready to go home.

She stood watching from one of the windows as the caravan of cars drove down the long promenade past the fountains toward the high and wide brick wall to exit through the gated portal onto the thoroughfare. She had spent ten days there at Shiloh with Mark, getting to know his family, who and what he was like as a child and growing up, and hearing about both sides of his family history.

She believed his family's request that she come back soon was genuine and heartfelt. However, she remained non-committal. Although Boston was an interesting city on many levels, the idea of living in "The Castle" didn't inspire her to agree. She believed that if she asked him, Mark would relinquish the hold Shiloh had on him and move away, even agree to join her in Summer County. He had made friends there during the year he helped the Fire Department set up its medic squad. He'd even donated four fully-equipped fire department ambulances to Summer County. However, the thing was that Mark needed to take on significant challenges. They made him feel as if he were making the kind of contributions that were life-affirming and life-altering. Summer County didn't offer him that. It already had a large number of über wealthy residents in the Alexander family alone who could be counted on to chip in for any local shortfall in the financial necessities through the Alexander not-for-profit foundation.

She didn't want to separate Mark from his family, who, she now believed, was the source of his strength. He and his other cousins, The Fives, they called themselves, were a tightly-knit group, and the next generation needed to continue Ashro and Shiloh's legacies. Mark would always hold true to that struggle. Her babies, if they were indeed Mark's, would need to learn about their heritage. Mark and his family would be the ones to teach them the lessons of their past. She would never deny them the right to know who and whose they were.

Mark came to stand beside Mary Ella while she watched out of the window as his family departed in a caravan. They were off for their various positions in and around Boston and beyond. She had been so quiet and introspective since breakfast ended. He wondered whether she was regretting her decision to leave today. He wanted her with him. However, he also believed that if he loved someone, he had to be willing to let her go. If their love was meant to be, she would come back to him. He had to believe that. In the interim, he would work on his recovery regimen to be ready for any eventuality.

"Are you going back to DWB, Mark?"

Mary Ella's question seemed to come from out of the clear blue yonder. He turned her to look at him. "I want to, but I can't just think of what I want anymore. I need to be with you, Mary Ella, but I don't want to take you into what could likely be dangerous situations anymore. The places we've been are too unstable now to go back there. Even if we weren't expecting these golden nuggets, I want you safe. It would kill me if anything ever happened to you because of me and my needs. So, I'm working on a plan to develop Townsend Medical Group Centers in the most economically depressed areas of the United States and its territories."

Mary Ella smiled broadly at him and put her arms around his waist. "Oh, Mark, that's a wonderful idea."

"I can't claim ownership of it." Mark shook his head. "The idea came from my grandmother. She has long held the idea that we should add a health and wellness foundation to our pharmaceutical arm. We can offer care at nominal costs based on need and dispense medicines we manufacture free of charge."

"Will you also offer hospital care?"

"Initially, I think I'll look at what facilities are already in existence in various places before making that decision. Shawn mentioned that veterans' facilities are not readily available in the places they are needed. So, I'll look at what the Department of Veterans Affairs has to offer. There are also certain Native American areas where health care services are spotty at best. Michael mentioned that McCoy Hotels scout locations all the time. They come across properties or areas where it isn't prudent or practical to put a hotel or inn but may be viable for a clinic. He'll share the lists and portfolios they have and, if I'm interested, we could co-build hospital and housing facilities like an inn for families to stay in while a loved one is hospitalized. It would be a tax write-off for McCoy Hotels."

"Another excellent idea."

"I know you're happy being back in Summer County. However, if I take this on, I'd like you to join me as Director of Nursing Services for all or any of the facilities I build."

Mark saw the surprise that covered Mary Ella's face and hoped the sparkle he saw in her eyes was a sign of excited interest.

"That's… *Wow*, Mark. That's a huge undertaking. Geeze, Mark." Mary Ella was flabbergasted, the idea reviving her energy banks.

"My research has already identified some places like Wheeler County, Georgia, Union County, Florida, and Issaquena County, Mississippi, where the per capita income per year is less than twenty thousand dollars. I want medical staff who will be willing to get out in the county to find and treat people where they live, not just in the hospital or clinic. I'm going to be fleshing out the plan over the next few months while I'm recuperating, so you have time to think about it. I'll share the plan with you as it is developed. While you're thinking about that, there's something else I want you to consider. Come with me."

She got into the buggy, and this time Mark drove. Every time they left one salon, she was fascinated with the décor or the areas they passed by or through. She was so fascinated with the frescos that she hadn't paid attention to where they were going. So, when they ended up in a salon with a view of the Charles River, it seemed somehow familiar, but not quite.

They sat in the salon for so long that Mary Ella finally turned to look at Mark. "This is a pretty salon, but why are we stopping the tour here?"

"We're in the salon where Allison used to be taken care of."

She looked around again and realized he was right. "It's Allison's bedroom suite?"

"Not anymore. Allison no longer resides here. I spoke with her parents and had her moved to their home. Although they don't need it, I've agreed to continue to pay for full-time medical care for her, but I'm not going to adhere to their wishes that I impregnate her so that she can bear them grandchildren."

Stunned, Mary Ella could only sit and share this monumental moment with him. After a time, Mark reached into his pocket and pulled out a small royal-blue box. Her mouth went dry at the thought of what she believed was about to happen.

"I've never asked you whether you're in love with me, Mary Ella. I'll admit, considering what I've put you through and what has happened to you, I'm afraid of what your answer might be. Still, I'm cautiously optimistic. So, I want you to have this because I'm in love with you. I know we have to determine your marital status, but regardless of that or the parentage of the twins, I want you and them in my life for as long as you'll have me."

"Mark, you're right. I don't know what my status is. If I'm legally the wife of someone, I must resolve that one way or the other before I can move forward. I know I love you. You're a very selfless and special man, but I'll admit your wealth and all of this." The swing of her hands indicating the castle, "It's daunting."

"I know. Maybe that's part of the reason I didn't tell you about my life before. I guess I knew it wouldn't work in my favor. Unless you've been born into it, I understand it's difficult to fathom. However, I don't have to be here all the time. We can build or buy something less ostentatious as a residence anywhere you want. We can live strictly off what we earn as a salary, but as I said, the hospitals or clinics will be not-for-profit entities. So, I'll leave the household budget up to you." He smiled, and she joined him.

Then he sobered. "Still, my family is as important to me as yours is to you. I'll need to come home and bring you and our children here several times a year, probably at a minimum, once a quarter. I would want to share our children with my parents, grandparents, uncles, aunts, and cousins as they grow up. I also want more children with you, as many as we can have without adversely impacting your health or break our budget." He grinned. "I want a future with you." He opened the box to reveal a gorgeous antique yellow solitaire. "It's up to you to decide whether you want with me what I want with you." Closing the box, he placed it in her hands, and then covered her hands with his.

"I won't put this on your finger unless or until you tell me to. With us, Mary Ella, it's going to be a one-and-done deal."

She nodded her understanding. Mark was giving her time to figure out her marital status and whether she was ready to make a lifelong commitment to him. She didn't know whether part of her reticence was because of her feelings for Eric or concerns about Kaseem. She only knew she needed time and space to make the right choice without regrets.

"Knock, knock." Satarah peeked into the cottage.

"Come on in, Satarah. I'm in the master bedroom," Mary Ella called out. She smiled to herself. The bedroom would be lost in one of the broom closets in The Castle.

Shortly, Satarah appeared at the bedroom door. "I heard you were back."

Mary Ella came forward and hugged her cousin. "Only just. I need to sort out my laundry and start a load. How are you and the family?"

"Everyone is well. Ari has the sniffles, but I believe that has more to do with the fact that I've not been where she expects me to be when she gets home from school. Douglas and I believe she is suffering a little bit of separation anxiety."

"Thank you for taking over for me. I'm sorry it's caused you and your family difficulties."

Satarah waved the sentiment off as she sat on the end of the bed while Mary Ella continued to separate her laundry. "Actually, it was fun working with so many of the nurses from my old crew. It was also a nice change of pace. Of course, I wasn't the big news. Everyone is curious about Mark and you. How did it go?"

"He was in pretty rough shape and needed time to recuperate before we flew from Germany to Boston. When I left there this morning, he was up and about. Oh, I sent some things from…"

"Germany," Satarah interrupted. "Yes, we got them. You had time to go shopping?"

"I needed to keep busy, and the hospital facility is like a major metropolitan area all indoors."

"So the map you sent would indicate. The kids got a kick out of the ball caps, and Douglas enjoyed the beer."

"Good." Mary Ella lifted a load of clothes and went into the bathroom where the stacked washer and dryer were located. Come to think about it, she never did figure out where the laundry was taken care of in The Castle. The clothes fairies just came in every day and took the clothes and linens away. They magically returned clean and fresh the same day. Not true here. She didn't do her laundry here before she left, and there was plenty of it, including two sets of bed linens.

"Mary Ella?"

"Yes?"

"What's this?" Satarah's voice sounded awed.

"Just a moment." Mary Ella started the washer before going back to the bedroom. She found Satarah holding open the royal-blue ring box. "Well, uh…"

Satarah shook her head. "Oh, no, Sister Woman, sit down and tell me what this is."

Mary Ella took a deep breath and sat. "Well, it's sort of a promise/engagement ring."

Satarah narrowed her eyes. ***"Wait!*** Rollback the tape. Did or didn't Mark ask you to be his wife?"

"Maybe."

Satarah shook her head in confusion. "Okay, you'll have to explain that a bit more."

Frustrated, Mary Ella tunneled her fingers through her hair, trying to get her thoughts in order. "There are things that I'm unable to talk about concerning Doctors Without Borders because some of it is classified. Still, Mark and I survived some pretty scary times. We both have some residual issues to resolve from that experience before we can move forward. Whether we can marry depends on the resolution of those things. So, yes, Mark told me he wants the babies and me in his life permanently. However, it hinges on how the next few months work out."

"Okay, that's about as clear as mud."

"I apologize, Satarah. If I were at liberty to tell you everything, believe me, I would."

"Okay, I won't press, but tell me, did you meet Mark's family?"

Mary Ella laughed. "Oh, girl, did I. Let's have a cup of tea. This is going to take a moment."

A while later, Satarah's mouth hung open while her tea had gone cold. She was astonished. "She can speak that many languages, read lips and sign, too?"

"Satarah, Chandra Rodgers is absolutely astounding. She soaks up information like a sponge, and she's so creative. Hold on. I'll show you." Mary Ella went to her duffel, brought a picture album back, and set it on the small table between them.

"Oh, this is so beautiful." Satarah ran her hand over the intricately designed cover.

"Chandra designed this. The colors are from the Ethiopian flag. This circle in the middle and star with many points of light are the country's anthem." Mary Ella opened the book to an image of Shiloh. "This is Shiloh, Mark's sixth great-grandmother."

"*Wow,* she's spectacularly beautiful."

"She is, and let me tell you a little of what I learned." Mary Ella surprised herself with her ability to retell the story of Shiloh. "This is her son, Ashro, and his wife, Dilly." She recounted that part of the story, too, aided by the pictures. "This is Ashro and Dilly's son's offspring." She went down the family groupings.

"*Wow*, there you are with Mark and his family. You look gorgeous, Mary Ella. The dress you're wearing is awesome."

"This was taken the first night I was at Shiloh. It was a special evening to welcome Mark home, but dinner each night is a dress-up affair."

"You mean you had to dress like this every evening?" Satarah asked, surprised.

"Oh, yes, and breakfast was not served in robe and slippers, at five-thirty in the morning." She laughed. "Lunch was more casual because the majority of the household was out and about."

"All of these people are doctors?"

"Yes, the majority of them are. For the most part, they met in medical school or during their residency programs at Harvard and then married. I dare say that they represent about thirty different specialties. There are a few exceptions, of course. Apparently, you've already met Michael Rodgers, Vice President of McCoy Hotels and Conference centers, and you know his wife, Kayla, and her sister Loretta. Loretta is married to Justin McCoy, owner of McCoy Industries. Kayla works for the US State Department. Loretta is still expanding her career on stage and screen.

"Then there's Michael's youngest brother Captain Shawn Rodgers, US Air Force. He's one of Benny's squadron leaders. This is his wife, Helen, and their daughter Rosemary who everyone calls Rosy."

Satarah's eyes widened. "Wow, is Helen a movie star or fashion model?"

"Neither. She's actually in the US Navy under Stacy Alexander's command."

Satarah's eyes narrowed. "Really?" Satarah deadpanned. "Coincidence, much?"

Mary Ella shrugged. "Hey, I don't make this stuff up. Then in this next branch of the tree is UN Ambassador Nathan Flack."

Satarah looked closer at the family grouping photo. "She looks familiar. Is she Jeff Logan's sister?"

"She is, yes, Dr. Savannah Logan Flack."

"I thought she looked familiar. Are these Nathan and Savannah's children?"

"They are, yes. They're little stair steps."

"You had quite an adventure." Satarah nodded before turning the next page. Then her breath caught. "This is some hotel. It looks like it's the size of the Biltmore in Asheville, North Carolina. Is this where you and Mark stayed?"

"Uh, yes, and no."

"Okay, enough with the cryptic remarks, Mary Ella."

Mary Ella sighed. "Yes, that's where we stayed, and yes, it's a couple of hundred square feet smaller than the Biltmore. No, it's not a hotel, it's Shiloh, Mark's ancestral home where he and his family currently live."

Satarah just stared at Mary Ella. *Oh. My. God.*

Mary Ella nodded. "And all the saints be praised."

"Mark's not just rich; he's a one-percenter," Satarah whispered as if the information was a secret. She held up the album and noticed the page seemed loose. She pulled the page, causing it to unfold, revealing a three-hundred-sixty-degree photo of Shiloh. On the back was an aerial view of the house, the land, and its position on the Boston waterway. There was also a floor plan for each of the house's six levels above ground and the three levels below ground. "Unbelievable." Satarah was astounded and looked at Mary Ella.

Mary Ella sat with one elbow on the table, her left hand palming her expressionless face. "Mark's family is a true member of W. E. B. Du Bois' **Talented Tenth.** They host balls to raise funds for all kinds of causes. There's no event held in or around Boston, which doesn't include many or most family members. They are patrons of the opera, the library society, the performing arts, MIT, and every political action at the local, regional, or federal levels. If I lived there with Mark, there wouldn't be one day we would not be expected to participate in some event. For New Years' Eve, they host a Black and White Ball at Shiloh, which in the past has been attended by thousands, including the President of the United States and foreign leaders and dignitaries. Chandra showed pictures of past events to me and the holiday decorations alone made me dizzy."

Satarah sat back in her chair, her arms folded across her baby bump, and stared at her cousin. "What in the world are you going to do?" Satarah shook her head. "I know this type of wealth has to make you uncomfortable, but this isn't about you anymore. It's about your babies' ancestry."

Mary Ella nodded, still not able to level completely with her cousin and best friend about what she was facing if, in fact, the babies she was carrying weren't Mark's offspring, but Kaseem's and whether she was legally married. When the washing machine signaled completion, she rose to tend to her chores while Satarah brewed another pot of tea. Mary Ella knew the discussion between her and her cousin wasn't over.

CHAPTER 30

Mary Ella parked under the carport, retrieved the groceries from the trunk, and let herself into Eric's home through the mudroom door. It was quiet with the wall of windows closed. She turned on the heating elements for the swimming pool. Going back to her car, she retrieved her overnight bag and took it upstairs to Eric's bedroom. When she returned to the kitchen, she used the remote control to turn on the music, loud. She didn't want to think for the rest of the afternoon. As she hummed along with a popular tune, she unloaded the two grocery bags, hunted up the pots and pans from the pantry, and utensils she needed before she washed her hands. Then she got to work.

Eric was finishing afternoon rounds when he received Mary Ella's text message asking whether he had plans for the evening. He did, actually. His brothers and he were planning a basketball pick-up game scheduled for seven at the academy. He sent back a text saying he was free for the evening and asking what she had in mind. Her return message was that dinner would be ready at his place by six. He said he'd be there and quickly found a replacement to play with his brothers. Then he sent a text to his brothers that something had come up.

When Mary Ella left to go to Mark Brooks, his family rallied around him and kept him busy as much as possible. Of course, he had heard that Mary Ella was back in her office on Sunday afternoon catching up on her work before she reported for duty that morning at six-thirty. He wasn't sure whether she would contact him once she returned, but he was thrilled to receive her text inviting him to have dinner at his home at six. Now, he just had to give his report on the video interviews he held with candidates who had applied for positions in his department and wait through the rest of the monthly department meeting before he could leave to go home to Mary Ella.

He hoped the fact she was cooking dinner for him was a good omen and not a death knell for the revival of their love relationship. He had decided to make his feelings known to Mary Ella and ask her to reconsider becoming his wife. He knew his chances were slim, but he was willing to toss his hat in the ring, so-to-speak, regardless of the competition for her love. He was banking on the fact he had grown up with her and known her longer than Mark Brooks.

Yes, she had rejected his marriage proposal once before and refused to leave the county with him when he joined the Army. Then she had left Summer County with Mark Brooks and stayed away with Mark for more than four years. She also returned pregnant with Mark's twins and left at the drop of a hat to go to Mark when she was contacted about him. Those were awesome odds in Mark's favor, but not enough to make him back down.

Eric admitted to himself that he was in love with Mary Ella Baker, and he loved her babies, too. He wanted to marry her, but he wouldn't stand in the way if she was in love with Mark. If her feelings for Mark weren't as strong as they should be, he would take his chances and stay in her life. He was secure enough in his relationship with Mary Ella to follow her lead and let Mark have unfettered access to the twins if that was what she wanted. However, he also wanted children with her. It wasn't a deal-breaker for him, but it was on his bucket list.

Now that the meeting was ending, he'd find out what his future might hold.

He was headed for the exit when Mrs. Alexander stopped him.

"That was an outstanding report you gave during the meeting, Eric. I was particularly impressed by the young woman from Portland, Oregon."

"Ah, yes, Dr. Marlene Sanders. Evidently, she and I were in med school together, and we both did our residency at Chicago Med."

"Did you know her well?"

"I wouldn't say I knew her 'well.' She was one of nearly eighty other med school students in the program. She wasn't in my study group. Her resume and the background information I found about her indicate she's done well since leaving Chicago. The good thing is that she's a rheumatologist like me and has experience in a group practice in Portland. I had Tom and Gordon look at her resume. Since she'd be sharing the suite of offices with us, they felt comfortable with what she presented. However, they also found other candidates they were impressed by. I think we rated the candidates fairly and equitably. There may be a salary range to contend with. Dr. Sanders indicated that she's flexible."

"So, I noticed. By the way, how is that other problem we discussed working out?"

It took him a moment to click into what she was referring to, and then he smiled. "You were right on the money. I did exactly what you told me to do. I sat down with the young lady in question and laid it on the line. She doesn't even look in my direction if we pass in the hallways. I appreciate your advice and your help in having her placed in a different department."

"You're a very handsome and eligible man, Eric. Women are going to want to grab your time and attention."

"Mrs. A, if you were still available, other women wouldn't have a snowball's chance in hell." He laughed.

"Ah, I hope you find someone who deserves you, but Bernard Alexander would win my affections hands down. Now, go on and get out of here. Have a good evening."

"He's a lucky man, and thanks, Mrs. A. I'll see you tomorrow." He smiled and left.

Sylvia Alexander pulled her cell phone from her pocket as she watched Eric Dixon leave the hospital. "Donald, this is your Aunt Sylvia. I just spoke with your cousin, Eric, about a Dr. Marlene Sanders from Portland, Oregon. I'll forward her jacket of information to you. I have my concerns about her reasons for wanting to leave a very lucrative position with a stellar medical group where she's in line for a partnership within the next two years to come to work in a small hospital in Summer County."

"Do you have any other reasons for your suspicions?"

"No, it's just a hunch. Something just doesn't fit."

"Okay, I've learned to trust your hunches. I'll look into it and get back to you, Aunt Sylvia."

"Thanks, Donald."

The scent of collard greens, candied sweet potatoes, and stuffed pork chops grabbed Eric before he had the mudroom door fully opened. Then he saw her. She was shaking her fanny to the beat of the music as she set the table for dinner. Leaning his shoulder against the door frame that led into the kitchen, he just watched her for a while.

When Mary Ella turned around to get the water glasses for the table, she saw Eric in the doorway smiling at her. "Hey, how long have you been there? I didn't hear you come in."

He reached for the remote and turned the music down a notch. "I wonder why." He watched Mary Ella come toward him. He would never tire of seeing that face, those eyes, and that mouth.

She stood on her tiptoes to kiss his cheek and started to turn away. "So, what's up, Doc?" She found herself ensconced in Eric's arms, his mouth and tongue taking possession of hers. When he released her, she smiled questioningly up at him.

Palming her face, he smiled. "Welcome home."

Her smile broadened and reached her pretty eyes. "Thanks, Eric, it's good to be home."

"I hope dinner is about ready. I'm starving, and the food smells great."

She looked at her watch. "Actually, you're earlier than I expected. The stuffed pork chops need more time. They're about two inches thick. I've stuffed them with cornbread dressing, green peppers, garlic, onions, and hot sausage. That's going to take a little longer to bake through and through."

"Mmmm," he moaned. "You're killing me, Mary Ella."

She laughed at him. "You have just enough time if you want to go for a swim or sit in the spa and have a glass of wine before we eat."

That's when he noticed the vapor rising from the pool and the spa. "That sounds like a plan." He nodded and went up to change into swimming trunks. He was accustomed to swimming nude, particularly when Mary Ella was there, but she didn't seem inclined to swim with him today. However, he spotted her overnight bag on the carriage stand and figured she planned to sleep in his bed tonight. That was fine with him.

He went into his closet and saw what she likely was planning to wear to work the next day, hanging in an empty space where Ginger's clothes used to be. No other woman's clothes had hung in his closet since Ginger left, and he liked the idea of Mary Ella's clothes taking up residence in that space. In fact, no woman spent time in his bed since Ginger left. He and Vernice spent their time together in hotels or on-campus in faculty housing. She had never been to his home.

Vernice called him while Mary Ella was away and wasn't pleased when he said he was unavailable. Uncharacteristically she had remarked this was the second time he claimed to be unavailable, and, if it happened again, it would be strike three, and he would be out. He didn't let it phase him. He changed his clothes and unearthed a pair of swimming trunks, a T-shirt, and a pair of flip-flops.

When Eric returned to the kitchen area, Mary Ella was working on her laptop on the center-post island. She looked up at him and had to do a double-take. Frowning at him, she quirked a brow. "Modest, much?"

"No, I just thought since you apparently weren't planning to swim, that I'd be a little more respectful of your presence."

She laughed. "Take it off, pal, and go *au naturale*. I'm a nurse, remember. Nudity doesn't embarrass me, and you have a magnificent body. Some men can't pull off that look when they're not wearing clothes, but you can. I enjoy seeing you nude and considering this is your home, don't mind me."

"Hey, you want me naked, you don't have to ask me twice." He grinned and immediately took off his clothes. He manually folded back the ceiling-high and glass walls, and, positioning himself on the deep end of his pool, he dove in. She watched his sleek form cutting through the water for a while. He did both the breaststroke and the backstroke. He truly was a beautiful specimen. She would have continued to watch him if a message from Chandra Rodgers hadn't popped up on her screen. For the next few moments, she exchanged messages with the young girl about identical and fraternal twins. Chandra asked for videos of the twins the next time Mary Ella went in for a regular check-up.

She agreed. That reminded her to make arrangements for her next appointment with Alfred. She accessed his appointment calendar and took the next available slot, which was on Wednesday afternoon at two. She entered the information on her calendar and went back to working on schedules for her nurses. Until she could secure more staff for the emergency room, she would have to contend with nine and ten-hour-a-day schedules. She had an appointment with Sylvia Alexander on Tuesday at ten. She hoped there was good news about the availability of nurses.

Mary Ella checked the timer and noticed Eric had finished swimming and was reclining in the spa with a glass of wine, and his eyes closed. She rose from the barstool and took off her pants. She grabbed a bottle of water and sat on the warm but damp kitchen floor with her legs in the churning waters of the spa.

Eric opened his eyes, smiling at her. "Modest, much? Fair exchange, ain't no robbery, pal, so strip.

Mary Ella laughed at him, put down her bottle of water to take off her shirt. She tossed it onto the sofa and then kicked water into Eric's face.

"Come on in." He held out his hand to help her.

She declined. "It's a little too warm for the twins."

"Ah, right." He opened a door in the spa to add colder water. When the spa water was tepid, he stood to help Mary Ella step down and recline on the submerged pool chair beside him. He also decreased the force of the churning water to avoid vertigo.

"Thanks, Eric, this is nice."

"Rough first day back?"

She nodded. "Satarah and Jenny did a great job in my absence, but I've been trying to find a way to reduce the number of hours my nurses have to pull duty. Some like the ten-hour days, others like the swing shifts, and for some others, particularly those with families, they need to be on regular six- or eight-hour shifts. I try to accommodate everyone, but sometimes it doesn't work out well. Everyone is being cooperative and patient, but I need between five and ten recruits like yesterday."

"I know what you mean. Tom, Gordon, and I have been interviewing allergists and rheumatologists because the load is getting heavier for the three of us. I'm one of only three rheumatologists in the state. So, I'm getting a large number of referrals. People shouldn't have to travel so far to see a specialist."

"I was talking with somebody about that recently."

"Really, who?"

"You haven't met him. Dr. Mark Brooks. He was here for about a year while you were away."

"He's the man you left with to join Doctors Without Borders before I came home."

Mary Ella nodded and turned to look into his eyes. "Yes. He and I became lovers while he was here, and he asked me to join him."

Eric nodded. "Yes, I know. Hester filled me in. He's the man you went to see recently."

"Yes, I was contacted by the military and NGO and flown to the Landstuhl Medical Center in Germany. Mark was brought there in pretty bad shape, and he was asking for me."

"Yes, I know the place. It was the first place I was stationed when I enlisted. In fact, I met Ginger there."

"I know. I met one of the security guides, Phil Gaines. He said to tell you hello."

"I remember him. That is kind of him. How is Mark now? You were away for quite a while."

"Mark arranged to be flown to Boston from Germany."

"What hospital is he in?"

"Uh, none. Mark is originally from Boston. His family is there."

"Wait, is he a member of the Townsend group of physicians and pharmaceutical family?"

Mary Ella nodded. "Yes, you've heard of them?"

Eric grunted. "Who in the medical community hasn't?"

"I hadn't until a few months ago."

"What? He's a member of the Townsend group, but you didn't know it when you met years ago?"

"We never talked about his family."

"They pretty much *are* Harvard Medical. Someone in the Townsend group authored many of my textbooks in med school. So, what is it that Mark Brooks plans to do?"

"I'll tell you over dinner. I think it's time to eat."

Mary Ella told him what Mark was planning while they sat wearing terrycloth bathrobes and eating. Eric is an active listener, asked appropriate questions, and offered suggestions based on his experiences.

"I imagine Brooks wants you to play a role in this awesome task. What has he asked you to do?"

"Director of Nursing Services."

"For the entire operation?"

"Yes."

Eric shrugged. "That's huge, Mary Ella. I don't doubt that you can do it, but with the twins so young, would you want to?"

"I didn't give him an answer. It's something I need to think about, but I'm just so tired of having to think at all."

He nodded. "Thanks for dinner. It was perfect. Since you cooked and thankfully made enough for leftovers, I'll clean up the kitchen. What do you want to do?"

"How about looking at a movie?"

"Sure, go ahead and pick something. I'll clean up and join you or, if you want to be alone, I can go into the den and read."

"See, it's that thing right there that you do," Mary Ella huffed.

"What thing?" Eric laughed at her quarrelsome expression.

"You're always so considerate, and you're not even trying. It's just who you are. I come to your home and talk with you about a man I just spent time with, and you don't even get an attitude with me about it."

"Okay, I'll bite. Why would I get an attitude?"

"You must know that Mark and I have been intimate."

"Okay, and you're not wearing his wedding ring, so I'm not concerned about that. You're an adult, not a child. As I recall, you have sex for comfort as much as you do for gratification. I imagine you did so with Mark Brooks. Still, you're home and trying to determine what's right for you and your life going forward.

"Mary Ella, you're honest to a fault. You don't play any head games, and you never have. There are men and women, too, who are out there slipping and sliding and peeping and hiding, but that's not you. I know you may not tell me everything going on in your life, but you would never knowingly hurt me or purposefully lie to me. You will always tell me the truth, and I can rely on your word if you give it. So, here's the thing. I'm in love with you. I have loved you since we were knee-high to ducks, and regardless of the choices we make going forward, I don't believe you can ever do anything that would make me stop loving you. We were friends first before we were lovers, and even if we are never lovers again, that friendship will always be there."

Eric took her tear-stained face in his hands and thumbed away her tears.

"Hurry up and clean up the kitchen."

Eric looked curiously at her, his brows bunched. "Why? What's the hurry?"

"I want to take you to bed for a little comfort."

He smiled enigmatically at her. "The hell with the kitchen. I'll clean it up in the morning when I make breakfast for you and bring it to you in bed."

"Oh, no, pal. Clean up first, comfort later."

"Okay, as long as you don't change your mind between now and then."

"I won't, but I want dessert first."

He looked at her quizzically. "We've called lovemaking by a few different names before, but now dessert?"

"*Haha.* I meant the edible kind."

"Uh-huh. That's doable." He grinned.

"As in your favorite dessert. Key lime pie."

"Second favorite dessert next to you."

"You're incorrigible."

"See, babe? That's what I mean. You ain't never lied."

Mary Ella's laugh was deep and heartfelt.

CHAPTER 31

He paced from side to side in the small interrogation room. He didn't know what was going on, but he wished they could get on with it. He was called in for a conference and had to leave his men in harm's way. They could hold their own, but after years of running with one group of terrorists and then another, they never knew when something could go horribly wrong.

It had happened when the doctor and nurse were taken. If they hadn't made any noise while making love, they wouldn't have been found. However, one of the forward scouts heard them by the limestone quarry and stopped to watch them make love. Then he had signaled Imad Mohammed Azul and the whole operation threatened to go to hell in a handbasket, a true clusterfuck. If he hadn't acted when he did, the woman would have been killed just for being naked, particularly with a man who was not her husband.

He knew who they were and the fact they were with the NGO rather than any counterintelligence organization. He had shadowed them often enough to recognize them on sight, especially the woman. Her name was Mary Ella Baker, and with her southern drawl, he figured she was from one of those southern states in the US. Over the years, he had been within touching distance of her both within Asia and Africa, but she was never far from Dr. Brooks. He knew she didn't recognize him because she only had eyes for Brooks. Most of the time, his head and face were covered, and he wore different disguises depending on the operation. Still, whether close enough to touch or further away shadowing those in the NGO, he felt something primal for Mary Ella Baker.

The first time he saw her, she was new to the NGO. However, Brooks was a veteran of the group Doctors Without Borders and a Marine. He knew Mary Ella to be a hard worker, regardless of where she was. She just dove into any situation and did whatever came next. Her tenacity turned him on. He considered them the dynamic duo. They worked well together. Brooks was a linguist speaking many languages and translating accurately what an injured person told him. They were credited with saving hundreds, if not thousands of lives, and rightly so.

Mary Ella was a phenomenal woman, not only in beauty and body, but also in spirit and kindness. She was someone he had to save though it almost cost him a two-year operation and his life. When Azul fisted Mary Ella's long, pretty, damp hair, he had long admired and then pulled his jambiya from its holster as if he were about to lop off her head in one fell swoop, he nearly sent the bastard to Allah where he stood. Instead, when he challenged Azul for her, the blood-thirsty bastard cut off her hair, rather than her neck. Then Azul yelled like an animal and charged him, throwing her hair in his face. The fight was brutal, and blood was drawn, but Azul was no fool. He recognized that they were too well matched for him to win handily. That's what he wanted Azul to think. Actually, he could have killed Azul with half the effort, but that would have created other problems. Rather than being seen as weak or losing the battle in front of his followers, Azul had beaten Mary Ella and settled for taking Brooks.

He had to marry Mary Ella immediately to protect her or she still could have been gang-raped or killed because of her nudity. He tried, but he couldn't save Dr. Brooks, too. He did his best to convince Azul that having a live American medical doctor as a hostage was a benefit.

After the marriage ceremony, conducted by the Iman, Azul and his henchmen watched as he consummated the marriage. He silently dispatched three of his men to join Azul when he carted Brooks' unconscious, naked body away. Azul also dispatched four of his own men to go with him and keep an eye on him. He believed Azul not to be an honorable man. He saw how Azul looked lustfully at Mary Ella's naked body, and he didn't put it past Azul to try to have her abducted and brought to him. He had to stay alert, watch his back, and keep her tethered to him treating her as any man might who was newlywed.

He had a niqab especially embroidered for his mother and abayas for his sisters, but he used the niqab to cover Mary Ella and battled to retrieve her tennis shoes. He treated her bruised and battered body in the limestone quarry and washed what was left of her hair. The rest of her garments and toiletries were stolen and weren't worth him fighting over.

They camped in the open most of the time. Although he tried not to hurt Mary Ella, they were being watched too closely by those who weren't too trusting of him and his band. Thankfully, she didn't fight him physically, but she tried to do so emotionally. After a time, he overcame the mental walls she'd constructed against him. He convinced himself that her moans, tremors, and orgasms were because she wanted him as much as he had long wanted her. Some nights he would lay awake next to her just looking at her in the moonlight and touch her intimately while she slept. She could orgasm from his touch alone. He was so deeply in lust with her that he might take her in her sleep, and she would cum for him and bring him over the brink with her.

Then he noticed while she was bathing some six weeks after taking her captive that she had lost considerable weight. He provided plenty of food for her, but as he watched her sitting with the women to eat, he noticed she was secretly sharing what he had given her with the other women whose husbands only gave their wives scraps once they had eaten their fill. As he watched covertly, Mary Ella would do it at every meal. If the men had seen it, he would have been forced to punish her to keep up the facade. He hoped she was not trying to commit suicide because of her captivity.

He realized then he couldn't wait for a convenient time. He had to get Mary Ella out of there, or she would lapse into ill health and die. Even though he was constantly being watched, he was able to get a signal out without jeopardizing the mission. Within twenty-four hours, he received the alert that Mary Ella would be secreted away the very next night. He made love to her one last time and told her she was going home. She was only half awake, but she automatically responded to him.

Whatever was used to knock them out kept everyone asleep well into the morning of the next day. He and his men pretended to look for her, but he wasn't sure how convincing they were.

Nevertheless, he was concerned for her and began to track her once she was sent home to some place called Summer County, South Carolina. He hacked into innocuous systems to find her and then sent an operative to bug her office equipment and other electronics. Initially, he told himself that he only wanted to ensure her health and wellbeing were intact. Yet, he realized that he was lying to himself. Over the years, he had fallen in love, not just in lust with Mary Ella Baker, although he realized she was in love with Dr. Mark Brooks. Still, there was nothing he could do about his feelings for her.

He had married Mary Ella to keep her safe and to feel that, at least, once in his lifetime, he loved deeply and only one woman. Considering his life and the constant dangers, he never expected to live to see her in person again. Still, he had their marriage recorded so that when he was dead, she would be notified and be free to move on with her life. Every opportunity he had to see her via the electronic equipment, he did. Then, for some reason, someone caught on to his traces. He didn't expect that to be the case in a sleepy, southern community in South Carolina. Still, someone had some awesome computer skills because every route he tried to get in to find out how Mary Ella was doing and to just gaze at her for the limited time he had, was met with blocks in places where they should not have existed.

If it weren't for her using her computer access codes to do research while she was at the beach, he wouldn't have known that she was alive and well. However, when she returned to Summer County, he couldn't track her anymore. He could only depend on his memories of her and how much he missed touching her, loving her.

Then he learned that Dr. Brooks had been rescued in an operation that netted a great deal of valuable information and high-value targets.

Now, he was back in the field, tracking terrorist agents who were said to be making dirty bombs for sale to the highest bidders. He had to find out where the meetings were going to be held and try to outbid others. If he could find out who was making the bombs and where, all the better.

He was dirty and smelled to high heaven. He wanted a shower in the worst way, but he had to stay in character or he'd lose his edge. However, he'd been pulled off the operation for some reason, and he was wearing a hole in the floor waiting.

"This is the operator known as Kaseem Ally Ghailani?" a voice asked, watching the man pace in an interrogation room.

"Yes, Sir. He's been brought in at your instruction but not told the reason."

"His reputation precedes him. I don't know of many who could so skillfully hack into highly-shielded systems without leaving a trace."

"He's even more effective in theatre, I mean when he's on the hunt."

"I know what you're referring to. I understand he's multilingual, Phi Beta Kappa at Stanford, and a member of Mensa. He's been trained as a Navy SEAL officer and a Mossad operative. He's still a SEAL with the rank of Captain on detachment to the CIA."

"That's correct, Sir. He was born in New Haven, Connecticut, to Abdel Karim Ayman Gupta from India and his African American wife, Farrah. Mr. Gupta owns and operates an antique store. His wife is a professor of international studies at Albertus Magnus, a small college in New Haven. They have four children, three daughters and one son, Adama Karim Gupta; Code Name: Kaseem."

"Divided."

"Excuse me, Sir?"

"His code name, Kaseem. In Arabic, it means divided. When was the last time he was stateside?"

The man flipped through the data on his iPad. "According to this, it's been more than five years ago, Sir. He hasn't asked for relief or downtime. He's dedicated to the missions and accomplished more than what's expected of him. There was only one incident where two NGO members were taken prisoner, but it's confirmed it was not within Kaseem's control. Both were returned earlier this year. He did have five fallen eagles related to the Brooks rescue."

"It's time for Kaseem to go home before the holidays."

Alarmed, the man sputtered. "Sir! He's needed in theatre! We need him here in the country! He only expected to be brought in for an unscheduled update! He left his team in theatre!"

"Bring them all in. I'll authorize a new team of insurgents who are battle-ready."

"You can't do that, Sir! I mean, yes, you have the authority to do it, but we're mission-critical! He's one of the best we've ever had!"

"Yet, a head of nursing at an obscure hospital peeped his hole card. He needs a break, so he's about to get one. Have him on a flight home in the next twenty-four and his team out of the theatre in less time than that. I'll have replacements ready to be briefed when the team is in situ. Finally," he held his credentials so that the man's eyes nearly popped out of his head, "I was never here."

"What's going on, Mary Ella?" Satarah asked. "I got your message that you needed a ride to the county municipal airport."

"I haven't a clue. I received a text for me to come to Connecticut. I presume it's to meet Mark, but I haven't reached him or anyone else in his family to determine what's going on. He's sending a plane to pick me up. It should be here in the next half an hour. Since I don't know how long I'll be away, I didn't want to leave my car at the airport. Do you mind giving me a lift?"

"Not at all. Did you have plans with Eric tonight?"

"Uh, no." She absently searched her drawers for what to pack. "He's in Miami for a five-day medical conference. Then he's going to Tallahassee to see Bishop over the weekend and catch a Florida State football game. He'll be back next Monday." She found the insulated bedroom slippers she was looking for and put them in a compartment of the duffle. It was bound to be chilly in Connecticut this time of the year. She needed warmer clothes than what she wore here in the fall. A few more things and her toiletry bag, then she would be ready to go.

"Why is he in Connecticut and not Massachusetts?" Satarah asked.

Mary Ella shrugged, mystified. "Maybe he had business there. I don't know. We've been communicating about the plan for the Townsend Clinics and Hospitals."

"Do you have someone to cover for you?"

"Jenny has been coming in several times a week. She and Bob are fixing up their home to put it on the market. Now that her maternity leave is over, she comes in part-time to make a little pocket change to help with the effort. She said they need to invest ten to fifteen thousand to bring their home up to date and ready for sale. Frank Dixon gave them a terrific deal. Bob is going to lend a hand when he can."

"Yes, Douglas told me. He and the boys are also going to give Bob a hand."

"Good." Mary Ella looked around the cottage, noting that everything was in its place. "I think I'm ready. At least this time I'm not leaving a pile of dirty laundry." She hefted the duffle, and Satarah locked the door behind them.

Satarah waited with Mary Ella while the jet landed and taxied to a stop. She noted the markings on the tail and fuselage and remarked to Mary Ella. "That's one of Vivian's Adventurer Executive Air jets. Didn't you mention that Mark's family owned jets?"

"They do. Although Mark ordered one of AEAs medically-equipped planes to fly us from Germany to Boston. He had me flown here on a smaller jet owned by his family. I don't think they have that many, but maybe the others are in service taking someone somewhere else."

Satarah shrugged. "That's possible. It looks like they're ready for you to board."

"Is this your only luggage?" a baggage handler asked.

"Yes, it is. Thank you," Mary Ella said when he picked it up and took it on board for her. Mary Ella turned, and she and Satarah embraced.

"You have a good time and tell Mark we said get well soon."

"I will. It's a good thing that this is a long weekend. Still, I should be back on Tuesday."

"Okay, I'll pick you up when you return."

"Thanks, Satarah. I'll let you know when my flight leaves Connecticut." She waved goodbye and was helped up the short flight of steps into the aircraft.

He was making his second loop around the lake and felt as if he hadn't even hit his stride yet. He was a long-distance runner in high school and college but barely had opportunities to stretch out his long legs and fly. The crisp cold air felt good and exhilarating against his cheeks. He had grown up here with his three sisters in an area just outside of the city limits of New Haven. He was the third child born to Abdel and Farrah Gupta.

His parents met at the Metropolitan Museum of Art, colloquially "the Met" in New York City nearly forty years ago. Since the Met was the largest art museum in the US, they counted their meeting as having been preordained. Abdel was there to see an exhibit of *objets d'art* recently arrived from India. He was planning to open a studio and gallery where he could showcase and sell his own creations and antiques he found for sale on the internet. Farrah was a Ph.D. candidate working on her dissertation on eastern art in Arab countries. They struck up a conversation, and forty years later, married with four offspring, they were still the two people they most liked to talk with.

The sun was going down in the west, and a thin layer of ice was forming on the placid lake. It was his fifth trip around the perimeter of the water when he saw his mother standing on the front porch of his cabin. She waved her mitten-covered hand at him, smiling broadly. He waved back at her and started his cool-down cycle.

"You remind me so much of when you used to race your sisters around that lake when you were younger," Farrah called out to him. "It's good to see you haven't lost your stride."

He laughed. "Yes, but you could beat all of us until we were in our teens. You won Olympic gold several times before you were out of your teens, and you could still kick it into high gear when we were in our teens."

"You come from a long line of people who routinely crossed the Serengeti on bare feet. You are part Maasai, remember?"

Through with his cool-down cycle, he walked up the short flight of steps and followed his mother's tall, svelte form inside his post-and-beam log cabin.

"When I saw you out at the lake, I brought down some stew and a loaf of bread I baked today."

"Thanks, Mom." He nodded while adding more logs to the fire in the great room. "What's Dad doing?"

"He's in his studio. He's determined to perfect his new interest in glass blowing."

"From what he showed me, he's done some credible work."

"He has, yes, especially since his hands cramp when he's working in clay or carving wood."

"How's his eyesight?"

"Better now that I've convinced him to wear his glasses when he works. He takes them off when he's in the shop working with customers. He says it makes him feel old and decrepit."

"Well, he is in his sixties, Mom. He's entitled. He's worked hard all of his life."

"He has, yes, and I hadn't seen him happier than when you surprised us by coming home."

"It's good to be here." He hugged her again.

"I'm going back to the house so that you can relax. Make sure your generator is hooked up. We're supposed to get heavy weather later tonight.'"

"I'll check it before I get in the shower. Thanks for the stew."

"You're welcome. There should be enough for leftovers. I'm going to the market for provisions in case this storm turns out to be a Nor'easter and keeps us housebound. I'll pick up groceries for you, too. I'll see you in the morning." Farrah waved and left.

He checked his wood bin and decided to bring in a few more cords in case it snowed overnight. While he was at it, he checked his pump. His cabin was built with a well-and-septic system and was powered by solar panels on his roof and geothermal energy underground. He hadn't been at his home in years. Still, with reverse polarization, his panels and underground units continuously fed electric energy to the grid so that now while he was home, his utilities cost him nothing to operate. Well, that wasn't all the geothermal system supported.

When he finished his chores, he activated his laptop. Sure enough, The Weather Service was calling for a nor'easter to blow through New England overnight. He likely wouldn't get any time to run, but if the lake froze solid enough, he'd be able to skate. His older two sisters might even bring their children over to skate, too. He'd enjoy that and have to check the thickness of the ice before he let them out on it.

When his stomach growled, he shut down his computer and went into the bathroom for a long, hot shower.

It was going on full dark when the jet landed at the New Haven municipal airport. A car and driver were waiting and took her duffle, loading it into the trunk after handing her into the backseat of the hired car. She couldn't see very much of the city as they passed through it and even less of the countryside as they drove away from the city lights.

She was incredibly curious about what Mark was doing in the Connecticut countryside instead of Boston continuing to work on his physical therapy regimen. Still, she settled back in the comfortable seat. When they turned into a dead-end street, she saw a rather large cabin lit up before them, but then she noticed the windshield wipers were going at a pretty good clip causing her to take her attention away from the house.

When the driver put on the high beams, she realized that it was snowing fairly heavily. She became concerned until the driver pulled to a stop at a smaller but more modern cabin where the lights were on, and smoke was billowing out of two chimneys.

"This way, Miss. Watch your step now. We have a bit of snow he-awh." His New England accent pronounced.

He carried her bag and helped her up the steps and into the nicely appointed but rustic cabin. It wasn't that large in the gathering room where she could see the kitchen, a dining area, a space for an office with a desk, and a living area. Something besides the pleasant scent of wood smoke was warming in a crockpot on an island in front of the kitchen.

She turned in time to offer the driver payment, but he waved it off. "It's been taken care of, Miss. Have a good evening." He tipped his hat and was gone.

It was warm inside with the fireplace going, so she took off her sweater coat and kicked off her shoes. She still had on her socks and her sweater dress that molded around her baby bump, her wider butt, and her breasts, which seemed couldn't be contained no matter what size bra she tried to wear. That's why she hated the contraptions in the first place and didn't wear them unless absolutely necessary. Her panties were a joke. They ended up making her feel like she was wearing bloomers or were so small they felt like slingshots.

As she moved around the space, she became concerned that Mark was not in the room. She moved toward the only other door off the gathering room. She looked in and heard the shower running. The fireplace in here was lit, too, and by the glow of the firelight, she saw a picture of herself on one of the bedside tables.

That was odd, she thought. The picture must have been taken years ago because her hair was loose around her head and flowing over her shoulder and down her back. She didn't remember Mark taking the picture before, but she picked it up to examine it more closely. She was smiling at someone just to the right of the camera and couldn't remember where they were by the scenery around her. She moved to the partially open door to the bathroom and called out. "Mark, I'm here. When and where was this picture taken?"

When she looked up at the nude man standing and looking as shocked as she was, her eyes rolled back in her head as everything faded to black.

CHAPTER 32

"*N*o, no, no!*" he shouted when Mary Ella began to crumble to the floor. He was out of the shower in a flash and caught her just in the nick of time. When he picked her up and carried her to his bed, she was limp as a wet noodle. The dress she wore molded around her like sealskin. He couldn't avoid seeing the ripples of movement in her swollen belly and touched it to feel the life growing inside her. He cursed in every language he knew and fumbled, trying to get her out of the clingy fabric so that he could cool her down. When he finally got her undressed, she wasn't wearing undergarments.

What was **wrong** *with her going without wearing underthings?* he silently fumed as he rushed into his bathroom to turn off the shower and wet two towels with cool water. *What the hell was he complaining about? She had no undergarments the entire time he had her with him!* He could try to convince himself that it was just to keep her cool in the extraordinary heat, but he knew that to be a lie. It turned him the hell on, knowing he could feel her feminine heat through the lightweight covering. His sex drive had never been that strong with any other woman. He had gone for years without, but with Mary Ella, he wanted her every moment of every day. Now, he looked at her and realized the result of his insatiable need for sex with Mary Ella meant he was likely going to be a father.

He had known it was a possibility. After all, he had seen the IUD on the ground, and if sex with her multiple times a day for nearly two months didn't produce a baby, nothing would. It was a thought that should have scared the life out of him, but somehow it didn't. He didn't think he would ever live a normal life; have a wife and children, and live to a ripe old age surrounded by grand and great-grandchildren. Yet he had married Mary Ella in a desert among hostility and terrorists moments after being willing to die to protect her. She screamed to defend her man, Mark Brooks, pleading with him to stop trying to get to her. She repeatedly told him that she would be all right. Still, in all that chaos, she never screamed that she loved him. He distinctly remembered that, considering Mary Ella and Mark were caught in the act of having energetic sex beside a limestone quarry. Brooks wasn't wearing a condom, so he assumed that Mary Ella must be on some type of birth control. He didn't see what was in her small toiletry bag, so he assumed she was on birth-control pills until he saw the IUD on the ground. That's what he got for assuming. As crazy as it was, he now had a pregnant wife on his hands with no idea how she found him here.

Back at the bed, he sat down on the edge and held her up with one arm placing one towel against the back of her neck. The other one he used to bathe her face of the perspiration that formed on her brow and across the bridge of her nose. Then he just looked at her; at the features of her face, he had seen almost nightly in his dreams. She was so real to him that he could almost conjure up her scent. She used eucalyptus oil on her skin and in her hair to keep the bugs away. In addition to being used for its aroma, the oil was a flavoring Brooks' medical conglomerate created for pharmaceutical and antiseptic uses. There were such things as antibacterial, anti-inflammatory, and analgesic properties, which helped treat a wide range of medical conditions. He bought a small bottle of the oil and used it on his beard and his hair. Every time he encountered or used that scent, he thought of her and wondered where she was and what she was doing.

Now, she was in his arms, waking from her faint. When she was nearly awake, her eyes widened in shock and likely fear as she scrambled backward away from him. She could go only so far before her back was against his leather headboard. He didn't want her to hurt herself, so he didn't try to stop her. She was afraid enough as it was.

"How… where did you come from? How did you get here? Where is Mark? Did you hurt him?" Mary Ella demanded in growing panic mode. She looked around the room that was still only lit by the fireplace.

"It's all right, Mary Ella. You're not in any danger here. I'm not going to hurt you. I certainly didn't do anything to hurt Mark Brooks. However, he isn't here. This is my home. My question is, how did *you* get here? How did you find me?"

"How did I…? Oh, well, holy hell. You speak English like a native, but that's not important. I was flown here, a car picked me up at the airport, and brought me here! I wasn't looking for you, and I certainly didn't expect to ever see you again in my life. I thought I was coming here to meet Mark. Now, it's your turn. Who the hell are you?"

"Wait. You said you were flown to New Haven and driven directly here to my cabin?"

"Yes, I didn't stutter! That's what happened!"

His senses went on alert. Something was off…way off. Whatever it was couldn't be good. He stood up, picked up his special phone, and went through the security checks activating a safety perimeter with shields up around his and his parents' home. Then he signaled his contact with the **DEFCON** 2, defense readiness condition and alert. His team used the US Armed Forces system developed by the Joint Chiefs of Staff (JCS) and unified, specified combatant commands alert to signal risk levels. The lower the number, the greater the risk. With any luck, his team was already erecting shields and was on the move to converge on his location.

Shortly, his phone rang. He carried on a conversation in Navajo with his handler on the other end of the line. He could not understand any of this. Especially being pulled out in the middle of an operation by someone who was so clandestine no one knew his name. Then his team was replaced in the theatre, and after debriefing, everyone was sent home. He was on a flight headed to Connecticut so fast his head spun. Now this? Who had brought Mary Ella to his home under the pretense that she was meeting Mark Brooks and why?

Still, he received the all-clear signal from his handler and wondered whether he had somehow been compromised. He was not dropping his guard, though. Someone was controlling this situation, and it wasn't him. Whoever it was knew Mary Ella Baker was his Achilles Heel. She was his weakness, which could actually or potentially lead to his downfall. He had been the thorn in the side of renegade countries or terrorist factions within certain societies for many years. If the connection was made between him and Mary Ella, she may have a specific vulnerability, which could also be detrimental to her and his entire operation. If there was breath in his body, he would never allow anything to happen to her…or his baby.

Mary Ella watched the man she had known as Kaseem, pacing the floor, mindless of his nudity. He spoke in a language she didn't understand on a cell phone, which didn't look typical of those commonly on the market today. His hair was still dripping wet and looked like black, liquid asphalt flowing over his broad shoulders, strong muscles, and firm chest. His pecs were well-cut, his abdomen concaved with a pronounced six-pack, hips narrow and muscular with a butt that was high and tight over long, long strong-looking legs.

With her training in anatomy, she could distinguish every fiber and sinew of his physique. Yet, somehow she couldn't entirely take her eyes off of any part of his smooth, well-toned, all-over, olive-brown skin. For some reason, he didn't seem this tall and imposing covered in traditional desert clothing.

Still, though she had never seen his body in the buff, the eyes, that pale, aqua-green was unmistakable. She remembered them in her sleep after she was rescued. She could almost cum spontaneously just by envisioning those eyes. There was more of him, which left an indelible mark on her psyche. For example, his penis is long, thick…and lethal.

He would not let her close her eyes when he was on her, between her thighs, inside her forcing her into cataclysmic orgasms against her will. He'd steadily look into her eyes, willing her to flow with him until her eyes would all but glaze over and go opaque with pleasure. Then he would cover her mouth with his hand, but not with his mouth, so she wouldn't cry out each time he brought her to completion.

Odd that she should remember now that he never kissed her mouth. He kissed her breasts, tugged her nipples into his mouth, rubbing his rough tongue over the tip of them until they peaked. Then he would touch her intimately, and she would nearly levitate up off the mat where they slept.

Oh, yes, there was much her damnable memory of him inside her wouldn't let her forget. Like the fact that he protected her at a potential cost to his own life. Like the probability that he instigated her rescue. Like the fact that his eyes were like lethal weapons to her psyche. They made her go damp at the sight of him. Like the way he was looking at her now naked in his bed. His eyes wandered down to her mouth and then lower to her breasts and half-round circumference of her belly and lower. She wondered whether he could scent her heat because his eyes lingered there, right there where her need was growing. Then his eyes took the journey just as slowly up to meet her eyes again, and she was done for.

He came toward her. "Did I do this to you, Mary Ella?"

She clutched her discarded dress as an ineffective shield. Still, he slowly pulled her clothing away, leaving her open and unprotected. He leaned forward, burying his face in her belly and simultaneously kissing and lathing his open mouth and tongue over the motion-filled sphere. It was perhaps the most incredibly sensual thing she ever experienced. The tears escaped, and the dam burst. He gathered her in his arms, cradling her while whispering soothing words in her ear. He was so gentle with her as he held her while she cried.

"I apologize, Mary Ella. I had no other choice at the time. I promise I'm not a monster or a rapist. Your life was seconds away from ending. So, I did the only thing I could to save you. If I could have done anything else, I probably would have. Still, I will not lie to you and say I was being completely altruistic. I want you."

She leaned back from his solid, bare chest, knuckling the tears from her cheeks, and quizzically looked into those amazing eyes. "I don't understand. You *wanted* me? How is that possible? You didn't know me."

For the moment, he let the distinction between "I want you" and "you wanted me" go. He reached into the nightstand and handed a leather wallet to Mary Ella. When she opened it, there was a picture of him with the Central Intelligence Agency's logo emblem embossed on the page. His name read: Adama Karim Gupta. The opposite page contained a headshot of him in a stark white uniform with colorful ribbons on his chest, his face solemn, clean-shaven, and wearing a hat bearing a US Navy

Trident emblem on the brim. According to this document, he was Adama Karim Gupta, not Kaseem, as she had known him for those months.

Mary Ella looked up at him, even more confused. "You're in the CIA?"

"My team and I are US Navy SEALs. We're attached to the CIA because of our appearance and linguistic abilities. We look like Arabs because we are or have roots in African, Arab, and Middle Eastern countries.

"I first saw you years ago…"

"The picture of me in the frame," Mary Ella interrupted. "That was when I first arrived, wasn't it?"

"Yes, I took the picture because my team was assigned to shadow members of DWB. If any of you got detached from the group, we had to rely on locals to help us find you. Generally, DWB members were never out of our sight. We provided a ring of security around you."

Mary Ella shook her head and looked skeptically at him. "I don't remember seeing you before you took me hostage."

"We're SEALs, Mary Ella, with Mossad training. You're not supposed to know we're there even if we're hiding in plain sight. We blend into the landscape of anonymous faces and forms as to be indistinguishable. There are more teams like us, and to continue our anonymity, we traded off assignments. Sometimes I wouldn't see you for months or a few times a year passed before my team was deployed to protect and defend members of the NGO. Your NGO wasn't the only one in operation. So, we have many different groups to shadow and protect while we gather critical intelligence. In the interim, based on the intelligence we gathered, we'd be inserted into various terrorist organizations on fact-finding missions or to disrupt or destroy as the situation required."

"In other words, you killed people," Mary Ella said pedantically.

He didn't answer. She was a smart woman. He didn't have to spell it out for her. "We were on a mission when we stumbled across you and Dr. Brooks. The team guarding you should have dispatched security for your protection, but they were waiting for replacement Army Rangers so they could shadow. The replacements never arrived. You got outside of their perimeter and were caught. Five good men paid the ultimate price, and the rest were so severely injured, they had to be taken out of the operation.

"Dr. Brooks, you, and three others were the only ones who survived. We wanted to neutralize the ones responsible, but they were a key to terrorist activities planned in the US and other countries who were members of NATO. We had to follow it up, find, and disrupt the plans. However, we also had a duty to protect you and Dr. Brooks. Three of my men infiltrated the ones holding Dr. Brooks, and I took on the responsibility to protect you. An unmarried woman in the situation you were in was fair game for any man in the group. When I had to split up our resources, which left me under-manned at fifteen or twenty to one, I had no other choice. Those odds weren't good, so I married you and kept you close.

"You're a strong woman, Mary Ella Baker. You did what was necessary to stay alive, even submit to me. You also continued to try to help the other captive females in the camp. I noticed you were losing weight because you shared the food I provided for you with the other women who were starving. It was brave and selfless of you, but if I'd let you continue to do that, the mission would have been in jeopardy, and the women would have summarily been killed for accepting anything, even food, from an infidel."

"That's why you arranged to get me out of there," Mary Ella said, understanding dawning.

Adama nodded. "Yes, but it wasn't selfless on my part. You see, I wanted you from the first time I ever saw you. You were like this precious sparkling stone. You fairly glittered with your excitement to use your skills and abilities to help people. Each time I saw you, you were undaunted by whatever tasks you were forced to tackle, and you succeeded. You wore this perpetual smile people who had no real existence gravitated toward.

"I gravitated toward your warmth and wished to high heaven I could bask in the glow you spread. Then one afternoon, out of the chaos and destruction I had just encountered with the loss of several of my men, there you were smiling and laughing with Mark Brooks, unaware of what was about to happen to you. How your life was about to change." He rubbed his warm palm back and forth over her abdomen. Then he buried his face between her breasts, breathing her in. "I wanted to save you, it's true, but I just wanted…you. I want this." He continued to rub her belly, "and I want you still."

"This is these." Mary Ella put her hand over his. "There are two babies in me, and I can't say with any real sense of certainty whether they are yours. As you know, Mark and I made love just before you married me and had sex with me. You continued to have sex with me continuously until the next morning."

"I had to…"

"I know. I understand why you did it. I was moments away from losing my life when that man dragged me by my hair in front of Mark and everyone else. You stepped in when he cut off my hair and protected me by marrying me. I understand your rationale for doing what you had to do to me." She then looked into his beautiful eyes, her tears brimming up and spilling over.

"Still, why did you have to make me enjoy it? I wasn't in love or even in like with you, yet I craved you and your touch. I never kissed you or even touched you intimately, yet when you looked at me, the way you're looking at me now, I damn near came unglued. Why would you do that to me? You could have done something, anything to make me not want to feel you inside me," she cried.

"I tried, Mary Ella. Initially, I thought I could pretend to have intercourse with you, fake it or do anything short of penetration, but—" He ruefully shook his head. Placing his palm against her jaw, he rubbed his thumb over her mouth. "I wanted this mouth. Yet, if I had this mouth on me, I would have been defenseless. I would have closed my eyes, blocked out the world, and just sunk into you. However, I had to stay alert and employ all of my senses. My remaining team members depended on me as I relied on them to cover my back.

"The terrorists were already suspicious of us because we never took women or girls as concubines or killed anyone during the raids. To the extent possible, we saved as many lives as we could. If we had knowledge of our route in advance, we got a message out, and teams were dispatched to protect the villagers, causing us to have to steer clear of as many places as possible. However, sometimes we had no notice and had to hope that satellites or close-encounter drones were tracking our whereabouts.

"The one thing I could not avoid was my insatiable need to mate… with you. I denied myself the overwhelming desire to kiss your mouth." Adama's eyes dropped to her lips. "You see, this touching of my mouth to yours is a sign of intimacy, of tenderness, something I couldn't let show to those who scrutinized my every move. So, I kissed your neck," his hand glided over her neck to her shoulder, "down your collarbone to your breasts," which he palmed and rubbed his thumb over her nipple and watched fascinated as it peaked, "and I could stay alert while giving myself permission to love you the way I dreamed of.

"When you, a strong, self-possessed, independent woman, didn't fight me, I saw your behavior as surrender, and it turned me on. Because, you see, Mary Ella, having you bound to me was a gift beyond belief."

"You were always gentle with me, Adama. You never hurt me when you came inside me. The other women wanted you because of that. They told me they wished you had chosen them. They asked whether you were a rich man and, if so, offered to be your second, third or fourth wife. You needed only to kill the brutal men who took them captive, and the women would have gladly been your slaves."

Adama smiled ruefully. "They didn't know or understand that no other woman was you, Mary Ella, and the only woman I wanted in bondage I already had."

Adama guided her head to within a breath of his mouth, hesitating only momentarily to determine whether she would pull away. When she didn't, he kept his eyes open on hers as his tongue languidly dueled with hers. She was so damn sweet to the taste. If he were not careful, he would overdose on her.

When she moved to caress his jaw, he took her hand and viced it together with her other hand behind her back. He knew she remembered. If he had allowed her free range of his body, her touch would have eviscerated him. So, he kept her wrists captive in his hand while his mouth traveled over her. He maneuvered her until she straddled his lap, and she trembled when he rubbed his hardened penis against the wide-open walls of her vagina. When he touched her there, intimately, her breath caught in her throat, and she began to moan in a very familiar way he remembered. He fisted himself and rubbed against her opening, and her Kegels began to spasm with just a hint of his preparation to enter.

Mary Ella was so beautiful with her head thrown back while he suckled one turgid breast tip and then the other until she was vibrating like a plucked bowstring. Adama wanted her on that razor-sharp edge where she blossomed, and her portal opened like an early rose with the dew still on the petals. He knew his Mary Ella, remembered every sound she made when her need was the greatest just before she was ready to peak. Though it was taking its toll on him, he gave her inch by inch more of himself. Her Kegels spasmed and began to draw on him. Mary Ella tugged her hands, trying to get free, but he kept her at bay with a thumb rubbing her clitoris as he fed her vagina more and more of him. Finally, he was seated inside her, his girth saturated with his pre-cum and her juices. He recognized that he was large, and many women could not comfortably accommodate his width and length. With Mary Ella, she was so tight, he had to take her slowly or he would cause her pain.

She rode him hard through four successive orgasms. By the time she tore through the fifth, she was spent, and he had to let go. On a strangled cry, Adama emptied himself into her. He had just enough energy to place her on the bed and under the covers. He lay awake, listening to the wind whistling outside, but his thoughts were troubled about this strange turn of events. Mary Ella was here in his home, in his bed, for a reason. He believed she was just as clueless as he, but it was necessary for him to think beyond this event. Someone brought them together. He was glad for it but still needed to know why.

CHAPTER 33

Slowly, Mary Ella woke, and her senses clicked in. She was not in Summer County in her bed. She was in New Haven, Connecticut, in the bed and cabin owned by a man she barely knew, a man who could so easily turn her into a sexual predator. She knew what he was about to do to her when he mangled her wrists together at her back and had her straddle his lap. She should have stopped him, moved away, and denied herself something she craved.

It had to be the possessive way he took her. It was different from the only other men she knew. With Eric, it was deep and soulful. There was a reverence between them. A beautiful dance tangled together because of years of being in sync.

She and Mark had a playful kind of coupling, making each other laugh through multiple orgasms. They saw stars together in the vastness of space and the adventures they enjoyed. They were a team wanting to be of service to those in desperate need.

With Kaseem, not Kaseem, Adama, it was a possessiveness, a tortured coupling that drove her relentlessly to ride a thin edge to nirvana. He held himself back from her, not permitting her to touch as she chose.

Three different men, three distinct lovers, and with each one, she craved something different. They gave her what she wanted, each in his own way. However, in her life, she had only had these three lovers. If she had to choose among them, she'd be at a complete loss.

She turned her head to look at Adama beside her. His eyes were closed and his breathing shallow, but she noticed the rapid eye movement under his lids as if he were scrolling back and forth across lines of text. The firelight illuminated his face. Through the months she was under his protection, which was how she chose to look at her time with him now, she never had an opportunity to study his face. Except for his mesmerizing eyes, he was usually completely covered. That was as much of a benefit to him as his ability to melt into his surroundings unnoticed. If anyone saw him naked, he would not be seen as the non-threatening personae he had to portray. He was handsome, yes, but his physique was a masterpiece of muscles and proportioned in every dimension. He was a titan, a warrior, and, yes, a killer. He had taken lives, likely in self-defense or in defense of the defenseless. It was probably difficult for him to acclimate to living outside of his relentless hunt for those who would perpetrate mass murder, but what of him? What would this lifestyle do to a man who, at his core, seemed decent and dedicated? She had no illusions about him and what she wanted.

Easing out of bed, she went to her duffle and pulled the sash from her robe. When she turned to face Adama, his eyes were open on her. His pale gaze dropped only briefly to the sash in her hand and back up to meet hers. He wordlessly watched her as she climbed on top of him. Taking his wrists, she tied them together, stretched his arms up over his head, and fastened them to the bedpost. She had no doubt he could have broken free, but he just wordlessly watched her. In his closet, she found two belts and a necktie. She tied his feet wide apart to the footboard, and with the necktie, she covered his eyes.

He didn't try to stop her. Instead, he just silently waited.

His hair fanned out over the pillow, but she ran her fingers through it, fisting the silky strands in one hand, and pulled just hard enough for his head to tilt back, exposing his throat. She started with a focused carnality to his mouth before she went for his jugular. With her free hand, she raked her nails between his widely-spread, muscular thighs. His arm muscles and shoulders bunched hard as rocks, but he gripped the sash to hold on, not to escape. She tasted his chest, biting, then soothing with her tongue. He gripped the sash tighter as she latched on to one raisin-like nipple with teeth and tongue while pinching and pulling the other between her thumb and forefinger. Under her hips, she felt his hard abdomen begin to convex and concave in rapid succession with an escalation in his labored breathing.

She kept one hand fisted in his hair so that he couldn't know what she would do to him next. His anticipation was her erotic lethal weapon as she nipped and then soothed where he least expected it. As she went lower, raking her nails up and down his moist body, she sat on his thick thigh muscles rendering him immobile. He wouldn't move for fear of hurting her, she knew, so she took full advantage of his vulnerable position and took her time driving him out of his mind. Each touch, bite or kiss was meant to arouse him to the brink of no return but then take him higher with no relief in sight.

She was unrelenting and kept it up until his beautiful body was pulled taut and moist. He was straining to hold on but craving a release she continued to deny him. Using his abdominal muscles, his back bowed clear off the bed as his body went board stiff, and his testicles shriveled to the size and consistency of walnuts. He cried out mindlessly as if tortured when she finally took him in and bathed, exercising him from tip to hilt.

When she released him from bondage, he slept.

When Adama woke, Mary Ella was not in bed beside him. It seemed strange not to have her tethered to him, to let her be free to move without his permission. Yet, she had turned the tables on him. She demonstrated how strong-willed she was. He didn't *let* her take control. She did so on her own volition and dominated his mind and body in a way no other woman ever had. How she knew what he needed was perplexing and potentially dangerous.

It was still full-on dark outside, so he realized he must not have slept long. He was accustomed to putting himself into a REM sleep, called a bat nap in the teams, but he could stay alert. However, what she had done to him took him deeper to the point of total lassitude. He raised his head and listened. She was in the gathering room, and from the sound of it, she was stirring something in a pot. His stomach growled, reminding him that he hadn't eaten since lunch earlier that day. It had to be at least eight at night. He let his head drop back against the pillow to think.

He was going to be a father, something he never expected, and the woman he impregnated was as mentally and emotionally strong as he.

He would have to alter his plan. No child of his would grow up without a father. If he had a son, he would carry on the family surname and need to be taught how to be a man.

Years ago, he put his estate in order and recently altered it to bequeath his holdings to his wife, Mary Ella. Now, he would have to specifically include his children. He owed no one a financial debt. His home, his cabin, and the land around it were already mortgage-free. All of the salary he derived as a government agent was automatically banked, and he never needed to touch it over the many years of his career. Should something happen to him, he had substantial coverage to give his children a good financial head start in life. Now, he only had to decide what he needed to do with his life.

Mary Ella wondered what Kaseem---not Kaseem---Adama thought when she approached the bed carrying a tray. He started to move to assist her, but she waved him off. "Sit, sit. I've got this." He did as instructed. She set the tray on his lap and sat tailor-style across from him. "Who made the stew?" She dug in, feeding him a mouthful and then herself. She kept alternating the feeding between them.

"My mother. She's not a natural cook, but she follows cookbook instructions fairly well and then improvises the rest."

"She lives close?"

"She and my father live in the cabin you must have passed to get here to my cabin."

She nodded, clearly remembering the larger cabin at the top of the rise. "Do you have siblings?"

"Three sisters; two older and one younger."

"Where are they?"

"My two older sisters are married with families. They live in Stamford."

"California?"

He chuckled and it turned his ruggedly handsome face into movie-star perfection. "No, Connecticut. Stamford is about forty clicks from here, midway between here and the city."

"The city?"

"As in New York City, where my younger sister lives and works."

"With a family?"

"No, she's single."

"What do your parents do?"

"My father is an artisan in clay and wood carvings. He's taken up glass art in the past few years. He owns an antique store in the city, as in New Haven, not New York."

She smiled at that as she continued to feed him and herself. "And your mother? Does she work outside of her home?"

"She's a tenured professor at a small college in New Haven."

"Do they know that you put your life on the line every moment of every day?"

Adama stopped smiling at her and looked away.

"I'll take that as a no." Mary Ella put the empty bowl of stew and tray aside and then handed a bottle of water to him. "So, if I'm carrying your babies, I'm to tell them what about their father?"

He brought his gaze back around to look into her eyes. "*I'll* tell them that they are loved by their father, grandparents, aunts, uncles, and cousins. That what I do, I do to protect them from harm. That I work to ensure there are no more wars or threats of holocausts on any continent in the world."

"You plan to be there to see them born, to read bedtime stories to them, to watch them take their first steps, go off to school, swing a bat, toss a football, teach them how to drive a car, go out on a date, go to college, marry, and have children of their own. You'll do all of this in-between fulfilling your duty to rid this world of those who would destroy it."

"With your support, yes, Mary Ella. I'm not the first or only Navy SEAL to have a wife and family. More than half of the SEALs get married and live productive family lives."

"The SEALs under your command, do they have wives or close family relations?"

"No. They don't have husbands either. I have both men and women under my command."

She nodded. "I stand corrected. However, do these men and women tell their parents, their siblings, aunts and uncles, and cousins how dangerous it is to be them?"

He tunneled his hands through his long hair, a sure sign of frustration. "I don't have all of the answers yet, Mary Ella. Until you came here today, I didn't have a reason to think about the 'what ifs.' I'm just coming to grips with the fact that my wife is pregnant."

"I'm still coming to grips with the idea that I'm someone's wife who I don't even know. Is this marriage thing real?"

He nodded. "It is, yes." He watched her closely for a reaction but decided this was not the best time to explain what she and their children would inherit upon his death.

"If these babies are not yours, which is a distinct possibility, would you agree to a divorce?"

"No, why would I? We were legally married."

"Without my consent."

"Your silence was your consent. It is written in the Hadith, *'No Muslim man has gained a benefit besides Islam better than a Muslim wife who is a source of his pleasure whenever he looks at her, who obeys him when he commands her and remains faithful to him when he is away.'* It is also written, *'A matron should not be given in marriage until she is consulted, and a virgin should not be given in marriage until her permission is sought, and her silence is her permission.'*"

"Well, with me three strikes and you're out. First, I'm not a Muslim. As you've witnessed, I don't do well with the whole 'obey' thing. This leads me to thing three. I will not remain faithful when you're away."

He grinned at her impudence. "Still not a game-changer. You're forgetting the other prong. Your silence was your permission."

She huffed a frustrated breath. "I don't understand the language well enough to know I could reject a Muslim man and wedding in the frekken middle of a war. Especially not when my head was about to be chopped off."

He grinned. "I'm half-lapsed as a Muslim."

She rolled her eyes. "You could have fooled me."

"Good. If I fooled you, I hope that I fooled others and my cover is still intact." He sobered and looked earnestly into her eyes. "Still, it's what I had to do to do my job.

He shook his head. "Listen, my mother is an American Muslim and an Olympic gold medalist. She didn't wear a niqab or abaya in any of her trials. She taught my sisters and me that it's not about what you wear on the outside, but what you wear on the inside.

"My father is Hindi from India. Imagine the damage which could have been done with a Hindu man and Muslim woman, but they've managed for more than forty years not to go to war over religious dogma. That's more than I can say for some countries. I don't see why we can't accomplish the same feat."

"Except to have even attempted such a *feat,* they had to have started out deeply in love with one another. We've started because you saved my life and have the ability to give me incredible orgasms—no love in the picture. I want to love someone as much, if not more than I love myself. I want someone to love me with every beat of his heart."

"Mary Ella, that whole 'love at first sight' thing is a myth. The first time I saw you, I wanted to sleep with you often and continuously. You gave me a boner that I was hard-pressed to survive. You radiate sex appeal, and you don't even know it, and you're not even trying."

He sighed and took her hands in his. "It takes time to build trust, love, and mutual respect. Those are the tenants of any relationship, regardless of religion. I believe we can build a marriage on the foundation we started with. I promise to give you as many orgasms as you want." He grinned at her. "Every time I've seen you, I've desired you even though you were clearly with Mark Brooks."

"You were probably just horny."

"I know how to control my libido because having sex with some women in certain countries can be detrimental to one's health. If I want sex, I pay for it with a woman who knows exactly what I want. I want you, Mary Ella, because, with you, there is no hidden agenda on either of our parts. We know and understand how our foundation was laid. You're carrying our future in your body, a body I continue to crave. I want more babies with you. So, the whole divorce thing for me is a non-starter. You're it for me. It's a one and done."

"Even though you don't know me?"

"Mary Ella Baker, daughter of your now-deceased parents, Robert and Elena McLeod Baker, Jr. Your paternal grandparents were Robert and Edna Mae Clark Baker, Senior. Your maternal grandmother was Imani. She was Native American, full-blooded Cherokee, and I believe barely in her teens when a man impregnated her against her will. He was Spencer McLeod, who died mysteriously a week later after raping her. There were certain herbs found in his stomach and system, which separately were not harmful but taken together would be detrimental to one's health, lethal in fact. Although it was suspected that he was murdered, no one was ever arrested in connection with his death. You were very close to her, and she shared her knowledge with you."

"Count yourself lucky to still be alive," Mary Ella deadpanned.

"I do. Of your remaining relatives, you're closest to your cousin, Satarah Josephine James Johnson. Other than me, you've only slept with two men, Eric Dixon and Mark Brooks, and you recently turned thirty-one."

"What's my favorite color and my favorite food?"

"Those are trick questions, Mary Ella. You don't have favorite anything. You're open to exploring new and different things. Cocktail party chitchat isn't in your vocabulary. You think outside of the box, but you don't tell everything you know or think about.

"I want time with you so that we can learn things together. Learn things about each other. You know only the surface things about me, but I've had the desire to know more about you for more than four years. You'll need time to catch up."

"I'm scheduled to be back in South Carolina on Tuesday."

He snorted a laugh. "If this nor'easter holds true, Mary Ella, you'll be lucky to leave New Haven before next weekend."

She frowned at him. "Are you sure about that?"

"I am, yes. So, let's put some more logs on the fire and settle in bed for the night. You can tell me all the things you've done, thought, and felt, starting with the first thing you remember when you were a kid. I need to make love with you again and to work hard to give you multiple orgasms before I sleep. So, talk fast." He laughed.

She raised an eyebrow at him, which made him laugh harder.

CHAPTER 34

The next morning dawned just as Adama predicted, with high winds and heavy snows. Mary Ella hadn't experienced snow like this since a blizzard years ago shut down South Carolina, and they had to contend with hundreds of accident victims on the interstate twenty-four-seven for more than a week.

As she stood looking out of the front picture window, she could barely see beyond Adama's front deck. He came to stand behind her, his chin on the top of her head, his left arm across her chest above her breasts, and his right hand soothing and stroking across her belly.

"These little people have been active most of last night and this morning. Are you feeling all right?"

"I'm fine." She sighed, leaning back against him, her hands resting on his strong left arm muscles. It allowed him free access to her abdomen. His warm touch was soothing and seemed to have a quieting effect on the twins. She appreciated that he woke during the night when she couldn't get comfortable. He sat up with her, her back against his chest while she sat between his muscular thighs. He stroked her belly for hours, much as he was doing now. Just before dawn, he gave her a hydro massage in his bathtub that had her drifting off to sleep.

His mouth trailed down the right side of her neck to her collarbone and back up again to her ear. She moved to allow him unfettered access and closed her eyes on a moan when his right hand dipped below her belly and found her damp and hot. She could feel his vertical ridge hard at her back as he inserted one, then two long, blunt fingers inside her while using one thumb to worry her clit. With his warm mouth on her ear, his left hand massaging her right breast, and his right hand bringing her to her peak, it didn't take long for her to crest.

He wasted no time carrying her still vibrating body back to the warmth of his bed. A while later, with her tucked tight into his right side, he kissed her hair just above her left ear and asked, "How about some breakfast? I think I can have it ready in a few short minutes."

She nodded. "First, I need to take a shower."

He led her into his bath and started the water. They showered together and washed each other's hair and body. He had such long, thick, raven-black, healthy hair that shined and curled when wet.

They dried each other, applied jojoba oil to each other's bodies, and then put on terrycloth robes before heading for the small kitchen bar. She sat on a stool as he brought a steaming hot, electric pot of oatmeal to the quartz countertop. He sprinkled brown sugar over it and spooned it up to test the temperature before feeding the first taste to Mary Ella.

"Why don't you have dishes?" Mary Ella frowned.

Adama laughed. "I don't cook, and I'm not here often enough to justify dishes. The pots, pans, and electric crockpots here are cast-offs from my family. Actually, I haven't been here in years. My sisters come and stay here from time to time with their families to take advantage of the lake. When I do make time to come home, I generally use paper products. Less cleanup or I eat with my parents or siblings, or I go out to a restaurant. My mother and sisters want to feed me, so I let them. They cook——" and halted, reaching under the cabinet for what Mary Ella recognized as a gun.

Just then, the front door opened. "Adama?" a tall young woman called out. "Come, I need…" she began and then halted. "Well, hello." She smiled broadly, coming forward, her hand extended. "I'm Kira Gupta, Adama's sister."

"Hello, I'm Mary Ella Baker," she offered just as Adama corrected, "Gupta."

Kira's eyes widened in surprise. "Okaaaay." She elongated, nodded slowly while skeptically looking back and forth between them. "I believe this is going to be interesting. However, first, Adama, I need help with the groceries I left on a sled beside your porch. Would you get them please?"

"Sure." He went to put on his sweats over the pair of Jockey's he was wearing.

Kira quickly unwrapped herself from her heavy weather gear and sat down next to Mary Ella on one of the kitchen bar stools, smiling broadly. "Okay, I had just planned to bring those groceries, but I think I'm too curious to leave now. Which is it? Baker or Gupta?"

"Gupta." Adama passed by on the way to his front door.

"It's a technicality that will be straightened out in the near future." Mary Ella's voice rose to make sure Adama could hear her as he went out the front door.

Kira's eyes got bigger, and her face was wreathed in joy. "You and my brother are married?"

"Well, yes."

"Cool!" she sang. "We didn't have a clue! He hasn't said a word. When and where did this happen?"

"Go away, pest." Adama voiced without heat coming inside with two bags of groceries. He dumped them on the island and started back outside.

"Mama sent me down here to cook for you, so I'm staying," she returned cheekily. "Especially now, so I can hear all of the details about your marriage and my new sister."

"No, she didn't. You don't cook any better than I do. Go back to the house and tell mama I'll do just fine."

"You may be good at a lot of things, big brother, but cooking isn't one of them, so I'm staying."

"Actually, I'm not bad in a kitchen." Mary Ella stood up to see what was in the grocery bags. Anything to distract Kira from asking pointed questions she didn't want to answer.

"Oh. My. Goodness! You're very pregnant! *WOW!*" She bounced up and down. "No wonder Adama came home so abruptly. When are you due?"

"I'm in my third trimester."

Kira clapped her hands like a child on Christmas morning and rushed her brother, hugging him tightly when he came through the door with three more bags of groceries. He laughed at her antics and barely made it to the kitchen with her hanging onto him.

"Mary Ella, may I hug you, too?"

"Of course." She accepted the gentle but warm hug from Kira.

Adama came to stand behind Mary Ella and put his arms around her. "Now, thank you for bringing the food and tell Mama Mary Ella, and I would like a little time to ourselves."

"Oh." Kira smiled and then gasped, *"Oh!"* with more emphasis, "Yes, of course. I'll see you later in the week." She winked as she put on her heavy weather gear again and hurried out the door.

Adama stretched his arms out in front of him and leaned against the edge of the countertop. His head dropped between his outstretched arms as he shook his head. "I thought we would have a little more time together to get comfortable with each other, but now that Kira knows you're here, we'll be invaded."

"Maybe I should try to go. I could maybe get a train out of New Haven into New York."

"No, Mary Ella, we might as well face this now, rather than later."

"Adama, I don't want to disappoint your family, but I intend to find a way out of this marriage."

"I understand that you want to try because you don't know me, but I'm asking you to wait until after our babies are born before you try that."

"You know as well as I do that if I wait until after I give birth, the babies will be Guptas. If they are not yours, Adama, I have to be fair and put Mark's name on the birth certificates instead of yours."

"If the twins are mine, Gupta will go on the birth certificates?" Adama was surprised.

She nodded. "Yes, of course, that's only fair to you. I will never separate them from you if they are yours, but I would not be the person I need to be for them if I'm forced to stay in a marriage that's not real to me with a man I'm not in love with."

He pushed away from the counter, walked toward her, and caged her in. He leaned down to look directly into her eyes with his arms around her and against the countertop where she sat on the barstool. "Then you may have to stay in a marriage with a man who will offer the type of love you need to be fulfilled and happy." He kissed her mouth deeply and then lifted her to sit on the countertop. With his forehead pressed to hers, he spoke quietly. "I want you, Mary Ella, for the whole of my life. When I go back into the theatre, I don't know how long that will last. I have missions I'm honor-bound to accomplish, but if I survive them, I'll come back, resign my commission as a Naval Officer and as a CIA agent, and take up gardening if you'll wait for me."

Mary Ella looked into his eyes. "I won't make a promise to you that I know I may not be able to keep."

"Then, for now, let's promise to make each other happy. One day at a time." Adama lifted her and took her back to bed. "Right now, you need the sleep you didn't get last night. I know how to put you to sleep."

It was noon when they showered and dressed again. They had left the groceries out on the countertop. So, they worked together, sorting through them.

Mary Ella frowned. "Are you a vegetarian?"

"No." Adama laughed. "I'm a meatatarian. The only thing I don't eat is pork. My hypocrisy does have boundaries."

"Okay, just so you know, I love pork chops, ham, and bacon from a pig, not a turkey. Although I use smoked turkey to season my vegetables, particularly greens, I've been known to add ham-hocks on occasion. Your groceries consist of a lot of vegetables. I don't mind that. I love vegetables, too, but where's the meat?"

"I have fillet haddock, chicken, and beef roasts. A typical Indian meal combines salty, sweet, creamy, spicy, hot, and pungent flavors. The basic menu usually comprises starch, a meat or fish main dish, vegetables, and chutney. Traditionally, Indian flatbread or basmati rice complements the other dishes to highlight a balanced group of flavors. So, it appears my sister was going to attempt to make several Indian meals for me."

"Okay, I don't mind cooking, but I don't know how to make traditional Indian meals."

Adama reached under the counter and brought out a book full of recipes. "Here you go. See what interests you, and if you have any questions, I'll call my mother."

She laughed at him and set about going through the book of recipes.

Two hours later, Adama leaned back in his seat, wiped his mouth, and tossed his used paper napkin onto his paper plate. He eyed Mary Ella. "For someone who didn't know anything about Indian food, you certainly are a quick learner."

"Thanks, the recipes helped a great deal, but the spices were new to me, so I didn't use a lot in the dishes."

"It was still perfect…" He halted abruptly, picked up his vibrating cell phone, and quickly read the text. "Uh, Mary Ella, I want you to remain perfectly calm, okay?"

"What? Why? What's…?"

"All in," Adama voiced aloud, and suddenly the room filled with seven men and four women all wearing BDUs or what is known in the teams as battle-dressed uniforms and carrying weapons.

She looked around at all of the faces, and some of the olive-brown and darker-hued complexions looked familiar.

"Capt'n, we received an alert."

"I know. I'm decoding it now." His brows bunched, and his focus remained on the phone's screen.

"Adama?"

"Hold on, Mary Ella." While still frowning at the message, his pale gaze was sharp and directed. Then he looked up and around. "Pac Man?"

"*Yo!*"

"I want you on point. See what you can sniff out."

"*Yo!*"

"Mac?

"*Yo!*"

"Show a little leg, and learn things."

"*Yes, Sir!*"

"I still don't know what the play is here, but I'll find out and follow up in a few days. Go."

"*Yes, Sir!*" they repeated in unison and then in deference nodded, "Mrs.," by way of a farewell greeting to her. Then they were gone as soundlessly as they'd arrived.

Mary Ella looked at Adama silently until he completed thumbing a message. When he looked up at her, his eyes were not focused until she spoke. "What the hell? You tell me to 'hold on one moment' when I'm suddenly surrounded by people with enough artillery and firepower to start World War III?"

He shook his head, frowning. "I apologize. That couldn't be helped. There have been multiple attacks, ambushes actually, on Army Special Forces, Green Berets. The President's wife, the First Lady of the US, is an active-duty Army Ranger. It was one of her teams that was targeted. It could have been accidental, but we think not. Two of the President and First Lady's sons are Army Rangers. We believe it was intentional, and my unit has been called back into the theatre.

"Before I was exfiltrated," Adama continued, "we were on the trail of Islamic militants in Mali and an ISIS terror group in Niger. They are suspected of having possession of dirty bombs. When we were called back to the Special Naval Operations Air Base in Sigonella, Sicily, another team was inserted to take my team's place. Various Islamist groups operate in Niger, with Nigeria-based Boko Haram carrying out attacks in eastern Niger and Algeria-based al-Qaida in the Islamic Maghreb operating in the west along with pockets of Islamic State fighters. You know where these areas are because you've worked in each of those areas more than a few times.

"These groups are finding a safe haven in West Africa as we continue to squeeze them out of Syria and Iraq. They tried to go to Libya, but we were there, so it didn't work real well for them there. Still, we've experienced cross-border attacks and kidnappings like what happened to you and Mark Brooks by AQIM fighters based in Mali. I was right on their heels when I was sent home and told to await further orders. A few days later, my entire team was pulled out of the theatre and sent home. As I said, another SEAL Team replaced us. The team they were backing up was the one hit. They took casualties."

"You want to go with them." Mary Ella voiced flatly.

He leaned forward, his elbows on his thick, muscular thighs, and took her hands in his. He looked earnestly into her eyes, his long, loose, curly, midnight-black hair fanning his face. "I do, yes, but I still don't know who brought you here and why. I need to know the answer to those questions and evaluate the threat to you and my family before I can leave. Is there anything else you can tell me about how you got here?"

"No, nothing." Mary Ella shook her head. "I've told you everything I know. I received a text message I thought was from Mark, but he didn't send the original text to me. He didn't send a jet to pick me up to bring me to New Haven. I don't know who arranged for the chauffeured car, either."

"Then who did?"

"I don't know. However, there was one thing."

"What is it?"

"Well, it probably doesn't mean anything, but the jet which brought me here is one of the private jets in the Adventurer Executive Airline fleet. Quiet as it's kept, the airline is owned by US Supreme Court Judge Vivian Alexander Montgomery. She and my cousin, Satarah, are also cousins on the other side of the family with Vivian. Vivian's mother and Satarah's mother are sisters.

"Satarah took me to the airport and mentioned that the jet I was about to board belonged to Vivian's company. However, I know for a fact that Vivian doesn't exercise management control over the airline or her other businesses. For the most part, her brother, Gregory Alexander, handles her estate and her husband's, Dr. Chuck Montgomery, in blind trusts, which are vast. I think Gregory has people working on various aspects of his sister's and brother-in-law's different businesses.

"For example, Vivian's cousin, Donald Dixon, is an attorney. He handles Vivian's and Chuck's legal affairs through her former law firm, Alexander, Carter, Chandler, Charles, Lightfoot, and Towson, PA, in Washington, DC. However, the text message didn't come from Vivian, Gregory or Donald."

"I know." Adama frowned while considering the information she provided. "I had your phone scrubbed for messages. My people haven't been able to trace the origin of the original text message you received. It was only available on your phone for a day. Long enough for you to read it to get here, and then it was gone."

"You had my phone 'scrubbed'?"

"Please, don't get upset, Mary Ella. I took the necessary precautions to try and determine how this occurred and what level of risk we're facing. I'm sure you want to know the answers to those questions, too. Someone sent you to me, and that's not normal. To the best of my knowledge, only a few people in my chain of command at Naval Operations or the CIA know anything about this place. I needed to know what was going on, and I'm sure if you knew something, you'd tell me. I don't want my family in jeopardy while I'm away. That includes you."

"Is that why you have a gun in the kitchen and another in your closet?"

"Yes, and concealed elsewhere in and around this property, but the team immediately came when I signaled them."

"*Wait.* Do you mean your team has been here all of the time I've been here? While we were having sex?" She voiced incredulously.

"They only got nervous the first time you tied me up." He looked at her straight-faced and shrugged. "The other times, they just relaxed and enjoyed the show as much as I did." He laughed at her horrified expression. "Seriously, Mary Ella, they could only hear what I allowed. If I don't use a stress word, they are on radio silence."

"Could they see us?"

He shrugged. "Well, yeah, this cabin is video and audio monitored."

"Where were they? Except for the ones who came in through the front door, they didn't look like they've been out in this blizzard like your sister did."

Adama shook his head. "I'm sorry, Mary Ella, I can't divulge that information." She was freaked enough that it wouldn't be wise to tell her that his team, as well as many others, were warm and comfortable in a bunker with all of the amenities below his cabin and his parents. None of his family members knew they were there. One of the entrances to the catacomb of passageways and hollowed-out areas underground was a mile away in a protected national forest and park.

"If they can find a way to leave New Haven to go to Niger, maybe I… why are you laughing, Adama?"

"We're SEALs, Mary Ella. We're trained to go where we have to go no matter the difficulty." The catacombs were large enough to drive eighteen-wheelers inside. His team had Humvees to exfiltrate when the need arose. However, they'd be on a submarine, courtesy of the New London Submarine Base at Groton, Connecticut, docked in one of the catacombs with water access in a matter of minutes. There was a large, secret base of operation in the New Haven, Connecticut, catacombs, many of its military units SEAL teams. Submarines entered and exited submerged through Black Island Sound. His team would be aboard one of them on a dead heat for the African continent in less than an hour. They'd transfer to a US aircraft carrier well out at sea and be flown into Italy and then a helo drop into the theatre of operations. From there, they would begin to hunt.

Most people knew of the SEAL teams based in Coronado, California, and Little Creek, Virginia. However, there were training sites all around the perimeter of the US. Even in the Great Lakes, teams were charged with the responsibility to keep the homeland safe. His team usually worked the Middle East, Asia, and Africa theatres. He was concerned that maybe his team was being reinserted when insurgents were plotting another ambush knowing their arrival was imminent. It raised the terrorists' profiles if they could boast at having killed even one member of an elite US Navy SEAL team.

He wasn't concerned overmuch. His team was among the best of the best, but he wanted to be there with them. He felt a bit better because he knew Wilde Wolf's Tiger Team had been activated to lead the hunt. Although the teams were interchangeable, they worked better when there were no missing pieces. Otherwise, they could be vulnerable.

He had gone quiet, thought Mary Ella. Adama apparently had a lot on his mind, and the reason she was inserted into his life at this time was clearly one of those things which concerned him. She needed to leave so that he could get on with his business. Then she could begin to finally come to a conclusion about the track her life would take. Now that she knew Adama would not cooperate in a religious divorce, she had to figure out her options. She'd talk with Donald Dixon, Eric's cousin, about it. He's an attorney and a friend, she thought. If anyone could figure this out, he could.

"Mary Ella? Mary Ella?" Adama tried to get her attention.

"Uh, yes?" His voice finally penetrated her maelstrom of thoughts.

"If you're tired, why don't you take a nap? I'll clean up the kitchen and join you."

She shook her head. "I'm not tired. I can help…"

"Remember, you didn't sleep well last night or this morning. Take an hour or so of downtime. I've put fresh sheets on the bed. I need to do a load of laundry while you get some rest."

She was weary, so she nodded her agreement and went into the bedroom. The fireplace was lit, making the room toasty warm. So, she discarded the robe, crawled into bed, and closed her eyes. She dropped into a dream-filled sleep featuring scenes involving three men: Eric, Mark, and Adama. She thought she knew with whom she belonged. The only question remaining was, who was the father of her twins?

CHAPTER 35

"I'm happy to see you back. How was the trip?" Satarah watched as Mary Ella gingerly settled into a tall, bar chair in the kitchen of The Summer House.

"It was a trip." When Satarah joined her at the bar, they hugged. "Thanks for sending Benson to pick me up from the airport."

"*Ha!* Like I could stop him?" She made herself comfortable next to Mary Ella. "Benson makes any excuse so that he can drive his car. He enjoys driving to and from school and his part-time job. He's picked up some extra hours working at JoJeff's dealership in the accounting department after school. He runs all of my errands for me. Besides, it's easier for him to carry your duffle than you or me," Satarah joked about her eldest sixteen-year-old son.

"Well, yes, for that reason, anyway. Is everyone up and out already?"

"Oh, yes, Doug takes the girls to school in his truck, and Benson takes the guys with him in his car. Doug just tails them to make sure Benson is driving responsibly, but enough about us. What about you and Mark? Why the impromptu get-together in Connecticut?"

"It wasn't Mark who sent for me."

"I don't understand." Confusion resided on Satarah's face. "If it wasn't Mark, then who?"

"I haven't got a clue, but when I got there, I was taken to this cabin on a beautiful lake. When I went inside, Adama was there."

Satarah frowned. "Who is Adama?"

"Kareem."

It took a moment before Satarah reacted. "*What!* How in the world did he get into the country, and how the hell did he find you?"

"He's not a terrorist. He's a US Navy SEAL attached to the CIA."

Satarah just stared at Mary Ella. "You've got to be kidding me! All this time, you thought you were married to a terrorist; instead, you were with an American hero?"

"Well, the hero part is right, but I am legally married to him. His name is Adama Karim Gupta. I suppose his military code name is Kaseem. We didn't get around to discussing that aspect of his service. It snowed for four days, but that didn't stop his parents, three sisters, and two brothers-in-law, including nephews and nieces, from arranging a big party to celebrate our marriage and the coming new additions. The day I left, the Gupta family held a farewell breakfast for me. They made it clear they want me to come back soon.

"I felt so disingenuous about the whole thing the same way I felt when I left Mark after having breakfast with his family, but Adama let everything happen as if our relationship is a normal occurrence for newlyweds.

"His father is Hindu, and his mother is African American Muslim, and, believe me, they know how to throw a party. Hindu weddings go on for days with copious amounts of food, drink, and dancing, but Adama ushered everyone out of his cabin after twenty-four hours. I was worn out. It was noisy and fun, but I could barely hear what anyone was saying because they play the music set on scream. The place was packed to the rafters. Adama's home is a modern one bedroom, one bath, open-concept, post-and-beam log cabin, but I'm sure it wasn't built to accommodate that many people.

"His three sisters decorated the cabin from top to bottom in these beautiful, shockingly bright colored cloths of reds and golds. The bedroom looked like a harem when they finished. They prepared so much food, I thought there would be loads of leftovers. After twenty-four hours, there were only scraps left and not a drop of alcohol. Mr. Gupta's six brothers and their families and Mrs. Gupta's large family and their three generations of offspring came, some from as far away as Philadelphia and Boston, on the spur of the moment to join the celebration. The nor'easter didn't deter them. The railroad trains were still running.

"I'll tell you, SaraJo, you know we can get pretty rowdy at get-togethers in our family, but their party was on steroids."

Satarah laughed. "So, how did you leave it with Adama, aka Kaseem?"

"He has missions for the CIA he feels he must complete. After that, he says he'll resign his commission as a Navy SEAL officer and resign from the CIA. His father owns a nice antique shop that Adama took me to see. He says he'd take over the search for unique pieces to buy and sell in the shop. His father is an artisan and really very good. He has this big studio at his home, where he does the majority of his crafts. He wants to spend more time doing that and is thrilled with the idea that Adama would do the heavy lifting with buying and selling items for the shop."

"How do you feel about that?"

"I don't know, Satarah. Sedate is not a word I would use to describe Adama. He says he wants his *'wife'* and children with him in New Haven. He plans to add more bedrooms and baths to his cabin to accommodate the twins and more children. He even introduced me to the Director of Nursing at New Haven General. She's a school chum of his. He did that in case I want to continue to work outside the home once the twins are born. He has it all planned out, even though he knows I'm not in love with him."

"What do you feel for him?"

"Heat."

"Okay, that's not a great basis for a life-long commitment."

"It isn't, no, but he believes that I will someday find myself in love with him."

"Did he say he's already in love with you?"

She nodded. "He's had a head start in that direction. Apparently, he's been tracking me ever since I joined DWB, but I was with Mark, so he backed off. I didn't even know Adama existed. Then Mark and I were captured, and Adama saved my life. I was honest with him. He knows I have feelings for Mark and even for Eric, but he's asking me to give our *'marriage'* a fair trial.

"He's given permission to me to tell you all of this, about him. He wants you to be able to reach him in case something happens with me before he returns." Mary Ella handed a card to Satarah. "This is how he can be reached through his handlers."

"When do you have to give him an answer?"

"When he returns from his current missions or after the babies are born, whichever occurs last. I need to know whose babies I'm carrying. I won't know that until after they're born."

"You didn't happen to collect another engagement ring, did you?"

"Well, he insisted I accept a ring he made when he was a child, and his father taught him to work with copper." She pulled it out from under her shirt by a piece of rawhide from around her neck and handed it to Satarah. The ring was attached.

"This is beautiful, Mary Ella. You say he made it when he was a child?"

"Ten years old, his parents told me."

"What are the markings on the ring?" Satarah handed it back to Mary Ella.

"It's written in Hindu. It says, 'trust in me.'"

"Hi, Donald. Thanks for meeting with me."

"Of course, Mary Ella. You said you need my help?"

"Well, yes. You see, I need to hire you to arrange for my divorce."

Not by a raised eyebrow did Donald's face change, Mary Ella noted. He sat patiently, listening as she explained the situation. "So, you see, I need to know whether I'm married under Sharia Law and, if so, how I can obtain a divorce."

"Do you have a dollar?"

Mary Ella thought the question strange but reached into her pocket and removed money. "Sure, here you go."

He took the dollar and pocketed it. "Okay, I'm now officially your lawyer."

Her brows bunched. "Donald, that can't be enough for your legal fees."

"I think it's a start. Now, I'm not an expert on Sharia Law, so this may take a day or two to figure out. However, rest assured, if you are sure you want out of this marriage, consider it done. The next matter to be addressed concerns the twins. If your twins are the offspring of Adama Gupta, what are you prepared to do about custody?"

"If the twins I carry are his, I would not want to deny him or his family access to them."

"Would you be willing to share joint custody?"

"I'd have to think about that, Donald. He's a Navy SEAL now, but I don't know whether he's serious about leaving the military. I've only met his parents, sisters, brothers-in-law, nephews, and nieces on two occasions. They appear to be fine people, but I would need to spend more time getting to know them before granting joint custody to Adama, particularly when the twins are very young."

"You hold no animosity toward Adama for this situation?"

"If I could change history and not put myself at risk, I would, but it is what it is, Donald. He saved my life. I can't get beyond that fact. If it were not for him, I would not be here today carrying these precious babies. They are the only ones who matter now. That trumps everything else that happened. I will not bring the twins into a situation where I'm at odds with their father over something that cannot be changed."

"If the twins are Mark Brooks' offspring?"

"The same goes. I have to believe that both Mark and Adama are honorable men. They are by no means perfect, but I've not experienced anything in their characters to be overly concerned about. However, it is no longer about me or their father or what we may want. What is best for the twins comes first, last, and only. I will teach them about their Cherokee and African American ancestries and expect their father to do the same with their ancestries. They will learn not only *who* they are, but also *whose* they are."

"All right, Mary Ella. I will figure out what to do about your marital status and draw up a custody agreement while I'm at it. Give me a few days, okay?" He stood.

When he reached for her, she hugged him. "Thank you, Donald. I appreciate this."

"You're welcome. More soon and tell my cousin I said he's a lucky guy to have such a strong, smart, and level-headed woman as a friend."

"I'll do no such thing, Donald Dixon. I'll leave that discussion up to you and Eric." She laughed and waved goodbye to him.

It was raining like a monsoon hit as Mary Ella stood under the *porte-cochere* at the emergency room entrance. She hoped the rain would slow enough to make it to her car without getting totally soaked. She certainly couldn't run, and the puddles were getting deeper.

"Well, hello stranger," a familiar voice came from behind her.

She turned and smiled up at Eric. "I'm no stranger than usual," she joked. "How are you, Eric?"

"I woke up breathing this morning, so I'll say it's not a bad start. How are you and the potato spuds?"

"They seem to be about the size of eggplants now, but we're well."

"That means you don't have long before you get to hold them in your arms."

"You're right, and I'm looking forward to it. Are you leaving early?"

"I am, yes. I pulled an all-nighter. I haven't done anything like this since I did my residency. I'm going home and crash. How about you?"

"I'm off duty, too. I was trying to wait for a break in the weather so that I can get to my car."

"You'll be lucky to get the break you're looking for. The hurricane, which was predicted to turn out to sea, changed its mind, and it's skirting the coast at Category four gale-force winds of one hundred fifty miles per hour. Then there's another storm following close on its heels. I believe we're going to get hit pretty hard."

"Oh, no, maybe I shouldn't go off duty."

"You've got competent staff to handle any eventuality, Mary Ella. You look like you could use a rest yourself."

"I really could. I haven't been sleeping well."

"Look, stay put. I'll get my car and pick you up and take you to your car. Then, why don't you follow me home? We'll throw something together for dinner and watch the weather report. Sound like a plan?"

"You just said you're tired. Shouldn't you get some rest?"

"I will, but I haven't seen hide nor hair of you since you got back in town three weeks ago. We can spend a little time catching up."

Actually, she had been avoiding Eric. Her life was so complicated at this moment that she didn't want to dump on him, but he was one of her best friends. She needed a friend right now, so she acquiesced. She liked spending time with him. "So, what's on the menu?" she joked.

The wind was picking up when Eric and Mary Ella rushed into the mudroom door of his home.

"Wow, this storm seems to be growing in intensity." Eric frowned. "I'll check the forecast." He went across the kitchen area to the family room space and, using a remote, turned on the flat screen.

The Weather Channel's Jim Cantore was standing on a beach as the storm surge battered his legs, and some brave camera person fought to keep the equipment from being ripped away by the strong winds.

"Yes, it appears that the hurricane will make landfall in Charleston, South Carolina, in a few hours. It's a fast-moving storm with sustained winds…" he continued.

"I guess that settles it." Mary Ella came to stand next to Eric while blotting the rainwater from her hair, face, and arms. When finished, she handed the towel to Eric, who did the same thing. "Maybe I should head back to the hospital."

"We're safe enough here. Frank built this house with block and brick with Cat five hurricanes in mind. I've also got electronic hurricane shutters on all of the windows and doors. The only vulnerable thing is the pool screen."

"What about the river? It's bound to crest above flood stage, don't you think?"

"Not according to the way this storm is tracking. It's spinning against the natural flow of the river."

"You're right. That might lower the river, rather than raise it."

"In any event, we'll keep an eye on it. So, let's see." He moved toward the kitchen space and opened the heavy freezer door. "Dad made chicken breasts stuffed with fresh spinach and feta cheese. How does that sound?"

"Like perfection."

"Good. It shouldn't take long. I'll just pop it in the convection oven to bake." After putting the Pyrex tray in the oven, he watched Mary Ella walk back and forth with her hands massaging her lower back. "Are you in pain?"

"Lower back. Do you mind if I use your spa?"

"Mi casa es su casa." After putting the rest of the food on to cook, he selected the temperature and started the water to bubble in the spa. Stretching and yawning, he decided he could do with a swim before dinner and went to change his clothes. When he returned, Mary Ella was reclining in the spa with her eyes closed. He turned off the flat screen volume and selected quiet music to play while he swam, and she napped. He didn't want her to be in there too long, or she might experience vertigo.

An hour later, they sat in terrycloth robes at the informal dining table, finishing off their simple meal.

Mary Ella sighed, contented. "Your father missed his calling."

Eric laughed. "I'll tell him you said that. He'll be pleased."

"Eric, I have a confession to make."

He shrugged his muscular shoulders. "Okay, so you didn't like the food," he joked, "or you want a third helping. Which one is it?"

"Ha!" She smiled slightly. "My confession is that I've purposely been avoiding you since I returned."

He poured more wine into his goblet and then took a sip. "Why would you do that?"

"You don't seem angry."

"I'm not angry, Mary Ella. I know you've been avoiding me, so I can only assume it has something to do with the impromptu trip you made a while back when I was in Miami. So, why don't you tell me what's going on with you?"

He recognized the move when Mary Ella palmed her face, scrubbing briskly and then tunneling her long, slender fingers through her damp hair as a sign of frustration. So, he waited, drinking his wine while the wind howled, and the rain lashed against the closed glass doors. His own fatigue was trying to set in, and, under other circumstances, he would have tabled this discussion with Mary Ella until the morning. Still, anything that would cause her to avoid him deserved an airing sooner rather than later. So, he relaxed and prepared to fight fatigue and listen.

"I was taken to see the man who may be the father of my children."

Eric's brows bunched. "Okay? You were taken to see Mark?"

She shook her head. "Mark may not be the father of my twins."

That got his attention. He sat forward with his arms crossed on the table and listened as Mary Ella told him of her capture, marriage, and ultimate rescue. The man who saved her life was not the terrorist she initially thought him to be, but a US Navy SEAL in deep cover. As she talked, he thought about the call he made to his cousin, Donald Dixon. When the President of the United States of America landed Air Force One on the tarmac at Summer County Municipal Airport in South Carolina, and snapped up his cousin, Donald, and Donald's pal, Lucas, everyone in the family knew not to say a mumbling word. He didn't know what Donald did in Washington, but whatever it was, he was still doing it. He had the presence of mind to ask Donald to check out Mark Brooks to ensure that he had not impregnated Mary Ella, and, rich man that he was, planned not to take care of his responsibilities to her.

Donald assured him that nothing could be farther from the truth. He believed Mark Brooks to be an honorable man and agreed to follow up. Now, somehow, he believed his cousin arranged the meeting between Mary Ella and this Adama Gupta, the only other man who might have fathered her twins.

When he was in the military, he heard about an über secret group created by the G7 that was so clandestine it didn't benefit from an anachronism. Washington, DC, was the home of the alphabet soup: CIA, FBI, NSA, etc. His cousin was no novice when it came to world affairs. Although Donald and Cecile lived what appeared to be an uneventful life, they traveled extensively. Donald often slipped in and out of town virtually unnoticed by most. So, his suspicions seemed firmly based while listening to Mary Ella, particularly when she said something that sharpened his attention.

"So, since your cousin, Donald, is the only lawyer I know other than Vivian, I asked him to look into what I needed to do, under Sharia law, to divorce Adama."

"What did he say?"

"Donald apparently knew someone who knew someone, and Adama signed the papers consenting to the divorce. I don't have to go to court or anything. However, I have to give him notice when I go into labor, and I am going to share custody of the babies with Adama if he turns out to be the father of my twins."

"Did Donald say how he was able to accomplish this?"

"No, but he told me at our initial meeting not to worry and to consider the divorce a done deal. You know your cousin better than I do. If Donald gives his word, stick a fork in it because it's done. I need for you to talk with him because he refuses to accept any legal fees from me for doing this."

"Forget it. I'm not going to ask Donald to take money from you." He laughed.

"You Dixons have a stubborn streak, ya know?"

"Thank you." Eric grinned. "How is your back?"

"Still a little painful."

"Okay, that's it. I'm sending you to bed. I need to clean up the kitchen, close the hurricane shutters, and crash. So, go, and I'll be up to check on you shortly."

She must really be uncomfortable, he thought, because she didn't argue with him but headed off to bed. He made quick work of his tasks and then checked on her. She was sound asleep when he entered his bedroom, and as was his habit, he crawled into bed and was fast asleep within moments.

CHAPTER 36

Eric rushed through his morning rounds. He, Tom Shelby, and Gordon Locke, the doctors with whom he shared a suite of offices, had two interviews to complete. The interviewees were both rheumatologists. Dr. Taylor Castellano, a recent graduate of Duke Medical Center in Durham, North Carolina, and Dr. Marlene Sanders, an experienced Chicago Med graduate who flew in from Portland, Oregon, just for the interview.

He wanted to get through his tasks as quickly as possible so that he could take Mary Ella and her twin boys home. So, he didn't feel like giving his brother, Byron, a lot of his time when he was stopped in the hospital hallway.

"Yo, brother mine, I hear you delivered twin boys in the midst of the frekken hurricane! Are you going to change your specialty from Rheumatology to Gynecology and Obstetrics?"

"You do what comes next," Eric joked, but it was no laughing matter when Mary Ella woke him at three in the morning. She was in the midst of labor pains that were less than three minutes apart. By the time he got his head around what was happening, the first baby was crowning. Fortunately, he had his medical bag in his car.

He made Mary Ella as comfortable as possible in his whirlpool tub before her water broke. His bathroom had the brightest lights in his home by which to see and help her through the delivery. It was also the best place to clean up Mary Ella and the twins after they were born. After he cleaned the boys, he wrapped them in a couple of his clean white T-shirts. Using a couple of dresser drawers as beds, he inserted pillows and clean pillowcases as makeshift mattresses.

"I hear the bridge over the Santee flooded, and you couldn't get Mary Ella and the twins to the hospital."

"It took several days before she and the twins could be transported, but by then, mother and sons were well acquainted."

"Sorry I missed it, but I was at a dentist convention in Las Vegas. I had to stay extra days because the hurricane settled in and moved slower."

"That's the convention you wanted me to attend with you, right?"

"Well, yes, you see, there are these twin dental surgeons I used to…"

"Uh, excuse me? Eric Dixon? Is this you?" A female voice intruded on his conversation with his brother.

He turned and found his arms full of a woman pressing herself intimately against him. His brother looked askance at him, his eyes questioning. Eric gave his brother a *"what the hell"* look and took a step back. She looked vaguely familiar, but he didn't recognize her. "Yes, I'm Eric Dixon. Have we met?"

"Oh, for heaven's sake, Eric, it's me, Marlene Sanders. We were at Chicago Medical together."

"Oh, of course. You're here for the interview today." He looked at his watch. "You're early. I believe your interview is for eleven."

When Byron cleared his voice, Eric recognized the signal for what it was. "Pardon me, Dr. Sanders, this is Dr. Byron Dixon. He's also on staff here."

She stuck her left arm under Eric's right arm before extending her right hand to Byron, a move that seemed possessive and entirely too familiar to both Eric and Byron.

"Oh, you must be one of Eric's brothers, right?"

"I am, yes. It's a pleasure to meet you, Dr. Sanders."

"Oh, we don't have to be so formal, do we? After all, I've known Eric for quite a while, and we'll be working together from now on. Just call me Marlene."

"Certainly, Marlene. Uh, Eric, don't you have to, uh…"

"Yes. Yes, I do. Thanks for reminding me. Perhaps you'd be willing to show Dr. Sanders around the hospital."

"I'd be happy to."

"Oh, Eric, I had hoped to have time to catch up on old times with you before the interview. Are you sure you can't spend the time?"

"I've some other things to take care of before the interview. Thanks, Byron. I owe you."

"Well." She dramatically sighed and then kissed his cheek before he could evade her and disentangle from her possessiveness. "If you must, but since I'll be here for a few days, I want to claim tonight's dinner with you. Maybe we can spend the day together tomorrow. I need to find someplace to live. I'm sure you know the best places. I'm staying at someplace called The Summer House. I haven't been there yet, but I understand the food there is very good."

"It is. Byron will tell you all about it, but I'm not going to be on duty after today for the next few weeks. So, I'll see you at the interview."

"Are you going away?" she stridently asked.

Eric didn't feel inclined to answer her question, so he nodded non-committedly, "Uh, yes. Something like that, so I'll see you later in the interview." He nodded again and escaped.

If she hadn't said who she was, he would never have recognized her. He recalled from her resume they did go through medical school at the same time, and they did their residency program together. Still, he was living with Ginger at the time and didn't have extra time to socialize between working, studying, classes, and Ginger. He certainly wasn't looking for a hook up now.

He made it up to the maternity ward and went straight to Mary Ella's hospital room.

"Ah, you made it, Eric." Dr. Quade nodded.

"Yes, I apologize for being late, Alfred."

"Not at all, Eric. I just finished Mary Ella's examination." He turned to Mary Ella, who was sitting on the side of the bed. "As I was about to say. You apparently release two or more eggs when you ovulate. This phenomenon is recorded in scientific research to occur in up to ten percent of all menstrual cycles, which means that the average woman releases two or more eggs at least once a year. You apparently do so much more frequently than once a year. Of course, as medical professionals, you know that when two eggs are released, and both are fertilized, this produces dizygotic or fraternal twins: a pair of children born at the same time to the same mother but each developing from a different fertilized egg. Such twins are therefore non-identical, being equivalent to normal siblings, and can be of the same or different sexes. In your specific case, those two eggs were fertilized by two different sperms and produced two boys.

"You also seem to have an abundance of egg production. Women in your situation have what's known as ovarian hyperstimulation, which causes the ovaries to produce multiple mature eggs during menstrual cycles. You're an excellent candidate for retrieving and donating mature eggs through a surgical procedure called transvaginal ultrasound aspiration. Egg donors spend around sixty hours for screening, testing, and medical appointments throughout the course of the procedure. Many women cannot conceive on their own and accept donated eggs to be fertilized with their partner's sperm."

"Are you saying that in my case, I can produce more than two mature eggs more than ten percent of the time during ovulation?" Mary Ella was astonished.

"Yes, that's exactly what I'm saying. You will likely produce twins, triplets or more, routinely for the whole of your reproductive life."

"Oh. My. Heaven." She looked at Eric, who stood feet apart, arms crossed over his broad chest, trying to hide the grin on his face with one hand. She narrowed her eyes at him, pulling a mean face. "When can I go back on the IUD?"

"It's not advisable, Mary Ella. Now that you've had twins, your intrauterine device is less effective."

"I used the IUD because I don't do well on the pill."

"Yes, I understand. I saw your medical record. For the immediate future, your only recourse may be the rhythm method or prophylactics."

Eric couldn't hold it in when Mary Ella's eyes widened. He laughed at her expression and had to excuse himself or he would have fallen out with laughter. He walked down the hall and happened to pass the nursery where Mark Brooks and Adama Gupta each sat covered in hospital overalls cradling their sons in their arms. Mary Ella had given birth to fraternal twins who were likely conceived on the same day, within hours of each other. Now he and Mary Ella knew how and why that probably happened and that she was one of those rare people who might produce twins or more each time she conceived.

He relished the thought as he watched the two men with their sons.

Mary Ella put the boys down for an afternoon nap. Eric's parents brought a couple of cradles to Eric's home for her to use. She was staying with Eric because Satarah had also delivered her and Douglas' son at home on the same day during the hurricane. Douglas had done the honors of helping Satarah bring their son, Douglas Junior, into the world. Although Mark and Adama were both in town to spend time with their sons, Eric took time off from work to be with her full-time.

Eric was downstairs watching as a new screen was being erected over the back of his house. Indeed, the hurricane had shredded the old screen, and his brother, Frank, and his construction crew were quickly putting up a new one. She went into Eric's closet specifically to retrieve the small blue velvet box in his jewelry cabinet and consider the consequences of what she planned to do.

Mary Ella was sitting on one of the bar stools when Eric entered the kitchen, carrying another one of his father's dinner casseroles. His parents, siblings, and Bernard and Sylvia Alexander came to see the babies, along with others. For now, the house had emptied, but more visitors were expected. There were baby gifts piled up in his library den. He and Mary Ella would have to sort through the baby clothes and wash them before they could wear them or be wrapped in the blankets. "I don't know if I have room in my refrigerator for another..." he started and stuttered to a stop. In the middle of the kitchen island was a blue velvet ring box. He put down the casserole and looked from the box to Mary Ella.

Without taking his eyes off her face, Eric rounded the island and sat on a barstool facing her.

"I've done a lot of things that I regret, but here's the thing, Eric. The biggest regret I've ever had was not marrying my one true love when you asked me all those years ago. Back then, I thought I was too young to be a wife and mother. I wanted to have a career and live a little before settling down, but I never thought my future wouldn't include you. Then you left and went into the Army. When Mark came along, I was still on the rebound from you leaving home. I didn't want you to go, and I was afraid to go with you. I think I've been rebounding ever since then.

"So, now I'm a little older, and, I hope, a lot wiser than I was ten years ago. I've got the career I wanted, and I've seen parts of this world I would never have seen if I had stayed here. That's good and bad, but there is still more I want to see, although I don't mean right away. I'm happy with who I am and where I am now. I believe I'm prepared mentally and emotionally to settle down. So, I'm asking you to roll back the clock and ask me again to be your wife with the assurance that I am deeply still in love with you, and I will definitely say yes this time."

"Okay, so thing two is that I could never, ever stop loving you, Mary Ella Baker. You're my best friend and the love of my life." He took the ring out of the box and fit it on the third finger of her left hand. "So, if you'll have me, I want to be your husband and the father of as many children as we can have for the rest of our lives."

"Oh, so you really had to go there?" Mary Ella chided.

"With the thought of what it's going to take to get you pregnant dancing like sugar plum fairies in my head? *Oh, hell yeah!*"

EPILOGUE

She shredded the letter from Summer County General Hospital into confetti. It advised her that, although they appreciated her interest in a position with their hospital, they were going with a different candidate. *Oh, hell, no!* That would never do! She had wanted Eric Dixon every day they were in medical school together. Every day he worked his residency program. She changed her specialty to rheumatology because of him. Every day he was married to that stupid GI Jane, she wanted him. It was hard finding a way to be friendly with the Ginger person so that she could find out every little detail about Eric, but then the woman got suspicious, so she had to back off.

Then she learned that Eric wasn't going to be there at a Chicago Med class reunion. He was living in some Podunk backwoods place in South Carolina called Summer County of all things, and he was divorced? She set her plan in motion to finally get her hands on him. That opportunity came when a job opened in the very same hospital in Eric's department with two other doctors. With her credentials, she knew she was a shoo-in until the damn letter came.

She was so sure of her ability to snag the position that she had already packed and put her condo on the market. She was on the verge of submitting her resignation when the letter arrived. Then, when Eric wouldn't return her phone calls, she had to resort to calling his brother, Byron, the walking gonad, and was told that Eric was on his honeymoon and was married to some damn nurse? *Oh, hell to the no!* This new woman had to go and soon! Eric was hers, and he'd know it before long. Wife number two would have to meet with a fatal accident.

First, however, she had to find a way to get rid of the wet-behind-the-ears candidate, Dr. Taylor Castellano, they selected to take the position she deserved! To her, he sounded like some damn Italian, but no matter. He would go, too.

"You really should let it go, Obadiah," JoJeff advised as he walked around his car lot with his clipboard checking the VIN numbers of the cars that had just been delivered against the list of vehicles he purchased at an auction. The man was getting on his last nerve, haranguing him about the fact no one would help him get what he thought was rightly his from Satarah.

"And that Mary Ella ain't no better! I hear tell she had two babies by two different men, too! And then she goes off and married Eric Dixon in a white gown like she was pure as the driven snow! What kind of shit is that, I wanna know? They say one of them babies came outta her womb a millionaire before it drew its first breath. And here you are over here when your lawful wife just had another baby by that northerner. He don't even belong in this county. Them carpetbaggers come down here and try to take over every damn thing. It's a pure d shame what that daughter of mine done! Just like that harlot of a mother of hers. Should have taken a firm hand to her years ago, but no, them old people said, '*spare the rod and spoil the child.*' Bunch of damn whoopee if you ask me. There's gonna be a reckoning, I promise ya that! I'm the head of my house and the leader of my flock! Them gals gonna bow down before me and give me what's rightfully mine before I'm through with them!"

JoJeff had long ago tuned out the ravings of Obadiah Baker. The old coot was his former father-in-law. He was off his meds again or stuck on stupid. SaraJo wasn't going to give Baker a thing, and why should she? Only because that store-front church of his couldn't afford to buy him a new Cadillac every year, he was working himself into a lather. That's why Obadiah was strutting around here now, looking to trade in his car for a brand new one. The one he had was only a year old, but the interior was for shit. The old coot ate in that car and tossed his garbage in the back seat. He never cleaned the inside or washed the outside, so JoJeff really didn't want to take the car in trade. He was tempted to tell the old buzzard to take the vehicle to another dealership.

So, he had cousins living large right there in Summer County where the Alexander clan made their home, did he? And here he sat in frekken Andersen Air Force Base in Guam in the village of Yigo, fifteen miles from the capital, Agana. He'd bet his last red cent those Alexander brothers, Kenneth and Benny, had something to do with derailing his plan to get back to the Pentagon in Washington, DC, where he should be. They're the reason he was busted down from Colonel to Second Lieutenant! All they had to do was go along to get along, but *oh, hell no!* Not them! Yeah, those goodie-goodie Alexanders were due for a reckoning, and he knew just the way to stick it to them, too. He picked up his phone and dialed a number he hadn't called in a very long time.

"Dr. Lambert, here," she answered on the second ring.

"Well, hello, Lisa. It's JC, here. I think I've found a way to stick it to your former lover, Kenneth Alexander, and his brother, Benny."

"Really? I'm all ears," she purred.

ABOUT THE AUTHOR

Ann Jeffries, the critically acclaimed author of the Family Reunion—Wisdom of the Ancestors Series, is a native of Washington, DC. As an only child, she enjoyed the benefits of a private school education at Allen in Asheville, North Carolina, and a public education at the University of Maryland. Ann began writing fiction for her own amusement.

Ms. Jeffries is the recipient of many awards for leadership and public service. A keynote speaker at colleges, universities, conferences, and conventions, she has extensively traveled the North American continent, Asia, and Europe. Among other endeavors, she is an entrepreneur, an avid supporter of public television, a genealogist, and a voracious reader.

Her pride and joy are her family members, particularly her Fabulous Four grands. She lives in Maryland and South Carolina.

Follow Ann on her website: www.annjeffries.net, Facebook @Ann Jeffries, on Twitter @Ann Jeffries and her publishing house site: www.newviewliterature.com. Her novels are available in both e-book and paperback. Her autographed copies can be found through annjeffries.net and also un-autographed on Amazon.com and barnesandnoble.com. All of Ms. Jeffries' novels are available in audiobook format through Audible, iTunes, and Amazon.